FIRST KILL

Jack Valentine took a breath, watching the Iraqi commander in the dark green uniform run to the car, his scope sight's reticle center mass on the man. He let out his breath halfway, held it, and relaxed, crosshairs dead on target. Then he added pressure with his trigger finger.

Boom! The rifle bucked against Jack's shoulder, and he watched through the scope.

The Iraqi commander was two steps from the back door of his Rolls-Royce sedan when the bullet struck his upper chest, sending red spray and debris exploding from his body. The shot took the man off his feet and drove him backwards to the ground.

Calm and cool, Jack drew back his bolt, ejected the spent cartridge slowly into his hand, never taking his eye off the rifle scope, watching the crowd of Iraqi officers pour out of the building, handguns and rifles drawn.

TERMINAL IMPACT

— A JACK VALENTINE MARINE SNIPER NOVEL —

CHARLES HENDERSON

BERKLEY
New York

BERKLEY
An imprint of Penguin Random House LLC
375 Hudson Street, New York, New York 10014

ISBN: 9781101988145

Berkley hardcover edition / November 2016
Berkley premium edition / September 2017

Printed in the United States of America
1 3 5 7 9 10 8 6 4 2

Cover art: Wadi rum sunset © Nicholas Olesen / Getty Images;
Flag of the USA © AXL/Shutterstock; Silhouette of military sniper at
sunset © studio0411/Shutterstock; Crosshairs with bullet
holes © Ivsanmas/Shutterstock
Cover design by Adam Auerbach
Book design by Laura K. Corless

For my brother, James Lindsey "Jim" Henderson

and

all my beloved Marine Corps HOGs
8541s, 0317s, fellow 9925s, and others who lead HOGs

and

In blessed memory of my dear Scout-Sniper brothers:
Staff Sergeant Shane Schmidt, USMC

and

Sergeant Rob Richards, USMC

and

Lieutenant Colonel, USA, Corporal, USMC,
Tom "Moose" Ferran

and

My mentor, Master Sergeant Bruce Martin, USMC

Fighters for Justice, Hunters of Gunmen
Brothers All

— 1 —

Eight, seven, six. The second hand on Jack Valentine's watch ticked.

Five . . . "Snuggle into the rifle, Jack. Like she's the woman you love. Yeah, baby. Breathe. Relax."

Four . . . "Close your eyes, bro. That's it. Go inside the bubble."

Three . . . "Now open up. Natural point of aim. Solid. Center mass."

Two . . . "Focus. Crosshairs sharp, clear. Target fuzzy."

One . . . "Hold that half breath. Ease the trigger roll. Squeeze."

Burlap fringe from his Ghillie-suit bonnet tickled Jack Valentine's face as a dry January breeze rustled the fuzzy strips of light green, dark green, and various shades of brown camouflage tied on netting that hid his face. Slowly, careful to not rustle the growth of dry dead foliage that hid him, he eased his fingers up and gave his itching cheek a rub.

The newly promoted Marine corporal and his spotter

partner, Staff Sergeant Walter Gillespie, affectionately known as Hacksaw, likewise Ghillied up, lay tucked beneath a weed crop on the raised border of a set of long and narrow farm fields. From this hide, they watched the main entrance of what appeared to be a Republican Guard command center, across a highway, nearly a thousand yards ahead of them.

Elmore Snow's special operations team had parachuted into position from a high-altitude low-opening jump the night before, two-man teams landing in three zones on the northwest side of the city of Hillah, Iraq, along Highway 84, which led to Hindiya and Karbala. Early that morning, January 17, 1991, Allied aircraft and sea-launched cruise missiles had begun the bombardment of Iraqi command and control centers, and antiaircraft-missile positions. The Persian Gulf War had now begun.

The mustang captain and his team's senior noncommissioned officer, Gunny Ray Ambrose, whom Snow had named Mutt during South American drug-war deployments, had moved northeast, edging around the outskirts of the city, past the palace that Saddam Hussein had built on a promontory hill overlooking the ruins of ancient Babylon, that he had also renovated into a new museum, honoring himself and ancient King Nebuchadnezzar. Saddam had even had his name carved in the bricks, boasting the lie SADDAM HUSSEIN, SON OF NEBUCHADNEZZAR.

Sergeants Kermit The Frog Alexander and Cory Habu Webster had skirted eastward, well past the captain and gunny's position while Jack and Hacksaw went west, then bent their trek southward toward a curious ring of lights that turned out to be the suspected Republican Guard command center that all three teams had sought.

They found a spot close enough to see what went on but far enough away to not draw attention to themselves. The sniper team had Ghillied up and lay in a hide because of random farmers and goatherds wandering by uncomfortably close. The Marines planned to stay put until nightfall, then move out west, beyond searching eyes, and find a place to eat, rest, and await next orders for movement.

Captain Snow reported the grid coordinates of the military targets to higher command over satellite-linked radio, and told the operations staff that neither Saddam Hussein nor anyone else important appeared to occupy the Summer Palace. The only people they saw there were caretakers.

As for Jack and Hacksaw, military traffic constantly streamed in and out of the Republican Guard headquarters, and only moments ago they had seen a dark blue Rolls-Royce sedan enter the complex and park by the building with the flagpole flying the Iraqi colors.

Two soldiers in desert-camouflage uniforms and burgundy berets hurried to the rear passenger-side door as the driver opened it. A trim, slight man in a dark green uniform with a bald head and a short beard got out, put on his burgundy beret, exchanged salutes with the soldiers, and followed them inside the building.

"He's got to be a regional commander. Flag rank, judging from the car," Captain Snow told his team on their heavily encrypted sat-link headsets.

"Shall we dance when he exits, sir?" Hacksaw asked.

"If you took the shot, do you have adequate egress?" Elmore asked in return.

"Once it's dark we do," Jack broke in. "Right now, sir, we take the shot, we best sit tight. We might get away with one shot. We're off in the boonies, where they likely won't look for us."

"What's the distance?" Snow asked.

"Range finder says 812 meters to the sedan," Gillespie reported.

"How do you feel about it, Jack?" Elmore asked.

"Quartering breeze off my right leg, nice and steady at three clicks, I can't ask for better shooting conditions. I'm all in, sir," Jack answered.

"One shot, one kill, it's all you've got," the captain said. "How about it, Staff Sergeant Gillespie?"

"We need to take the shot, sir," Hacksaw came back. "Even if Corporal V misses, just think how it will fuck with these dudes' heads. They won't know whether to shit or go blind, paranoia fucking up their dope."

"Bear in mind, Staff Sergeant, lots of important ears might be listening to you at the national command center as well as Riyadh," Elmore cautioned his swarthy Marine. Then added, "Stand by while I clear the mission."

An hour had passed, and Hacksaw began to grumble, "I got a brick crawled straight up my ass and parked. What I wouldn't give to take a leisurely shit and read the newspaper with a hot cup of black coffee."

"Scoot down behind us and pinch off a loaf. Nothing's stirring," Jack grumbled back. "Just make sure you drop your turds where I won't crawl in them."

"You got it, bro," Hacksaw said, and inched himself

backwards, off the two-foot-high raised berm overgrown with weeds. "I hate taking a shit lying down, but a man's gotta do what a man's gotta do. Sure glad I don't wear panties. This might leave a stain."

Jack fought the urge to laugh and focused on what he saw through his rifle's twelve-power scope sight.

Just as Hacksaw farted and released a steaming load, Elmore Snow came on the sat-link.

"We're a go on the shot, but as a stopgap, should the target decide to depart the area," the captain said.

"What'd ya mean, stopgap, Skipper?" Jack asked.

"We've got a Nighthawk inbound with a GBU-27 to deliver on that Iraqi command center," the captain answered.

"That's like a mark 84 laser-guided smart bomb, isn't it? Two thousand pounds of high explosive, sir?" Jack came back.

"Roger that, a bunker buster," Elmore said.

"Just checking, sir," Jack answered. Then he added, "Seems like I recall the lethal blast radius of a two-grand bomb throws fragmentation four hundred meters up and out."

"Roger that," the captain confirmed.

"Won't it get just a touch breezy out here, across the flats, Staff Sergeant Gillespie and me lying on this two-foot-high berm eight hundred meters away from the target? Just weeds for protection?" Jack asked, worried.

"You should be fine," the captain replied. "I've called it in closer, but not much. You'll get some dust up your snot locker."

Jack Valentine shrank over his rifle and looked through

the scope again, watching the headquarters main door and the blue Rolls-Royce parked in front.

"Hacksaw back at you, sir," the staff sergeant said over his sat-link as he eased alongside Jack and put his eye back on the high-power spotting scope equipped with infrared and night-vision technology. "Had to scatter a little rat bait out in this farmer's tater crop if you know what I mean."

"Did you copy my com?" Snow asked.

"Roger," Gillespie answered. "Why the mark 84? Last I checked, that bomb puts down a thirty-foot-deep crater, fifty feet across, and blows through sixteen feet of concrete or fifteen inches of solid steel. Kind of overkill for a two-story spread-out office complex."

"Wizards in the head shed think this headquarters may sit atop a good-size bunker system," Elmore explained. "Obviously a flag officer inside, the one you spotted, and maybe more.

"Given the war began before daylight this morning, we believe they could have a command and control center underground. You said lots of traffic in and out, and that blue Rolls-Royce has our G-two people convinced you happened upon a major honeypot."

"Does this mean we can come home early?" Hacksaw joked.

"Maybe you're half-right, Walter. We may get to bust out of this burg and redeploy," Snow answered. "As soon as I know anything, I'll let you boys know, too. We'll all likely beat feet to the rally point and await pickup there."

"Anything going with Frogman and Habu?" Gillespie asked.

"They've got a flight of four Tomcats loaded with mark 82s inbound on targets. We're trying to coordinate those strikes with yours. How about your laser? It set up? We need to get that target painted," the captain followed.

"Just pulled it from the drag bag and setting up as we speak," Hacksaw answered.

"While you're in the bag, go ahead and pull out the camera and put on the long lens," Snow told him. "If this commander with the blue Rolls emerges from the head-quarters, I want pictures of him."

"If he comes out of the building, he's probably leaving, sir," Jack said.

"That's where you have the green light to splash him," Elmore replied. "I want Walter to snap his pictures, nonetheless, and you take your shot. Be nice to identify this guy."

"Got you covered, Skipper," Hacksaw broke in. "Laser is up and painting the target. I'm on the camera with a nice view of the car and front door. Awesome lens. Very clear. By the way, sir, it looks like the driver is talking on a radio."

"Now he's stepping out," Jack added, seeing the driver's door open.

"What's the ETA on that Nighthawk?" Walter asked.

"I just checked, and the pilot says he's less than two mikes out," Elmore came back.

"May be too late," Jack said, seeing the general emerge through the front doors, square away his burgundy beret, and jog down the steps. Instead of escorting the senior officer, the driver ran to his station, started the car, and left the general to let himself in the backseat.

"Your range is hot, corporal. Wind unchanged. You've got your dope. Fire at will," Hacksaw said, snapping the camera as fast as the motor drive could run the film past the shutter.

Jack Valentine took a breath, watching the Iraqi commander in the dark green uniform run to the car, his scope sight's reticle center mass on the man. He let out his breath halfway, held it, and relaxed, crosshairs dead on target. Then he added pressure to his trigger finger.

Boom! The rifle bucked against Jack's shoulder, and he watched through the scope.

Two steps from the back door of his Rolls-Royce sedan, the shot took the Iraqi commander off his feet and drove him backwards to the ground. As the bullet struck his upper chest, red spray and debris exploded from his body.

Calm and cool, Jack drew back his bolt, ejected the spent cartridge slowly into his hand, never taking his eye off the rifle scope, watching the crowd of Iraqi officers pour out of the building, handguns and rifles drawn.

"Report," Elmore said on the satellite radio.

Sirens began wailing, and Iraqi soldiers, rifles ready, poured from every wing of the command complex.

"You ever piss in an ant bed, Skipper?" Hacksaw laughed, still snapping pictures. "Corporal Valentine just broke his cherry. Score him one kill. A general at that! Nice. Real nice."

"Your laser still painting the target?" Elmore asked.

"Yes, sir," Hacksaw replied, just as a whistling whining screaming sound from the sky came down and the entire command-center complex suddenly erupted in a massive, ground-shaking, deafening explosion. Dirt, debris, bodies, cars, trucks tumbled in the air as a great brown-and-gray cloud rose a thousand feet into the late-afternoon sky.

"We best di di mau, Boo-Boo," Hacksaw said, gathering equipment into the drag bag and rolling down the back side of the berm. Jack slid out, too, hot on his partner's heels.

On February 24, 1991, Allied ground forces rolled across the line of departure into Iraq. Saddam's three-hundred-thousand-man force occupying Kuwait fled the land. Many of them surrendered to the Americans, while others faced death from their own Republican Guard, who shot deserting Iraqi soldiers on sight. In four days, Allied forces conquered the Iraqi army and restored Kuwait to its rightful owners. General Walter Boomer and his Marines waded through Kuwait the first day. Carl von Clausewitz and Sun Tzu would have been proud.

On the second day of March, Elmore Snow and his team of five Marines sat at a table on the mess deck of the USS *Iwo Jima*. Like a family admiring baby pictures, they passed around copies of choice reconnaissance photographs they had taken during their deep special operations mission.

"What do we do?" Hacksaw asked, holding up a photo he snapped of the dirtball mushroom cloud that used to be the Republican Guard headquarters.

"We fuck shit up!" Jack laughed.

"And the pièce de résistance," Gillespie added, holding

up a photograph of the Iraqi general just as Jack's bullet struck him. Stop-action death. The center of his chest exploding as the bullet lifted him off his feet.

Hacksaw grinned at Jack. "Corporal Valentine put the hammer of justice on this sand flea. Fucked him up!"

"Hammer." Raymond Ambrose smiled over his cup of coffee, looking at Jack. "I name you, Hammer."

Elmore Snow raised his coffee mug with his men and toasted their new addition. "Here's to Hammer," he said.

"And here's to the loss of virginity," Jack added.

"So, Corporal Valentine, what do you think of South America?" Elmore asked the young Marine.

"I'm fluent in Spanish," the corporal said, and smiled back. "Mexican, I should say. My mom, you know."

"I read that in your SRB," the captain said, nodding.

"Did you also see where I put in for Basic Underwater Demolition/SEAL training?" Jack came back. "I'd really like to go, Skipper."

Everyone at the table looked at the green young corporal sideways.

"What the fuck, over?" Hacksaw said. "BUD/S is redundant, shitstain. You done done it. What's those deck apes gonna teach a badass Para-Frog Scout-Sniper Force-Recon hard-baked little bitch like you?"

Then the staff sergeant scooted close to Jack and wrapped his tattooed, muscled arm around the corporal's neck. "Listen to me," Walter said, wrinkling his brow, "this is your daddy talkin' to ya. A Navy SEAL ain't nothin' but a sailor tryin' to be like a Marine. You got that?

"Fuck me to tears, boy. Stop thinking such silly thoughts. You need to pack your trash and go down to

South America with us men and kill yourself some of them cocaine cowboys we been huntin'. You got the good eye, the trigger, and the Hammer!"

Jack looked at Elmore. "Sir?"

Captain Snow took a little coffee and thought what to say, then spoke slowly.

"Staff Sergeant Gillespie in his crude and rude way told you right, son," he began. "BUD/S is a basic school, just more of the same thing you learned at Amphib-Recon. Yes, they get into a bit more detail, but at the end of the day, you will learn little to nothing new, and it will not put points on the board for promotion. It's virtually meaningless, given your training.

"Navy personnel who graduate BUD/S go from there to advanced training, just like we do, either as Underwater Demolition Technician, frogmen, which most of them end up doing, or move into the kind of training you've already accomplished, that allows them to be designated a special operator of the Sea, Air, and Land.

"I disagree with Staff Sergeant Gillespie's assessment that a SEAL is nothing but a sailor trying to be like a Marine. Maybe a sailor trying to be like a Force Recon Marine, perhaps. But do not grow a superior attitude about them or Delta Force operators, either. They're all good men, very well trained. But so are we. Don't forget that."

"So, you say no to my request?" Jack asked.

"I think you should focus your goals in a direction that will benefit our Marine Corps foremost and yourself secondly," Snow said, and drew smiles around the table.

"Without question, Marine Corps first, sir," Jack agreed. "Don't get me wrong."

"You're ambitious, Jack, and you want to be the best at what you do." Elmore smiled at the corporal. "Like I said when we first met, you remind me of me. Some years back. The better warrior you are, the better for our Marine Corps."

The captain looked at the photographs, then at Jack.

"That shot you made," he continued. "Over eight hundred meters and a running target. You shot him center mass, in the chest, one shot. That impresses me."

"One shot, one kill." Jack smiled. "That's what Gunny Carlos Hathcock always taught his snipers. Right? One shot, one kill."

"The deadliest thing on the battlefield is one well-aimed shot," Gunny Ambrose added. "We all know Gunny Hathcock."

"Corporal Valentine," Captain Snow said. "Here's what we're going to do. Trust me."

The "trust me" phrase drew a round of laughs.

"Seriously, son." Elmore smiled. "Trust me. I want you with us in South America. I can use your skills. There's an old thorn in my side in Medellín, Colombia, I want to check off my to-do list. His gunslingers killed Leroy Griffin, the sniper we called Dirty Harry. Good Marine. Outstanding sergeant. I want you to put a bullet in the motherfucker's ear."

The whole table erupted into hoots and fist pounding. Hearing the Christian gentleman Elmore Snow say a very, very rare motherfucker meant serious business.

"A year with us down there, you'll pin on sergeant, and I will personally see to it that you go to Quantico for the Scout-Sniper Advanced Course and Instructor

Course, too," the captain finished, and put out his hand. "We have a deal?"

Jack thought about it and began to smile as he looked around at the Marines who surrounded him. A small team, but a family.

"Jack," Gunny Ambrose added, "I've chased Elmore Snow around this planet since he was a staff sergeant, and I was a corporal. We go back a piece. Always exciting. Always rewarding."

"Deal, sir," Jack said, and shook Elmore Snow's hand.

— 2 —

A double-spanned bridge crosses the Euphrates River in northwestern Iraq, taking Route 19 across it from the east westward where it joins Route 12 and slants northwestward to Syria. The bridge plants its longest span briefly on a small island community called Hawija Haditha, near the west bank, then it crosses a shorter span into the city of Haditha proper.

Six kilometers north, the massive earth-filled Haditha Dam, nine kilometers long and 187 meters high, impounds the mighty Euphrates's flow from its Turkish headwaters after crossing Syria into Iraq. Its river twin, the Tigris, also begins in the Taurus Mountains, fifty kilometers east of where the Euphrates gathers itself, both collecting waters from ancient Mount Ararat and surrounding peaks. With the Tigris on the east side and the Euphrates on the west flank, defining between them ancient Mesopotamia, the basin of Noah's great flood, the cradle of civilization and the Garden of Eden, they carry life-giving moisture and fruitful promise across desert lands southward to their Persian Gulf outlet, which empties into the Indian Ocean. No other river systems on earth have more greatly cultivated humanity's rise and mankind's civilization than these two.

Strategically and economically vital, the Haditha Dam stores two cubic miles of water in 193 square miles of surface area that forms the Buhayrat al-Qadisiyah reservoir. Within the nearly two-hundred-foot-high, concrete, double-decked spillway systems at the dam's center, six Kaplan hydroelectric turbines capable of generating 660 million watts of energy turn day and night. Restored in 2004 by the United States Army Corps of Engineers, Haditha Dam sends 350 megawatts of power into Iraq's grid, the second greatest share of electrical power for the nation. Mosul Dam in Iraq's Kurdish region, on the Tigris River north of Baghdad, produces the greatest share, 750 million watts.

Should al-Qaeda manage to blow the dam or kill the power, it would devastate Iraq's electrical grid. If insurgents managed to break open the dam, floodwaters would fill the Euphrates River valley, wiping out cities along its banks. Thus, Iraqi government and American forces keep a close watch on its security and structure. However, six kilometers south, in and around Haditha, jihadists, who traveled down Route 12 from Syria, gathering from places like Lebanon, Jordan, Turkey, eastern Europe and western Asia, and other conclaves that breed radical Muslim zealots, keep the city wild, woolly, and dangerous.

American forces assigned to this sector do not sleep but catnap while another warrior keeps watch. As Jack Valentine says, "It's a target-rich environment."

This day at Haditha Bridge's most visible point, nearest the city from Hawija, hundreds of terrified onlookers lined Haditha's riverbanks and streets. They watched the Jordanian-born Palestinian terrorist, Ahmad Fadeel al-Nasal al-Khalayleh, who had named himself Abu Musab al-Zarqawi, mount the roof of a wrecked taxi with its dead driver still sitting inside, his brains splattered across the windshield, and rant at the people on a bullhorn, while waving an AK-47 automatic rifle. He shook it in the air and occasionally let go rounds to punctuate his tirade, cursing the city's non-combatant citizens.

From the Iraq war's onset, and even before it, in the 1990s, Zarqawi led a Sunni Muslim blood-and-torture campaign, *al-Tawhid wal-Jihad*, against Shia people, Christians, and anyone from the West occupying any part of the Islamic world or just pissing him off in general. From birth, as a Palestinian, he hated Israel and its long-standing Judeo-Christian ally, the United States.

At the onset of the Iraq War, that jihad grew into *Tanzim Qaidat al-Jihad fi Bilad al-Rafidayn*, al-Qaeda in Iraq, escalating a greater, nationwide insurgency against the predominately Shia-led, post–Saddam Hussein Iraqi government and its American overseers. Today, as Zarqawi shouted threats, waving his rifle, demanding Haditha's allegiance to his AQI army, he declared all-out war.

Haditha listened as the stockily built, average-height man with the cropped-short beard and hair, a black knit kufi on his head, and wearing a solid black shalwar kameez, with a Ninjutsu hood hanging down its back, and a green, deep-pocketed Russian ammunition vest over the top of the ninja-style terrorist outfit, proclaimed in Palestinian-accented Farsi, the language of poor Persia and the Shia, "I am Emir of al-Qaeda in the Country of

Two Rivers! You will bow down to me and serve my army, or you will die!"

Below Zarqawi, a long line of noncombatant Haditha men and their sons, even their youngest male children, singled out because of their community leadership and cooperation with the Americans and government, knelt on the bridge where the gathering crowd could see them. A hundred gun-wielding al-Qaeda jihadists were scattered around the throng, keeping the people standing in place, while other Zarqawi gunmen combed the surrounding blocks and marched more people to the riverbank-and-streets viewing area and forced them to watch.

Behind the kneeling men and boys, AQI insurgents dressed in executioner black, like Zarqawi, hoods and masks covering their heads and faces, exposing only their eyes, stood ready with long knives drawn.

Zarqawi gave his dark minions a nod, and they commenced sawing off the heads of the men and boys, and even the smallest children.

On a desert hilltop more than fifteen hundred meters away from his target, on the east side of the river, two hundred yards east of where it bends like an elbow toward the southwest, Gunnery Sergeant Jack Valentine blinked at what he saw in his twelve-by-fifty-millimeter Schmidt and Bender telescopic gunsight.

"You seeing this shit?" Sergeant William "Billy-C" Claybaugh fumed, watching through an experimental, twelve-to-forty-power refracting spotting scope. The optical system had a Leupold Mil-Dot reticle and range grids built in it for distance and moving-target speed calculations. Sitting on a squatty little tripod, the new scope, sent to them by brothers in the Marine Corps Scout-Sniper Association, in one of their black-plastic-footlocker "care packages," had a Leupold sixty-millimeter-diameter, nonreflective, light-gathering objective lens with laser filter to guard against eye injury from amplified light on the battlefield. At the back end, the scope also accommodated an assortment of high-tech attachments, such as night vision and infrared. Still years away before anyone considered that this new system or anything like it had a snowball's chance in hell of getting in the sniper-kit inventory, it was the envy of everyone using the old twenty-power M49 scope.

"I'm taking the shot. That's gotta be Zarqawi!" Jack said, watching as heads and bodies fell off the bridge. Both Marines could hear the echoes of Zarqawi's rants as the men and boys fought their best fights, hands tied behind their backs, dying horribly.

"Don't do it," Billy-C argued. "Listen, Hammer. We got no backup. Just that motorized dip-wad platoon out of Hit supposedly cleaning up some IED mess somewhere between Barwana and Haqlaniyah."

"I'm taking the shot, Bubba," Jack insisted. "I cannot abide watching murder. Not little babies. Give me the fucking range. Now!"

"Feet or meters?" the sergeant came back, looking in the lenses.

"Both," Jack answered.

"I'm reading 5,143.21 feet," Claybaugh called out. "That's 1,524 meters, give or take a cunt hair."

"Wind!" Gunny Valentine snapped. "Hurry, Bill, or we'll lose him!"

Leaning on his side and holding his handheld Kestrel weather meter into the air, Billy-C called out, "Southeast to northwest, 12.6 miles per hour, right up your ass. At least we have that going for us, but then again, it has a little chop, dropping to eight, bouncing to twelve. Temperature, too fucking hot, ninety-one. Humidity, 8 percent. Barometer says 30.06. You might hold to favor a bit on the left side and up, given air density, the long distance, bullet drop, and clockwise spin."

"You think too much, Billy," Jack said as he fired his 7.62-by-51-millimeter NATO, Remington model-700, short-action, M40A3 sniper rifle.

Both Marines saw the bullet splash the roof of the taxi, striking between Zarqawi's feet, blowing dirt out the car's open side windows.

"Fuck!" Jack huffed, slammed the bolt, and tried a second shot, but the al-Qaeda leader had already taken cover, and it missed, too. Meanwhile, Zarqawi's army opened fire, hosing the streets and sky in every direction as Haditha's civilians ran for cover.

"Hey, Gunny! You gonna shoot or what?" a voice crackled on the small green two-way radio that lay next to Jack Valentine at the thousand-yard berm.

He jerked awake and yawned. The memory of the horror at the bridge already fading. Then he picked up the radio, and said, "Keep your panties on. When you hear that target go pop, you can pull it. Until then, don't worry me. Got it?"

"Yes, sir," the voice crackled back.

Jack looked through his riflescope and mumbled under his breath, cross and groggy, "Fucking newbies."

Then he settled into his work, focusing on the new rifle's sight reticle, letting the black bull's-eye on the target more than a half mile away get good and fuzzy in his crosshairs.

North Carolina early-morning dankness smothered the Carlos Hathcock thousand-yard high-power rifle range at Camp Lejeune, used by the Second Marine Division and Marine Special Operations Command Scout-Sniper School where Gunnery Sergeant Jack Valentine was senior sniper and chief instructor. Cool breezes coming off the nearby Atlantic sent swirls of thin fog across the long green to the targets.

Controlling his breathing, holding it as he relaxed and laid pressure on the trigger, Jack let go his shot.

Two seconds later, down the target went.

Jack picked up a black, government-issue pen, tried to plot his target call in his data book, and couldn't get the ballpoint to write.

"Fucking crap!" he snapped, and threw the pen as hard as he could, still lying prone.

His target then rose in the air, with a large white spotter sitting in the center of the black.

"Here, try this one," a voice behind Jack said.

The gunny looked over his shoulder, then up at a towering giant of a Marine holding out a clear-plastic Bic pen in his hand.

"You are one tall motherfucker, you know that?" Jack said, and took the pen and plotted his call but wrote nothing for the hit.

"So they tell me," the tall Marine said.

"How long you been standing there?" Jack said, frowning at the man.

"Maybe twenty, maybe thirty minutes," he said.

"Really? That long?" the gunny asked.

The tall Marine nodded. "I sat down awhile behind you, too. Then I got to my feet, to give you a nudge, when I heard you snoring."

"Snoring?" Jack laughed. "Fuck me. I might have shot you, you know?"

"Roger that," the Marine said. "Then the guy in the butts called on your radio, so I backed off."

"Lucky you. I had a bad night," Jack grumbled. "Getting ready to deploy a team to Iraq. Back to some of my old haunts, I'm guessing. Maybe up north of Ramadi, badlands out past Hit."

"Yeah, I know the area," the tall Marine said. "I worked on a sniper team out of Ramadi. Mostly hunted there and down to Fallujah. But we made a few runs up your way."

"You ever make it up to Haditha?" Jack asked.

"Couple times," the staff sergeant said. "Took Route 12 past Haditha once, on up to Al Qàim, on the Syrian border. Looking for Zarqawi and killing lots of Qaeda up and down the road. Left 'em scattered like dead jackrabbits."

"That's where they pour in the country," Jack said, and let go a laugh. "Good old asshole Zarqawi. I was just reliving one of my recurring nightmares of him while I was snoring on my gun. I had a shot at him, you know. Too far off for that weak-ass .308. Put one between his toes."

"I heard about it," the Marine said. "I heard about you, too, Ghost of al-Anbar."

Jack laughed. "Fucking ragheads. Ghost of al-Anbar my ass. What a joke. They've got a name for everybody nowadays."

"Not me," the Marine said.

"Lieutenant Colonel Elmore Snow running MAR-SOC, his dream finally come true, us fielding as his inaugural special operations team, those sand fleas will hang one on you, too," Jack said. "By the way, we're calling my platoon Ghosts of al-Anbar, using Ghost for our call sign. I am sick to shit of that cliché crap like Reaper."

The tall new guy with no name yet stared downrange and bit his lip, thinking.

"They cheated your shot, you know," he said, looking at the white spotter in the center of the black bull's-eye.

"Yeah, I know," Jack answered. "I put one out in the white at two o'clock, on purpose. Assholes want to hurry up and go to the schoolhouse, so they resort to lying."

Jack went back on his gun, focused, and fired. His next shot blew the white spotter off the middle of the target.

"Now that's a legit bull." He smiled at the tall Marine, getting to his feet and offering the man his hand.

"I see that," the towering staff sergeant said, shaking Jack's hand. "Terrence Martin, Gunny Valentine. I'm reporting aboard from Pendleton by way of Okinawa."

"They call you Terry?" Jack said, picking up his radio and growling to the crew in the butts, "Pack it in."

"No, folks call me Cotton," Staff Sergeant Martin said.

"Cotton? How's that?" Jack said, tossing his data book,

brass, and ammunition in a satchel, then taking his rifle and ground cloth in hand.

"I played college hoops at Texas Tech," Martin answered. "Bobby Knight named me Cotton because I could hit the bucket from just about anywhere. Drive up the lane or three off the arc. Coach Knight used to say, 'Nothin' but cotton' when I shot. The net on the hoop made of cotton, ya know. Back in the day. It's polyester or something now."

"Nothin' but cotton." Jack smiled. "I like that, Cotton."

"It works," Cotton Martin said.

"Division One college ball. No NBA contract?" Jack asked, heading along the road from the Hathcock Range to the group of redbrick buildings at Stone Bay firing range, just off the coastal waters on the bottom end of Camp Lejeune.

"At six-foot-six, I'm considered medium to short in the NBA," the staff sergeant said, walking alongside the gunny, to his left, abreast and in step, which Jack also noticed. "Lots of hot-shooting guards in the game. They've got all the Steve Nashes they want. I knew if I made the NBA, it would only be a fluke. So when nine-eleven hit, that was as good an excuse as any to tell Coach Knight I'm done with basketball. I heard my country calling."

"How'd he take it?" Jack asked, laughing. "I hear that guy throws chairs."

"Gallantly," Cotton said.

"You are a college boy, using words like gallant around people like me." Jack laughed. "Define how Bobby Knight took it gallantly."

"He wished me well, and even said he would join up, too, if he wasn't so old and fat, and pissed off all the time," Martin joked, as the two Marines cut across the grass parade field opposite the range-facility headquarters. Outside it, two Marines dressed in desert camouflage stood by the flagpole, holding the American Colors while the Officer of the Day checked his watch.

Just as Jack Valentine and Cotton Martin stepped through the doorway of the Scout-Sniper School, a scratchy record sound came on the Stone Bay public-address system. Jack stood at attention, looking outside. So did Cotton.

Still outside, running hard across the parade field, came the two knucklehead newbies from the butts. When the first blast of the bugle announced attention to Colors, the two Marines stopped, turned, stood at attention, and saluted the flag. They correctly held their salutes while the National Anthem echoed across the camp. At the last blast of the recorded bugle, calling order arms, the two Marines broke back into their hard run to the schoolhouse.

"Good boys," Gunny Valentine said, and smiled at Staff Sergeant Martin. "They might do."

"I've seen some guys go ahead and run it out, ducking inside during Colors," Cotton added.

"Me, too," Jack said. "Then they regretted it."

The two Marines from the butts burst through the handprint-littered glass double doors that led into the Scout-Sniper School facility. Gunny Valentine stepped around the corner, blocking them, his arms folded.

"You're late!" he barked.

"Gunny, we was pulling your targets," the first one said, a short-sized Latino corporal.

"That's no excuse," Jack came back. "Staff Sergeant Martin and I had a leisurely stroll, and even stopped for coffee and crullers along the way. We made it on time. What were you two jokers up to?"

"Gunny, we had to take down the targets and stack them, and that sergeant in the range house, he made us sweep up the shit you blew all over the deck when you busted that spotter," the second corporal, also Latino but taller, said.

"By the way, Gunny," the short-sized corporal said, "nice shooting."

"Go ahead and kiss my ass some more, shit-weasel." Jack frowned at them. "Before we go in the classroom and meet the rest of our little zoo, how about some names."

"Staff Sergeant Claybaugh didn't tell you?" the taller corporal said.

"That a rhetorical question, or did you really mean what you just asked?" Staff Sergeant Martin cut in.

He got blank stares from both Marines.

"Rhetorical means you already know the answer to the question," Gunny Valentine barked.

"No, I mean," the shorter corporal stammered.

"Obviously, Staff Sergeant Claybaugh didn't tell the gunny your names, or he would not ask you your names," Cotton Martin huffed at the two bewildered souls.

"Right." The shorter of the two corporals nodded. "I'm Corporal Jesse Cortez, and my partner here is Corporal Alex Gomez."

Cortez added with a smile, "We call him Jaws."

"We do, do we?" Jack said, raising both eyebrows. "Jaws? Catchy name."

"He comes from South Central in Los Angeles," Cortez explained. "Alex did some enforcing work for some of the holmes out there. On the side, when he tried to make it in pro boxing. That's what they called him, Jaws. We gonna sic Jaws on your shit, they tell some poor bastard that don't pay up."

"What's your story?" Jack asked the talkative partner of the newbie duo.

"I grew up in San Antonio," he began. "Born in El Paso, at Fort Bliss. My dad was in the Army. We got sent to San Antonio when I was like two, and he retired there. I ride bareback and saddle broncs in the PRCA. You know, bucking horses. Rough stock, we rodeo pros call it. I rode in the Camp Pendleton show just before me and Jaws headed out here for duty in this new lash-up, MARSOC."

"Can either of you shoot?" Martin asked. "Or did Colonel Snow pick you for your personality and good looks?"

"We can shoot," Jaws offered. "Both of us."

"Sniper school at Pendleton?" Jack asked.

"There and at Twenty-Nine Stumps," Gomez answered.

"Me and Jaws will take on anybody at this school, except maybe you, Gunny Valentine. We know about you, dude," Jesse Cortez boasted.

"We'll see," the gunny said, and looked the shorter corporal up and down. "So you're a rodeo star? I saw a few in my time. I was born in El Paso, too. Raised there. My mother's Latina, gave me my good looks."

Both corporals smiled.

"You any good with those broncos?" Jack asked Cortez.

"One of the best, bro." Jesse smiled. "I'll show you my collection of championship buckles sometime."

"So, you're a big star?" Cotton asked.

"Just say Jesse Cortez to anybody in the PRCA, and they know me," the corporal boasted. "I've been on ESPN like four times. Phoenix and Houston, then twice at Fort Worth."

"How about Las Vegas?" Jack asked.

"NFR? Damn close, Gunny," Cortez said, straining his neck to one side and pursing his lips, showing a touch of frustration. "Just out of the money. If I got one more ride, I'd make it. With this war and shit, I don't know. Not anymore."

Jack looked out the dirty glass on the double doors and thought for a moment. Then he looked at Jesse Cortez.

"How about Bronco Star," the gunny said. "Bronco and Jaws. That's a catchy pair."

"Bronco Star and Jaws," Martin said. "It is kind of catchy."

"What do you think, Bronco Star?" Jack smiled at the corporal. "That work for you?"

"Only if you spell Star with two *r*'s." Cortez smiled back.

"Oh, I like that." Jack grinned. "Bronco Starr like Ringo Starr."

"Hey, it's got to be cool for me to wear it," Corporal Cortez popped back.

The four Marines walked to a set of metal double doors. Above them was a carved dark wood sign with black bold letters, HOG WALLOW, burned in it. Beneath them, smaller wood-burned words wrote, HUNTERS OF GUNMEN LIVE HERE.

Bronco Starr and Jaws stepped up and pushed the handle, but Gunny Valentine stopped them.

"We operate on Lombardi time," he told them, and got another pair of blank looks, as if neither man had ever heard of the legendary football coach. Jack rolled his eyes.

"So I gotta go Barney Fife on you two yo-yos?" Jack sighed.

Bronco and Jaws stood there, eyes wide, question marks blinking on their foreheads.

"I say be here at 0800, that means 0745. Fifteen minutes early. Always," Jack explained. "If Colonel Snow calls a meeting, I'm there a half hour early, and that means you be there before me. Never arrive after me. Clear?"

"Gunny," Bronco half whined. "Why not just say the time you mean? Eight means eight, seven forty-five means seven forty-five."

"You should've been a lawyer, Barney," Jack grumbled with an even deeper sigh, and held the handle as Cortez tried to push open the doors. "You know, Bronco, those glass doors out front need a good washing. Get some cleaning supplies down the hall, in the janitor's room. You'll recognize it from the pine-oil smell, and you Nimrods get that glass shining like a diamond on a black goat's ass."

Jaws frowned at his partner and tightened his lips as he headed down the hall, huffing with each step. "You and your mouth. Always got to run your trap and try to get up on the man. Why don't you ever just shut the fuck up? Bronco Starr my ass. You can jump up and kiss my ass, Jesse."

"Dude, wait up," Corporal Cortez called after his cohort. "Gunny was gonna do it to us anyway, bro. I saw that dirty glass coming in, and I knew we was getting tagged to clean it. Come on, dude. Don't be pissed at me."

Jaws never slowed down.

Bronco stopped and called at Jaws in a long, loud whine that echoed down the halls, "I'm sorry!"

Cotton Martin smiled as he opened the door to the HOG Wallow, where thirty hopeful Marine Scout-Snipers temporarily assigned to the new platoon waited, and let Gunny Valentine enter first. "Age before beauty."

"Faces before assholes," Jack fired back.

Liberty Cruz stepped from the shower, dried her long black hair with a white towel, then wrapped an oversized pink bath towel around her tall, well-shaped, athletic body. She popped open the bathroom door and saw the handsome man she had taken home last night from a reception for security and law-enforcement executives at the Washingtonian Hotel in downtown DC still there. He was scrolling through pages on her laptop, not noticing her, focused on snooping in everything private on the computer.

She casually padded cat quiet to a mahogany humidor she kept on top of her bedroom bookcase and took out a Montecristo Especial Number Two Havana cigar and silently snipped off the end with a cutter she kept in the fine wooden box. Sensually, she licked the thirty-eight-ring-size cigar, sliding its full length inside her mouth and drawing it out. Then she took out a gold lighter, popped a flame, and drew the fire into the end of the six-inch-long Panatela, sucking a mouthful of the sweet smoke and letting it go.

Without batting an eye, cigar clenched in her teeth, Liberty, a Special Agent of the Federal Bureau of Investigation and the only woman assigned to its Special Operations branch at Quantico, reached behind a book on the second from the top shelf and took out a loaded and chambered Sig-Sauer P-226 nine-millimeter pistol, the same handgun carried by US Navy SEALs, and pointed it at the man.

He smelled the cigar's aroma and casually looked over his shoulder, seeing the tall, statuesque, dark-haired beauty wrapped in the bath towel, smoking the stogie and holding the gun on him.

"I ought to have a camera," he said, unruffled.

"You know, it's loaded," Liberty said.

"The cigar, the gun, or you?" He laughed. "Maybe all three after last night."

"You've got a lot of nerve, Cesare," she said, and unwrapped her shiny black hair and let it fall, still damp, covering her shoulders. She shook it hard and took another long drag off the cigar.

"Just checking a few things," he said.

"You set me up, didn't you? So you could check a few things." She frowned. "And I kind of liked you."

"You fell in love," Cesare Alosi said, throwing his empty Sicilian-American charm at her. "So did I."

"You're too damned good-looking for your own good," Liberty Cruz said, dismayed. "Yeah, the name got me, too, I'll admit. The *GQ*-looking guy in the trim dark suit, dark eyes, olive skin, perfectly slicked-back black hair, and a name like Cesare Pierfrancesco Alosi. It got me. That and a few too many belts of Jack Daniel's."

"You had me, too, Liberty." Alosi sighed. "The long cool woman in the black dress, working for the F-B-I. Just like the song. A tall walking big black cat." And he began to sing, "With just one look I was a bad mess, 'cause that long cool woman had it all."

Liberty laughed and let down the gun.

"You need to leave," she said.

"But Special Agent Cruz," he pled, "I'm in love with you! Love at first sight."

"You love me so much you're snooping out my laptop?" she said, her teeth now clenched and the gun raised again. Something about this too-pretty man pegged her bullshit meter in the red. His insincerity seemed too well played, practiced. "Your name really Abdullah from Goatville? Some kind of jihadi spy?"

"Actually," Cesare said, getting to his feet and starting toward her, "you might recall me telling you how I am deploying in a few days to Iraq with my company, Malone-Leyva Executive Security and Investigations. We're under contract with Department of Defense, working in al-Anbar. I'm going over there and may not come back alive. Doesn't that at least draw some of your sympathies for me and justify our lovemaking last night?"

"Not so fast," Liberty said, motioning with the gun for him to stop his advance and sit back down. "Going to Iraq doesn't draw water with me. I know other people, a lot more worthwhile than your sorry ass, who're going to Iraq, too."

"The guy in the pictures?" Cesare asked. "A Marine gunnery sergeant. Handsome fellow. Gold wings and lots of ribbons. Tough guy?"

"You might just find out if you fuck around with me," Liberty threatened. "Or I might just shoot your worthless butt here in my bedroom. You're dressed, and I'm showered clean. I came out of the bathroom, found you snooping, and I killed you. Home invasion. Make my day. How about that?"

"But what about all those FBI agents and supervisory special agents who saw us leave together?" Alosi mused.

"Just try me," Liberty Cruz threatened, and now her face turned red as the throttle controlling her anger engines went forward.

"I'll leave," the slick mercenary supervisor said, easing to his feet, his hands raised. He knew when he had reached a limit and didn't want the beautiful Latina to lose her good senses and her temper and empty the magazine in him. Just as in their lovemaking, women like her never stop with one shot. They go a full fifteen-round capacity.

"Gunnery Sergeant Jack Valentine," Cesare Alosi said, going downstairs and through her living room, heading for her Georgetown town-house front door. "He writes some romantic stuff in his email to you."

"I'll fucking shoot!" Liberty raged.

"Ciao," Alosi said, waving, skipping down the steps to the P Street Northwest sidewalk. He stopped and looked back at her, still holding the gun in her right hand and the cigar in her left, the bath towel breezing open, exposing way too much of Liberty Cruz to the world. "If I see Gunny Valentine in Iraq, I'll be sure to give him your regards. Oh, and dear. Do cover up. Your puberty is showing."

Liberty threw down the cigar and grabbed her bath towel closed around her nakedness.

"You better not say a fucking word to Jack Valentine!" she yelled. "You hear me? Not ever!"

Two weeks of togetherness, and Gunny Jack had his platoon trimmed to eighteen finalists. The dozen culled out went to battalion sniper platoons or to the newly formed Marine Special Operations Battalion for additional training and seasoning.

Lieutenant Colonel Elmore Snow, wearing the new Marine Corps desert-camouflage MARPAT pixel-pattern utility uniform with the slanted breast pockets, crisp and squared away, stood at the front of the classroom and said nothing for a long time, studying each face.

After five minutes of silent, cold gray eyeballing, several of the Scout-Snipers began to fidget. Jaws stared back, locking his dark brown eyes on his senior commanding officer.

"He wants to do Mexican sweat, I'll show him how a real Mexican plays that game," Alex Gomez thought to himself. Then he wondered if the colonel could read his mind, maybe his face. So Jaws worked hard to show no expression. Just a hard-assed stare.

Bronco Starr broke first, seventeen minutes into the standoff.

"What's going on, sir?" Cortez asked.

Snow took a breath, looked at Gunny Valentine, and smiled. "Broke the old record by two minutes."

Then he strolled down the center aisle where the men sat at schoolroom-type desks, their eyes and faces following him. He made an about-face, smiling, and walked back to the front of the room.

"Very good, gentlemen," he said. "I do have your undivided attention."

"Sir, we could have saved seventeen minutes," Bronco said, a bit perplexed. "You had our undivided attention from the get-go."

"But you're just a touch impatient, Corporal Cortez, aren't you?" the colonel came back.

"I don't think so, sir," Jesse politely argued. "I just don't like wasting people's time."

"I'm wasting your time, Corporal?" Snow said in a voice that could crack plaster at a hundred yards.

"Oh, no, sir!" Cortez exclaimed, and got to his feet, snapping at attention. "Sir. I didn't mean it like that. It's just all that staring and waiting. For what?"

Elmore Snow smiled at the corporal.

"Take your seat, young man," he said in a friendly, fatherly voice. "My point with the silence and the waiting is very simple. Patience in our business is everything. We are a handpicked Special Operations team with a mission to go to Iraq and work the entire theater. We're not going there to work a base camp or patrol a road. We are going there to hunt."

Snow paused, waiting for the dramatic moment, then added, "Hunt the devil himself. Abu Musab al-Zarqawi.

"That, gentlemen, requires persistence, ingenuity, and the utmost profound patience.

"We are part of a greater, Joint Special Operations Command that combines our Marine operators with the best that Delta Force has to offer, the best that Air Force Pararescue, Combat Control and Special Operations has, and the best of the Navy's SEALs. Our operators today scour the mountains in Afghanistan for Osama bin Laden, our number one target. And soon we will scour the Iraqi deserts for an even worse devil, in my opinion, Abu Musab al-Zarqawi."

"Gentlemen," Gunny Valentine said, walking to the front of the classroom, on cue, and taking a position to the left of the colonel. "Staff Sergeant Terrence Martin and Staff Sergeant Bill Claybaugh, whom you now know well after our two weeks of evaluating and testing each of you for fit on this team, will lead our two nine-man squads. I will lead the platoon. Captain Mike Burkehart, a Force Recon mustang officer, whom I have known for many years, joins us Monday as the platoon officer-in-charge. Lieutenant Colonel Snow will command our platoon, and two others like it.

"Do not write letters or make phone calls home telling Aunt Sally or your best friend Jody Boy, or your girlfriend he's keeping warm while you're gone, or your mama and daddy what you're about to go do, or that this team even exists. Everything we do is classified top secret.

"You're deploying to Iraq as a MARSOC detachment, augmenting Marine Corps Scout-Sniper operations in al-Anbar Province should anyone ask. Do not say any bullshit like, I'm going on a secret mission, or go buy a T-shirt that has TOP SECRET stenciled on the back. Am I clear?"

The whole room answered, "Yes, sir!" as if they were back in boot camp and Gunny Valentine was their senior drill instructor.

"Our weapons systems will include the standard M40A3 sniper rifle," the gunny continued, "shooting our faithful 175-grain Sierra .30 caliber bullet launched by 7.62-by-51-millimeter cartridges. Added to that we will be shooting the M40A3 sniper rifle with the Remington 700 long action, similar to the one the Army shoots, and that gun will be chambered for the .300 Winchester Magnum caliber ammunition, also shooting the same Sierra MatchKing bullet as our .308, but one hell of a lot flatter, hotter, and farther. We will also have six Barrett Mark-82 .50 caliber long rifles, and six Barrett .50 caliber Bullpups.

"Bill Ritchie, out in Utah, at EDM Arms, has built us a dozen .338 Lapua Magnum rifles that he guarantees will drive nails at two thousand yards. That's the gun I am looking forward to carrying in my hands. We've also got a set of M40A3 rifles with threaded crowns chambered for .338 Lapua Magnum as well, for special applications.

"Zarqawi got away from me because I was shooting that weak-ass .308 NATO, and had fifteen hundred meters to cross. Too much drop, and I dropped it between his feet. That's not happening twice.

"Rifles will be here Monday," Jack concluded. "We have the coming two weeks to get them and our ammo tuned to our liking. Then we're off to the sandbox. You've got the weekend free, so go have some fun. Someone said that C. J. Quinlan has a HOG party at his Rally Point tomorrow evening. I might see you there."

Billy Claybaugh barked from the back of the room, "If you get put in jail, you better break out or kiss your ass good-bye. If I have to come to the Onslow County brig or some other drunk tank up or down this coastline, I will fucking kill you. I will rip out your throat and piss on your collarbones."

Several Marines shot him the finger as they left the classroom.

In the back, Cotton Martin had Gunny Valentine's cell phone. It had buzzed and he was exchanging text messages with someone.

When Jack first saw it, he thought he recognized the phone and checked his pants pockets to be sure. Gone!

"What are you doing?" Jack asked, running to Cotton and grabbing for the phone.

"Getting you laid." Cotton grinned and held the flip-top Moto with the tiny screen high over his head. "You're pissed and grouchy, all crabby like an old hen with PMS. You need to get your pipes cleaned, brother."

Jack kneed him in the nuts and grabbed the cell phone when Martin doubled over.

"Fucking asshole," Jack grumbled, looking at the string of text messages. "Do you know who the fuck this is?"

"Same chick I saw in the pictures on your laptop. Liberty Cruz," Cotton said. "Billy says she's FBI. One fucking hot agent, if you ask me."

"You're looking at my laptop?" Valentine bleated.

"Billy-C was looking at your pictures, and I saw all the eye candy over his shoulder. That tall dark drink of fine wine you got on there. Shots of her in that tiny bikini were killer," Cotton said, pulling at his belt and shaking his balls back down his pants legs. "You fucking hurt me. You know that, Jack?"

"I hope you die," Valentine said, and flipped the phone shut as he walked outside.

He punched in Liberty Cruz's speed-dial cell number, and she answered on the first ring.

"Damn, you must feel guilty about something," Jack said, "answering on the first ring. What's up?"

"I am so excited about this weekend." She swooned. "I've got a room booked in Jacksonville for us, and dinner reservations at Thig's Barbecue House. You're always telling me how you love that place. We're going to get some of their fall-off-the-bone ribs and swine wine barbecue sauce. Oh, Jack, I have missed you so bad!"

"Where are you?" he asked, not having a clue about the text-message conversation that had gone on while he had briefed his snipers.

"I told you, Jack!" Liberty exclaimed. "I'm here in Jacksonville. SERE School. I check in Monday. I had a choice of Florida or Camp Lejeune, and I chose here. You're here. Why then would I go to Florida?"

"Sorry, babe." Jack sighed. "It's been a rough week. My brains are fried."

"You put some pretty serious stuff in those text messages," Liberty chirped. "I hope you're not too fried to live up to all that bragging."

Jack torqued his jaws and considered how he could get even with Cotton Martin. Billy-C Claybaugh was in on it, too. He was back there, next to Cotton. Both of them sending the text messages. Valentine had hoped for a quiet weekend alone in his little cottage down by the Swansboro docks. Maybe do some fishing, and finish the seascape painting he had been dabbing in oils for the past several weeks. Painting and drawing relaxed his mind, and his artwork was quite good.

When he retired from the Marine Corps in a few years, he thought of disappearing down to Santa Maria, Mexico. A little village below a trout lake in the mountains of Chihuahua, 150 miles southwest of Juarez. He and his dad used to go there when he was a kid. Crystal-clear water and fat fish. Simple country people and no pressure.

He also loved Liberty Cruz, ever since high school. Nobody else. He had his one-nighters, but no one of a relationship status. He had Liberty and wished she could understand the beauty of his simple life's dream.

Her ambition and obsessive mind-set for accomplishing her agenda of wealth and the big house on the Riviera had kept him from ever asking her to marry him. Yet she was the only woman Jack Valentine had ever loved.

"Why don't you pick me up and we'll just find out," Jack said. "I'll leave my truck here at the schoolhouse for the weekend. We'll bury the phones and get lost in our lust. How's that sound?"

Liberty laughed. "Oh, Jack. I'm on my way!"

"We can swing by my place in Swansboro, let me pick up an overnight kit and clean clothes," Jack said.

"Still not wearing underwear, Jack?" Liberty giggled.

"Nada." Jack grinned. "Commando through and through. I also have a big watch."

"Oh yeah!" Liberty laughed, and hung up.

When Cesare Alosi checked in with his headquarters in Baghdad, he met three former Marine Scout-Snipers now working for Malone-Leyva. One had retired as a master sergeant, and the other two had left the Marine

Corps in the mid-nineties. A bit on the mature side, he thought, but still solid.

As the stylish boss, in his tan 5.11 operator's shirt and matching trousers, bloused over roughed-out Army Ranger jump boots, and a black operator ball cap on his head, smelling of the latest Versace men's cologne, put out his hand, Hacksaw Gillespie had a good laugh as he shook it.

"Sorry, boss, but you smell too good for these parts," he mused. "I recommend you keep the flu-flu in the locker, or you'll have one of these Iraqi sweet peas trying to park his pork up your caboose."

Alosi let go of his paw and put his hand in his pocket. He didn't bother shaking hands with Kermit Alexander or Cory Webster. All three of the mercenaries, now working for Malone-Leyva as contract hit men and executive bodyguards, wore black "do-rag" bandanas tied over their heads like Hulk Hogan. All three wore moustaches and goatees, too.

They dressed in cargo jeans and Under Armour T-shirts and wore Advanced Operator vests with the pockets stuffed with gadgets. Their legs were Velcro strapped with semiauto .45 caliber pistols, sporting flashlights on rails.

"So," Alosi said, and paused for effect, eyeballing Hacksaw, then Kermit The Frog and Habu last. "You guys are like what? Pirates?"

"Yarrrr!" Hacksaw grinned back, flashing gold-capped front teeth and pointing to a diamond ear stud. Then he slipped on a pair of Ray-Ban black-framed shades. "We got to look badass for the clients. Didn't you read the handbook?"

"I wrote the handbook," Alosi said.

He walked around the men's office, which also doubled as transient sleeping quarters, should a team have to work days and nights. The place was a wreck. Trash was on the floor, and beer bottles filled three overflowing garbage cans.

"Home sweet shit hole," Hacksaw said.

"I agree," Cesare said. "I thought you guys were Marines. You know, squared away. Disciplined."

"We didn't sign on to do maid work or housecleaning," Kermit snapped back. "You want home sweet shit hole cleaned up, hire a maid."

"Yeah," Habu chimed in, pissed off, already not liking this dressed-up sweet-smelling Don Juan.

"I'll do just that," Alosi said, went to the desk, swept crap out of the chair, and sat. "What are your stories?"

"I retired from the Corps a few years back, E-eight and glad to leave," Hacksaw said, stepping up to do the talking. Kermit and Cory were happy to have him do it.

"Staff Sergeant Webster there ran a sniper gun and our old boss, Gunny Mutt Alexander, spotted for him. I worked as a spotter with another Marine," Hacksaw said. "We hunted cocaine cowboys down in Colombia and Chile back in the eighties and nineties. Killed a whole raft of them."

"Really?" Alosi said, a smile crossing his face, and he cocked his feet on the desk.

"We was in the Gulf War, the first one, for a short bit, but got back down south where we enjoyed the work more, and the women, if you know what I mean." Gillespie grinned.

"Don't misunderstand Hacksaw. We didn't party," Webster interjected. "We worked hard. Killed a lot of bad guys."

"You were all Force Recon then?" Alosi asked. "They got the drug-interdiction missions down there, if memory serves me right."

"Correct, sir," Kermit offered. "Captain Elmore Snow led us. Great man. I'd follow him to hell and back."

"I've heard the name," Cesare said, then looked at the three, considering their ages and experience. "You ever hear of a Marine Scout-Sniper, Jack Valentine? I think Force Recon, too, gold jump wings and lots of shirt salad."

All three men laughed.

"He's our bro, bro," Hacksaw said. "Shit, I spotted his first kill. Down by Hillah, during the Gulf War."

"Really?" Alosi beamed. "He's headed over here, you know. Leading a MARSOC team, they say."

"Awesome!" Habu said. "Oh, you'll like Jack. Everybody likes Jack!"

"So I gather," Cesare said, still smiling. "Some more than others."

The three Marines didn't quite know how to take the last comment but let it slide.

"You know," Hacksaw said, looking side to side as if someone might eavesdrop. Then in a low voice added, "Jack Valentine put the bullet in Pablo Escobar's ear."

"I thought Colombian National Police shot him when they raided his hideaway town house in Medellín," Alosi said. "All the Wikipedia and Google stuff says it."

"Bullshit! Pure bullshit," Hacksaw said, and looked at his boys. The other two nodded at their new boss.

"Jack Valentine shot Pablo Escobar in the ear from three hundred yards using an Australian Special Air Service M55, Tikka sniper rifle with a ten-power Leupold scope, shooting the .22-250 Remington cartridge with a 52-grain hollow-point boat-tail Sierra MatchKing bullet," Kermit Alexander said. "Like a bolt of lightning. Four thousand feet per second! I was there. So were Habu and Hacksaw, and Sergeant Major Ray Ambrose and our officer in charge, Captain Elmore Snow. We all saw Jack make that shot."

"We were down there in Colombia in '92 and '93, with the CIA running special operations dovetailed into that Los Pepés uprising they had going on," Cory Webster explained.

"Yeah, I've heard about the Los Pepés thing." Alosi nodded.

"Jack got that Aussi gun off a British SAS operator working with our group and the Los Pepés brigade. Sad story there. His whole team got bushwhacked by Escobar's men," Webster went on. "Sergeant Valentine had made close friends with that Tommy, an outstanding SAS paratrooper and special operator. Easy to get tight with soldiers like that. When we found him and his lads dead on the road, old Jack got real mad. Trail was still hot, so we went on the hunt.

"Just one valley over, we found the bastards, doped up, counting their loot. We killed every last one of the dirty bastards with no mercy. They threw their hands up, but we shot 'em anyway. We wasn't police, and they needed killin'.

"They had the dead Brit's rifle among the other stuff they stole, so Jack took it. He cleaned it up and put it to good use.

"That was one hot shootin' gun, and our boy knew how to use it. When Sergeant Valentine killed Pablo Escobar, that was the last round he ever fired with that rifle. I guess it closed the book for him and that British boy. Grave sealed. Justice served."

"What happened to the rifle?" Cesare asked.

"We shipped it stateside with our gear, and Jack took it home," Hacksaw said. "Knowing him, it's tucked away someplace. He'd never get rid of it. Too many memories."

"So, once again, history and Google are wrong." Alosi smiled. "Jack Valentine killed Escobar, not the police."

"Colombian National Police couldn't hit a bull in the ass with a bass fiddle." Gillespie laughed. "But with us working some deep-cover black ops, the CIA felt all too happy to give those shit turds a day in the sunshine. Besides, Escobar's big brother put the hit on them. We didn't need that grief. Best let them have the credit."

"We found Escobar hiding out in a fancy apartment and called the sheriff," Habu told Cesare. "Police surrounded the building and Pablo went out the second-story French doors, climbed over the wrought-iron railing off the little patio, and tried to escape down the red-tile roof. I remember it like yesterday. Jack Valentine was on the rifle, and Captain Snow had the binoculars on Escobar. He gave the command to shoot him, and Jack dropped the bastard like a sack of rocks. Blew the wax out of his ears and the holy dogshit out of his head."

"I look forward to meeting this man, Gunnery Sergeant Jack Valentine." Cesare Alosi smiled.

"Oh, you'll like him," Hacksaw said. "Everybody does."

"Yes, you said that." Alosi smiled.

— 3 —

A black Cadillac Escalade with armored doors, floors, and bulletproof glass led two others just like it out of the United States embassy compound, Baghdad. A Marine and Army security contingent joined them as they blew past the blast gates onto Haifa Street rolling west, guns up, throttles down. The high-speed wagon train had just turned onto the Qadisaya Expressway to intercept Airport Street, which led to Baghdad International, when suddenly the Escalade out front slammed brakes to a full stop. There it sat, dead center of the fast track of the high-walled concrete-flanked four-lane.

Two up-armored, M1025 sand-tan Marine Humvees, with M2 .50 caliber machine guns on 360 turrets up top, had the VIP sedan, the second black Escalade, sandwiched between them. The third black Escalade followed next, with a fully loaded Cougar HE, six-by-six, Mine Resistant Ambush Protected troop truck close behind. A six-man squad of unhappy Army infantry rode inside the MRAP with its crew while a lone warrior manned an MK19 forty-millimeter grenade-launching street-sweeper machine gun from the truck's well-fortified dorsal turret.

Several times daily, caravans like this carried American embassy diplomats, CIA field operators, and staff workers to and from the airport for flights, or meetings with Iraqi state bankers, walled inside airport security, or to and from skull sessions at the Al Faw Palace, a postcard picture of imperial luxury surrounded by a reflecting-pond moat in the heart of Camp Victory. The base sat next to the airport, within the same high walls of security, where the American-led Allied coalition headquartered its bosses and key planners. And the home of Elmore Snow and his MARSOC team as well.

Jack Valentine rode shotgun while Billy Claybaugh drove the front Hummer, a good interval behind the lead Escalade and ahead of the VIP car. Cotton Martin rode shotgun in the Hummer following the sedan with Sergeant Clarence "Cochise" Quinlan driving. Corporal Petey Preston ran the Maw-Duce in the turret, with Corporal Randy Powell assisting him.

Elmore Snow and his twenty-two-man MARSOC team had landed in Iraq two weeks ago and had not seen the outside of Camp Victory since. Except for the opportunity to run security on a couple of high-speed caravans from the embassy to the airport. It was something for his operators to do while they waited to slide into the tall grass on their primary mission, hunting Abu Musab al-Zarqawi.

Jaws manned the turret on Valentine's Humvee while Bronco assisted him. Corporal Cortez kept protesting that he should run the .50 and Corporal Gomez should assist him.

"Alex, come on," Jesse whined. "We can take turns, dude."

Jaws ignored him, both hands on the gun, as if he owned it.

Gunny Valentine was ready to throw Bronco Starr out the door when the lead Cadillac smoked tires to a dead stop on the expressway.

"You locked and cocked, Jaws?" Jack yelled to the backseat. Both Billy-C and Valentine had their M4s up and ready.

"I've been locked and cocked, Gunny," Gomez answered. He spun a 360, looking for a target, and shouted down below, "Not a thing happening out here. No gunfire. Nothing. I don't get it."

Bronco leaned between the front seats, looking out the windshield.

"Why they stop, boss?" he asked.

"Just be ready to feed ammo," Jack answered, searching everything that surrounded them.

"Sniper?" Bronco asked.

Then the radio crackled from the lead Cadillac, manned by security contractors from Malone-Leyva, "We're taking heavy fire!"

"So we stop and make ourselves better targets?" Staff Sergeant Claybaugh fumed.

"I don't see a thing!" Jack said, pissed off.

Before Jack could get on the radio and ask the embassy security officer what he wanted to do, gunfire erupted from the up-front black Escalade.

"We've got shots coming out the Escalade," Jack reported on the radio. "Zero incoming, but automatic fire going out all ports of the lead car."

Several bullets skipped off Valentine's Humvee, and Jaws ducked low in his turret.

"Do I return fire?" he shouted down, swinging the .50 in big arcs, searching for targets.

"At who?" Jack yelled back. "All the shit's coming out that Escalade. Nothing incoming!"

"What the fuck are those guys on?" Billy-C asked.

"Dude from Camp Liberty told me these private-security punks be shooting steroids, hard drugs, meth and shit, and stay drunk all night," Bronco offered.

Valentine looked at the insanity ahead of him. "Makes sense to me."

Just then, the three-man crew in the lead Cadillac came rolling out, hitting pavement, lighting up the world with a SAW and two Uzi burp guns. They ran a mad dash to Jack's Hummer. Behind them fire exploded out of the abandoned car, flames and black smoke boiling skyward.

"Pop the back, Bronco," Jack ordered. "Soon as those turds get aboard, Billy, roll this motherfucker hard to Camp Victory."

Jack put the radio to his mouth and called to all following vehicles, "We're hitting it, high speed to Victory. Try to keep up."

As soon as the trio of Malone-Leyva security pros got inside Jack's Hummer, Billy stomped the gas pedal and dodged around the burning Escalade.

"What the fuck!" Jack blew at the Malone-Leyva trio, dressed in tan M-L logo ball caps, sunglasses, tan 5.11s, black Under Armour T's, and Advanced Operator Kevlar vests, pockets crammed with gadgets.

All three men stunk of booze, chemical-laden sweat and body odor, and urine. One had pissed himself when the shooting started, and now he tried to get his wet pants off, crammed in the back of the Hummer.

"Fucking wait!" Jack yelled at him. "Just fucking lay in your shit for five minutes. It won't kill you."

"You saw that RPG, didn't you?" the crew leader asked the Marines.

"Weren't no RPG, dude," Jaws said, holding on to his big gun while Billy-C drove hard.

Behind Jack's Hummer, the two Caddies and Cotton's truck poured on the gas while the MRAP roared full-tilt boogie to keep up, blowing black smoke out its pipes. Shrinking in the mirrors, the abandoned Escalade sent a towering plume climbing skyward. A common sight in this city of exploding cars and bomb vests.

The contractor leader looked at the corporal and took off his sunglasses. "Was too! Motherfucker! RPG came right across our hood!"

Jaws turned sideways, looking down at the idiot, ready to boot the mouthy bastard, but caught the gunny's squint.

"Heavy fire! Shit, bro. You had to have taken some, too," the contractor fumed.

"I ain't your bro, and I saw nothing," Jack said. "My corporal saw nothing. No RPG. Sure as shit one didn't blow."

"Dud most likely," the scumbag said.

Billy-C studied the leader in the rearview mirror. Jack took in the man's need for a shave and a haircut, and his bloodshot eyes. One fucked-up piece of shit. Skin pasty, cheeks gaunt but big bones and chin. Muscles and no fat. Eyes sunk in his skull and watery red.

Then there was that smell. Oh, that smell. Not the liquor, but that other stink that oozed from their filthy hides. Drugs and steroids. Steroid unmistakable in the piss.

Bronco put his face close to the window, focusing on the world and wanting fresh air. Then he looked at the contractor boss.

"How come you to torch your wagon, dude?" he asked.

"Shot all to shit. Totally fucked," the leader said.

Bronco shrugged. "Is now."

As Jesse Cortez said it, the leader gave Bronco a mean squint. "Don't I know you?"

"Could be," the corporal said. "You tried to do the Basic-Recon course at the School of Infantry, out at Pendleton, when I went through out of boot camp. You sprained your ankle or something, didn't you?"

"Broke it," the guy said, and smiled, and put out his hand to Cortez. "Good to see you, bro."

Jesse shook it but didn't like it.

"Hey," Billy-C called from up front. "Didn't you used to be at three-two? Like a year or so ago?"

The dude smiled. "Yeah, that's me. Didn't know if you recognized me, all bulked up and built nowadays."

"Takes a minute," Claybaugh said. "You look like you got that Mickey Rourke thing going on. Your face kinda grown a chin and big cheeks."

"Dude, that's age," he said, not liking the passive-aggressive way the staff sergeant hinted at the steroids.

Billy-C nodded. "Right. These days a guy ages a lot in a year."

"Still can't think of my name, though," the Malone-Leyva crew chief said, half a smile on his face.

"Oh, I think I recall some kind of hyphenated red-clay grit sort of John-Boy name," Claybaugh drawled out.

Jack's guys laughed and Bronco tuned in with a smile like Sylvester just ate Tweety Pie. Then when he saw Billy-C couldn't quite pull it out, he blurted, "Ray-Dean Blevins."

"Yeah, that's it!" Claybaugh called out, leading the caravan down the off-ramp from Airport Street, main gate of Camp Victory dead ahead. "But they call you something else. Coochie or Cootie. Yeah, that's it, Cooter."

"Cooter's a pussy," Ray-Dean said, then added, "It's Cooder, with a D, not a T."

Jack grinned. "On *Dukes of Hazard*, they spelled Cooter with a T."

"I spell it with a D, okay?" Blevins popped back.

Staff Sergeant Claybaugh looked in the rearview, and said, "Corporal Blevins. How the fuck you been, dude?"

Ray-Dean gave Jack a go-to-hell glance, then spread a condescending smile at Billy-C. "Gettin' rich as shit while you lame-ass losers still be living off food stamps."

As the caravan closed behind the lead Hummer, a security force came out from behind concrete barricades by the blast-proof steel entrance to the American head-quarters compound, and began their vehicle check. Thumbs-up, and a soldier waved the two Escalades and three military trucks to proceed inside Camp Victory.

"Who're your friends, Cooder-with-a-D," Jack asked, looking at the other two contractors.

The one in wet pants nervously spoke first. "Gary Frank. I used to be a Marine sergeant in public affairs. A forty-three thirteen. Radio and television. Malone-Leyva hired me to work PR for them. I got put on security duty for a couple of weeks to get me some front-line experience, and see how the company does business. Pretty exciting so far." The guy finished with a big smile.

Jack nodded at the guy and felt sorry for the schmuck.

"And you?" Valentine said to the dry-pants contractor.

"Fred Stein," he answered. "Hard stripe sergeant, US Army Rangers. Signed on with Malone-Leyva five months ago. I finish this tour next month. Then I'm going home to work construction with my dad's little company in Tennessee."

"You sound relieved," Jack said.

"Security contracting. Not my cup of tea, it turns out," Stein answered.

Jack nodded, kind of liking the guy.

Bronco began giggling like a child with a dirty secret. Jaws gave him an elbow. "Don't fucking say it."

"What?" Billy-C grinned, stopping the Humvee at the dismount area at Al Faw Palace, the caravan halting behind him.

The VIP car's passengers couldn't depart the Escalade behind Jack fast enough. Then the two crews of the remaining black SUVs made a fast circle and lit cigarettes. The MRAP Cougar pulled around the stopped cars and headed to its home shed at Camp Liberty, inside concrete walls on the north side of the Victory compound.

While Cooder-with-a-D and his crew climbed out to join the Malone-Leyva crowd, Bronco laughed to Staff Sergeant Claybaugh. "Frank and Stein! Get it?"

Claybaugh grinned at Ray-Dean Blevins. "So long, Cootie." And got a middle finger shot back at him.

After they left, Billy-C wheeled the Hummer toward their MARSOC set of white hard-walled homes that looked more like ship containers than living quarters and offices. Jack sat on the right seat, and Bronco and Jaws settled in back. Cotton Martin and his crew followed in their truck.

"You know," the staff sergeant said to Jack, "Corporal Blevins weren't a bad sort, as a Marine. I'd give him a 3.8 out of 4.0, if you asked me to write a pro-con on the dude."

"He's a pure zero in my book," Jack said.

"Cooder didn't break his leg at Basic Recon, either. I was there," Bronco chimed in. "He faked that sprain. He's all kinds of big talk. Wore a Recon T-shirt but never earned the 0321 to go with it."

It was just past nine in the morning when they parked their two trucks, and everyone headed to his air-conditioned quarters to check email and clean guns.

Just as Bronco and Jaws headed out, Gunny Valentine called to them, "I want that piss smell out of my Hummer before you guys sky out."

They both wheeled in their tracks and tried sad faces on their gunny. It didn't work. Then Bronco bucked up.

"How about Cochise and Randy, Guns?" Bronco said. "They just walk?"

"Cotton wants his truck cleaned, that's his call," Jack said. "I own you two Spartans, and I want my Hummer decontaminated. Spring lilacs or new leather needs to greet my nose next time I sit down in that truck. I do not want to smell any faint whiff of contractor. Got me?"

"Right, Guns," Jaws said, and headed toward the Humvee, grumbling. "You running your mouth did this, Jesse. Always got to have shit to say."

"He was going to do it anyway," Cortez whined. "Bro, it ain't because of what I say."

Bronco turned for help from Gunny V, but got his back.

Elmore Snow stepped in the MARSOC headquarters hooch and swatted the dust off his pixel-patterned Marine Corps desert-camouflage utility uniform with his flop hat. A sign made of wood from an ammunition crate and black words that read, HOG WALLOW, hung above the door outside. Jack had hand painted the sign and stylized Marine Scout-Sniper emblems, upward-pointed arrow with overlaid SS, at both ends of it.

"Sir, you mind doing that outside?" Jack said, looking up from a book propped on his leg. He had his feet cocked on his desk and a cup of hot decaf green tea tipped against his lips.

"You look relaxed after a hard start of a day," Elmore said, and pulled up the metal chair by Valentine's desk. "What you reading?"

"*Riding the Rap*," Jack said, and closed the book. He put his feet on the floor and took another sip of hot tea.

Elmore nodded. "You already read *Pronto*, I guess."

Between sips, Jack said, "Yup."

"What about this gunfight?" Lieutenant Colonel Snow asked.

Jack grinned. "What gunfight?"

"Oh, I don't know. How about the one that destroyed a three-hundred-thousand-dollar armored Cadillac. That one sound familiar?" Elmore said.

"Like I said, Elmore, what gunfight?" Jack answered, his eyebrows raised at his boss.

"This report that Malone-Leyva's chief of security submitted to the United States Department of State two hours ago, asking for reimbursement of the cost for their lost vehicle, says there was a gunfight, Jack," Snow said, and laid the stack of stapled papers on Valentine's desk.

"Boy, that's fast," Jack said, picking up the handful of bullshit witness statements and cover-sheet claim. "Not even four o'clock, and they've already submitted paperwork. I guess that's the difference between private enterprise and government. It'd take our boys a week just to collect statements."

Elmore looked down his nose as Gunny Valentine leaned back in his chair and cocked his feet back on his desk.

"Funny thing, Jack," the colonel said. "Army guys in the Cougar said they were too far back, but their man in the turret definitely heard gunfire. So, why haven't you or Staff Sergeant Martin signed off on these claims? Those soldiers aren't lying."

"Oh, I never said there wasn't gunfire, sir," Valentine answered, and took a sip of tea. "We had lots of shooting. My Hummer's dinged with bullet creases. We just never had a gunfight. No ambush. No enemy."

"So you're saying that the Malone-Leyva vehicle never took fire but fired at nothing?" Elmore asked.

"That's about the size of it," Jack said.

"What about the rocket attack?" Snow asked.

Jack laughed hard. "My ass! Nobody shot any RPG, and no Hajis on the road ambushed that Escalade. That half-drunk, steroided-out fool, Ray-Dean Blevins, went psycho as we sped along the boulevard, and I guess his PTSD must have kicked in. I don't know. Just giving him any benefit-of-the-doubt reason for stopping in the middle of the fucking expressway and opening fire on nobody."

"What about the lost armored car? Burned to smithereens," Colonel Snow asked.

"You've got two nitwits with no experience led by a drug-induced fool who starts screaming that they're under attack," Jack said. "They start shooting, scared shitless. Hell, that poor child Gary Frank wet his pants! They pulled pins on incendiaries, bailed out of the car behind crazy Cooder-with-a-D Blevins, beating face against pavement, and blazing guns at zero bad guys. Colonel Snow, that's it in a nutshell. No gunfight. Just stupid."

"You and your team in our two vehicles are the only real eyes and ears on the event," Snow said, and jotted notes on the face of the report. "Your statement in total is what you just told me?"

"In total, sir," Jack said. "Cotton and his boys will say the same thing. No gunfight."

"You know, Malone-Leyva will not like this one bit," Elmore said. "Maybe you and the boys just sign off on this and let it slide?"

"No way, sir!" Jack said, sitting straight up and stamping both boots on the floor. "I'm surprised at you, sir, asking me such a thing."

Snow smiled. "I had to ask. Just in case."

"Why?" Jack frowned. "That's not me, sir. I don't care what the fuck is expedient or avoids trouble. As far as I can see, Malone-Leyva or any of the other bloodsucking mercenary outfits shouldn't even be suited up here."

"I can't help but agree. But we don't run things, do we?" The colonel sighed, and Jack did, too.

"You know, they could be a problem," Elmore added. "State Department will not approve this claim without your signing off. That asshole who runs the show over here for Malone-Leyva will be none too happy. He's a real head of steam, I hear. Friends in high places, like that US senator from Nevada, Cooper Carlson. Always ragging our asses. Could be trouble."

"Fuck them, sir," Jack answered, and looked at the book he'd been reading.

Elmore followed, "And the horse he rode in on. I know."

Jack blinked deadpan. "Just like Raylan Givens told Dale Crowe Junior, I don't take it personal. Malone-Leyva can piss up a rope. Ray-Dean Blevins is not my problem. He's his own problem. What old Cooder-with-a-D will have to do now is ride the rap. It's all anybody can do."

Jack opened his book back up, and Elmore Snow picked up his paperwork, put on his hat, and left.

"**F**ucking Jack Valentine!" Cesare Alosi yelled as he threw the twenty pages of denied claim for the three-hundred-thousand-dollar fully armored Cadillac Escalade across his office.

As it smacked the wall and fell dead on the floor, Walter Gillespie, who had just entered the office, ducked.

"Bad news, I gather?" he said, and Alosi glared at him.

"I thought you said Jack Valentine was a good guy," Malone-Leyva's head of operations in Iraq asked the man he had promoted to chief supervisor.

"He is," Hacksaw Gillespie answered.

"We're out three hundred grand because of Valentine. I don't call that good," Cesare fumed.

Gillespie scrunched his face and squinted at his boss. "This wouldn't be about our loose cannon Blevins putting the torch to his SUV last week, would it? You know, that boy is past due for the psycho ward."

"I don't fucking give a shit!" Alosi seethed. "Every one of you are way past due for the psycho ward."

"Well, present company excluded." Hacksaw grinned.

"No, present company especially included," Alosi said, still fuming.

"What the fuck you need done?" Gillespie asked.

"I need Jack Valentine convinced that on second thought, he did see an RPG shot across the front of my Escalade, it disabled as a result of the attack, and my crew returned fire at an ambush," Alosi said.

"That ain't happening," Hacksaw said, shaking his head.

"It will happen!" Alosi screamed, his voice cracking from rage that sent the veins bulging in his face.

"What the fuck you want us to do, kill him?" Walter asked, sarcastic.

"Yes!" Alosi said. "Unless he signs off on this claim,

kill his ass. Then start taking down his men until someone signs off. Get their attention."

"Jack's an old friend, boss. Out-fucking-standing Marine. One hell of an operator," Hacksaw said. "I'm not doing anything that hurts him or his men."

"I'll can your sorry ass, you don't do as I order," Alosi said.

"Go ahead, asshole," Hacksaw came back. "I'll cash out the remaining full year of my brand-new chief-supervisor contract. Go home happy. Rich. And sing like a bird. Non-disclosure agreements don't cover crimes. I can overlook a few things I've seen done here, but not this."

Cesare took a breath and knew Hacksaw had him. However, he had others in the company that would be all too happy to work some dirt for him.

"That was my temper speaking. Blowing steam. I don't mean anything. Fuck it, I'm just pissed off," Alosi now said, showing his calm, professional side. "I apologize, Top Gillespie. Forget I ever said such nonsense."

"We all get pissed off, sir," Hacksaw said, and shook hands with his boss.

"Forgiven?" Alosi asked, smiling as he shook hands.

"You got it, sir," Gillespie agreed.

He went to the wall where the report and denied claim lay on the floor, and picked it up. Several pages had come unstapled on impact, and the retired Marine special operator master sergeant gathered them, too.

"I'll go over to Camp Victory and have a talk with Jack," Hacksaw said. "I've been meaning to visit him. Let him know I'm here. Can't hurt to ask if he'll reconsider and let this thing slide. At the end of the day, sometimes we have to get into the gray just a little bit, between the black and white, the good and bad of things. When it serves a greater good, Jack can be reasonable. Like keeping harmony among us and MARSOC."

"Good way to look at it, Top." Alosi smiled.

Gillespie spread a big one back, showing off the gold-rimmed pearly-enamel front grill he'd had installed in Miami's rapper central with part of his high pay from the last pump with Malone-Leyva. The new implanted teeth replaced the chewing-tobacco-ravaged originals he had lost.

As the mature but still athletic and sturdy retired Marine opened the office door, Alosi called to him.

"Say, Top," Cesare said, "put a call out to Ray-Dean Blevins and have him report to me ASAP."

"You got it, boss," Hacksaw said, and left.

_ 4 _

"*Allahu Akbar! Allahu Akbar!*" chanted the Iraqi jihadist who had parked a stolen taxi at the corner of a busy intersection on Baghdad's south side. He sat in the rear seat, looking out the back window, and spoke as he watched through the viewfinder of his digital camera, recording his voice under video as two US Army Humvees approached on the boulevard that entered the opposite side of the intersection.

He chanted more rapidly now, as several rocks and some cans came tumbling off the roof of a building overhead onto the American vehicles, occupied by soldiers not normally engaged in direct combat. This early morning, they had ventured out to take care of some administrative errands on this normally quiet side of the city.

A can hit the windshield of the lead Hummer, and the driver slammed on the brakes. He jumped out of the truck, angered, and pointed his rifle at the roof of the building above him. He shouted something that the taxi's driver running the camera did not understand.

"*Allahu Akbar!*" another Iraqi insurgent chanted under his breath. He hid in a hot, tight space, padded with a blanket, inside the rear fender of the taxi, and put the crosshairs of his makeshift sniper rifle's telescopic sight on the angry American who stood in the street with his M4 raised, ready to shoot, searching the rooftops.

The sniper and his partner who drove the taxi and shot video of their jihad, which others would post on the Internet, had taken a Russian-made AK-47 and wired tight on top of it an old three-power hunting-rifle scope. They had also welded a homemade sound suppressor on the muzzle of the rifle, to silence their shots. It fit perfectly inside the taillight hole on the rear fender of the taxicab. The missing taillight and lens gave the sniper a clear shooting port and reasonably good field of view.

Sweat poured off the Iraqi gunman's face as he lay inside the car's fender, and he followed his crosshairs on the American soldier as he walked into the middle of the street. *"Allahu Akbar,"* the sniper said as he put pressure on the trigger.

He tried to remember everything that his Islamic brother from the east of Europe had taught him about relaxing, breathing, focusing on the crosshairs, then holding his breath without strain while gently adding pressure to the trigger until the shot broke.

"Ahmed, let the shot always fire with surprise. This way you know that you did not force the trigger, and the bullet will always strike exactly where you had your sights aimed," the Chechen jihadist they called Juba had told him. Ahmed was not this gunman's name but his Muslim brother who had once held acclaim as a precision marksman in the former Soviet Army called everyone he trained in Iraq, Ahmed.

Someone opened the door of the second Hummer and yelled at the soldier standing in the street, craning his neck, turning his head in every direction, looking for the kids who must have thrown the rocks and cans at them.

"Let's go!" the soldier in the second Hummer shouted.

"Allahu Akbar," the Iraqi running the digital camera chanted again and again, and captured on his video the sudden impact of the silenced .30 caliber projectile as it struck the American soldier loitering in the street. The bullet exploded through his neck, sending a spray of red just above his body armor. The shot's force threw the man to the pavement.

Blood gushed from the downed American's neck as he writhed on the street. He tried to cry out for help but could make no sounds from his shredded larynx except that of air escaping his lungs from his final gurgling breaths.

Iraqi shopkeepers and early-morning customers casually moving along the sidewalks now ran in every direction, hiding inside every available door. In a heartbeat, the normally bustling quad of streets and shops sat empty. The people disappeared from sight like cockroaches leaving the kitchen when lights come on.

Three soldiers jumped out of the two sand-tan vehicles, rifles out, ready to shoot in any direction. Another soldier, without a rifle but shouldering a green satchel that had a red cross painted inside a white circle on its side ran to the wounded man and tried to save his life.

It is a woman, the sniper realized as he put his cross-hairs on her. She had taken off her helmet, and he could see her long, black hair rolled in a bun on her head.

"Allahu Akbar," the sniper said as he shot her in that rolled knot of hair, killing her instantly. All of it captured on video to be seen later on multiple al-Qaeda fan-base Web sites, worldwide.

Just after the sniper had killed the woman soldier, and she crumpled, dead, the jihadi driver jumped over the seat and got behind the steering wheel. As he started the taxi, he sent a cell-phone text cue to several trucks and cars that now converged on the intersection.

As the traffic surge came through, the driver hit the gas and sped away in the mix of delivery trucks and cars.

None of the soldiers, nor any other witnesses, ever realized where the shots came from. One Iraqi shopkeeper said he might have noticed a taxi sitting at the corner, but he wasn't sure. Taxis frequently sat there, waiting for fares in that busy part of town.

"**G**angway!" Jack Valentine yelled as he used the edge of his boot sole to pull open the door to the MAR-SOC, Iraq detachment operations offices. They sat inside a white hard-walled, white-roofed block-type one-story structure that looked like a giant refrigerator turned on its side. Similar to the quarters in which Jack and his tribe lived, it had tiny high windows and air conditioners sticking out all four corners of the supposedly somewhat-bullet-repellant walls.

A new crimson sign posted on white pipe stanchions out front proclaimed with bright gold lettering who lived in this house, United States Marine Corps Forces Special Operations Command, Iraq. The newly coined MARSOC emblem, an eagle, globe, and anchor inset within a large black spade-like spearhead, dominated the sign's center. Beneath it read a slogan in gold script, ALWAYS FAITHFUL—ALWAYS FORWARD.

On the lower corner of the big sign, a smaller red one with yellow lettering read, LIEUTENANT COLONEL H. E. SNOW, COMMANDING. Opposite it, a similarly small strip read, GUNNERY SERGEANT J. A. VALENTINE, STAFF NONCOMMISSIONED OFFICER IN CHARGE. On the hooch door, yet another sign, a varnished cedar plank with bold black lettering burned into the wood, read, HOG WALLOW (FORWARD).

The gunny blindly hefted two large boxes, one stacked atop the other, reaching from his knees to over his head and as wide as his arms could hug.

"That sniper they call Juba killed two more Americans," Staff Sergeant Billy Claybaugh yelled to Jack when he saw the boxes and the gunny's feet peddling under them. "Both Army. Office types making some kind of off-the-wall admin run to south Baghdad. Whatever the fuck that's about. Like letting children wander off a playground if you ask me."

Jack grunted and huffed as he came inside the office. "Yeah, I heard about it at the post office. A little help might go a long way."

Billy-C grabbed the box off the top. "One was a female lieutenant and the other a sergeant. Dirty shame. Gunny, why didn't you get one of the boys to go with you for these?"

"Didn't know they'd arrived," Jack said. "I just happened by the headquarters mail drop and those Air Force jamokes working in there was kicking our boxes around and tripping all over them. Given a little time, they would have rat-fucked the whole load. So I grabbed shit and fled. I left the rest of the MARSOC mail out in the seat of the truck. Elmore got another letter from his wife."

"Good. He can pick it up on his way out," Billy-C said. "You buy that Juba stuff, the Phantom of Baghdad?"

"I don't know," Jack said, feeling in his pocket for his Cold Steel lock-blade knife. "Intel guys at the two-shop say al-Qaeda made up this Juba character, and it's really a bunch of different gunmen, mostly lucky shooting Hajis making kills at short range. Nothing impressive, like now they got their version of Carlos Hathcock."

"Both these was head shots," Billy said. "Well, actually, one a neck shot and the other a clean head shot."

"We need to get after 'em, brother," Jack said, pushing his knife into the tape of the first big box. "Entirely too many Americans getting hit by snipers these days. We need to engage some countersniper action to put a stop to it."

"Fuckin' A," Billy said as he headed for the truck to grab the mail off the seat for everyone in the detachment.

Just as Staff Sergeant Claybaugh shoved open the HOG Wallow door, it hit Lieutenant Colonel Elmore Snow slam in the kisser. Wham!

"Oh shit, sir!" Billy-C cried out. "You okay?"

Elmore shook his head like rattling rocks in a box. "No worse for wear. Carry on, Marine."

"I guess you heard about those two soldiers got killed by Juba the Phantom of Baghdad, first thing this morning?" Claybaugh said to the colonel.

"Bloody shame, that," Snow said. "We stress sniper vigilance, but I guess some people forget where they are."

"Yes, sir," Billy said, and dashed outside to the truck.

The colonel eyed Jack, who had his knife out, cutting open the tape to the top of one of the big boxes. On the side of the pasteboard, dark blue print read, JACKSONVILLE CUSTOM IMAGES COMPANY.

"What's in the boxes?" Snow asked, walking over and trying to peek inside the one Jack had just opened.

"Oh, just a few Tinkertoys I had made up for the kids," Valentine said, and grabbed a handful of black-and-red-embroidered patches from a plastic bag and handed them to his boss.

Snow looked at the four-inch-by-three-inch red-trimmed diamonds with a black ace of spades on a gray field that had an overbearing, evil-eyed white skull trimmed in red and black in its center. Below the black spade and white skull, was a set of white dice with black dots showing snake eyes.

"You drew this?" Snow asked, admiring the artwork.

"Yes, sir." Jack smiled.

"Nice," Snow said, and tried to hand them back.

"No," the gunny said. "Those are yours. I got three hundred of them made for our team. Plenty to go around."

"These are not kosher on Marine Corps uniforms, you know," Snow said, stuffing the patches in his utility-trousers pocket.

"Oh, goes without saying," Valentine said. "We'll sew them on our kit bags and maybe on the pocket of our vests. A little team identity."

"Sounds good," Elmore said, and took a second glance

at the very large boxes. "But it looks like more than patches here."

"Oh, just a little decor for the hooch, sir," Jack blew off. "Nothing really."

"Hey, Jack," Snow said casually. "I thought I'd mention that a couple of CIA operators, boy named Chris Gray and his partner, Speedy Espinoza, may come knocking on your hatch in the next few days. Help them out all you can. They're tasked with finding Zarqawi. And we want to kill him."

"I'll roll out the green carpet," Jack said, and puzzled a second. "Chris Gray? Sounds familiar. I knew a Chris Gray at Second Force Recon back in the Gulf War."

"One and the same," the colonel said. "Espinoza's Marine Corps, too. Flew the EA-6B Prowler for a while."

"Spy in the sky," Jack said. "I'll do all I can for them. Last time I saw Chris, we were lance corporals. Then you kidnapped me."

"I should have grabbed him, too," Elmore said. "He's a solid operator. So's Speedy."

"Never fear, they'll be at home here," Jack assured his commander.

"Meantime, I've got a flight out to Dover Air Force Base in about three hours," the colonel said, glancing at his watch. "Then a puddle jumper down to Jacksonville. We have the MARSOC Colors unfurling and inaugural appointment-of-command ceremony on Friday afternoon."

"Real shame, sir," Jack said.

"What do you mean?" Elmore said.

"Some one-star we don't know will take command of

this creation that you dreamed up back when we were killing cocaine cowboys around Medellín, many moons ago," Jack said. "You're the guy that sold this idea to the Marine Corps, convincing them we needed our own organization, like the SEALs and Delta Force."

"I'm not in this for credit or praise, Jack," Elmore said. "What we've got exceeds even my most ambitious dreams. I couldn't be happier."

"Well, sir," Jack grumbled, "I don't have to like it, and neither do the boys. Every one of us says they need to kick you up to full colonel or even go ahead and jump tracks to brigadier and put you in charge. It's your show, and nobody in the American armed forces knows as much about special operations as you do."

"I'm flattered, Jack"—the colonel smiled—"but it's a lot more complicated than just Marine Corps Forces Special Operations Command. We're coordinated into the armed-forces-wide Special Operations Command. It's a whole joint forces structure under Central Command, and it unites all special warfare forces of the United States."

Jack rattled off, "I know, sir. We got SOCOM opened shop in Florida, and JSOC under them in Afghanistan, and I guess we'll have our own Joint Special Operations Command here in Iraq, too, giving you yet another star to salute. I've heard all that alphabet soup. If you ask me, it's just another excuse for career-serving officers to get stars put on their collars."

Elmore Snow smiled and put his hand on Jack's shoulder. "Oh, how right you are, young Spartan. The political opportunists will certainly seize the day. However, you and every Marine in our detachment here, and the command back at Lejeune, benefit. We're quickly becoming our own Marine Corps occupational field.

"Scout-Snipers will no longer fall under the 8500, marksmanship training field, but will more appropriately expand the Marine infantry 03 field. Your 8541 MOS will change to 0317. And who knows? The next step may well be a primary MOS that is Special Operations."

"Elmore, sir," Jack said, and looked to see no one else lurked anywhere in the operations offices, "I would love to see you in command and wearing a star. Just saying. You're the toughest, scariest Marine I ever knew. Soft-spoken but swinging a big stick. You'd make a great Commandant of the Marine Corps, sir."

Colonel Snow put his head back and laughed. "Jack. Son. You're plying the lather just a little thick. I'll be lucky to see full colonel. I'm a snake eater, not a politician. I was a sergeant who got lucky and made lieutenant, and got sent to Beirut. Then I got to teach young leaders at the Infantry Officers Course, and worked hand in glove with our incoming Marine Corps commandant, General Jim Conway. Remember how Colonel Conway gathered up our team in Iraq, back in the Gulf War? He doesn't forget his friends. Believe me. Great things are coming for all of us."

"Yes, sir, and the Marine Corps has done itself proud naming General Conway our new commandant," Jack said. "Pete Pace as Chairman of the Joint Chiefs of Staff is good for all us Scout-Snipers, too. You know how he loved Gunny Hathcock. So why don't those guys who truly know you put you in command of MARSOC for real?"

"They know that I do best crawling in the weeds,

shooting bad guys," Elmore said. "You only see the commander side of me, and the friend that would give his life for any one of you Marines. But, up where the flags fly high, I struggle. I'm that guy with the grass stains on his pants."

"Trousers, sir." Jack grinned. "In the Marine Corps, men wear trousers and women wear pants."

Elmore laughed and gave Jack a playful shove.

"Other than the command ceremonies," Elmore said, "I've also got to check on how Second M-SOB is coming along. We've got two detachments we're trying to send to Afghanistan, to join JSOC and hunt Osama bin Laden. I'll be gone to Lejeune maybe three weeks. Be back here sooner if all goes well."

"Afghanistan. That's where we ought to be, sir," Jack said, without thinking too much. "Not a whole lot popping up here in our favor, locating Zarqawi. Osama's a much bigger prize. It'll be my luck some deck ape with a burp gun will whack the bastard before I can get him lined up in my gunsights."

"He's not a prize, Jack. He's just a man. We work best where God sends us," Elmore said.

Jack shrugged. "That's what these Hajis keep saying. Right before *Allahu Akbar*, and they push the button on the bomb vest. God is great! They're doing it for God. We're going where God sends us. All this death and evil done in the name of God. Really, sir?"

"The god they pray to is not my god. Not the God of Abraham and Moses. Not God the Father, Son and Holy Spirit, our triune God who is Love," Elmore said, and it made Jack wince to hear it. Talk of God always made him uncomfortable, mostly because he carried so much sin and well-earned guilt.

"Some say it's Satan, not God," Jack said, and looked to make sure the shop was vacant. He reckoned that Billy-C must have cut out to deliver mail to the crew, and that was good. None of the gang needed to hear very much of Elmore Snow's radical Christian perspectives about Islam. The boys might grow fangs and go on killing sprees, all in the name of doing God's work.

"In the year AD 610, when Muhammad was in the desert outside Mecca, encountering his angel inside the cave called Hira, on the mountain named Jabal al-Nour, and this angel, supposedly Gabriel, informed him that God had named Muhammad a holy prophet, giving birth to the Islamic faith, he was out there worshipping the god of the moon. A demigod the Mesopotamians had named Sin. In Arabic he's called Hubal," Elmore began, and rested his leg on Jack's desk. "You know who Sin is?"

"The devil?" Jack said.

Elmore went on, "In the ancient faiths of the Arabic regions, long before Islam or Christ, the Mesopotamian people worshipped the moon god, Hubal, or Sin, as their supreme god, believing him the father of the sun god, Shamash, and of Ishtar, the goddess of the bright star that is the planet Venus. Together, the three gods formed a holy triad that controlled the universe.

"Depictions of Sin, or Hubal, showed him as this wise and unfathomable old man with a flowing gray beard, an all-knowing and all-seeing god of all creation. He wore a headdress of four horns surmounted by a crescent moon.

"On nights when the crescent moon came in confluence with Venus, Ishtar embraced by her father, Hubal, this was the most powerful moment in any year. Thus, as Muhammad established Islam, he used the crescent moon and star as one of its symbols."

"I didn't know that," Jack said.

"Hubal strikes a remarkable likeness to Ba'al, the Hebrew demigod that the Children of Israel bowed to in idolatry when they fell away from God," Elmore explained. "God visited His wrath on His people because they fell into wickedness, worshipping idols of Ba'al and even sacrificing their own children to him. For all intents and purposes, Ba'al is Satan. And we know from even our childhood Sunday school classes that Satan is the great liar, tempter, and purveyor of all evil, the cunning deceiver who wants us to worship him as god."

"So, Muhammad is out in the desert worshipping the devil, and God sends Gabriel to visit this joker?" Jack said, priming the pump, now having fun fueling Elmore's love of long, drawn-out explications of insights born from his exhaustive historical, social, and cultural studies of what makes enemies tick. For Colonel Snow, every pebble on the enemy's beach has a revelation beneath it, and he turns over every stone.

"A very good question indeed," Elmore said. "Perhaps old Lucifer fooled the young prince."

"That would make sense," Jack said.

"Muhammad's father, Abdullah ibn Abdul-Muttalib, and the whole Muttalib family ran the Kaaba in Mecca. Today the most holy site in Islam. But in those early days, the Kaaba was the temple where Hubal the moon god resided among 360 gods that the people worshipped, all called Allah in those times, meaning the gods, one god for each day of their calendar year. That was until Abdullah's death in AD 570. Six months before Muhammad was born," Elmore went on.

"In fact, after Muhammad's encounter with the angel, and he began to spread the word and fear of Islam across the lands, he destroyed all the demigods in the Kaaba, except the idol of Hubal. Which I am told stands in the Kaaba today and represents Allah."

He cocked an eye at the tall coffeemaker sitting at the side of the office, and asked, "That oil fresh?"

"I was just going to get a cup, sir," Jack said. "Decaf okay? That's all we serve around here."

"Decaf is what I like," Snow said, and filled a clean mug that had sat, turned upside down on brown paper towels next to the pot.

Then the colonel returned to his perch on Jack's desk and carried on with his history lecture.

"With his father dying the year he was born, Muhammad was sent to the desert to live with his mother and the Bedouins, which they thought was healthy for a child. Fresh air and camel dung.

"The lad's mother soon expired from that healthy desert life on the move, when the lad was three or four years old. So little Muhammad went to live with his uncle, Abu Talib ibn Abdul-Muttalib, his father's brother.

"Uncle Talib, now the Muttalib in charge of the family business, ran the Kaaba. So you've got to figure that young Qasim Muhammad al-Muttalib ibn Hashim, known to us as the Prophet Muhammad, very likely did not worship the God of Abraham, the father of Ishmael, to whom

Muhammad claims kinship but there is no proof of it. More likely, like his father and mother and uncle and kin before them, he worshipped the moon god, Hubal."

Elmore took a big drink of coffee and let that sit with Jack to ponder.

Nothing better to do, Jack enjoyed relaxing with his decaf and hearing Elmore prattle, so he tossed out more bait.

"So you're telling me that Muhammad was out in the desert six hundred years after Christ, worshipping the devil in a cave, when he claims that an angel appeared and told him he was now a prophet of God?" Jack concluded.

"Correct," Elmore said. "Do you suppose that God Almighty would visit His own herald, Angel Gabriel, on a man out in a cave one night worshipping Hubal and Ishtar under the crescent moon and Venus?"

"I wouldn't think so," Jack said.

"Thus God declares this devil-worshipping swordsman His prophet? Does that make a lick of sense?" Elmore ranted, raising his voice as Billy-C came back to the hooch.

"What devil-worshipping swordsman we talking about?" the staff sergeant asked, seeing the two Marines drinking coffee and going and getting himself a mug of it, too.

"Muhammad," Jack said.

"Oh hell yeah!" Claybaugh chimed in. "You know, my grammy back in Alabammy told me these Islams is a bunch of devil-praying zealots from the dark side. And I needed to watch my step over here, or they'd hex me."

Elmore frowned at the Marine. "I'm talking verifiable history, Billy, not raging superstition or advocating hate at anybody. Most of these ignorant people believe they worship the true God of Abraham, not Satan. I'm just explaining how Satan has likely misled them. It would explain why Muslim extremists perpetuate so much evil in the world. God is Love, not hatred and murderous bloodshed."

"Unless you provoke His wrath," Jack added.

"God's wrath is nothing to joke about, Gunnery Sergeant Valentine," Elmore cautioned. "God destroying people is not the same thing as Muhammad riding on his rampages, putting Christians and all kinds of other people who would not convert to Islam to the sword. Committing bloody murder!"

"So when the Christians put the Muslims to the sword in the Crusades, that was a good thing?" Jack asked, baiting his longtime friend. He had heard Elmore's rants before and enjoyed their entertainment.

"I think it was terrible!" Elmore said sincerely. "I don't believe God sent the Crusaders. They took it upon themselves to slaughter a lot of innocent people, along with the jihadi villains that sacked Jerusalem. We suffer many of our problems today because of that misguided Christian zeal. The Crusades were perpetuated by kings and villainous popes, not God. We should have sent missionaries to save the Muslim people, not the Knights Templar to eradicate them."

"Way I understand it, boss," Jack said, "the Muslims started that fight by massacring Christians and Jews, and taking Jerusalem. The Crusaders came here for pretty much the same reasons we're here today."

"Yes, that's true," Elmore answered. "Don't forget that the Kurdish Sunni king, Saladin, wound up ruling Jerusalem along with Egypt, Syria, and all lands of the Levant in 1187, and sent the Crusaders home on their shields. We should bear that in mind. Especially today. We can handle things better. We need to win these people's friendship, not their scorn."

"Sir, I think if we sent missionaries over here instead of armies, they'd end up with their heads rotting on pikes," Billy-C said.

"We have Christian missionaries here today, son," the colonel said. "All kinds of Catholics and Evangelicals. In fact, one of the oldest Evangelical Christian churches in Iraq was built in Mosul by the Presbyterians in 1850. Many Presbyterians, Baptists, and other Evangelical Iraqis live here today. There's a Presbyterian church in Kirkuk, Saddam Hussein's hometown. We just have to try harder to win these people to the Lord."

Jack and Billy-C saw the colonel's sincerity, and that gentle side of his good heart that they loved in the man. He held no malice for anyone, nor hatred. He was the classic noble warrior, a Bible in one hand, a sword in the other, and poetry on his lips.

"I guess we need to love these bastards while we light 'em up," Jack said, and flashed a wry grin at Billy.

"Kill 'em but don't hate 'em. And just kill the ones that need killing," Elmore said.

Jack laughed. "Colonel Snow, I can't help but love you, sir. We've walked down these roads together a lot of years, and you do not change. You've never hated anybody, but you have killed plenty of bad hombres. You're a special man."

"I thought the Good Book says, 'Thou shalt not kill,'" Billy-C said, and looked at Jack, then at the colonel, honestly puzzled. "Ain't us killing them just as bad as what they're doing? Except they leave a lot of innocent folks murdered in their wake. We pick and choose ours."

"King James Bible says, 'Thou shalt not kill,' but that's not a true translation of the actual Hebrew that God wrote with His fiery finger on that stone tablet for Moses," Elmore said.

Jack looked at Billy-C, then at Elmore, a bit surprised. He had always heard the Ten Commandments told as "Thou shalt not kill."

"Yes, all our lives we have heard, 'Thou shalt not kill,' thanks to King James. But God truly wrote on the stone and told Moses, 'Do not murder,'" Snow said. "The correct translation says 'murder,' not 'kill.' A very big difference in the two words. Billy, we do not murder . . ."

Elmore stopped before he said it and Jack finished it for him. "'Bastards,' sir? Or did you mean 'motherfuckers'?"

"Evil ones," Elmore mumbled, hiding a grin.

Jack and Billy both laughed.

"I've only ever heard you say one profanity, sir." Billy-C broke up. "Motherfucker! That's your one cussword for everything that pisses you off. Motherfucker."

"Only rarely. When I'm truly mad, much to my chagrin. It slips out. I manage to keep all the others off my tongue, though, but that one choice blister agent leaps out of my mouth when I trip off the emotional cliff." Elmore laughed.

"You are the consummate officer and gentleman, sir, our poet warrior and scholar," Jack said, and a light came on in his mind. "Oh, and speaking of poet warriors, did you hear from our old pard from fun times in South America, Black Bart Roberts?"

A smile crossed Elmore's face at mention of his old Force Recon running mate who claimed direct descendancy from the original Welsh pirate of the 1720s, Captain Bartholomew Black Bart Roberts.

"I did get word that he is here," the colonel said. "Out west in the Denver operations area, based near Al Asad Air Base, near Hit, I believe, commanding one-five. We'll have to catch up and partake a thimble or two of Jameson's Irish elixir with him when I get back from Lejeune. I've got a bottle of eighteen-year-old Limited Reserve stocked away in my stash of contraband."

"I'll keep that in mind while you're gone." Jack grinned. "I like it, too. I can't afford it, but I like it."

"I know, Jack." Elmore grinned. "Lots of things you like but can't afford and yet seem to manage somehow. Like that pretty girl of yours, Liberty Cruz. You ever going to make an honest woman of her?"

Jack shook his head. "We're still working on that question."

"Lot of years to be pondering such an idea," Snow said. "She's still at Lejeune, you know. Finished SERE school in flying fashion, I hear, and now she's training on various high-power rifles. Strange one, that girl. She'd fit in around our club quite nicely. You ought to propose."

"I think that's what she's gunning for." Jack sighed.

"The wife, you know, June, invited her for dinner with us one night while I'm home this trip. She and Liberty are thick as thieves. Our little girl Kathy, now graduating from training bras and middle school, sees Miz Cruz as the person she wants to be. I don't know if that's such a good thing or not, given Liberty's career choices, and her taste in having you as her man. I think they planned this dinner because the ladies want to check up on you. She apparently tells June you're pretty brief in your few emails," Elmore said.

"Naw, we're good. Don't worry about it. I keep it short and dry because I've got a lot of assholes around this shop eyeballing my laptop, and email and pictures," Jack said, looking straight at Billy-C, who smiled big.

"Oh, okay," Elmore said, then wrinkled his forehead. "What about Black Bart? You sounded like you had something working in your craw."

"Right," Jack said. And then, as if it were no big deal, "He gave me a blast on the horn yesterday. Wants us to run a little thing with him and his boys out in the Anbar for a day or so. Nothing to worry about, sir, but something good to do. Helps him out. He was supposed to send you over the plan and everything, so you could approve us going along."

"Captain Burkehart can look at it and give it my okay," Elmore said.

"Well, sir, Skipper's up at the puzzle palace stuck in operations all the time, and we hardly see him," Jack said. "Colonel Roberts has this thing going down pretty darned quick, and we need to jump if we ride with his boys."

"Bart's got it set up? Transport, planning, all that?" Snow asked.

"Yes, sir. Top to bottom," Jack answered. "He takes good care of folks. You know him."

"Yes he does," Snow agreed. "Fine Marine, Lieutenant Colonel Roberts. Great combat leader. A bit rough around the edges, and a mouth that matches his Black Bart name. But a good man."

Elmore Snow checked his watch, looked at the boxes, then at Jack. "Go ahead. You've got my blessing. Just make sure that Colonel Roberts sends me a copy of his after-action write-up. And if you manage to capture any intel on Zarqawi, or his henchmen, make sure we get exclusive first rights to it. Don't go sharing that with SEALs or Delta Force before we can swing in the saddle ahead of them."

"You read my mind, sir." Jack smiled.

"Oh, and keep the doors closed to those private-contract security mongrels I see lurking around more and more these days," the colonel added. "I don't like them, and I do not trust them."

"Couple of our boys hooked up with them now," Jack said. "Hacksaw, Kermit, and Habu work at Malone-Leyva. Hacksaw's been trying to get hold of me the past few days."

"I know," the colonel said. "He reached out to me, too. I'm still thinking about it. Mercenaries. That's all they are, you know. Hired guns with no law over their heads."

"Roger that, sir," Jack agreed.

Staff Sergeant Claybaugh remembered the letter from the colonel's wife and grabbed it off the stack he brought back to the hooch after holding mail call for the team.

"You got this from your wife," Billy said, handing the letter to his boss.

Snow smiled as he took it. "Thank you. A nice fat one. I'll read it while I wait to board the plane."

"Stay frosty, sir," Jack said.

Elmore headed to the door and looked back at the boxes. "Make sure that whatever unholy raiment and bunting you may hold in those boxes remains inside this hooch. Do not decorate the outside with black draperies, skulls, or any other hideous ornaments. Please. Not this close to the flagpole. I remember what you did for graduation at the instructor school at Quantico, building that monument of bones and skulls under the yard sign."

"The commandant loved it, sir," Valentine retorted.

"Oh, it amused him," Elmore said, "but had the school not been way off the beaten path, out there at Marksmanship Training Unit, he would have ordered those bones buried."

"Sir, they were just hog bones from our cookouts and a few plastic human skulls mixed with the roasted pig heads," Jack said. "No pork to pick around these parts, and nobody's collecting any skulls except maybe the bad guys'."

"Just keep our exterior orderly. We don't need negative attention," Elmore said, and departed to catch his flight.

Billy-C looked at Jack. "Wonder why we can't find a pig to roast around these parts? I could sure go for some barbecued ribs."

Jack looked at the Southern-fried staff sergeant, started to say something but instead blew out a big breath.

"Eleven hundred, Guns," Claybaugh said, checking the big white-faced government clock Jack had had mounted over the entrance. That way when he looked up to see who came through the door, he could note the time.

Bronco and Jaws hated it because they always showed up at the last minute. Never on Lombardi time.

"That's right, you've got security duty on that wagon train headed down Fallujah Road," Jack said. "You boys roll out of the chocks at what, thirteen hundred?"

"Straight up," Billy said.

Jack went to the wall map and took a look at the route.

"Lots of nasties on that trail," Jack said.

"Guaranteed one of those KBR semis hauling bacon and beans going to pop an IED, big as shit," the staff sergeant said. The tone of his voice told Jack that Billy-C had a little honest worry going on.

Gunny Valentine put his hand over his boy's shoulder and gave it a good squeeze. "You got this, dude. Right?"

"Cotton's got a team in the other Hummer one truck behind me." Claybaugh nodded but bit his lip.

"Keep plenty of interval between you and those trucks. That MRAP out front of the lead truck may find the pressure-plate mines, but not the command-detonated ones. Give yourself room," Jack said, then thought. "Load your team heavy this trip. Lots of bullets. Throw a two-forty golf machine gun in each truck to back up your Maw Duce. You hit a cross-fire ambush, you can light up both sides of the road."

Billy-C looked at the map, then his watch.

"Hey, brother, you got this!" Jack said, and gave a hug to his staff sergeant, whom he had first met when Billy was a lance corporal in Bosnia-Herzegovina. There Claybaugh had taken his first scalps as a sniper, killing Serbs trying to murder Bosnian Muslims three years after the

Bosnian government had signed a treaty. Even today, the border sniping continued. Both Jack and Billy had decided that NATO's trying to keep that peace was a waste of time.

Today, those Bosnian Muslims that American troops had protected from Serbian slaughter had joined with other Muslims in Chechnya and the Caucasian region, and infiltrated Iraq as al-Qaeda terrorists, killing Americans.

"I don't want to fuck up," Billy let out, and took a breath. "Why not put Cotton on lead? He's good, like you."

"If I didn't believe you had your shit in one bag, Billy, you'd be back at Lejeune," Jack said. "You're not going to fuck up. What's to fuck up?"

"Getting guys killed, that's what," Claybaugh said. "Like you said, it's a real nasty piece of road."

"Trust your training, brother," Jack said, and held on to Claybaugh's shoulders while looking him in the eyes. "You're lead because you need the snaps. Everybody's nervous, first ride out the chute, as Bronco Starr likes to put it."

Billy bit his lip. "Believe it or not, I'd feel a lot more confident if I had him and Jaws with me on the guns."

"They're stood down, with me," Jack said. "They pulled night watch, so they've got rack time. Besides, I'm putting them to work painting my black accent wall this afternoon."

"Black accent wall?" Billy-C said, and broke a smile.

"Yeah, this whole side of the hooch," Jack said, and pointed at the wall that ran the full length of the building.

"And all that shit in these boxes?" Billy grinned.

"I got a giant flag with our logo, and all kinds of other good shit," Jack said. "We'll have this place looking like a proper Special Operations sniper hooch in no time."

Billy smiled. "Home of the Ghosts of Anbar."

Then Jack pointed at the center of the intended accent wall, and said, "I'm painting a five-foot Punisher skull right there."

"I'd love to be here when Elmore sees it," Billy said, laughing. "He'll shit green marbles."

"Yeah, I know." Jack laughed. "We're warped."

Billy looked at the gunny. It felt good to laugh.

Jack smiled at him. "Got an idea. Grab some mono-lithic .50 for the duce. It cuts through walls like a buzz saw."

"Mind if I take a couple of Barretts, too?" Claybaugh asked. "One for each truck? Load 'em with Raufoss rounds? They'll bust through all kinds of shit. You never know."

"Sounds good," Jack said. "Take what you need. And never fear, brother. Shit goes south, I'm up with you on com. Holler help, and we'll roll out the cavalry."

Cesare Alosi looked out his office window in the American compound next to the US embassy in Baghdad. Rat-hole city crawling with crap. Like every other third-world night-mare he had ever lived, yet he kept coming back for the money. He liked it better here than Islamabad or Kabul. Nice dinner parties with the American and Allied civilian workers, more and more of whom crowded the Iraqi capital each day. Alosi liked dressing up and dining out. Even here.

Paris. He loved Paris more than any place on earth. New York was a close second. Maybe he could get her to fly to Paris with him, when he took a month off at the end of this four-month cycle.

Cesare thumbed through his calendar, counting the weeks, then looked again at the framed photo he had of Liberty Cruz, printed off a snapshot he had taken with his BlackBerry the night he had gone home with her. The lights outside the Washingtonian Hotel gave the long cool woman in the clinging black dress a halo effect as she had flashed a devilish smile for his camera.

"Not that drunk," he thought. "She's into me like wicked whiskey."

A smile crept across his face as lurid thoughts of Liberty whirled in his head; her sexy body and his dirty mind left him aroused.

A knock came at his office door, and the attractive Iraqi girl he had hired as a secretary put her head inside.

"Sir, I tried to reach Mr. Taché for you, but he has gone for the week with Mr. Decoux," the girl who went by Irene said. She did not use her Muslim name and held this job in secrecy from her family, who lived south of the Iraqi capital, near Hillah.

"Where'd they go?" Alosi asked.

"Mosul and that region along the Tigris," Irene said. "The girl at their offices said that they had found another trove of privately owned family antiquities, some more than three thousand years old. They hope to purchase the best among them and send them to Paris."

"Very good," Alosi said, and dismissed her. Then he looked on the shelf above his credenza at a small brown-clay oil vase and matching oil lamp that Davet Taché had given him. Two thousand years old, from the Tigris region in Turkey, Monsieur Taché had sent them as tokens to remind Cesare that he and his partner, Jean René Decoux, were not French rug merchants but connoisseurs of fine art objects.

At a party, Alosi had offhandedly called the two import-export businessmen from Avignon, rug merchants.

"We trade in art, antiquities, and precious objects," Davet had tastefully corrected Cesare.

Alosi liked the two gentlemen from France very much. They were a breath of class in this dreary city.

He looked back at his phone and checked his watch.

"No word from that rube, Ray-Dean Blevins?" the Malone-Leyva boss yelled out his open door rather than pushing the intercom button on his desk phone.

Irene put her pretty head inside Cesare's office. "Mr. Blevins has just come through the lobby. Should I send him straight in?"

"Please, and close the door behind him," Alosi said.

Blevins came in, looking bad and smelling worse.

"You're a sight," Cesare said, and caught a whiff. He waved his hand under his nose, and turned up the fan on his air-conditioning unit. "Your shower broken?"

"No, sir," Ray-Dean said, and scratched his crotch. "It's working fine."

"Then you should use it," Cesare said.

"We work up a sweat out there, sir," Blevins said.

"That's more than workingman's sweat," Cesare said. "You've got a whole mixed cocktail of stenches coming off you like an open sewer. Steroids, booze, meth, its waste product seeps out the skin, and stinks."

"I don't have to listen to your insults," Ray-Dean said, and turned toward the door.

"Stop!" Cesare ordered. "I could shoot you right here, and there's not a fucking thing anyone can or would do about it. American legal jurisdiction does not cover us in Iraq, and the local government could give a shit if you or I commit murder or get murdered. So you'd better listen to me when you step in my chambers."

Blevins turned back and sagged on one hip, glaring at his boss.

"And next time I call you to report, I want you freshly showered and wearing something more fragrant than your dirtiest T-shirt and shit-stained pants," Cesare barked.

"You called me here, for what?" Ray-Dean said, still sagging on his hip, and now resting the heel of his hand on his .45 pistol strapped to his upper thigh. If the man wanted a gunfight, he would give him one. He hadn't slept in two days, and had a bad headache from last night's booze, drugs, and whores.

"I thought you were going to keep me informed about these MARSOC operators? You claim to be friends with a couple of them," Cesare said, and put his .45 auto on the desk as he spoke, so Ray-Dean could see it.

"I said I know a couple of them," Blevins answered. "I didn't say I liked any of them. And I sure the fuck never said I had any friends over there."

"But you still made a deal with me. What's their status?" Cesare asked.

"Security patrols," Blevins said. "They're running shotgun for a KBR convoy of tractor-trailers down Fallujah Road this afternoon."

"Who all knows about it?" Cesare asked.

"Like you told me, I make sure the hookers hear about it." Blevins shrugged.

"Good," Cesare said.

"You know, it doesn't make sense, you wanting us to compromise those guys, telling those whores classified shit like that," Blevins said, disgusted.

"Marginally classified. And who else do you suppose those whores are fucking besides you assholes?" Alosi asked.

"Iraqi soldiers, cops, a few Allied soldiers, maybe Americans, too. Shit, I don't know," Ray-Dean slurred out.

"Reporting all to al-Qaeda, I suspect," Cesare added.

"Then we sure as shit don't need to be giving them information that can end up killing Americans," Blevins fired back. "That's treason."

"That's business," Alosi corrected his man.

"What, so we can get more security duties and special operations?" Ray-Dean said.

Cesare Alosi smiled. "Precisely."

"MARSOC and those Army guys stuck on security aren't in business," Blevins argued. "They're not our competition."

"They are the competition, you fool!" Alosi snapped.

Blevins stuck out his jaw and took a grip on his gun, not liking the insults hurled at him by his boss.

Cesare picked up his .45 and cocked the hammer, not pointing it at Ray-Dean but still sending a message.

"Cooter," Alosi said. "That's what your pals call you, right? Cooter, like a pooter but with a C."

"No, sir," Blevins came back, his lips curled above his brown-rimmed teeth. "It's Cooder with a D."

"Right. Cooder," Cesare said. "I stand corrected."

Then the swarthy boss with his slicked-back black hair and pearly teeth rested his gun's butt on his desktop, pointed the muzzle straight at Ray-Dean, and explained, "It's simple economics. As long as the less-expensive Jar-heads or Doggies provide adequate security, we sit here making nothing. However, if the Marines or Army look like they cannot adequately protect these caravans of sup-plies and important people, then the government comes to us. Get it?"

"I got it a long time ago," Blevins said, and took his hand off his gun and crossed his arms, still not breaking eye contact with Cesare Alosi. "I'm just saying it ain't right. What we're doing. Americans can die from it."

"Americans die every day in this war," Alosi retorted. "Most often because some bonehead fool sends them out underarmed and ill prepared on a poorly planned mission. They're fighting this war like the cavalry of the old West. Ride out of Fort Apache at dawn, kill Indians, and ride home. Proves nothing and wins nothing. Do they expect to kill all of an ever-increasing army of insurgent soldiers?"

Ray-Dean took a big breath. "That it, sir?"

Alosi shook his head. "Yeah, that's it."

Blevins started to leave, then turned back at his boss. "I thought Hacksaw and his buddies that's supposedly so tight with Gunny Valentine might help you out."

"Not hardly," Alosi answered. "They're not mainlining drugs and fucking Iraqi whores. They may dress like pirates, but unfortunately, they're too straight for my needs. They'd never compromise their lofty sense of ethics for anyone or any amount of money. Dumb-ass losers."

"Then why do you keep them around?" Blevins asked.

"I have to," Cesare said. "My boss, the owner of this company, likes them."

"Oh." Blevins nodded.

"But I always come up with a solution to every kind of problem that gets in my way. Haven't you noticed?" Cesare smiled. "People get killed on the job every day. That's why we pay astronomical salaries and keep our queue of ready replacements filled. You just never know when one day's your last. It's a dangerous business."

"That why Hacksaw and his boys run a lot of duty down by Fallujah and Ramadi? You want them dead?" Blevins asked.

Cesare shrugged, lowered the hammer on his pistol, and slid it to one side of his desk. He gave Ray-Dean Blevins a cold, narrow smile as he leaned back in his tall, executive-model leather swivel chair.

"Cooder. Don't forget. I've always got you by the balls. You willfully destroyed our three-hundred-thousand-dollar armored Cadillac Escalade that Jack Valentine stuffed up my ass. Oh, that festers, my man. It festers.

"I simply dangle it over your head, and that gets you to do anything I need," Alosi reminded the man. "We can take the cost of that car out of your pay anytime you start sprouting morals and want to quit being my boy, or you can do what I say."

"There are limits," Ray-Dean said.

"Not around here." Cesare smirked.

_ 5 _

Midday sun sent heat waves dancing off the concrete where four KBR semi-tractor rigs sat as workers running forklifts finished loading the long box trailers with pallets of shrink-wrapped supplies, outbound for delivery to the logistics drop point that served the camps around Fallujah, Ramadi, and Hit.

Billy Claybaugh had Lance Corporal Rowdy Yates pull across from a sand-tan Cougar MRAP HE where a dozen infantry soldiers and their lieutenant sat in the shade of the six-by-six mine-resistant troop wagon. Cotton Martin's driver parked the second Hummer alongside the other MARSOC truck.

The Army lieutenant gave Billy-C a wave with the tip of his index finger off the lip of his helmet. Claybaugh answered him with a hip-low cowboy-style slide of his hand.

"Go ahead and stretch your legs, boys," the staff sergeant leading the MARSOC security mission told his Marines, and gave Cotton Martin a sign to dismount, too.

None of the Marine special operators smoked cigarettes or used tobacco in any forms. They didn't want dependency on nicotine eating at them when they worked in a hide days on end, nor to have effects of the drug making their sights on long-range shots bounce any higher than the low ebb of a slow pulse and calm heartbeat. Like professional athletes, they avoided caffeine, too, and had eating habits that ensured that their bodies remained at peak performance. Free-weight workouts, aerobics, martial arts practice, most of the men held various degrees of black belt, and long runs daily kept them fit and tool-steel hard. No fatsoes or skinny weenies in this outfit. Just trim muscle and clear minds. Jack Valentine had that uncompromising rule, among others, that made his Marines different than any run-of-the-mill hard charger. They looked it, too.

Most of the infantry soldiers sat in their truck's shade sucking on high-octane energy drinks and cigarettes, and spitting tobacco juice on the blistering concrete and watching it fry. Even the lieutenant had a lip full of Skoal. As staff sergeants Claybaugh and Martin gathered their cadre of eight Spartans and sat them in the shade of the two Marine Hummers, the soldiers gave them those telltale sideways leers that always say, "So you think you're hot shit?"

The Marines knew their shit was righteous and blew off the condescension. Cotton shot the soldiers a slack smile, then turned his back on the mutts.

Breaking the tension, the lieutenant walked over to the two staff sergeants, and asked, "Who's in charge?"

"That'd be me, sir," Billy said, and put out his hand for the lieutenant, who shook it.

"You've got our channel on your comm link?" the lieutenant asked, pulling a notebook out of his pocket.

"Roger that, sir," Billy answered. "Staff Sergeant Martin and I both will have you up on command channel. Just talk, and we hear you. Each member of our team's on intercom as well, also linked to our operations office. You can patch in, if you like. You want a radio check?"

The lieutenant shook his head no as he scribbled in his notebook, then said, "We'll run one when we pull out. I want to make sure the truck drivers have us on comm, too."

Just then the first semi cranked its engine, boiling black smoke from both stacks. Then, one at a time, the other three started as each operator got his rig ready to roll.

The lieutenant sized up the truck drivers and guessed where they came from. "Tennessee, Arkansas, Texas, and Oklahoma, my bet. Overweight rednecks with plugged arteries from a life of fatback and taters. Trying to cash in on a rich payday so they can live what they got left of their miserable lives at home, instead of one day keeling over dead at some far-off interstate truck stop."

"Since you're taking bets, I say one's a 'Bama boy. Maybe a Georgia peckerhead and a Kentucky hillbilly. I'll throw in one coal knocker from Pennsylvania, too, just to be different," Billy added. "Poor folks gambling their lives after a poke of fool's gold, driving trucks over here. Look at 'em, wearing ball caps and T-shirts, like they's only gonna roll up I-65 to Montgomery or Nashville."

"Yup," the lieutenant said, and spit a brown splat of Skoal on the concrete apron in front of the airport warehouses where big cargo planes from stateside supply centers unload an endless stream of pallets stacked with boxes shrink-wrapped in clear plastic, like those that now filled the trailers pulled by the four big KBR trucks. "I feel for these boys. They're my people. Trying hard for their families. Let's try hard for them, too. Keep these fellows from dying today."

Billy nodded at the lieutenant, liking him. "Yes, sir."

Cotton Martin gave a mount-up nod to his three gunmen, corporals Clyde McIllhenny and Byrd Clingman, and Sergeant Bobby Durant who ran the M2. Martin's other man, Corporal Hubert Biggs, a muscled hulk just a hand shorter than Cotton, came off a dairy farm near Kerrville, Texas, and went by the nickname, Hub, since childhood, slid onto the driver's seat as the six-foot-six-inch-framed staff sergeant took his spot at shotgun in the right-front seat, pushed all the way back.

As the Army infantry officer walked toward the Cougar to mount up his dozen soldiers, Billy Claybaugh called to him, "What's your name, sir?"

"Phipps," he answered, looking over his shoulder. "Jeremy Phipps. Fayetteville, Arkansas."

"Go Hogs!" Claybaugh called to him. "Staff Sergeant William C. Claybaugh at your service, sir. Mobile, Alabama."

"Roll Tide," the lieutenant answered, and walked on.

When the Army Cougar HE packed full of troops rolled out, the convoy fell behind the tan monster with the forty-millimeter grenade-launching main machine gun swinging a full 360 turn in its armored turret, making sure everything still worked. Two of the semis pulled behind the MRAP, and Billy had Rowdy Yates roll behind them. Then two more big trucks fell in, and Cotton Martin and his team of four brought up the rear.

As the supply convoy left the gated barriers of Baghdad International Airport military compound, which also held Camp Victory and Camp Liberty within its maze of razor wire and high hard walls, Billy-C felt his nerves start to tighten from his belly to his jaws. He and most of the other Marine Scout-Snipers he knew called it the Lump. Nobody ever liked getting the Lump.

"You boys stay frosty, ya hear me?" Claybaugh told his crew over the MARSOC channel that linked all ten Marines plus Jack Valentine on a squawk box at the operations hooch.

"Yeah, boss. We cool," Cotton answered.

Lance Corporal Rowdy P. Yates's mother had named her son Rowdy after her favorite Clint Eastwood Western character, from the old black-and-white TV series *Rawhide*. The *P* in his middle name stood for Paden, his father's first-choice character from his all-time top-of-the-ladder Western movie, *Silverado*. Emmett, Jake, and Mal had plenty of grit going on, but Paden had it all. Quiet, cool, and capable.

The twenty-year-old lance corporal cut his teeth watching videotape television, if he watched anything on the boob tube at all. Where he lived in the wild wide-open Wyoming wilderness, their best broadcast signal came with snow and jagged lines. They had no cable and couldn't afford satellite. So Burke and Rhonda Yates had bought VHS movies and TV shows off the clearance racks at the discount store for years. When their boy Rowdy started high school, they bought a DVD player and opened a whole new vista of entertainment.

While Burke regarded *Silverado* and *True Grit* hands down the best Westerns ever made, and Rhonda enjoyed her TV series like *Gunsmoke*, *Bonanza*, and *Rawhide*, and they all loved Jackie Gleason and Lucy, their boy Rowdy thought *Monty Walsh* and *Quigley Down Under* beat out all others. The idea of Matthew Quigley nailing all those long shots with his 1874-model Sharps buffalo rifle with a thirty-four-inch barrel, shooting the .45-110 caliber metallic cartridge with a 540-grain paper-patched bullet made Rowdy dream big.

He even went to wearing his Wranglers tucked inside his tall-topped, high-riding heeled Olathe buckaroo cowboy boots, and on his topknot rode an extrawide-brimmed heavyweight beaver Stetson with a Gus crease on the crown and the fore and aft of the brim dipped low over the young cowboy's eyes and neck with a soft roll at the sides. Just like Quigley or Monty would wear it. Always pearl snaps for shirt buttons, too.

Rowdy's moustache, however, did not want to grow quite right. It sprouted thin and had gaps. So the only girlfriend Rowdy ever had, Brenda Kay Nevers, eventually talked him into giving up the project, until he grew thicker stalk, and he shaved it off.

"Ain't no bushiness to it, son," she'd say. "Makes your mouth look dirty. Like you been suckin' hind teat on dad's old sow."

His senior year at Campbell County High School, where he played football for the Camels and tie-down calf

roped on the rodeo team, Rowdy bought a Quigley replica 1874 Sharps long-range rifle, complete with double-
set triggers and long-range flip-up sights on the small of
the stock, in addition to the buck-horns on the barrel,
along with all the brass trim, identical to the one Matthew
Quigley used. Rowdy had saved money from two summers' work to afford the expensive and fully functional
work of art made by the Shiloh Rifle Company of Big
Timber, Montana. The same folks that made the very gun
that Tom Selleck used in the movie.

"Over three grand for a smoke wagon," his dad marveled.

As Burke Yates had taught his son, never buy something you don't use, and if you buy it, use it well, Rowdy
Yates mastered his Quigley Sharps long rifle. He practiced
vaporizing prairie dogs and splattering running jackrabbits at five hundred yards, open sights, on the fly. Fall
hunting season after he graduated high school, the boy,
still seventeen, killed a seven-by-seven-point trophy bull
elk with the rifle. Put the animal down with one shot at
1,206 paces.

Burke had told the young man in the big hat not to
risk such a long shot, just too far off. But Rowdy dropped
the hammer anyway. He fired the shot and waited. When
the heavy bullet went thump, the big elk raised his head
and craned his neck back, then collapsed. Burke Yates let
out a hoot.

"Best shooting I ever saw!" he exclaimed, and the boy
didn't say a word but just grinned under his big hat.

While the family had hoped their son would have one
more Christmas at home, the Marine recruiter surprised

Rowdy with an early seat at MCRD San Diego, the day after Thanksgiving. He hung his Quigley Sharps over the fireplace with his hat, in mom and dad's den, and asked Burke to keep it oiled and clean for him until he got back. The long gun still hung there when Rowdy headed to Iraq. Oiled and clean, under his big hat, ready to shoot, as always.

Rowdy Yates was the only Marine Elmore Snow had ever known besides himself who ever lived at Crazy Woman Creek, Wyoming, much less got born and raised there.

Snow Ranch, known around those parts by its brand, the Standing-S, twenty-one sections of land homesteaded by Hector E. Snow, Elmore's great-great-grandfather and namesake, sat at the bottom of Headgate Draw, just west of where Crazy Woman Creek pours into the Powder River. Yates Ranch, that carried the Sky-Y brand, an arc above the Y, likewise homesteaded generations ago and passed along father to son, lay just south of the Standing-S.

Elmore Snow grew up riding horses and chasing cows on that same wild land where Rowdy Yates had learned ranch work from the boots up. They knew the same hills and hideouts, and best places to take a girl for a kiss. Both of them had endured those long bus rides morning and night to and from school at Gillette, seventy miles by road and thirty-five if a fellow could hitch a ride on a crow's back and fly direct.

Thus, Rowdy Yates had a leg up with Lieutenant Colonel Elmore Snow when it came decision time on composing this MARSOC, Iraq team. Those home ties and the intimate knowledge of what kind of man comes from Crazy Woman Creek, Wyoming, helped trump the stump of his junior rank. Kinship of growing up in the same place on Mother Earth that most people never realized existed convinced Elmore that in this instance a lance corporal could measure up. Rowdy also seemed a lot older than his years, probably because the wellspring of his life and many influences came from a time more like Jack's and Elmore's, and they related well to him.

Even so, Rowdy P. Yates still had to make the grade as not merely a qualified Marine Scout-Sniper and Force Recon operator, but a superior man with a gun, and have keen senses about all those other things rolled into one body of muscle and bone that makes the MARSOC operator all things capable. No task too difficult or too off-the-wall that he cannot accomplish the mission with what he holds in his kit. Creativity, ingenuity, and enterprise define his nature. He's at home by himself, confident and fearless. A master of field skills, camouflage, and craft. He will adapt to conditions and overcome all challenges, and he will always accomplish the mission regardless of obstacles. It takes special warriors to fight special warfare, and Rowdy Yates filled that bill.

Right out of boot camp, Rowdy got married while home on leave. Brenda Kay, his girl from high school, never wanted anyone but Rowdy, and he had never wanted anyone but her. She and her family lived just west of Headgate Draw, off Crazy Woman Creek, on a small ranch with good timber, up high. They had a cozy stone house up there and ran cattle in the meadows that they opened from logging where they could. She and Rowdy had gone to those sweet secret places that Elmore Snow had also shown June, his bride from Gillette.

Now Brenda Kay Yates sat home at Midway Park enlisted-housing area on Camp Lejeune, North Carolina, two thousand miles from Crazy Woman Creek, Wyoming, and her family, eight months pregnant, waiting, worrying, and praying for her man.

"You sure it's a girl?" Billy Claybaugh asked Rowdy, joking with him as the lance corporal drove the lead Hummer in the convoy of KBR tractor-trailer trucks heading down Fallujah Road. "Maybe it's a boy, but he had his leg or his hand in the way. Or his pecker's so little like his daddy's that you can't see it without magnification."

Rowdy laughed with the others and took the jab in stride. They were brothers, and that's what brothers do. Tell a guy he's got a little pecker.

Before they had left the MARSOC home base, Rowdy Yates had just gotten pictures of his soon-to-be-born daughter in an email that Brenda Kay had sent him. She had gone to the doctor, and they took ultrasound images of the baby, and announced that they were fairly sure it was a girl. Filled with joy, Rowdy had shown everyone from Captain Burkehart and Gunny Valentine right down the line to Bronco and Jaws.

"Staff Sergeant Claybaugh," Rowdy drawled back, "my pecker may be short, but it's wide and satisfying. I'm proud of every pound of it."

Everybody laughed more because they had all seen Rowdy with his pants off. None of them wore underwear.

It was a thing that special operators did, avoiding crotch rot. Free-balling commando style. Big watches and no drawers. A long-held tradition among Force Recon Marines and Navy SEALs.

As a result, living as they did, in close quarters, there were no secrets and no surprise packages.

Cochise Quinlan manned the .50 caliber machine gun and Petey Preston fed him ammo. Randy Powell rode in the jump seat and would run the M240 Golf machine gun if they needed it. The additional man made life a tight fit in the Hummer with the extra boxes of ammunition that Billy-C had stacked in the back. Just in case. Along with the Barrett .50 caliber Bullpup sniper rifle and two of the Vigilance VR1 semiautomatic .338 Lapua Magnum sniper rifles that Bill Ritchie and his son, Keary, at EDM-Vigilance Arms had built for Jack and his boys.

"Jammed up and jelly tight," Billy-C had said when his Marines started complaining. "You'll thank me later, when we get in the shit."

Cotton Martin thought it was overkill but went ahead and loaded his Hummer with the gear and ammo his cohort had prescribed for the mission. No questions asked. Billy was in charge of this detail, and the tall Texas staff sergeant supported his authority. When his crew began to complain about the tight conditions, Cotton backed Billy-C up and said he or Gunny V would have made the same choices.

As they left the pavement and now rolled on hard-packed clay and crushed rock, the Army Cougar that led the convoy ran fifty yards ahead of the first two KBR transport trucks pulling box trailers filled with food and supplies. Each of them also kept fifty yards' space between their bumpers. Billy-C chased fifty yards behind them, leading the other trucks, followed by Cotton and his crew. All seemed well.

"Staff Sergeant C," Cochise chimed down from his perch. "Just the other day, Rowdy, me, and Petey was taking us a piss off the Euphrates bridge. Rowdy started whizzing first and said, boy, it's sure a long way down to that water. Then Petey lets his monster fall, and says, yes it is, and that water's cold. Then I unfurled my snake. Pretty quick, I let those boys know, that river's deep, too!"

The whole crew laughed again. So Rowdy took up for himself. "You know, I bruised mine up pretty good when it dragged the rocky bottom. Water being so swift and all. Bruised it up something fierce."

Everybody moaned.

Billy-C was glad they could joke. It took the edge off his nerves. Boring. He loved boring. Boring to the point that men start measuring their dicks and telling lies.

As they had left Baghdad, mostly wide space lay between them and any houses. Not much cover to support an insurgent ambush. However, less than a mile ahead, Staff Sergeant Claybaugh saw the tight spot he had dreaded. Walls, buildings, junk cars. Lots of places to set up an ambush.

"Heads up and eyes out," Billy-C reminded his crew.

Captain Mike Burkehart pecked furiously at his computer, across the office from Lieutenant Colonel Elmore Snow's vacant desk. Several wall lockers lined the bulkheads of the small white MARSOC headquarters office. In the rear of the building, the captain and the colonel had set up their living quarters in small, walled-off rooms with a single bathroom and shower serving both officers.

A knock came at the front door, and Burkehart looked up as the bright outside light came through when it opened. A geared-up combat Marine stepped inside, an M4 carbine rifle slung on his shoulder and mature creases lining his tan face.

"First Sergeant Alvin Barkley, Charlie Company, One-Five," the Marine said. "Looking for Lieutenant Colonel Elmore Snow."

"You missed him by half a day, First Sergeant," the skipper said. "I'm Captain Mike Burkehart. Officer in Charge of the MARSOC detachment, and executive officer to Colonel Snow. Can I help you?"

"I hope so, sir," Barkley said, and took a brown, nine-inch-by-twelve-inch envelope out of a green map case. "Lieutenant Colonel E. B. Roberts, one-five battalion commander, gave me direct orders to hand carry this operation plan to Colonel Snow. I've been busting my hump since daylight to get here from out in the Anbar by Hit. Deeply regret missing Colonel Snow. Will he return soon?"

"He's gone stateside for three weeks," Burkehart said.

"We've got a team of your MARSOC operators tasked to support this operation," the first sergeant said.

"Colonel Snow told me about it before he left," the captain said. "Gunny Valentine briefed me, and he'll lead the team. You can take that envelope back with you or leave it with me."

First Sergeant Barkley thought about it and started to put the envelope back in his map case but stopped.

"Sir, I just don't know what to do," he said. "Colonel Roberts didn't trust email or the classified guard mail couriers with this, and wanted me to hand carry this hard copy direct. Too many compromises these days. But I hate to go back and tell him I couldn't deliver the package."

Captain Burkehart reached out and took the envelope from the Marine. "Leave it with me. Absolutely safe. I've known Black Bart Roberts for years. Tell him you left it with Mike Burkehart, Snow's X-O, and he'll be fine with it."

"Be sure you lock it up, sir," the first sergeant reminded the captain, and opened a logbook for Burkehart to sign.

After endorsing receipt of the plan, Captain Burkehart pointed to the three-drawer classified-documents safe in the corner of the office. "I've got some other classified materials that I'm wrapping up. I'll secure your op plan with them when I'm done."

"Thank you, sir," Barkley said, and shook hands with the captain. "I'll let the colonel know that all is well on this end, and your team will be joining us."

"They launch out of here in a day or two, so the gunny tells me. I'll read the plan and get myself fully up to snuff. Worry not, Marine," Burkehart said.

"Sounds righteous, sir," Barkley said. "I've got my company chopping up by Haditha Dam in the morning, setting up our end. Trying to clear the scum up and down the river."

"Good luck with that. Easier said than done," the captain said, walking the first sergeant back to the door.

"Don't I know it, sir," the first sergeant said, and shook the captain's hand again.

"Tell Colonel Roberts that Captain Burkehart sends his regards," the skipper said.

When the Marine departed, Captain Burkehart laid the envelope on the colonel's desk with other papers he planned to lock in the classified safe, once he got his work done.

As he sat down at his computer, another courier came through the door with a handful of similar-looking envelopes. Saying nothing, the captain merely pointed at the colonel's desk. The courier laid them on top of the envelope and other papers, and left.

While Jack Valentine had the double album *Traveling Wilburys Collection* playing on his CD boom box, keeping corporals Jesse Cortez and Alex Gomez tranquilized while they painted the finishing touches along the corners and edges of the black accent wall, he mixed several shades of gray and white paint in plastic throwaway cups. He had used white chalk to sketch on the black wall the outline of his massive evil-eyed skull with long teeth exuding a terrible snarl, and no lower jaw. Punisher style. Except Jack had decided to paint his own stylized version of Le Croix Pattée, the footed cross, worn by Knights Templar during the Crusades, on the skull's forehead.

He had gotten the idea from Elmore Snow's lecture on Muhammad and the Crusades. Why not? The cross of the Knights Templar might provoke the enemy even more than a mere Punisher-inspired skull by itself. Besides, everybody these days sported some version of that skull. Le Croix Pattée, painted blood red and trimmed in black, would pop.

On the desk nearest him, Jack had set his intercom radio tuned to Billy-C's security team's channel. He could hear the boys laughing and yakking while George Harrison, Bob Dylan, Jeff Lynne, Tom Petty, and Roy Orbison sang about a woman called Maxine riding a llama through an old parking lot, and she never came through here again. Or words to that effect. Jack liked the song because of its old-school Flamenco style. The rhythm and the bass run held his heart.

His mother's roots reached deep in Mexican musical and dance culture, and extended to Cordoba in the Andalusia region of Spain, where the Flamenco was born. Jack's grandfather, Pablo Francisco Guerra de Cordoba, whom the villagers called *El Capitan*, a tall, stately man, had come to Mexico as a young gypsy and danced the Flamenco in the *Ballet Folklorico de Mexico*. Jack was very proud of his grandfather, and his aunts and uncles, too. All musical artists, like his mother, a great Flamenco dancer herself. Thus music and art were in the gunny's blood, and a great passion in his life.

"We shoulda gone on that convoy, Guns," Bronco said, interrupting Jack's musical daydream, hearing his buddies on the radio, laughing, sounding like they were having a lot more fun than him.

Jaws said, "Shut the fuck up, Jesse."

"You always in my shit, Jaws," Cortez whined. "Thought you was my bro, dude."

"Shut the fuck up," Gomez repeated. "We get this done,

we can kick back. Drink a brew and watch a movie, maybe. Those guys, they're happy now but that's Fallujah Road they're running. I'd rather be here, under the cool A-C, painting. Not ducking lead."

Bronco thought about it, and nodded. "Right on."

Jack began sketching the skull's teeth longer, exaggerating them with uneven points like dripping wax.

He stepped back and cocked his head to one side. Bronco and Jaws came alongside him and cocked their heads, too.

"Whoa, Guns," Bronco said. "Gnarly skull."

Jaws nodded and let a smile creep out.

"Gnarly," Jack agreed, and glanced at Jaws, seeing the rare smile. "You approve?"

"Righteous," Jaws said.

Immediately after his morning meeting with Cesare Alosi, Ray-Dean Blevins had done his best to kill a pint of vodka, pissed off about feeding Iraqi whores information on US military security operations. He knew he had become worthless scum, but even scum will sink only so low. Making American forces look bad, to the point of compromising lives and safety, so that Malone-Leyva could generate some business, went way too far, even for him.

He soon killed the pint and clanked it in the trash with several other dead soldiers. When he couldn't find more to drink, Ray-Dean fell across the foot of his bed where he dazed out for an hour. When he awoke, he stumbled into a hot shower, gave himself a good shave, and put on clean clothes.

Now, Ray-Dean looked at himself in the bathroom mirror, flashed his teeth, and checked his breath. Still a little vodkaish. So he took another slug of minty-fresh mouthwash, gargled and swished it good, then he swallowed the whole glob. Why waste good alcohol?

He kept a room in the same hotel where most of the American press corps resided, along with a good number of mercenary soldiers like himself, working for the several security contractors. Hacksaw Gillespie, Habu Webster, and Kermit The Frog Alexander kept rooms here, too. They had clued him in about nightlife with the American and European reporters. Great food, great drinks at the frequent going-and-coming luaus they threw. More female correspondents in Baghdad these days, all ready to face the war-beast in the daylight, and screw their drunken brains out at night.

When he got to the elevator, a French freelancer working for an American news agency based in London stood in the car headed to the lobby. Her first name was Francoise, and Ray-Dean could not recall her last. Some mouthful of frog soup that he couldn't pronounce right anyway.

She wore a leopard-print silk top with no bra, or if she had one on, it was far too thin to do much good. Her ample breasts jiggled and bounced every time she moved. Black synthetic something covered her lower half, pegging her muscled legs down to her ankles. The clinging thin spandex gripped tight around an inviting plump camel toe, the crotch seam pulled deep down the center of her roomy snatch.

Francoise smelled of strong, day-old perfume and well-used pussy. Her scent made Cooder's dick hard. He didn't try to hide the growing bulge in his 5.11s, either, but gave her a nasty smile.

"How about an afternoon cocktail?" she asked him in her sultry French slur of tipsy words as the elevator eased toward the lobby.

"Love to, sweetness, but I've got business. Maybe later if you're still around," Ray-Dean told the woman whose face could make a freight train take a dirt road, but whose love monkey he had slam-danced many a worthless night.

When the lift hit the lobby stop, Francoise gave Cooder-with-a-D Blevins a wet red-lips smack on his cheek, then she click-clacked off toward the hotel bar.

Ray-Dean thought about following her and maybe getting a quick blowjob, but he checked his watch. No time for folderol. He didn't want to risk running into any old acquaintances, especially Gunny Valentine, returning from a totally fucked-up patrol when he visited the MAR-SOC compound at Camp Victory.

Just a friendly drop-in and howdy-do with brother Marines, he rationalized as a cover for his dark mission. A few light and hearty laughs with the usually talkative storekeepers and gunsmiths, get a little updated dope on what's happening, then he'd duck out.

As he slid into his new Escalade, which replaced the one he had burned, he reached in the console glove compartment and took out a bottle of Givenchy men's cologne. He pulled off the lid and gave himself a nice spritz. Then Ray-Dean pulled the shifter to drive and headed across town toward the airport.

Hot, bright sun glared off the hood of the Hummer, and Rowdy Yates blinked through his sunglasses. He took them off and pushed back his helmet, wiping sweat off his face with the back of his hand.

"Wish we could go faster. Get a little breeze blowing through this truck," he said, putting the sunglasses back on and adjusting his helmet.

"Just think cool," Billy said, and gave the boy a pat on the shoulder.

"We're like three pigs in a blanket back here, boss man," Corporal Randy Powell said, extra ammo boxes pressing him against the door.

Petey Preston sat on the other side of Powell, equally jammed. "Chico's right, Staff Sergeant. All this extra guns and ammo is overkill. I'm sorry but shit, dude."

Cochise Quinlan gave Petey a kick in the shoulder with the side of his boot, enjoying better air manning the Maw Duce in the open turret. "We get in the shit, and you'll be kissing Billy's ass."

"Yeah, Cochise, you got the breeze up there on the duce, and we're down here smelling each other's farts," Petey came back, and gave Quinlan a hard elbow in the thigh.

"Put a sock in it and keep your eyes open," Billy-C said from up front. Bad vibes rode up his spine as the convoy rolled through the tight spot. His stomach twisted into a knot, just as it always did before a fight. Jack called it built-in radar, and paid attention when Billy Claybaugh's jaws tightened.

"You feeling the Lump?" Rowdy asked, knowing that look on Billy-C's face. They'd all heard Gunny V talking about Claybaugh's inbuilt early-warning system. Some people have the hair stand up on the backs of their necks, but for Billy, his gut wrenched. He got it just before an ambush, when all the warning signs made his nerves edgy and his stomach tied itself up. He also got it when competing in gold-medal matches on the Marine Corps Shooting Team. That's when his coach named it the Lump.

Billy looked around. Mud houses, high mud walls. Two-story block houses with flat roofs. Open windows. Junk cars. Trash piles. Lots of places to set up guns for an ambush. The Lump made his ears turn red and his jaws clench hard. He had it bad this time.

"Keep your intervals wide!" Billy yelled on the command radio, seeing the two KBR semis ahead of him rolling way too close and the lead vehicle running way too slow. "Lieutenant Phipps, can we pick up the pace, sir? Let's open some space between these trucks."

The six-wheel-drive Army Cougar blew out black smoke as the driver pushed down the throttle and opened the gap between him and the first tractor-trailer. Rowdy tapped his brakes, slowing way down, and the trucks behind him nearly stopped from the accordion effect of all the vehicles trying to increase distances between bumpers.

Just then a command-detonated mine buried deep under the road blew a back wheel off the MRAP. A heartbeat behind it, a second mine, even larger, took out the entire tractor of the lead semi and destroyed half its trailer. They'd be lucky to find body parts of the driver.

The man running the KBR truck behind him jumped out of the cab, taking a panic-stricken run for it. A sniper's bullet cut him down, dead, as his feet hit the ground.

"Ambush!" Claybaugh let go on command radio and intercom, a surge of adrenaline taking hold of him.

Rowdy Yates had his left hand resting on the top of the steering wheel and had his window down. He was about to say something to Billy Claybaugh when a 180-grain .30 caliber bullet fired by a 7.62-by-54-millimeter rimmed Dragunov sniper rifle struck him just under the left armpit. The al-Qaeda Iraq sniper had placed his shot in the arm opening of the young Marine's body armor. The heavy Russian bullet took out the lance corporal's heart and lungs while he blinked, surprised, looking at Billy-C. Rowdy wanted to say something but died before he could make a sound.

"Sniper!" Billy Claybaugh yelled on his microphone as Rowdy Yates fell into the staff sergeant's arms.

Cochise Quinlan did not wait for orders. He opened fire with the duce at the ambush's left flank as soon as he saw the truck driver fall dead on the road. Then he trained his stream of .50 caliber monolithic brass projectiles at a second-story window that looked a likely hide for the sniper who had just killed his young brother.

"Get that 240 up and running, and cover the right!

Light those motherfuckers up!" Billy yelled as he pushed Lance Corporal Yates off him and leaned down as several AK bullets splattered the glass on his door window and the windshield.

"Cotton," Claybaugh shouted, as Petey Preston went to work feeding ammo to Cochise and handing belts up to Randy Powell, who opened fire with the .30 caliber machine gun. "We're in a cross fire from both sides of the road. At least a dozen sources. Beaucoup bad guys high and low."

Machine gun fire began working from Cotton Martin's Hummer as the Army lieutenant with the infantry squad in the Cougar came on the radio.

"You Marines still mobile?" he called.

"Roger, we're both mobile," Billy said, but added, "My driver's dead."

As the Army officer spoke, heavy fire from both sides of the road focused on the MRAP. An RPG glanced off its side and exploded as the turret gunner sent several forty-millimeter grenades at the building from which most of the machine gun fire came and the rocket had launched.

"Gather the drivers from the rear KBR trucks, and bring both those Hummers up here so we can form a defense and deploy my infantry," the lieutenant commanded.

Billy had just pulled Rowdy over his legs, and squeezed himself under the dead Marine's body, getting into the driver's seat, when a B-40 rocket hit the passenger side of the Hummer and blew away that wheel.

"We're stuck, sir," Billy came back on the radio. "An RPG just took out our front end."

"Shit," the lieutenant answered. "Consolidate your two vehicles there and get those KBR drivers under cover."

Cotton Martin pulled his Hummer alongside the two semis behind Billy-C and laid down suppression fire with both his machine guns while the two surviving KBR drivers squeezed inside with the Marines. Already, both cabs of the big trucks looked like Swiss cheese.

"Pull asshole to belly button behind me, Cotton," Billy said, seeing the second Hummer coming up, taking heavy fire.

"They aim to overrun us," Cotton said. "We need to get deployed and roll an offense at them. Turn the tide!"

"You there, Gunny V?" Billy-C called on his intercom.

"Billy, I'm right here, and cavalry's coming, just like I promised. Reaction force launching your way as we speak. Give me a sitrep when you can catch a breath," Jack Valentine said over the radio to Staff Sergeant Claybaugh, trying to sound calm while his heart beat double time. All interior decorating had come to a complete stop. Bronco Starr and Jaws stood close by their mentor, intense, listening to the gunfight and combat chatter of their mates that came over the intercom speaker.

"Gunny, let's mount up," Jesse Cortez pleaded.

"Fuckin' A, dude," Alex Gomez followed. "Let me drive, and we'll get there in fifteen minutes."

Jack wanted to do it but knew better. A reaction team of reinforcements had already moved out for business. Gunships had launched, and what battle Billy and the boys had going on would likely be over before any of the MAR-SOC tribe could possibly arrive to help.

"Rowdy's KIA," Billy-C came back. "I've got machine guns laying down cover fire, and we're deploying teams right and left to go on assault. Enemy strength substantial. Twenty or thirty. But we gonna kill these mother-fuckers!"

"Kill 'em all, brother," Jack snarled back. "Light 'em the fuck up!"

Bronco dropped to the floor and sat, staring at his boots. Jaws stood with his skull-ringed biceps and tattooed arms crossed. Jack stood by him, resting his chin on his fist, listening to the fight.

"He was going to be a dad," Bronco said, not raising his head. "Rowdy, I mean. He showed me the ultrasound pictures of his baby girl this morning."

"Fuck it," Jaws said. Then he looked at Gunny Valentine. "Those cocksuckers in the head shed got us on these silly shit details long enough, Guns. It needs to stop."

"That's right, Gunny V," Bronco added. "They got battalions of doggies just sitting on their asses. Let those assholes run security. Better yet, give it to those scumbag civilian security contractors. Better they die than one of us."

Jaws came back, "Why we not out there huntin' these Haji motherfuckers anyway and killing 'em all? I thought we had Zarqawi on our list. Why ain't we hunting that motherfucker?"

"I feel you, boys," Jack said. "You got my vote. Time this extracurricular horseshit stopped. Fuck the military politics. I'm telling the skipper. We're going full MARSOC ops out in the Anbar, hunting Zarqawi or whoever the fuck else we can shoot in the meantime. Every fucking one of us I can drag on Black Bart Roberts's operation. If we're going to die, we die on our terms. Not some dog-meat security duty leading supply trucks. Total fucking bullshit!"

"Fuckin' A," Jaws said.

_ 6 _

The entire front half of a two-story stucco house cascaded to the ground after Cochise Quinlan poured two and a half belts of .50 caliber Browning machine gun monolithic ammunition through the building's vital supports. The 746-grain solid brass bullets cut through the corners and center supports like a chain saw on soft pine. A salvo of forty-millimeter high-explosive grenades fired from the MRAP's mark 19 finished off the structure, once Cochise had broken its spine.

When the house fell, its entire roof collapsed atop its broken walls and floors. Dirt and gray smoke boiled skyward behind the gush of air that rushed from under the roof as it went down. Like drunken sailors lost in a fog, half a dozen Qaeda gunmen staggered out of the mess dazed, each man blinded from dirt-clogged eyes, bleeding, delirious from explosion trauma, and their bodies caked with dust like floured chicken ready for the deep fryer.

As the building fell to rubble, Billy-C watched from behind a low adobe wall, with Petey Preston and Randy Powell. He couldn't help but smile. An awesome sight.

Poetic justice to the dirty bastards who had lain in ambush inside the now-destroyed house.

Staff Sergeant Claybaugh carried the new short-barreled Barrett Bullpup and a satchel full of mark 211 .50 caliber tungsten-core Raufoss multipurpose, explosive-incendiary, armor-penetrating ammunition. A Raufoss round will blow through a wall, or even a sheet of ballistic steel plate, then explode behind it. The multistage explosive-incendiary properties of the round do a total job on anyone fighting behind a wall or armored barrier.

Corporals Preston and Powell each had an EDM-Vigilance, VR1 model, .338 Lapua Magnum semiautomatic sniper rifle, and had stuffed their packs and vest pouches tight with ammo. The three Scout-Snipers spaced themselves thirty meters apart and formed sectors of fire that fanned across their entire left flank. Billy lay between his two cohorts, covering the middle with his big-bore gun.

When the front half of the two-story house came down, the gang of Hajis inside the second-story room had no place to go. They clung to what they could but soon fell into the rubble. It reminded Billy of breaking open a rotten log filled with termites. After the grenade salvo from the MRAP, those not killed came staggering out, firing their rifles.

Petey Preston busted two gunmen with his Lapua Magnum. Randy Powell splashed three more with his Vigilance. Billy-C laid crosshairs on the back of the sixth man, who clutched a Dragunov for dear life and tried to run after seeing his cohorts die. The staff sergeant coolly squeezed off a .50 caliber Raufoss round that nailed the

Haji right between his shoulder blades. The man exploded like a watermelon dropped off a tall building.

"He's the one that got Rowdy," Preston yelled over the intercom. "You see that Russian sniper rifle he had?"

"Roger that," Billy replied. "He was shooting out of that top window, right in line with our truck. We get the chance, I'm taking that rifle home with us and mounting it on the HOG Wallow wall back at Camp Swampy."

"Put Rowdy's name on it," Petey said.

"Fuckin' A," Billy came back. "His picture by it, too."

One of the two KBR truck drivers manned the .30 caliber machine gun on Billy-C's Hummer and helped Sergeant Quinlan keep belts fed in his .50. Two men, two machine guns, and no extra help. Everybody else had deployed to cut the heart out of the ambush.

Likewise, in Cotton Martin's Humvee, Bobby Durant ran the Maw Duce and the other KBR driver manned the M240 Golf .30 caliber machine gun. Luckily, both truck drivers had prior Army infantry experience and knew how to rack a machine gun, pace their fire, and not melt the barrels.

Lieutenant Phipps did everything he could to help in the fight, keeping the crew busy on the MK19 grenade-launching machine gun, ducking fire while lobbing all they had against the sizeable enemy force. Despite the one building taken down and its rat pack of fighters now killed, seven other Haji gun nests kept pouring lead on the MRAP. The dozen infantry soldiers could do little more than hunker inside the armored truck and wait for a break to kick open the back doors.

Two brave souls inside the Cougar HE popped open

the top hatches at the back of the truck in an attempt to fire machine guns at the al-Qaeda attackers, hoping to set up a base of cover fire so that the rest of the troops could scramble outside and go to work. Rooftop guns quickly poured their wrath on the opened lids, and sent lead and copper fragments spraying inside. When the soldiers finally got the hatch covers closed, four men had suffered flesh wounds in their arms and legs.

"Can you Marines move up to cover our position so we can get the fuck out of this death trap?" Lieutenant Phipps called to Billy-C and Cotton.

"Roger dodger. On our way, sir," Cotton answered, and started maneuvering his team forward.

Machine guns on the two Humvees shifted their fire to the buildings that flanked the front of the caravan and began focusing their streams into open windows and rooftops.

"Air strike about now'd be real nice," Cochise Quinlan sang from behind his .50, ammo links rattling in the Hummer like popcorn pouring out the popper at the Carmike Majestic in downtown Chattanooga. The former Marion County, Tennessee, sheriff's deputy who went active duty from the Marine Reserves when the planes crashed into the World Trade Center and Pentagon rode the big gun hard, trying to shut down the enemy's rooftop fire on the column's left flank.

"A reinforced Marine infantry company would work even better," Cotton Martin came back.

"Meantime, we make do," Billy-C added. "Boys. Tuck it up. We gonna leapfrog to the front. Fire and movement. Cochise and Bobby, you and the truckers work those machine guns so the rest of us can maneuver up. Once we get them solja-boys outta that tin can, where they can sling a little lead, then us snipers'll go do our thing."

"Kill 'em all, Billy. Let God sort 'em out," Jack Valentine broke into the conversation on the operations-office radio.

"We kilt a bunch of 'em, Gunny, but they's a whole bunch more still needs killin'," Claybaugh answered, now in his mental groove. "Shore wish't you an' the rest of the tribe was here with us, to enjoy the moment. Share the wealth. I feel downright greedy havin' all this fun, and you girls sittin' there with your hands in your lap, nothing better to do than gather round the campfire, braid each other's hair, and sing 'Kumbaya.' As you say, we got ourselves a target-rich environment. Except right now, we'uns is mostly the targets they's a shootin' at."

As the machine guns focused on the front two buildings on both sides of the road, the seven MARSOC snipers on the ground kept the remaining four enemy positions covered. Any shots or movement in an open window, from a rooftop or around the junk on the ground drew hot lead from Marines.

With every fifth round coming from all four machine guns a red tracer, fires in the shot-up debris and in several of the buildings began to burn. When Billy-C saw the erupting flames, he got an idea.

"Lieutenant Phipps!" Billy called on the command channel. "You boys got any sort of incendiary grenades for that mark 19? Maybe like illuminations or flares?"

"Stand by one and I'll check with my gunner," the

Army officer said. A few seconds later, he answered, "A couple or three belts of green and red clusters, and a belt of illumes, but mostly we've got H-E-D-P fragmentation rounds. Why?"

"Have your gunner load up with the incendiaries. Anything that ignites a fire. Those willy-peter illumes are dandy. Lob it on all these buildings and set 'em ablaze," Billy-C said. "Smoke from fires started with our tracers is blowing south. If we set the neighborhood ablaze, lots of smoke, it'll totally fuck up the Haji's shit. Smoke inhalation, burning eyes, you know the drill. And it won't be in our faces at all. Besides, a fire might burn a bunch of these sand rats out of their holes, so we can shoot 'em."

"I like your idea, Sergeant," Jeremy Phipps said. "We'll give 'em all we got. Maybe we can get out of this tin can before they figure out how to put an RPG into it."

"Right, sir," Claybaugh said. "Light 'em up!"

In a few seconds, the MK19 began hosing red and green flares, and white phosphorus illumination rounds into the windows of every building within reach. Three belts later, rising flames and smoke enveloped the whole neighborhood.

Just as Jack looked up, the operations-hooch doors burst open, and the six remaining MARSOC-Iraq snipers and both detachment armorers rumbled inside. The eight men huddled around the gunny's desk, picking up on the action over the intercom radio's speaker.

"Smedley says Billy-C and the boys gettin' hit hard,"

Sergeant Sammy LaSage, whose name everybody had shortened to just plain Sage, growled. "What's the damage on our side?"

"Three dead. Two truck drivers and one of our own, Rowdy Yates," Jack said, looking around the crowd that now made up the rest of the Iraq detachment. "Staff Sergeant Claybaugh just set the world afire, down by Fallujah. Rough count, our guys splashed a dozen Hajis, and they're still fighting."

"Target-rich. We ought to be there," Sage said.

"Billy's got this," Jack said.

"No doubt, Guns," Sergeant LaSage agreed. "I'm just saying it seems a shame we're not there to help out."

Valentine smiled. "Billy said nearly the same thing."

Sage nodded. "Right on."

Sammy LaSage grew up in Albuquerque and got drafted by the Colorado Rockies baseball club out of Manzano High School. He played two years of single-A shortstop for the Modesto Nuts before giving up the dream. Then he enlisted in the Marine Corps when he decided that playing more years of farm-team baseball with holes in his jeans, cold chicken in a box lunch on the team bus, and a rattrap pickup truck to drive did not quite cut it. Cooperstown would not be his.

So with his high school diploma and not much else, Sage went looking for more meaningful work. Not many demands outside the diamond for a five-foot-nine-inch athlete with a rocket arm, quick hands, and a good eye for a cut fastball.

Down to his last nickel and a quarter tank of gas in his

twenty-year-old Dodge, Sammy LaSage took note of a Marine Corps recruiting office next to the Church's Fried Chicken store, where he had just filled out an employment application, on Juan Tabo Boulevard just south of Manuel. He didn't have to think much about it to decide that a Marine uniform fit him better than a chicken outfit, so he filled out an application there, too.

Good eyes, quick hands, and strong arms worked well for the Marine Corps, too, and Sage found his new home and life.

Bronco and Jaws served on Sergeant Sage's team, along with a dark green Marine named Craig Heyward, a corporal from Garland, Texas, the Dallas suburb where Hank Hill and his oddball *King of the Hill* family and friends also lived. Propane and propane products made Garland great, and Calvin Johnson was proud of that fact, along with the Dallas Cowboys, who Hank Hill and the boys also loved. God bless Tom Landry!

Thus when Jack Valentine began calling Corporal Heyward Ironhead, the young man who lived and breathed Cowboys blue had mixed emotions about it. Sharing the same name with the hard-hitting NFL running back who gained righteous fame on the New Orleans Saints and Atlanta Falcons, long-standing rivals of Dallas, rubbed against his grain more than just a tad bit. He didn't like it at all. But that hardly mattered to Jack. Ironhead was Ironhead, and that was that.

The other four Marines who jammed in tight with Sage and Ironhead, surrounding Gunny V, Bronco, and Jaws, Jack had lovingly named the Mob Squad. He also called them by a few other creative names like "Mario Brothers" and "Donkey Kong." But "Mob Squad" seemed most popular.

Sergeant Carlo "The Iceman" Savoca, a six-foot-tall, good-looking Marine, born and raised on Staten Island, headed up the Mob Squad. His father and grandfather, and as far back as he knew, men of his family for many generations carved Italian marble and granite for a living. They didn't just make grave memorials but architectural works of art and fine sculptures. People called Sergeant Savoca the Iceman because nothing ever rattled him. On the trigger, he was all business.

Also a native of New York City, Corporal Salvador "Sal the Pizza Man" Principato called the borough of Queens his home. His dad was a cop, a lieutenant on the Big Apple's SWAT team. Sal's father had survived the falling towers of the World Trade Center on September 11, 2001, among the last policemen to clear the street before everything came crushing down. Now, five years later and counting, Lieutenant Salvador Principato Senior fought the early stages of lung cancer and mandatory retirement.

Sal Principato had openly wept with his father as the families said good-bye to their Marines as MARSOC Detachment, Iraq, boarded their flight at Cherry Point. Both Marine and New York policeman wore their uniforms proudly that day.

Corporal Nicholas "Nick the Nose" Falzone, the third of the four-man Mob Squad, lived at the opposite end of the Verrazano Bridge from Sergeant Savoca, in the Bay Ridge section of Brooklyn. His mother and father owned a popular restaurant on Fourth Avenue just past Marine Avenue, toward Ninety-ninth Street.

For Nick Falzone, a nickname like Nick the Nose didn't bother him. But he warned everyone, including Gunny Jack and Colonel Snow, and especially Captain Burkehart, who always loved using nicknames, to nix it on the Nick the Nose anytime anyone from his family was around. They wouldn't understand the affection that went with it and would feel insulted by it. Nick's father, Anthony, carried a nickname of "Big Tony" from childhood. Little Tony Falzone was a kid up the block that grew up with his dad, also from a Sicilian family, but no relation. While Big Tony Falzone had never even gotten a parking ticket, and took pride in building and owning his own business the hard way, Little Tony Falzone had gone with the mob, robbed an airline with three other Bay Ridge boys, and now was spending the rest of his life in Attica.

Last but not least, Corporal Marcello Costa came to the team already named Momo. His mother in Hoboken, New Jersey, heard Frank Sinatra call one of his buddies Momo, so she decided her son, Marcello, should be Momo, too.

Jack Valentine loved the Mob Squad. He hadn't put them together, they chose each other. Sergeant Savoca had suggested it early in their training, even while paring down the detachment to eighteen operators plus Jack, the captain, and the colonel, two armorers, and the one supply and administrative clerk they called Smedley.

"Make a hole. Let me in where I can hear the radio," Staff Sergeant Dennis J. Drzewiecki, chief detachment armorer said, pushing from the rear. He and his armory partner, Sergeant Andre Romyantsev, whom Jack Valentine called Rasputin the Devil, mostly because he and everyone else on the team had trouble getting Romyantsev off their tongues, had followed the crowd to the operations hooch when they heard that some of their brothers had hit trouble.

Jack had shortened Staff Sergeant Drzewiecki's name to simply Sergeant D, for the same reason Romyantsev became Rasputin.

"Gunny," the staff sergeant added. "Captain Burkehart told me to tell you that he's headed up to MAF operations to catch a ride with the assessment team. They're heading out to the ambush site right behind the reaction force."

"With you and Rasputin here, who's minding the store? Smedley? Again?" Jack asked.

Drzewiecki nodded. "Yup. Corporal Butler has the con."

"You know, he ain't the sharpest tack in the pile," Jack said, and looked around at his men and saw the smiles. They, too, knew that Ralph Butler, whom they nicknamed Smedley, had real issues with Marine Corps common sense and skills beyond keeping documents filed, making correct entries in service records, which Captain Burkehart supervised closely, and maintaining inventory of detachment supplies.

Sergeant D cleared his throat, as if he had more to say, but then simply added, "I keep an eye on him. He's trained to pee on the paper, Gunny, and we don't let him out of the yard."

As he came to know the staff sergeant, Jack had come to highly regard the man. A deep well, and nobody's fool. The best gun maker in the Marine Corps, with Rasputin the Devil a close second.

Dennis Drzewiecki grew up in Whiskey Run, Pennsylvania. People who didn't know better assumed him a backwoods coal thumper, as the name Whiskey Run might imply. And Drzewiecki let them believe it. For Jack, Whiskey Run fit right in with Crazy Woman Creek and seemed totally out of place as a neighborhood on the west side of Pittsburgh. Jack also learned with more than a decade and a half in the Marine Corps that a man's hometown didn't make him smart. Elmore Snow from Crazy Woman Creek stood testament to that fact. And poor dead Rowdy Yates, too.

Jack felt bad as he thought of Rowdy, listening to the intercom chatter with Billy-C and his brothers fighting on. They would mourn their fallen Spartan later.

Looking around at his Marines, Jack knew one thing as certain as death and taxes—his warriors, even Smedley Butler manning the phone in the headquarters office, had bonded as a family. A few months ago, he had his doubts, especially with someone as far off the normal track as Andre Romyantsev. Rasputin the Devil was an outstanding armorer, smart hunter and outdoorsman, and outstanding rifle shot. A little reconnaissance and sniper training, and Rasputin could do double duty, but beyond that, he was really a different sort of animal.

Jack thought Rowdy Yates was unique, but not nearly as special as Rasputin the Devil.

Sergeant Romyantsev was born in the Yukon Territory when his parents tried life off the grid, before it became fashionable among antisocial political zealots of the new age. Although his Canadian birth certificate lists Whitehorse, the territorial capital, as his birthplace, Andre took his first breath in the family cabin on a trail nearer to Dawson City, in the Klondike.

When Andre turned fourteen, his parents repatriated to the United States and opened their own gun store and repair shop in Anchorage. They had not set foot on native soil since his father, Grigory Romyantsev, burned his draft card in 1972. His mother, Tapeesa Ipalook, was only thirteen when the two of them dropped out of sight and ventured to the Yukon from Palmer, Alaska, their hometown.

Tough as a boot and virtually bulletproof, Andre never caught cold, never had a runny nose, and seemed impervious to weather. He had his mother's Iñupiaq color and black hair, and her beautiful pixie eyes and smile, but his father's tall Russian build.

When a Marine came to his father's shop, ordering a big-bore rifle for hunting brown bear and Alaskan moose, the idea of seeing the rest of the world appealed to the tall, tan-skinned young man. Andre found a recruiter and signed up when he turned eighteen. Then he told his parents.

Grigory Romyantsev hit the roof, not wanting his son anywhere near the American military. Tapeesa and her entire Iñupiat clan celebrated her son's becoming a warrior, and Marines stood at the top of their list of heroes. They held a big party in Palmer for Andre, and tossed him high in the air from a blanket, in the Iñupiaq tradition, celebrating his departure to the Marines.

More adaptable to cold than hot, Sergeant Andre Romyantsev found working under the air conditioner in his T-shirt and PT shorts most to his liking while the Iraqi world outside the armory burned in the desert heat. When he followed

Sergeant D into the operations hooch, that's what he wore. Flip-flops, PT shorts, T-shirt, and a bush hat.

"Rasputin," Jack Valentine said, eyeballing him behind Staff Sergeant Drzewiecki, "if I need fresh utilities with zero wear, I can always find a set in your wall locker."

"Help yourself, Gunny V," Romyantsev said. "Unless we're standing parade or inspection, I intend to wear what works in the shop."

"Fucking Eskimo," Jaws grumbled.

"Fucking El Centro gangster," Andre shot back.

"South Central, ass-wipe," Gomez growled. "El Centro's some shit hole down on the border near Arizona with orange groves and coyotes."

"Jaws. Who peed in your Wheaties?" Jack said, turning from the radio and Billy-C's gunfight to look at Gomez. "Cut Rasputin a little slack. He may not know Pico-Union from Alameda, but what the fuck do you know about Alaska?"

"Fucking cold, polar bears, and I don't give a fuck if I never see it. That's what I know," Jaws came back.

"You need to branch out, dude," Rasputin said.

"Branch this," Gomez said, grabbing his crotch, then grumbled as he turned back at the radio, "Fucking Eskimo."

Heavy black smoke boiled out of the buildings as the fires took over the neighborhoods on both sides of the road. The gunner on the MRAP had belted up more high-explosive dual-purpose grenades and now belched them from his MK19 machine gun into the flaming structures.

With each explosion, a fountain of red embers blew into the sky.

"Now we're cooking!" Billy-C said on the intercom. "Watch for movement and shoot what moves. Nothing but bad guys out there."

Jeremy Phipps kicked open the back doors on the Cougar, and a dozen grunts plus a medic poured out of their tight-fitting entrapment. Six warriors and the doc followed him on the left side, and five ran right, tailing their top kick, Sergeant First Class Connor Bower, a genuine Boston Southie with an attitude, hailing from Beantown's Irish hood near the Red Line's Broadway Station off Dorchester.

The main gun operator in the forward turret with his assistant feeding up fresh mark 19 belts of grenades, two more gunners, top hatches open and running a pair of M240E1 machine guns mounted at the truck's rear, and the driver with a second assistant gunner, both hustling ammo, stayed inside, pouring cover as their infantry deployed.

Braving a burst of hot-running enemy lead, the Army lieutenant from Fayetteville had just gotten his sixth man set along the low mud fence that flanked much of the road when three AK rounds found him. Two of the bullets took him off his feet, slapping into the back of his body armor, more painful than damaging. However, the third slug shattered his left elbow and left his arm twisting like a wet rag.

Phipps pulled himself up to the mud wall, bleeding badly, and announced on his radio, "I'm alive, boys. They just winged me."

The medic, who had taken cover ahead of the officer, just missing the AK burst, threw a compression wrap on the lieutenant's arm and hit him with a shot of morphine.

As Jeremy Phipps's eyes rolled up, more from shock than drugs, Connor Bower came on the command radio with his unmistakable Southie brogue. "L-T's down, but okay. I got command now. Sah-gent Bower, if yah askin'. Hah 'bout you jah-heads? Ready ta kick some ass?"

"Fuckin' A, dude," Claybaugh came back.

"We'll run straight at 'em, then push around our end," Bower said. "You jah-heads cover the flanks on your end and kill 'em when they flee. Don't let any a dese rat bastads escape. You gat dat?"

"We're already on the move," Billy answered.

Bullets flying, Bower left a sergeant in charge of his right echelon and ran to the back of the Cougar. He slammed his hand against the steel doors while hot lead slapped all around him. "Open up! Wounded man comin' in!"

Then the medic and another soldier dragged the half-conscious lieutenant back to the MRAP, where the driver and an assistant gunner pulled him inside.

Billy-C watched the fearless sergeant leading his warriors, enemy lead in the air and him standing amidst it.

"You guys catching this John Wayne moment? That's one insane motherfucker," he said on the MARSOC intercom. "I like him."

"Insanity don't make him bulletproof," Cotton Martin said, then splattered an al-Qaeda gunman with an AK who appeared at the corner of a burning building, taking aim at the crazy Irishman. His .50 caliber Barrett sent the enemy's head tumbling high in the air like a football over a goal post while an arm and a leg flew right and left, and the rest of the body sprayed red chunks on the stucco wall.

"Fuck!" exclaimed Byrd Clingman, who the crew had named Jewfro, because of his curly brown hair. "Downright spectacular when those Raufoss penetrators hit somebody."

As Connor Bower scattered his warriors on both sides of the road into well-dispersed assault lines, and began to move them forward and push an angle on the Hajis' lower flanks, using fire and movement tactics, Billy-C spread his two snipers even wider from his center position, curving around the enemy's opposite end.

"Hook on around, Cotton. We'll blindside 'em when they run for it," he told Martin, who had also spread his operators and maneuvered to hook around the enemy on his side of their ambush positions.

With everything on both sides of the road now ablaze, funneling fire and smoke through the neighborhoods parallel to the Fallujah-bound road, al-Qaeda gunmen began to dash out of back doors and gallop down alleyways.

Hub Biggs, the tall boy out of Kerrville, Texas, had stayed even with his Scout-Sniper partner, Corporal Clyde Avery McIllhenny, whom the team called Hot Sauce.

Point of fact, Clyde McIllhenny came from Lafayette, Louisiana, was a member of the Tabasco Sauce McIllhenny family, and was the great-grandnephew of one of Tabasco's more legendary bosses, Brigadier General Walter Stauffer McIllhenny, who led Marines on Guadalcanal in World War II.

Tabasco Mac, as his fellow Marines had nicknamed General McIllhenny, in addition to his heroism, for which he received the Navy Cross and Silver Star, also had great talent with a rifle and pistol, earning Distinguished Marksman in both disciplines. Likewise, Hot Sauce had a natural marksmanship talent, and sought to earn Double Distinguished ranking like his famous uncle who had made Tabasco a Marine Corps staple.

"Yo, Hot Sauce. You seeing this?" Hub Biggs said in a soft voice over his comm link.

"You talking about the dude who ducked behind the car?" McIllhenny answered.

"You see what he's doing?" Biggs asked.

"Not hardly," Clyde came back. "I's waiting for him to run, then pop him on the fly. Looked like he's carrying a scoped rifle. You got a shot?"

"Oh yeah," Biggs answered.

"What ya waiting on? Weather to change?" Hot Sauce said.

"I just feel bad taking advantage of a man with his pants down," Biggs said. "Poor bastard's got the runs. Must be all the excitement. Soon as he got behind the car, he dropped bloomers and let fly. Squirting like a fire hose."

"Dog would a caught the rabbit had he not stopped to take a shit," McIllhenny said. "Bust that side mirror over his head. See what he does."

Biggs laughed as he took aim and squeezed off a shot.

The mirror exploded over the sick gunman's head, and the man fell backwards, into his puddle of shit.

Then the Haj rolled to his knees and lurched for his

rifle. That's when Hub Biggs put his second shot square in the man's back, sending him skidding through his own fresh shit, face-first, drawers down.

"That's a sight you don't see every day," Cotton Martin said. "You're one warped motherfucker, Hub. You do know that, don't you?"

"What was I supposed to do?" Biggs asked.

"I don't know," Martin answered. "Maybe just shoot him right off the bat?"

Ray-Dean Blevins pulled the seat of his 5.11s out of the crack of his ass when he stepped out of his Escalade. Then he checked his breath as he headed to the MARSOC-Iraq headquarters hooch.

Inside, Corporal Ralph C. Butler sat at Captain Burkehart's desk and put the finishing touches on an email to his mother, Janine, back home in Red Bank, New Jersey. She taught third grade at Red Bank Primary School, and had raised Ralph on her own since the boy was three years old, and his father was killed.

Ralph's dad, Trooper Ely Butler, a New Jersey State Police motorcycle officer, died when a hit-and-run stolen delivery truck sideswiped him as he was writing a speeding ticket on a highway shoulder near Fort Monmouth. They never caught the killer although the stolen delivery truck turned up quickly, abandoned on a side street in Eatontown. The only eyewitness, the real estate agent getting the ticket, driving her Lexus eighty miles per hour up Route 35 because she was late for a property closing, saw nothing.

When Ray-Dean knocked on the front door and stepped inside without waiting for an invite to enter, as if he belonged there, Smedley gave the Malone-Leyva mercenary the stink eye. He swung around and clicked off the intercom speaker, too, where he had been listening to Billy-C and the crew turning the tables on the jihadi ambush.

"Can I help you?" Butler huffed, immediately suspicious of the heavily accessorized, steroid-juiced intruder carrying the low-slung Glock 21 strapped to his thigh.

"Oh, it's okay, Corporal Butler," Blevins said after checking Smedley's name on the embroidered tag above his pocket. "I'm an old Force Recon Marine from the way back. Half the guys in MARSOC are buddies of mine."

Butler still kept the stink eye going on Blevins.

"So you say," Smedley said. "You got a name?"

Ray-Dean gave him a cockeyed nod.

"Hey, I'm cool with your being careful and shit," Ray-Dean said, taking a seat on the corner of Colonel Snow's desk and eyeballing the pile of envelopes, postal mail, and various papers laid there. He picked up a *Marine Corps Gazette* and thumbed it open.

"Captain Burkehart's not here, if you're looking for him. He won't be back for a good while either," Smedley then offered, hoping Blevins would leave. "Can I give him a message?"

"Like I said. I'm an old friend of a lot of the guys here, not the captain. I don't know him. My boss is up the street at a conference, and I'm killing time. That's all. Thought I might swing in here and catch up with some of my bros," Blevins said with a shrug, keeping his butt in place on the corner of Colonel Snow's desk and relaxing even more with the magazine spread open, as if he might read it.

He looked again at Ralph's name tag above the pocket on his utility jacket and pointed. "Name like Butler, I bet these ass-wipes call you Smedley, don't they. Am I right?"

Butler just stared at the jerk.

"So, Smedley," Blevins picked up. "Who's on campus? Toss me a few names, and I'll tell you if I know them."

"How about you toss me a few names," Smedley answered.

"Staff Sergeant Bill Claybaugh," Ray-Dean offered. "Me and him was real tight back in the day at three-two."

Butler nodded. "He's on patrol."

"Down to Fallujah?" Blevins said.

Smedley pursed his lips. "Yes."

"My bet, they hit the shit, didn't they," Ray-Dean said. "You always hit the shit down that way."

"Going on now," Smedley said.

"On that run, it's not if but when. Bad karma. Totally bad karma," Blevins said, shaking his head, showing Butler his dismay. "Our guys got it under control?"

"Couple of truck drivers dead, and one of our operators," Ralph opened up. "But Staff Sergeant Claybaugh and Staff Sergeant Martin have it handled now. Last I heard on the squawk box, they're kicking some righteous ass."

"My boy, Billy! Hard as woodpecker teeth," Ray-Dean said. "Gunny didn't go with them?"

"Gunny Valentine's down at operations. He's on the net with them," Smedley said, relaxing into the conversation.

"How about Jesse Cortez? He out with Claybaugh?"

Blevins asked. "I went through recon school with his lame ass out at Pendleton."

"Bronco?" Butler smiled. "He's at operations, too. Gunny's got him and another guy on work detail."

"Typical Cortez." Blevins laughed. "Extra punishment duty, right? Jesse's alligator mouth always talking himself into shit his hummingbird ass can't handle. Fucker's always on E-P-D."

Smedley laughed. "Yeah, that's Cortez. But he's one of our best snipers. Him and his partner, Jaws, are badass in the field."

"Jaws," Ray-Dean said. "That's the big Mexican dude, looks like a gangster with the tats and shit?"

Butler nodded yes. "Alex Gomez. We call him Jaws."

"So, mind if I camp here until my boss gets done?" Ray-Dean asked, seeing that Butler had finally relaxed his attitude toward him.

"You're a Marine, right?" Smedley asked, looking for a little reassurance.

"I hope to shit in your shoulder holster. Force fucking Recon," Blevins said.

"What was that name again?" Smedley asked, relaxed but still wanting to be sure about the man.

"Sergeant Blevins," Ray-Dean said, lying about his former rank. "I go by Cooder, with a D."

A smile spread across Butler's face. Cooder-with-a-D rang the bell. He'd heard Gunny Valentine ranting about this asshole, and how he insisted on spelling Cooter with a D instead of a T, because of the pussy connotation that the Cooter with a T had.

"Mind if I help myself to a little coffee?" Blevins said, already pouring a cup.

"Sure," Smedley said, and gave a look at his near-empty mug, then noticed the rapidly building pressure in his gut. Irritable bowel syndrome, triggered from nerves, caused by the strange visitor. He gave Ray-Dean, who was thumbing through pages of *Marine Corps Gazette*, a look. "You know how to answer the phone if anybody calls, right?"

"What do I say, 'MARSOC, how do I direct your call?'" Ray-Dean answered.

"That works," Butler said. "I need to make a head call. You mind picking up the phone if it rings?"

"No sweat, GI," Ray-Dean said. "Take your time. Take a nice long shit if you want. Like I said, my boss is in that meeting, and I'm just killing time."

Smedley nodded and trotted to the restroom that connected between Colonel Snow's room and Captain Burkehart's.

As soon as the lad shut the door, Ray-Dean Blevins turned to the pile of envelopes on Colonel Snow's desk and his eyes focused on several folders with red strips down the edges and big letters stating SECRET stamped on them. Then he saw the fat, nine-inch-by-twelve-inch manila envelope with CLASSIFIED TOP SECRET stamped in red ink on its face. It had "Hand Carry Only" handwritten on it and underscored three times. Then "Lieutenant Colonel E. B. Roberts, Commanding Officer, First Battalion, Fifth Marine Regiment" written in ballpoint ink on the upper left-hand corner and "Lieutenant Colonel H. E. Snow, Commanding Officer, MARSOC-Iraq" written in the same handwriting in larger letters on the center.

Ray-Dean had heard scuttlebutt that one-five was planning a big operation, and he guessed that this envelope contained information about that project.

"For fuck sake," Cooder-with-a-D laughed under his breath, and as he heard the toilet flush, he stuffed the envelope down the back waistband of his cargo trousers and pulled out his shirttail. He hurried to the door before Smedley Butler could get back to the front office and yelled at him, "My boss just sent me a text message. I got to run."

Smedley gave him a wave, then glanced at Colonel Snow's desk and ensured that the *Marine Corps Gazette* lay back atop the pile of mail and other folders, envelopes, and papers. Then his eyes caught the red-striped borders on the classified folders.

"Skipper's going to get us all put in jail," Butler griped as he gathered up the folders and envelopes stamped SECRET and CLASSIFIED. One by one, he registered them into the classified-documents log, assigned them a file number, and put them away in the safe. He had no clue that one was missing.

After the bulk of surviving al-Qaeda gunmen managed to break from the ambush and scattered at a hard run, a gang of more than a dozen well-armed fighters rallied among a clutch of mud-and-stick farmhouses with adobe fences and brush-arbor animal shelters surrounded by withered vegetable gardens, goat pastures, tall weeds, rocky hills, and gullies through which a sorry excuse for a road zigged and zagged. Here, what was left of the main force of Hajis now prepared a countering ambush against Sergeant First Class Connor Bower and six of his grunts, who pursued them along that dirt road. The enemy, however, did not see Billy Claybaugh, Petey Preston, and Randy Powell mounting a hill on their flank overlooking the entire scene, nearly three-quarters of a mile away.

The staff sergeant and his two corporals had cut a diagonal for the high ground that Billy had anticipated would give them a distant but commanding overwatch where they could see the fleeing al-Qaeda and keep an eye on his Army brothers, too. He was right.

Cotton Martin and his Marines along with the truck drivers and the remaining soldiers from the MRAP worked at clearing the ambush area of holdouts left behind to offer cover fire while their main al-Qaeda Iraq force fled. One by one, these zealots died hard.

Once Billy-C, Petey, and Randy fanned into positions on the hilltop overwatch, they began scoping the enemy positions. Rather than just shooting a few of them at best, while the remainder escaped up the nearby gullies, he wanted to get the Army warriors in position to cut off any escape.

"I've got overwatch on you, Boston, and you've got a dozen to fifteen Hajis just ahead of you, holed up in some mud houses and shit," Billy said on the command frequency to Sergeant Bower. "I'm guessing they'll try to cut you guys down after you make that turn in the road just ahead."

"Roger that," Bower replied. "You got any targets?"

"Lots of 'em," Billy said. "But lots more will escape unless you boys block the gullies and road, and kill 'em when they come runnin'."

"I'm guessing you've got a plan?" Connor Bower came back.

"Sort of, I suppose," Claybaugh said. "Just take a few steps up in the rocks on each side of the road and implant automatic fire there. Then send two riflemen to the right and two left, and they take positions on the high ground over the gullies leading away from the farmhouses. You might miss one on the flanks, but I'm guessing that when you open fire in those spots, the Hajis will think you spread yourself thin, sweeping around their flanks to attack, and left the middle open. We'll kill 'em in their own kill zone."

"If they're set to ambush us, how you going to flush them out?" Bower asked, his South Boston brogue strong as the anticipation of yet another fight tightened his jaws.

"I've got a little something that just might rattle 'em loose," Billy said. "Give me a call back when you're ready for me to kick off this rodeo."

Billy and his Marines watched the soldiers climb up the gully walls and take position on the high ground at the right and left of the farms. He already had his eye to his riflescope and finger on the trigger when Connor Bower offered one word on the radio.

"Go," Bower said, and Billy-C broke his first round.

One of the gunmen had hidden behind a water trough made of stones, clay, and tar. While his front was amply covered from the approaching American soldiers, his back was wide open to Billy. The .50 caliber Raufoss round disassembled the Haji in a burst of body parts.

Two other jihadi brothers had taken ambush positions behind some adobe feed bunks, and when their friend exploded only a few feet from them, it sent them running for a nearby adobe wall. The first man vaulted over the top, but the second gunman caught one of Randy Powell's .338 Lapua Magnum 250-grain hollow-point boat-tail Sierra MatchKing bullets between his shoulder blades.

Three more Hajis squatted behind the mud fence and had the wall of a house two feet behind them. When they popped their heads up and fired their AK rifles at nothing, Petey Preston splashed a Lapua round on the wall behind them.

The three Marine Scout-Snipers waited for movement among the houses, but not a soul stirred.

"They're hunkered down." Randy sighed.

"And they're not moving," Billy-C said. "Let's see what happens when I start blowing holes with Raufoss rounds."

Claybaugh then took a breath, steadied his crosshairs on the adobe wall where he anticipated an al-Qaeda gunman squatted, and let one go.

A hole the size of a dinner plate blew through the mud fence, and the adobe wall of the house behind where the gunman had squatted glistened red and wet with blood.

"Fuck! That's nasty!" Powell said, and fired his magnum at the house, trying to ricochet lead at one end of the wall and hold the enemy in place while Petey Preston put shots on the opposite side.

"Once more," the staff sergeant said, and squeezed off another explosive penetrating shot. It, too, blew a big hole in the fence and left the house sprayed with blood and bits of another dead al-Qaeda.

Billy cycled his bolt and chambered another big round,

and in the periphery of his riflescope he caught movement in a window. Someone stood just to the side of the opening, so he moved his crosshairs there and blew a hole in the house.

As the shot exploded, the round must have barely grazed the man standing there with his back against the wall by the opening. He came spinning out the window, half-alive, his right arm and a good part of the right side of his upper torso torn off. He hit the ground dead.

That was all the remaining al-Qaeda needed. They poured out of their positions and ran for the gullies, where several gunshots turned them around. Rather than running toward the deadly sniper fire, they chose to try to make it around the first bend in the road, where the overhead rocks and hills gave them closest cover.

Billy, Randy, and Petey chased them with shots, making sure they all got around the corner.

"You got 'em," Claybaugh said on the command channel as Connor Bower and two of his solja-boys opened fire with their machine guns and mowed down the rest of the Hajis.

Ray-Dean Blevins waited until he had driven outside the secured perimeter of Camp Victory before he stopped his Escalade, pulled the envelope from his waistband, and opened it. His eyes scanned down the cover page of the First Battalion, Fifth Marine Regiment's top secret operation plan. As the impact of what he had stolen took hold, he let out a breath that ended with, "Fuck!"

For about two beats, he considered trying to sneak the

classified package back to the pile of crap on Elmore Snow's desk. Then he thought again.

It was bad enough just getting his hands on a shred of any kind of information that might get Cesare Alosi off his ass. But this was way too much, and putting the envelope back now, way too risky.

He pounded the steering wheel with both fists. The magnitude of what he had stolen went far askew of the boundaries of even his corrupt sense of right and wrong. Way over the top of anything Cooder-with-a-D anticipated he might swipe for his boss.

"Why the fuck would anyone with half a brain leave something this deadly just lying in a pile of mail?" he said, looking at the red TOP SECRET stamp on the op plan's cover page. Then he rationalized, "Assholes fucking deserve to have it stolen."

Blevins thought about burning it, or tossing it in the trash somewhere back on post. "That'd serve 'em right." But he had to have something to hand to Alosi, or it was literally his ass.

"Fuck this," Ray-Dean finally resolved, as he did so many other perplexing matters, and tossed the envelope on the passenger seat. "What's done is done. Let the chips fall," he said as he tromped on the gas on the company Escalade, heading back to his hotel in the relative safety of the Baghdad Green Zone.

Ray-Dean went straight to his room, tossed the envelope on his bed, then did an about-face and shot the gap down to the hotel lounge, a poor attempt at a luxury cocktail bar serving an ever-changing variety of smuggled liquor and homemade Iraqi moonshine.

Most of the "good stuff" came from a British para-trooper major turned private-security operator named James, who came from Leeds in England. With an Iraqi named Ajax, a procurer of anything one might want, legal or otherwise, he had opened a well-hidden but very popular joint called the Baghdad Country Club.

James and an enterprising blue-eyed Kurdish business-man named Ahmed, who owned nearly all of Iraq's duty-free rights, had partnered in late 2005 and began trucking in booze from the north. A very dangerous business in a mostly Muslim country with restrictive alcohol-prohibition laws and radical booze-hating zealots at every turn.

No less than twice a week on differing days and never the same times, and sometimes more often, depending on demand, the hotel hospitality manager had a laundry truck stop at the Baghdad Country Club and restock the bar with whatever James from Leeds had available. Load-ing the hotel laundry truck always involved a game of cat and mouse to avoid detection, especially by the club's nosy neighbors, moving the boxes wrapped in bundles of bed linen and towels. Ironically, the Baghdad Country Club sat behind a wall in a garden behind a second, foliage-covered outside wall, next door to the powerful Iranian-controlled, Shiite-based Supreme Council for the Islamic Revolution in Iraq. But then, Baghdad has always lived as a city filled with contradictions.

Hacksaw, Habu, Kermit The Frog, and many of the other Malone-Leyva operators frequented the Baghdad Country Club, a watering hole that James and Ajax had patterned after the infamous Rick's Café of *Casablanca*, but most nights, the place seemed more like Chalmun's Cantina in the pirate city Mos Eisley from *Star Wars*.

Cooder-with-a-D was not nearly the social animal and war-story teller that the pirate trio Walter Gillespie, Kermit Alexander, or even Cory Webster were. Baghdad Country Club, with its mix of contractors and reporters, mercenaries and gunrunners, hookers and hoods, had a little too much social mix for Ray-Dean's taste. He mostly drank alone.

When Blevins stepped through the beaded curtain that hid the goings-on inside the dark hotel lounge, he locked eyes on Francoise, the loud-smelling French reporter with the inviting snatch. She sat in a booth, basking in the red glow of a candle in a net-wrapped ruby-glass snifter, nursing a tall brown drink with half-melted ice and a cherry floating on top. In her fingers she held a long, thin pink cigarette with a gold ring above a black filter tip that she lipped deep in her ample mouth, sucking her lungs full of designer-flavored smoke.

"Got another one of those?" Ray-Dean said as he took a seat across from her and tossed his sweat-ringed Malone-Leyva operator's ball cap on the table.

"Sure," she said, and passed him the gold-trimmed pink-and-black flat cardboard box.

Blevins took one out and lit it with the candle. As he exhaled, he smiled. "Whatcha drinking?"

"Supposed to be Long Island Iced Tea," Francoise breathed back, her husky voice saying fuck me between the lines. "Only God knows what they used as liquor."

"Long as it gets the job done, who cares? In this place? Be thankful you've got ice," Ray-Dean said, snapping his fingers at the bartender, pointing at Francoise's drink, then pointing at himself. The barkeep nodded and took a glass off the counter and began mixing Blevins a Baghdad version of the wicked cocktail.

"So . . ." Francoise said, cigarette smoke curling out of her mouth, then swirling up her nostrils. She leaned toward Ray-Dean so he could see down her blouse, pressed her breasts' cleavage together, and smiled at him with her eyes sagging half-shut. "What's news?"

Cooder-with-a-D leaned toward Francoise and let his eyes go half-shut as he smiled back at her. "Want to go to your room to fuck?"

Then he smiled more. "Or . . . We can go to mine."

"Got anything to drink up there?" she asked.

"Old Fuad keeps a stash of Stolichnaya vodka that he sells me, straight out of Moscow by way of Istanbul," Ray-Dean said. "I'll pick up a bottle to keep us warm."

"I like Beluga." Francoise shrugged. "Have you had it? It's new from Russia. Everyone in Paris is drinking it."

"This ain't Paris," Blevins said, as the bartender brought him his Long Island Iced Tea. "Like I said, you're lucky to get ice. And Stoli sure as shit ain't rotgut."

"I'm waiting for a friend," the French reporter said. "You know Paolo? The sound tech for CNN, he's from Milan."

Ray-Dean took a sip off the top of his tea. "Naw." And he gave her a second look. "You'd rather fuck him than me?"

She shook her head and added a horny smile. "I thought he might join us. A *ménage à trois*. You like?"

Cooder laughed. "Fucking nasty bitch."

She smiled more. "He's bisexual, you know."

"Oh, fuck no!" Blevins let out so loud it made the barkeep turn and look. "I'll go for you and another bitch, but no dudes. I make it a rule. I don't cross swords."

"You've never tried it?" Francoise asked.

"No, and never will," Ray-Dean came back.

"It is so hot to see a man with a man, and then me with them both," she breathed hot, licking her lips.

"You want to fuck? I'll fuck you 'til your eyes pop. I'm all the man you need," Cooder bragged.

Francoise shrugged and smiled more. When she had Ray-Dean's full attention, she tapped her finger on her nose.

"Yeah," Cooder said, "I know what you want. I got a bag of blow so good it'll make you wet your pants. Couple hits, you'll want to fuck a lamp pole."

Francoise licked her lips. "Does talking so vulgar make you excited? It does me!"

Ray-Dean grinned. "Yeah, baby. I'm so hard right now, my dick can cut diamonds."

"*Bon.*" She smiled.

Captain Mike Burkehart rolled hard and fast behind the assessment team's command Humvee, driving Colonel Snow's MARSOC Hummer that Corporal Butler normally piloted. The skipper had grabbed an unsuspecting Marine private first class nicknamed Eugene the Jeep, who was cleaning a coffeepot in the operations office at the time, and told the lad to ride shotgun with him. Another operations Hummer with a machine gun topside rode tail-end-Charlie behind them.

When the MARSOC executive officer approached the

ambush scene, he could only think that this was how Hiroshima must have looked right after the atom bomb exploded there, or pretty close to it. Fire consumed everything on both sides of the road, pouring black smoke in the air. Little of any kind of structure stood, most everything that used to be houses burned in fallen piles with only bits and pieces of the buildings pointing skyward among the unchecked flames.

Smoke obscured the afternoon sun. The whole place felt hotter than hell and looked like hell, too.

First elements of the reaction force had landed by Black Hawk helicopters and immediately begun securing the area surrounding the ambush site, searching for any enemy stragglers. Their reinforcements arrived just ahead of Captain Burkehart and set up checkpoints at both ends of the village.

When the skipper stepped out of his Hummer and looked for his Marines, he couldn't find any of them except the zippered black bag that held Rowdy Yates. The Army team had thoughtfully laid the Marine's body aside from the two dead KBR truckers, likewise bagged and tagged. They had only found parts of the body of the one driver who had died in the bomb blast.

"My Marines," he asked the Army captain who commanded the reaction force. "What's their status?"

"On their way in," the officer told Burkehart. "Should be here any minute. They chased down the main force that initiated this ambush and by all reports killed most of them. Last enemy body count was twenty-eight. We estimate they had somewhere between thirty and fifty combatants. Not bad shooting. Not bad at all."

"We secure here?" Burkehart asked, giving the area a scan. Lots of rear-echelon gagglers running around lax and slack like highway patrolmen at an interstate wreck scene. The Marine Mustang captain knew better than to just prance around the open spaces like a spring fawn. He kept covered.

"Oh yeah," the soldier assured him with a casual shrug.

As the Army captain walked away with a talkative and overly excited master sergeant decked in clean uniform and newly issued combat gear jabbering at his side, Mike Burkehart noticed Cotton Martin maneuvering with his three Marines through the debris field on the right side of the roadway. He, too, remained cautious of a possible unseen enemy straggler hidden in some rat hole.

"Skipper!" Cotton let out, glad to see his captain, Hot Sauce, Jewfro, and Hub Biggs smiling behind him. "As they say, the proverbial shit hit the fan here. We had an overwhelming enemy force laying for us." Then as Staff Sergeant Martin got close enough to speak in a low voice, "They had it planned to the T. Somebody on the inside had to have fed them all our dope. Cost us one of our own."

Both men gave the body bag that held Lance Corporal Yates a long look.

"Maybe they had eyes on you when you departed the wire," Burkehart said, raising his eyes.

"No way they could see us then and have time enough to put together an ambush of this size and complexity, and with the kind of weaponry they used," Cotton said, looking cold at the skipper. "They knew we's coming from the get-go. They were set up in the upper rooms and rooftops, hides in junk piles and old cars. That's not some quick setup. No, sir. They got inside intel. I'm sure of it."

"Any word from Staff Sergeant Claybaugh and his team?" the skipper asked.

"Last check? I'd say he'll come through that smoke on the left, over yonder, any second," Martin said, pointing toward the smoke pall on the opposite side of the road.

He had no sooner spoken and was still pointing when the silhouettes of the three Marines came into sight. Billy-C saw the captain and Cotton, and gave them a wave. Then he broke off from Petey Preston and Randy Powell, and jogged to the body of the dead sniper with the bloody Dragunov rifle lying gripped in his lifeless hands.

"What's up with that?" the captain asked, seeing the staff sergeant break off from his two *compadres*.

"War trophy, I suppose," Cotton answered, seeing Billy bend over to grab the sniper rifle from the dead enemy.

Corporal Powell had kept moving, but Preston waited for his staff sergeant, his Vigilance rifle cradled across his arms, ready, just in case.

"Billy says that's the motherfucker that killed Rowdy," Cotton added.

"Going up on the wall at the Hog Wallow?" Burkehart said.

Cotton nodded. "Yup. I expect so."

Billy-C held the Dragunov up for the captain and Staff Sergeant Martin to see, then bent over to pick up something else just as a lone rifle shot cracked from a smoldering rubbish pile a football field away. The impact of the bullet sent Claybaugh headfirst into the dead Iraqi insurgent's body.

Petey Preston caught the movement in the rubbish pile and shot the sniper as he tried to flee. The impact of the Lapua Magnum took off an arm and made a mess of the chest, killing the man before he hit the ground.

Randy Powell made a beeline for his downed staff sergeant as Billy-C scrambled back to his feet.

A bloody patch spread across the seat of Claybaugh's trousers, as Corporal Powell ducked under Billy's shoulder and helped him walk, the Dragunov still clutched in his hands.

"Laid open my left ass cheek," the staff sergeant said as he hobbled toward the captain, Cotton, and the others with Randy Powell as his crutch. "But I got that dead motherfucker's rifle."

"Guess you bent over at just the right time," Mike Burkehart said.

"Motherfucking AK bayonet. Dead guy had it on his belt," Billy said, holding up the multipurpose knife and fighting tool that also slides onto the muzzle end of an AK-47 rifle. "I've been wanting one of these suckers for a long time."

"Got shot in the ass for your trouble, too," Cotton said. "I guess you paid the price for it."

"Guy that shot him paid a bigger price," Corporal Preston said, coming in behind Claybaugh and Powell.

"One dumb motherfucker's all I can say," Captain Burkehart added. "If he'd just lain still in that trash pile, and let Billy take that rifle, he'd still be alive. Army already cleared that area, so when we left the scene, he could have just gone home."

"Sometimes a rattlesnake just can't help himself but bite a guy," Claybaugh rationalized.

_ 7 _

Cottonmouth and a splitting headache roused Ray-Dean Blevins to a foggy realm of consciousness. The smell of coffee, toast, eggs, and bacon made him open his eyes.

Laughter. Screechy female laughter. Then a familiar male voice made him raise his head to see who else was there.

Francoise stood in front of his kitchenette cookstove, scrambling a skillet filled with eggs while Cesare Alosi dabbed dry freshly cooked turkey bacon with paper towels.

The Malone-Leyva boss wore a black company T-shirt and tan 5.11 cargo trousers, a Glock 19 strapped to his upper thigh, and a black M-L operator's ball cap tilted on the back of his head. The French reporter wore one of Cooder's drab tan company T-shirts and nothing else. Her ass cheeks played peekaboo below the bottom hem.

"How'd you get in here?" Blevins grogged out at his boss, staggering up from the bed. Then he realized he was naked and sporting morning wood. So he grabbed the top sheet off his bed and wrapped it around his waist.

Seeing his package, Francoise giggled like a teenage virgin ditching Sunday school with the bad boys. She made a show of hiding her eyes, as if she had a degree of modesty, then went back to scraping the pile of eggs around the pan.

Alosi gave it a slight headshake, rolling his eyes, then smiled at Cooder as if he knew it all. "Your little friend Paolo let me in as he slipped out this morning. Odd fellow, that one. And boy, did he look haggard. Hard night at the races? Three of you? Really? My, oh my . . . Bet you had fun."

"It's not what you think!" Ray-Dean shot back, pulling the sheet up high to his chest like a shy girl at a topless beach, and wrapping it tight under his armpits.

"I'm not judging you." Alosi laughed. "Who you fuck and how you three fucked. That's your business. I don't want to know even the slightest details of what went on here last night. Seriously. None of my business."

"Well, it's not what you think. That's all," Blevins blustered as he threw the sheet in a wad on the bed, pulled on his trousers, and hurried to the table where he noticed that Cesare had left off reading the First Battalion, Fifth Marine Regiment operation plan, opened to the back-page appendices. He gave Alosi the stink eye.

Seeing the frown, Cesare offered, "Look, dude. I apologize for waking you. Not really thinking, I put on a pot of coffee. The aroma woke Francoise, and she insisted on cooking breakfast. I pitched in to help, and I guess we got a little silly and a bit loud. I honestly intended to let you sleep. I just wanted a cup of coffee to sip while I read that operation plan I found on the floor as I came through the door. Nice work, Ray. Top secret no less. I suppose it came from your visit with your friends at MARSOC? That right?"

"Yup," Cooder said, taking a Malone-Leyva polo shirt off a pile of clothes atop an overflowing hamper. He sniffed it, gave it a shake to air out the body odor, then put it on.

"Very good work indeed, young squire," Cesare said, pouring a cup of coffee and bringing it to Ray-Dean.

"Look, boss," Cooder said, taking the cup, then casting his eyes down at the operation plan. "Maybe we should throw that thing in the shredder and pretend we never saw it. Soon as I knew what I had, I got a really bad feeling. Seriously. This ain't any small-change security detail. No, sir. We're talking a full-scale battalion operation from Hit to Haditha Reservoir. Lots of American lives at risk here."

"Let me do the worrying," Alosi said, and wrapped his arm around Ray-Dean like his new best friend. "After all, we're on the same side. Right? Would I do anything to compromise the security of those Marines or any other American presence here? We're in business to help them!"

Ray-Dean pulled away from the clutch of his boss. "Right. Just like you helped those guys yesterday. I hear two KBR drivers and a MARSOC Marine got whacked in that ambush, plus some other dudes got wounded. Paolo, that squirrely guy you saw on his way out this morning, told us all about it. He's a sound tech with CNN, and was there with the news crew covering the story. One Marine killed, another one wounded. Couple Army guys with minor wounds and their lieutenant hit pretty bad. You don't think that bothers the shit out of me? I may seem like a worthless shit turd to you and a lot of other people, but I'm still a Marine."

"Look, Ray. It's business. On the positive side, I picked up a little CIA work on this operation, and I got a call from KBR's in-country boss late yesterday, and they pitched us a security contract for convoy-protection management. It's worth millions!" Alosi rationalized. Then, with a nonchalant shrug, he added, "You break a few eggs to make an omelet. Right? People do get killed in a war."

Blevins frowned. "What's in it for me? This new security contract worth millions from KBR. I get a bonus?"

"Yeah," Cesare said. "That Escalade you burned. Consider it off the books. Plus, I'm putting a fifty-grand kicker in your direct deposit this month for the op plan you brought us. Does that soothe your guilty conscience?"

Ray-Dean nodded yes, then half smiled. "Like, what difference does it make now? Right?"

"Right!" Alosi bubbled, and put his arm back around his new best friend. "We go on living, you and me. Nice cars, pool in the backyard. Big boat. Pussy on the quarterdeck. All the good shit that comes with serious money. Right?"

Cooder-with-a-D gazed at Francoise, looking sexy in his T-shirt, holding a platter heaped with scrambled eggs, her plump, bald snatch peeking out, and he smiled.

When Billy Claybaugh pulled open the door to the MARSOC operations hooch and heard the weird Arabic music, it stopped him in his tracks. A hellish scene.

The great skull painted on the black wall loomed over Jack Valentine, who sat transfixed to his laptop computer screen, watching a video taken off one of the many al-Qaeda

Web sites. Then came *"Allahu Akbar"* chanting from the sound track, mixed with the sounds of gunfire.

"Jack! What the fuck, over!" the staff sergeant said as he hobbled on a set of aluminum crutches, heading to Gunny Valentine's desk as fast as he could scramble. He knew what his sniping partner watched, and it wasn't healthy.

In 2005, six Marine Scout-Snipers and their platoon's Navy Hospital corpsman, all from a reserve unit in Cleveland, fell victim to an ambush south of Haditha. Most of them died on the spot as an al-Qaeda gunman shot video of the grisly scene and later posted it on the Internet. One Marine, still alive, was dragged through the nearby village and brutally sacrificed as a crowd cheered.

The Marines had been betrayed by the Iraqi soldiers assigned to support the operation, who knew many sensitive details about the plan and deployment of the ill-fated sniper team. Once the Iraqi and Marine leadership identified the traitors, they sent a reinforced rifle platoon of Marines to apprehend the men.

En route to the village where the culprits had fled, the Marines again suffered betrayal, again compromised by Iraqi traitors inside their tent. This time fourteen infantrymen from that same reserve unit died in a well-executed ambush. In less than two days, Cleveland, Ohio, lost twenty-one of its sons to al-Qaeda Iraq gunmen.

This all occurred only days after Jack and Billy-C had taken the shot that missed Abu Musab al-Zarqawi as he stood on the roof of the taxi on the bridge into Haditha, lording over the public execution of men and boys that day.

"Recharging my mental batteries," Jack said without looking up.

"Fucking up your mind, I say," Claybaugh said, and slammed shut the lid of Jack's notebook PC. "You know how seeing the video of those Cleveland Scout-Snipers getting ambushed fucks up your dope. It fucks up mine just watching you watch it. Hell, Jack, I trained those guys with you, don't forget. I knew them, too. Fuck, dude!"

"They died because of us, Billy," Jack grumbled. "You can't deny it. I took that totally impossible shot, and pissed off the madman. You know he came specifically hunting the Marine Sniper who nearly killed him. We went home, but twenty-one of our brothers died because of us."

Billy fell onto the chair by Gunny Valentine's desk, holding out his leg stiff to protect his sore ass, landing on the good cheek. After an exhale from pain, he looked at his longtime friend and started to say something more. But then the Alabama staff sergeant with nearly always something smart-assed to say just shook his head, words failing him.

"I should have said no," Jack complained. "When the skipper came back with yet another road-guard mission. I should have nutted up. My lack of balls? Got you shot and got Rowdy killed."

"We got compromised, Jack," Claybaugh said. "Somebody tipped off al-Qaeda. That's not your fault."

Jack clenched his jaws. "You wouldn't have been there if I had been the man I'm supposed to be. I was rolling with the flow. Getting this deployment done, following orders, not making ripples. You got shot, and that's on me."

"Hey, I'm fine, brother!" Billy came back. "Like a razor slashed across my ass cheek is all. A few stitches, and I'm back in the weeds. Ready to rock and roll."

"You can't say that about Rowdy Yates," Jack reminded his sniping partner. "In a few hours, when the sun comes up at Camp Lejeune, Elmore's going to make the widow's death notification with the chaplain and the Casualty Assistance Call Officer. We're down a man, and he was a good one."

"They're all good ones," Claybaugh said.

"Yeah," Jack said, lifting the lid on his computer but then shutting it back down. Then he looked at Billy-C and put a smile on his face. "How's your ass?"

Claybaugh grinned. "A horizontal smile to go with my vertical. But the sideways one hurts like a son of a bitch."

"Let's see," Gunny Valentine said, motioning for the staff sergeant to stand up, turn around, drop trousers, and unveil his wound.

As Billy complied, britches at his ankles, bandage off, bent at the waist with his bare butt pointed at the gunny, Rasputin and the Mob Squad barreled through the main door.

"Whoa! Dude! Cover up! That's one memory I don't want," Sergeant Romyantsev said, leading the four others and suddenly encountering Billy-C bent over bare-assed a foot from Gunny Valentine's face.

Sergeant Carlo "The Iceman" Savoca and his top corporal, Sal "Pizza Man" Principato, swooped in close for a good look. Nick "the Nose" Falzone and Marcello "Momo" Costa stepped back with Rasputin. They had no desire to look at Billy Claybaugh's naked bum or his wound.

"You need to get a tattoo with that scar, like eyes. You know, like on a smiley face?" Principato offered, and put his finger on the stitched wound.

"It does look like a smile across my cheek, don't it," Billy said, looking over his shoulder at the boys giving his butt close scrutiny.

"Like, have a nice day, asshole." Iceman laughed. "You know, the smile face talking to your bung."

"Shouldn't you, then, have the whole cheek tattooed yellow?" Rasputin offered, now moving in close to see, too, interested by the smiley face comments.

"Yeah!" Billy said. "Like two big black eyes and a black outline around the smile, surrounded by a big yellow circle that takes up my whole ass cheek. And shaded like 3D. You know?"

They all laughed.

"You've got to do it, Billy," Sergeant Savoca said. "Soon as we get back to Lejeune. We'll all chip in."

"Not to change the subject," Jack Valentine said, "but to what do I owe the pleasure of not only having the entire Mob Squad grace my presence, but Rasputin the Devil emerge from his dungeon?"

"This operation with one-five out in the Anbar. Staff Sergeant D said we're all going. Even him and me both. That true, Gunny?" Sergeant Romyantsev asked.

Jack Valentine looked at his Mob Squad, then Rasputin, and spread a big smile, cautious. "Would you like to go?"

"Gunny. That's why we wear tree suits," Sergeant Savoca

said, wedging his two cents into the conversation. Then, looking at Romyantsev, added, "Rasputin will even put on clothes."

Gunny Valentine looked at Romyantsev standing there with his arms folded, wearing a black *Metallica: Some Kind of Monster* tank top, neon-green P-T shorts, and flip-flops. "This operation. We'll need the entire detachment. Except for Captain Burkehart, Smedley, and Billy-C. They'll stay back and hold down the fort."

"So, it's not a handpicked team, like I heard at first?" Savoca said.

Jack shook his head no. "I changed my mind. After what happened yesterday, that silly horseshit stops. We're going on mission to do what we came here to do. Kill Zarqawi."

"Fuck yeah!" Pizza Man let go. "Balls out!"

"We're assigning teams to each of one-five's infantry companies, and a composite group to the battalion's command element. We'll brief everyone on the breakdown, overall objectives, and who goes where right after noon chow," Jack went on.

"Mob Squad, heads up. You're chopping out to Haditha Dam tonight. Link up with a hard-core Force Recon knife fighter, First Sergeant Alvin Barkley, top kick at Charlie Company. You're first team out. I hope you've got your kits packed and ready."

"They've been packed and ready," Savoca said.

Jack gave Savoca a hard, cold look, then eyeballed each of his three Mob Squad cohorts. "Report to First Sergeant Barkley directly, Iceman. Got it? And none of your boys' silly it's-just-business shit. Barkley's no-nonsense old

Corps. Hard as woodpecker teeth. He's even got muscles in his do-do. So don't fuck around with this guy."

"What do you mean hard-core knife fighter? You serious?" Momo Costa asked, now a little worried about dealing with a potential wild man.

"Fuck yeah. Serious as a heart attack," Jack said. "Couple years back, over in Afghanistan, then–Gunny Barkley emptied his M9 pistol in one crazy Taliban hell-bent on killing him. Fifteen nine-millimeter rounds center mass in the dude, and he's still coming.

"So Barkley takes out his trusty ivory-handled, sixteen-inch-long Dan Dennehy custom-made Bowie knife he always wears strapped on the side of his leg, and gutted the motherfucker, belly button to chin whiskers.

"When Billy and I were in Fallujah last pump, Barkley did a Haji there with his knife. Almost the same story. Man's legendary."

"Fuck, dude." Momo laughed. "That's cold."

"Fuckin' A, that's cold. Cold as shit," Jack said.

"Hey, you better have a big-ass pigsticker if you're depending on a fucking M9. Total piece of shit that lightweight gun," Pizza Man added. "My trusty .45 hardball 1911's the only way to go to war."

"The .45 compared to the 9. Like a truck over a Volkswagen," Rasputin said. "That's 230-grain hardball. It's a hammer. Hard to beat in a gunfight."

"Unless you're shooting 230-grain .45 plus-performance jacketed hollow points. Puts your lame-ass Marine Corps hardball to shame," a scraggly, scratchy voice chimed from the rear of the gathering.

Jack stood up and grinned. "Hacksaw Gillespie! You old horse thief."

"Hammer, my boy, Hammer. The fabled Jack-Hammer of Justice!" Walter Gillespie beamed, showing a mouthful of gold grill, right at home with his Ray-Bans, a diamond stud planted in his ear, and black-silk do-rag tied on his shaved head.

While lines furrowed deep on his face, embracing a more salt than pepper heavy-duty Fu Manchu moustache wrapping around his mouth, the old Spartan's trim body looked as young as ever. Hard muscles rippled tight beneath his black Under Armour high-tech fabric T-shirt, and even covered by the baggy 5.11 operator jeans, Hacksaw's legs looked ample and strong below a narrow waist. He sported a well-defined six-pack under his shirt and not a hint of belly fat. This salty, well-seasoned guerilla fighter had few equals when it came to combat.

Behind Walter Gillespie, Kermit Alexander and Cory Webster stood equally fit, wearing similar hired-gun outfits, black-ops do-rags tied on their shaved heads, Ray-Bans, and full-blown Fu Manchus.

All three men sported rings of human skulls tattooed around their biceps, each head representing a kill. Hacksaw had three circles of thirteen per row on his right upper arm and two wraps of thirteen skulls on his left. Most of his sixty-five kills, cocaine cowboys in South America. Jack had splashed forty-nine down there, including Pablo Escobar.

"Elmore said you boys were in country, hired on as gunslingers for Malone-Leyva," Jack said, greeting his old war-fighting *compadres* with bear hugs. "Where you been hiding?"

"Under your nose. Been by here four times to see ya," Hacksaw said. "You're always out babysitting diplomats or some such happy horseshit."

"I see you got new teeth," Jack said, eyeballing Walter's glittering mouth. "Makes you look like hip-hop gone bad."

Hacksaw laughed. "My boss called us pirates."

"Well . . ." Jack said, sizing up the motley trio. "You do look like pirates."

"Fuck you and the horse you rode in on, ass-wipe," Kermit Alexander said. "Hip-hop gone bad sounds better."

"How about you, Habu?" Jack said to the never-talkative Cory Webster.

"Don't like either one," Habu said. "Think Little Stevie Van Zandt and the E Street Band. Ray-Bans and do-rag going on, rockin' on his Rickenbacker. That's more me than fucking pirates or hip-hop gone bad."

"Thought Stevie Van Zandt played a Fender," Billy-C said, leaning on his crutches, and offering a hand for the three old snipers to shake. "Staff Sergeant Claybaugh."

"Glad to know you, Claybaugh. Little Stevie plays both brands," Cory said, and shook Billy's hand.

"He's that dude, Silvio, on *The Sopranos*. Right?" Momo Costa asked.

"Yeah," Iceman said. "That's him. Figures you'd know Little Stevie better for *The Sopranos* than Springsteen."

Momo shrugged, nodding much like Silvio did on *The Sopranos*.

"These are some of my HOGs," Jack said, realizing

the need for introductions. "We got my Mob Squad here. Corporals Momo Costa, Sal the Pizza Man Principato, Nick the Nose Falzone, and their boss, Sergeant Carlo the Iceman Savoca."

"That's fucking rich," Hacksaw said. "Mob Squad. Figures you boys would be big on Tony Soprano. I like him, too. Fucking cold steel, that one."

They shook hands as Jack continued, "We got my number two gunsmith here, Sergeant Andre Romyantsev, better known around here as Rasputin the Devil."

"Call me Andre," Romyantsev said as he shook hands with the three old pirates.

"And you met Staff Sergeant Claybaugh," Jack added. "We call him Billy-C. He and I've pulled a couple of pumps together before this one. Stone killer with a sniper gun, and one hell of a spotter. He'll put you dope on, first shot."

"Glad to know ya, Billy-C," Walter Gillespie said. "Retired Master Sergeant Walter Gillespie here. Just call me Hacksaw. That black guy there is none other than Kermit The Frog Alexander, and his asshole buddy there, Cory Webster, known to us as Habu. One deadly motherfucker. I was Jack's sniper spotter back in the day, and broke the boy's cherry."

He looked at Jack. "Remember that, Hammer? Fucking Iraqi general. Blew his shit straight to hell. Then, in about two seconds, screaming from the sky, comes two grand of holy shit. Mark 84 smart bomb blew the fuck out of that place. Only way we confirmed the general's kill was I took pictures before the bomb hit. One hell of a memorable way for a Marine Scout-Sniper to step across that first kill threshold."

"Gunny Valentine really take out Pablo Escobar?" Momo asked.

"Yes he did, young son," Hacksaw said. "Old Jack the Hammer of Justice Valentine put fifty-two grains of .22-250 Sierra MatchKing lead straight through Escobar's left ear. Surgical as it comes. I don't think he even got wax on the bullet. Turned out that motherfucker's lights at three hundred yards, downhill, cross-compartment. Hell of a shot! History says the Colombian National Police killed old Pablo, but in truth, it was Jack done it. I ought to know. I was right there by him, calling wind and range."

"Enough of the old-home-week nostalgia," Jack gruffly interrupted as his buttery-eyed crew of young Scout-Snipers soaked in the story of their gunny's glory days. "You just come by to say hello, Hacksaw, or did you want to suck my dick while you're here?"

"Fuck you, child." Gillespie laughed. "Actually, I did come by just to say hello to an old friend. My boss, also, asked that if I did see you, I should try to persuade you to sign off on his toasted Escalade that fucking space cadet Ray-Dean Blevins put the thermite to a while back."

"Suck my dick, and I might think about it," Jack said.

"I'll let that fucking Cesare Alosi suck your dick," Walter said. "I delivered the message, and that's all I said I'd do for that slimeball Sicilian piece of shit."

"Really do like the guy, huh?" Jack laughed.

"Oh, fuck yeah!" Hacksaw let off. "Motherfucker's been sending us down to Fallujah and Ramadi every day of the week since he got here. Trying to get us three killed, I think. He hates my fucking ass almost as much as he hates yours."

"What's it worth to him for me to sign off on that Escalade?" Jack asked, curious.

"Oh, he'd definitely suck your dick, and probably swallow, too," Hacksaw grumbled. "Piece of shit, that one."

"He gay?" Jack asked.

"He might suck cock, but I don't think he's totally Fruit-Loops," Gillespie said. "He's got a picture of one dark-eyed beauty on his desk. Guaranteed eating material. She's way too pretty to just fuck. She kind of reminds me of that sweet thing you had back home. While we was down in Medellín. What's her name? Liberty something?"

"Liberty Cruz," Jack answered, and gave his gang of grinning MARSOC operators a cold, no-smart-assed-remarks look. "She's a special operations agent in the FBI nowadays."

"You don't say," Hacksaw said, and grinned at Jack's crew of snipers. "You'll have to get the Gunny here a little drunk, and maybe he'll tell you about getting that pink ribbon full of sweet-smelling hair in the mail, when we was deployed to South America on drug-interdiction operations."

Then Hacksaw looked at Jack. "Did Elmore ever realize what kind of hair was tied up in that ribbon?"

Jack shook his head no.

"So, the little cheerleader's a G-man now?" Hacksaw said, still grinning at the boys, knowing they were dying to ask about the hair and pink ribbon but knew better than to say a word more.

"Yeah, she just finished SERE school at Lejeune," Jack said. "Got an email from her this morning. She sent a picture. But I'm not so sure I want to show you."

"Oh, please! Can I see?" Billy chirped. "I love eye-fucking her shit. Hacksaw, you gotta take a look. This chick is way too hot for this dumb-ass gunny. She's like a fucking movie star, but better."

"Alright, Hammer, let's see how your little cheerleader has grown up. Come on, beam it up," Hacksaw said.

Jack opened the lid on his laptop and looked at the glassy eyes of his Marines and his old friends, licking their chops like they were about to see good porn.

"No fucking comments. Got it?" Valentine said as he clicked the arrow on the email and opened Liberty's latest picture, full screen.

Liberty Cruz stood there in a nice-fitting tank top and well-fitting tailored cargo pants, snugging her in all the right places. She had her long, black hair let loose and wild around her gorgeous face. Topping off the whole she-warrior special-operator image, in her hands she held an M40A3 Marine Corps sniper rifle.

"Mmm, mmm! Don't she make that mantelpiece look good?" Billy-C exclaimed of the long cool woman holding the rifle.

Hacksaw, Habu, and Kermit said nothing. Noticeably silent. Then nodded approvingly but uncomfortable.

Jack looked at them. "Something wrong?"

"Naw!" Hacksaw lied, recognizing the woman from Cesare's desk. "Hell, Jack, she grew up real pretty. Kind of left me speechless. Your boys are right. She's way too hot for a dumb-ass gunny like you."

"Fuck you, ass-wipe," Jack said, closing the lid on his computer.

"Look, Jack," Hacksaw said, checking around to be sure no one unauthorized lurked anywhere near. "We're headed out to Hit. Battalion operation we got assigned to support this morning. Contracting for the CIA. You know Chris Gray and Speedy Espinoza? Couple of former Marines gone spook?"

"Know them both," Jack said, smiling. "Chris and I served together in Force Recon, back in the Gulf War, when I joined your crew. Good men, both of them. I know all about the operation, too, Hacksaw. We're heading up that way."

All three old operators laughed, delighted.

"No shit?" Hacksaw said. "I kind of dreaded this one, just to be honest. Like Alosi stuck our pork in the fire this time to end all our troubles. Now, with you boys coming up? Why, it'll feel like old times. Shit, now I'm happy. I ought to call my boss and let him know how happy I am, just to piss him the fuck off."

"Got something else for you, Walter." Jack grinned. "You know that crazy flat-hat, Black Bart Roberts, commands one-five?"

"Fucking Black Bart Roberts? No shit!" Walter Gillespie sang out. "Now he's a pirate! At least the great-grandson of a pirate, for real. I thought that name E. B. Roberts on the brief sheet I read from Chris Gray looked familiar. Why, shit, Jack! We're gonna have a hell of a good time."

"You're heading that way now?" Jack asked.

"Joining a truck convoy leaving here in an hour," Hacksaw said, and let out a big sigh. "Wish we could chop up there by air. That road's dangerous."

"Tell me about it," Billy said, leaning on his crutches.

"Yeah, we heard about your bad luck, Claybaugh," Gillespie said. "We pulled into the opposite end of that ambush about the time they hauled you out to Charlie Med. You're the poor fucker got shot in the ass. Right?"

"That be me," Billy said. "Just a graze, though, but it's got me on a light-duty chit for a week or two."

"And your boy, the one got killed?" Hacksaw said, a solemn, respectful tone in his voice.

"Lance Corporal Rowdy Yates," Jack said, shaking his head, and all the snipers looked down at their toes, as if they suddenly joined in a moment of prayer.

"Sorry to hear it," the grizzled old Marine said. "Losing a brother's never easy. I still grieve our boy Dirty Harry. Sergeant Leroy Griffin. The Scout-Sniper that Hammer replaced, back when he was a skinny little corporal. Griffin got killed down in South America, back in our cocaine-cowboy-huntin' days. Never gets easy, Jack. I guess you know it."

"Yeah, I do," Valentine agreed. "Elmore's meeting the widow first thing this morning at Lejeune."

"Widow, huh?" Walter said, shaking his head.

"Baby on the way, too," Jack said.

"Fuck. That sucks a big one," Hacksaw said, taking a deep breath. "Look here. I'm making lots of money. Old man that owns Malone-Leyva loves me. Pays me rich coin. We get off this mission, I want to put fifty grand in a kitty for that girl and her baby. Start a fund. Get all the Marine Corps Scout-Snipers kicking in some jing-wah, too. Old Moose Ferran, out in Colorado Springs with the

Scout-Sniper Association, I'll get him to put something together righteous for her and the kid, God bless 'em."

"That's good of you, Hacksaw," Jack said. "That means a lot to me. It'll mean a lot to Elmore, too."

"Old Elmore Snow," Gillespie said. "Him and Mutt Ambrose used to scare the holy horseshit out of me with some of those goofy missions they'd dream up. Still kicking ass and taking names, then preaching Jesus on Sundays I guess?"

"Fierce as ever, and not shy about sharing the Gospel." Jack smiled. "And what of Master Gunny Ambrose? I lost track of him when he retired."

"Mutt?" Hacksaw said. "He's running a rescue down in San Antonio for homeless kids, runaways from abusive situations. Him and his wife. I saw him just before I flew over here."

Jack smiled. "Not at all surprising."

"I hunted him down after he disappeared off the Scout-Sniper community radar. Feared him dead, but he's doing real good. Real happy down there in south Texas," Hacksaw added.

"Glad to hear it," Jack said.

"Mutt Ambrose, one of the best ever. And Elmore Snow? He is the best, Jack. I do love that man," Hacksaw said.

"We all do, Walter," Jack said, and every head in the room nodded.

"He made our glory days, well . . . Glorious." Gillespie smiled.

"Yes he did, brother. Glorious. And still does," Jack said.

Road dust and exhaust fumes mixed with burned-oil stench, smoking from the worn-out diesel engine of the Russian-made farm truck. Wafting through the floorboards, it left Giti Sadiq ready to toss her cookies. For the past two hours that she had rumbled southwestward down Iraqi Route 19 from Baiji toward Haditha, she swallowed hard to keep from spewing chunks. And, with each pothole they hit on the battered roadway, her morning nausea only got worse.

Two hours on the road and their destination coming in sight, she felt every bit as green as the faded paint on the cab of the rust-bucket old KamAZ five-ton stake bed in which she rode, overloaded with wooden crates filled with produce for delivery in Haditha. A dusty brown tarp riddled with holes and tied to the sideboards with an eclectic collection of scavenged ropes flapped on top of the tipsy towering load.

Beneath the tarp rode boxes of dates, apricots, and pomegranates, bundles of dried hot red peppers, cotton-cloth sacks of garlic, and big hemp-burlap bushel bags of onions. Lots of fresh sweet and hot peppers, garlic, and onions on this load, whose smell swirling with the truck fumes and goat stink of the graybeard driving, farting at regular intervals, only made Giti feel all the worse.

This pungent load of eye-burning, nose-scorching produce hopefully cloaked the truck's other load: a four-foot-tall-by-four-foot-wide-by-eight-foot-long plywood shelter installed behind the cab and buried under the boxes and bags of farm-to-market goods. Hidden inside it rode six al-Qaeda jihadists, tucked uncomfortably around a cache of Kalashnikov automatics with extra high-capacity magazines, two Dragunov sniper rifles, four Russian B-40 rocket-propelled-grenade launchers, and several cases of ammunition and rockets for the weapons.

Giti only knew the graybeard driving the truck, Omar Bakr al-Nasser, by the strike of his murderous hands and the unceasing hardness of his third member, stabbed between her thighs as he raped her at will. Members of his growing Jamaat Ansar al-Sunnah army, now allied with al-Qaeda Iraq, called him Abu Omar. Father Omar. However, for Giti, he was hardly any sort of father, nor any ilk of kin or husband of even the loosest definition, but her owner.

She served Omar's will as one of three captive girls taken from the rural Tigris River countryside at Al-Shirqat, a town about halfway between Baiji, to the south, and Mosul, to the north. They belonged to this hateful old dog with stinking bad breath and putrid teeth, who smelled worse than wet goats covered in shit because he never bathed. Always sweaty and foul, and always hard.

Giti feared with nauseating certainty that she had gotten pregnant, and knew that as soon as Abu Omar learned it, he would toss her to his wolves, who would all have a good time defiling her. Then they would kill her. And her child. That's what he did to another slave he knocked up, just after he took Giti and the two other Christian girls from Al-Shirqat.

While Giti lived for survival's sake as a Muslim, she secretly prayed to Jesus Christ, her Lord and Savior, and one of the three persons, Father, Son, and Holy Spirit, of the one true God of her small Presbyterian life. She prayed to God the Father through His Son, Jesus, for relief. She begged Him for deliverance from her horror. She longed for God's mercy but got none of it. Her faith lacked strength of conviction, and she felt shame for it. She should have died protesting for Christ. Instead, she had feared death, and put on the Muslim shawl to remain alive. Enslaved and terrified.

Early in her life, under Saddam's reign, Giti's family had worshiped God as Evangelical Christians under a government policy of narrow tolerance. Christians, as with the Sunni Muslims, along the upper Tigris valley had supported Iraq's Ba'athist socialism and Hussein's regime. In return, Saddam tolerated them.

Her father and mother had married in the little Presbyterian church in Mosul, located on the city's Right Coast, near the corner of Nineveh and Nabi Jorjis Streets, which stood in the shadows of the Al-Nabi Jarjis Shrine, Al-Hadba'a Minaret, and Al-Noree Grand Mosque.

Then, with the fall of Saddam Hussein and the arrival of the Americans, which installed Iraq's Shia-led government, Muslim Ba'athist socialists became jihadists of Ansar al-Sunnah, that became Ansar al-Ahlu Sunnah and Ansar al-Islam, and that became Jamaat Ansar al-Sunnah. They swore death to the Shia's Mahdi Army and their allies in the Iraqi and American governments, and to all Christians. Thus Abu Omar murdered Giti's father and two younger brothers. He cut their throats and took off their heads as Giti and her mother and baby sister watched. Then he turned his pistol on the mother and her child, and offered them life if they embraced Islam and renounced their Christian faith. When they refused, he shot them point-blank. First the child. Then the mother.

Abu Omar Bakr al-Nasser later put his people in the Sadiq family farm. The farm that Giti's father and grandfather and great-grandfather had scratched from bare ground with their blood and sweat, and made flourish over generations. It now became a resource for the Ansar al-Sunnah army. Because Abu Omar had found her desirable, he took Giti as a slave, along with two other Christian girls from Al-Shirqat.

With her family still warm on the ground, their blood running into the soil that once grew their crops of wheat, oats, and lentils along the rich Tigris lands, Abu Omar gave the other Christian women the chance to live by turning from Jesus Christ and bowing to the Muslim faith. All they had to do was bow down to Muhammad.

Most of the women and children did this by kneeling before Omar and declaring themselves Muslim, but a few refused. One at a time, the graybeard shot them with his pistol. Even the smallest child.

Like every charismatic leader, Abu Omar Bakr al-Nasser had his grand scheme for the world. He foresaw a great land of Islam, the mountains lowered and the valleys raised. A return to the splendor of Persia, the Levant, a time where no borders contain the Muslim people, and Arabs rule without equal.

Just as the prophesies foretell, Moslem brothers of the west will look across this plain and see their Moslem brothers of the east, and Moslem brothers of the east will likewise look across that plain and see their Moslem brothers of the west. Omar prayed to Allah for the prophesies of the Hadith, a world united in Islam, to come now, without further delay. Hasten the Mahdi, who will bear Muhammad's name and his father's name, and will be the protector of knowledge, the heir to all the knowledge of all the prophets and aware of all things, to now be born and lead Islam with justice and peace in a world torn by injustice and tyranny. He believed that violence and chaos would hasten the birth of this Guided One, the Lord of the Ages, and his time of Islamic Ummah would finally come.

Abu Omar preached these Sunni beliefs, steeped in his Ba'ath Socialist ideals, to his growing army, and embraced the Palestinian Abu Musab al-Zarqawi and his al-Qaeda Iraq camp as brothers in common cause. The enemy of my enemy is my friend.

Likewise, others from outside the Sunni Muslim world came to this united jihad. Pilgrims of other Islamic sects from Europe, the West, and the Far East. Together, they shared the common dream of an Arab-led Islamic state and a united world of Islam.

"How much farther?" a voice in the darkness behind the cab spoke through the open back window, the glass removed to make it a crawl space in and out of the hidden compartment.

"We approach Haditha now," Abu Omar answered the man, glancing over his shoulder. "There may be road-blocks with inspections before the bridge. You will have to push those crates closed in front of the window and remain silent until we move again."

"My poor eyes and nose will never recover," the man they called Juba said in French.

"It cannot be helped," Omar answered. "The Americans have dogs that can smell people and explosives hidden in cargo. The hot peppers, garlic, and onions interfere with the dogs' smelling. Trust me. You will recover in a day."

Juba and one other of the six men hidden in the box came from Chechnya. Born and raised in the Chechen region of Ichkeria, he and his partner had declared jihad under the flag of the Caucasus Emirate.

Dzhamal Umarov had become known among jihadists as Juba over the past two years, whom they also touted in their propaganda as the Phantom of Baghdad. A sniper menace to the Americans. He had trained as a sniper in the Russian army, along with his spotter, Khasan Shishani, whom the Arabic-speaking Sunni now simply called Hasan.

While less than fluent in Arabic or Farsi, both Umarov and Shishani spoke beautiful French, fluent without accent. Thus to communicate with Juba and Hasan, Abu Omar spoke mostly French, interspersed with Arabic, and they understood each other very well.

After the fall of the Soviet Union, Juba and Hasan had disappeared for several years of their youth to the south of France. They lived around Avignon, working in the lavender fields and vineyards, driving cars and guiding tourists, posing as French natives and students at *Université d'Avignon*. They maintained an on-again, off-again residence in Avignon, and quietly developed a history with French-citizen documentation, student identification cards, and ultimately obtained French passports under the names Davet Taché and Jean René Decoux.

Documented as French citizens, they lived well in Baghdad, posing as import-export businessmen from Avignon. Their long-held French residence served as their home office.

Dzhamal Umarov roamed freely in the world as Davet Taché, and Khasan Shishani likewise lived as Jean René Decoux. They both frequently dined at the French and American embassies, getting to know military officers, contractors, and diplomats, and socialized with many in the Western media. They were both dashing, well-mannered, and finely dressed French rogues, braving the dangers of war-torn Baghdad for profit and adventure. And everyone loved them.

They both had claimed service in the French military as *Troupes de Marine*, in the Ninth Infantry Regiment, *9e Régiment d'Infanterie de Marine*. Davet Taché even wore a French Marine beret badge above a set of jump wings on his stylish leather bomber jacket. Both he and Jean René wore miniature French paratroop emblems and service rosettes on their suit lapels: veterans of foreign military service.

The two men spoke, lived, and looked like authentic French businessmen and armed forces veterans, keenly clued in on military tactics and strategies, as well as economics and business. Yet without question, they both lived to die for Islam and the jihad.

Long ago, they had made it a habit to never speak to each other or anyone else in their native Caucasian language. They spoke French. To the Americans, they spoke English with their natural French accents.

The four others in back with Juba and Hasan were

their driver, Mahmoud, who doubled as a bodyguard, and their three full-time bodyguards, Ali, Jalal, and Yazen. The six men had driven in two cars from Baghdad to Baiji. Juba and Hasan rode in the backseat of their Daytona metallic-blue lead Mercedes sedan, with Mahmoud driving and Jalal riding shotgun, while Ali and Yazen followed behind in the Taché-Decoux Trading Company's Zambezi silver Range Rover. They parked the vehicles with their hotel's valet service, checked in, changed clothes, and quietly slipped away, unseen.

They spent the night with Abu Omar, enjoying good food and warm company at his farm, north of Baiji, and before first light, struck out for Haditha, hidden under the mountain of stinking produce. In Haditha, Juba and Hasan would train a new class of snipers in Abu Omar's jihadi army. They would teach the shooters how to hide in plain sight, or in a rubbish pile, in the fender of a car, or in a darkened room away from the window.

In five days, Juba and Hasan, and their crew of four would return to Baiji, where they would change back into their business clothes and return to Baghdad from their trip up the Tigris buying ancient artifacts and jewelry, family heirlooms that dated back a thousand years.

A baker's dozen Iraqi soldiers wearing drab green flak jackets and dull green helmets backed up four Haditha policemen, similarly dressed, who ran the Route 19 roadblock a half mile east of the bridge across the Euphrates River that entered the city. The same bridge where just more than a year ago, Abu Musab al-Zarqawi had murdered a score of leading citizens and their sons, terrorizing the remainder of the city's leaders to fall in line behind al-Qaeda Iraq. It was the same day that Jack Valentine had taken his shot at Zarqawi and missed.

Backing up the squad of Iraqi soldiers and four policemen running the roadblock, First Sergeant Alvin Barkley sat behind an M2 .50 caliber machine gun atop an up-armored Humvee with a reinforcing ring of sandbags piled around the gun turret. He and twenty-two of his company of Marines had come here today to ferret out a reported influx of enemy fighters and arms resupply.

By State Department agreement with regional and national political leadership, Iraqi soldiers and police had to run the roadblock with American forces as support on request. Not Alvin Barkley's idea of how to run security. Too many holes in the net. Too many Iraqi cousins let slide without a look. Too many trusted friends waved through.

The Marine wiped sweat from his eyes with the back of his hand before he looked through his green-rubber-covered binoculars at the approaching truck. He began rolling the focus knob with his fingertip as he watched it come closer.

Through the mirage, dancing heat waves, and dust-devil swirls, Barkley brought into focus the cab and the two people riding inside the rust-bucket old rig tipping and tilting its towering load as it rattled along the rough road. He sharpened the focus on the gray-bearded old Haj behind the steering wheel. Then he put eyes on the teenage girl riding on the passenger side, a Muslim shawl over her head, draped loosely to allow airflow around her face.

Young. Pretty. Out of place with the grizzled old man behind the steering wheel.

"Sergeant Padilla," Alvin Barkley called down to a Marine with a Belgian Malinois working dog on a leash, "you and Rattler get ready. We got a live one coming our way."

"Roger that," Jorge Padilla answered. He tightened his grip to short-safety on Rattler's leash, taking a wrap halfway down the lead. Cued, the big black-and-brown brindle Belgian braced, just enough to let his handler know he stood ready to work.

Rattler had a full set of titanium teeth that replaced most of his original choppers, installed one by one in the several years after he had finished his basic training at Lackland Air Force Base, San Antonio, Texas. A land shark's land shark, his aggressive bite in the attack mode had eventually broken all of his original canines and uprooted several molars.

When Rattler clamped on, he did not let go, sometimes breaking teeth but never relenting. Although the titanium implants served the dog well, some of them also gave way under his enthusiasm and also required replacement. Thus, veterinary dental specialists had to devise a way to more substantially anchor Rattler's titanium teeth, and resorted to titanium reinforcing rods and screws anchored to his skull bones, and installed larger, stronger teeth to withstand his fierce bite.

Now with his mouth filled with the oversized sparkling silver, nearly indestructible metal teeth, giving Rattler a hellish smile on his mostly black face, he could now, quite literally, tear the fenders off a Honda or rip the arms off a man.

The Malinois wore a Marine Corps desert-pixel-camouflage tactical vest with his corporal rank insignia stitched on its sides. His working dog uniform. Sergeant Padilla had Rattler's name and USMC embroidered just below the two chevrons and crossed rifles.

As military working dogs go, Rattler performed at the top of the game, a total land shark, living for the "Kong," his chewy red-rubber-ball toy that his handler, his "Kong Dispenser," used to reward him after every task. Rattler loved his job, loved the "Kong," but loved Sergeant Jorge Padilla most of all. They had lived as inseparable partners for the past five years of the dog's six years of life. And now Rattler smiled with anticipation of the game. His tongue hanging out, teeth glittering in the sun, lopping drool off his lips.

Alvin Barkley looked down, admiring the sleek but muscular dog with just the right amount of drop in his hips to win anybody's Belgian show. He could breach nearly any barrier, or quickly find a way around it, and had a special knack of leaping through windows. Best yet, the athletic animal had smarts that rivaled many human Marines. Perhaps surpassed even a few in Barkley's company.

The first sergeant reckoned that having Rattler around gave his Marines an incalculable edge on the often-hazardous road-guard duty.

His long Dan Dennehy custom-made Bowie strapped to his leg, opposite his special-ordered Lippard Model 1911A2 .45 caliber Close Quarters Battle Pistol tied to his other leg, Alvin Barkley slid low behind the big machine gun and aimed the muzzle right at Abu Omar's ugly face.

"Open your blouse," Omar Bakr al-Nasser ordered Giti Sadiq as he pushed on the brake pedal. The worn-out pads squeaked and ground metal to metal against the drums as the towering old truck rolled to a stop.

"No!" the girl protested without thinking, reacting immediately modest, and clutched the top of the simple, gray-cotton shirt that she wore. Then she took her shawl and wrapped it tight around her head and shoulders, gripping it firmly around her, but now realizing and dreading the abuse she knew would come.

Abu Omar looked hard at her, his lips curled. "Do it now!"

Tears filled Giti's eyes as she released the shawl, so that if fell open, loose again, away from her ample breasts. Then, one by one, she unbuttoned the blouse and untied the chemise she wore beneath the shirt, so that her bare breasts showed easily to anyone who might look inside the truck.

Not satisfied that she showed enough, the old devil reached across the cab and gave the girl's blouse and undergarment a yank open. "You sit there now, so they can see what they like," he told her. "Stop your sniveling . . . and smile!"

When the first Haditha cop stepped on the running board and looked inside the cab, he immediately saw the girl sitting there with her blouse opened. He motioned for another policeman to go to the other side and check it out.

Then, smiling two gold front teeth at Abu Omar, he said, "What is this, grandfather?"

"A servant," Omar said, and gave the cop a nasty smile in return. "She does my bidding. Anything."

"Anything?" the cop asked, sweat popping on his face, and he brushed his black moustache with the back of his hand as he looked hard at Giti's breasts rising and falling as her breathing increased.

She looked straight ahead and put her mind back in Al-Shirqat. Her childhood. Playing with the new goat kids, petting them and cuddling them, and her father scolding her for doing it.

"Do not fall in love with them, Giti," he had said. "Soon enough they will be meat on our table."

It made her cry, and now tears filled her eyes.

"Smile for them, girl," Omar ordered her, and she did her best to do it.

"Look this way," the cop on the passenger side said, from the running board, his head inside the cab only inches from her. "Come on," and he pulled her face toward him with his fingers.

He smelled terrible, rank body odor, and his breath rotten like his teeth, caked with crud from decay.

Giti forced a smile at him, then turned her eyes back to the front, where she saw an American Marine with a big knife strapped to his leg walking with another Marine and a fearful-looking dog. Her heart began to pound.

Inside the plywood box beneath the stacks of vegetables, Dzhamal Umarov, known among al-Qaeda as Juba and among the Americans as Davet Taché, and Khasan Shishani, known as Hasan and as the Frenchman, Jean René Decoux, had armed themselves with AK rifles. Their four men, Mahmoud, Ali, Jalal, and Yazen, likewise filled their hands with loaded rifles, all of them ready to martyr themselves for jihad in a bloody fight.

Juba pushed the boxes apart and put his head between them. "Whatever these men require to look the other way and let us pass, I will pay double. Tell them that. Tell them I will reward their commander as well. I have a good deal of money. But if they choose to let us die here, so will each of them and all of their families, and God will send them all to Hell. Is that clear?"

"You heard that?" Abu Omar asked the senior cop, and got a nod back.

"Good," Juba said. "Now let's get moving."

"What's going on here?" Alvin Barkley called to the four policemen crowded on the running boards, gawking inside the truck. He could see the young woman, tears on her face and her blouse opened.

The senior cop, the one who did the talking with Abu Omar, called out to the Iraqi army sergeant in charge of the squad of local soldiers. He said something in Arabic that none of the Marines understood and their Iraqi translator ignored.

The Iraqi sergeant intercepted Barkley and ordered him to back off and let the cops do their inspection.

"It is okay. Trust me on this," he assured his American counterpart.

Alvin Barkley didn't like the look of any of it. He could see the girl frightened inside the truck, her eyes wide open, tears on her face, and a smile forced on her lips.

"Some servant girl this old man has. She's nothing," the Iraqi soldier told him.

First Sergeant Barkley looked down at the sergeant. "Best you back off, cousin."

"You cannot take command here," the Iraqi protested, and now the senior cop stepped off the truck running board and came over.

"This is an old farmer we know, coming here for many years," the policeman said. "He only carries vegetables for the market. He's old. Harmless. Look at him."

"What's in the truck, under all that shit?" Barkley snapped at the cop. "Hell, he could be hiding a ballistic missile under that load."

The cop laughed. "He's an old man with a servant girl to help him. Do you think they will jump from that truck and kill us here?"

Barkley looked at Sergeant Padilla and Corporal Rattler. "Check out the truck, Sergeant. Any of these guys get in your way, turn Rattler loose on 'em. Give him that 'Hot Sauce' command you showed me."

Padilla grinned, remembering how Barkley had suited up in the training pads a few days earlier, playing Rattler's dummy, and he gave the Malinois his attack command. "Rattler! Hot Sauce!"

The first sergeant had stood a hundred feet away from the working dog, and in a heartbeat Rattler had "housed" the Marine, bowling him so hard off his feet that Barkley flipped in the air and body slammed the ground. It left the first sergeant dazed, and left the men from his company watching the demonstration laughing their asses off as Rattler locked jaws on the downed Marine and dragged him in circles.

As they approached the truck, Rattler stayed right at

Padilla's side, focused only on one thing—work. The Kong awaited after a good job done, and the big Belgian loved his reward time.

The men on the truck froze as the fearsome dog began working around the front of the truck, checking and sniffing first low, then high, and back low as Sergeant Padilla stepped along, the lead now dropped low and relaxed for Rattler to do his thing.

As the dog went up the side of the truck, one of the cops whimpered, and Padilla had to remind Rattler to focus on the detection work, sniffing for explosives, weapons, and hidden people.

Abu Omar sat at the steering wheel, sweat beading off his face now. He watched the dog go low, then high, then low along the sides of the truck. The peppers and garlic seemed to be working. He breathed a bit easier.

Omar said over his shoulder to Juba, "I think everything will be fine. He smells nothing. Relax."

"I cannot relax until we are rolling again," the Caucasian terrorist posing as a distinguished middle-aged French businessman answered. "We will come out shooting, killing as many as we can. Make sure these brothers surrounding our truck know this, too."

Abu Omar nodded, and the cops on both sides of the truck nodded back.

Sergeant Padilla noticed that Rattler had begun acting differently as soon as he went high on the side of the truck, relaxed down low, but changed mood as he went high again. The mood changes were subtle but distinct cues. Intentionally discreet so that they did not tip off anyone but the handler.

Once Jorge and Rattler had made the circle around the truck and all seemed clear, he led the dog back to the first sergeant and acted casual for the tense Iraqi audience, as if all were well.

"Rattler alerted all the way around. They're hiding something under that load," he said in a low voice as he walked past Barkley.

The first sergeant turned and whistled at his platoon of Marines. "Let's untie that tarp and take down all those crates of produce."

"No, no, no!" both the Iraqi Army sergeant and the senior policeman said together. And just as suddenly, the baker's dozen of Iraqi soldiers surrounded the truck, ready to repel any Marines who stepped closer.

"The motherfucker's got shit hidden under all that crap. I intend to see what he's got!" Barkley barked at the two senior Iraqis.

"You do not have the right to inspect," the army sergeant reminded the Marine. "You are only here to support our searches."

Meanwhile, the senior cop had already begun to talk fast on his radio, letting his police commander know the trouble, and the payoff.

Then the platoon's radio operator shouted from Barkley's command Hummer, "I got somebody from State Department on the horn. They've got orders dispatched to Colonel Roberts that we are to pack up and leave this roadblock immediately."

"Son of a bitch!" Alvin Barkley bellowed. Then he looked at the smiling cop and Iraqi sergeant. "You motherfuckers know he's got shit hid under that load. My bet, explosives or guns, or both, and he just put money in your pockets. Fuck you people! Fuck all of you!"

As the angry Marine walked to his command Hummer, he put his hand above his head and waved it in a big circle.

"Load up!" he shouted.

As Alvin Barkley slid onto the passenger front seat of his truck, he looked in the backseat at Corporal Rattler and Sergeant Padilla. "They're carrying some kind of bad shit that we'll regret letting go. You watch and see. This one's coming back to bite our asses."

"Definitely shit under all those boxes," Padilla affirmed as he patted Rattler, who had his Kong in his mouth, happy.

"Let's get the fuck up to the reservoir, where we can kill some of these Haji assholes," Barkley told his driver.

Dinner at Elmore and June Snow's home last night dragged on long and sad, the pall of Rowdy Yates's death dominating the evening. The call from Captain Burkehart had sent the colonel into a funk. Then that night, since misery loves company, what Elmore and June had planned as a cheery farewell evening for Liberty Cruz evolved into a slog through dinner and a late night with John Jameson's best whiskey and Jack Valentine war stories. Elmore tried his best to find the lighter side with his tales, underscoring each round of two full bottles of eighteen-year-old Limited Reserve with his hearty "*Sine Metu*," without fear, Latin toasts, but invariably even his best yarns turned dark.

Clouding everything, Elmore knew that when his head hit the pillow, the next moment when he opened his eyes, he would have to face the inevitable: deal with that dreaded knock on the Yates front door and break the news to Camp Lejeune's newest widow. He fought off sleep as long as he could, and his wife and Liberty tried to help. Yet dawn will come for the condemned, regardless, just like the impending drop of the headsman's axe.

With no sleep and a throbbing hangover, Liberty Cruz caught the dawn US Airways flight out of Jacksonville's Albert J. Ellis Airport, landing at Ronald Reagan Washington National just in time for morning rush hour and a slow go to her office at FBI Headquarters on Pennsylvania Avenue.

Throughout the flight and the bumper-to-bumper drive, she thought of poor Elmore, and the even-sadder Brenda Kay Yates. Liberty counted herself lucky that she did not hold office or rank to have such casualty-call duty put on her shoulders. She didn't have the heart for it. But then, she thought, who does?

Elmore Snow wore his dress green uniform and barracks cover with gold braid on the bill. As he mounted the steps to the Midway Park government quarters assigned to Lance Corporal Rowdy Yates and his pretty wife, Brenda Kay, he checked his emotions, swallowing a lump in his throat the size of his fist. As the Casualty Assistance Call Officer, a veteran captain, leaned to push the doorbell, the Marine lieutenant colonel took hold of his hand.

"Just a second, Skipper," Snow said. "I knew this lad real well, and his wife. Give me a second more."

"Take your time, Elmore," the base command Protestant chaplain, Fred Woodhouse, said. A Navy commander, today in his formal dress uniform, Chaplain Woodhouse also knew Brenda Kay Yates quite well, along with Elmore and June Snow, and their daughter, Katherine, from their regular attendance at his Sunday worship services and Wednesday night Bible study.

"I think it will just get worse, the longer you stand here, sir," the captain suggested.

"He's right, you know," Chaplain Woodhouse said.

"Yes. I know," Elmore said, and reached in front of the captain and pressed the doorbell.

Footsteps tromped across the floor, and the door came open. A pregnant and very beautiful, and very young-looking Brenda Kay Yates greeted them. When she saw Elmore Snow, she smiled.

"Look at you, all dressed up," she said, her voice filled with sparkle. "Chaplain Woodhouse? You, too? All dressed in your class-A uniforms? Why . . ."

Then it struck her. Nobody smiled, and Elmore had tears already pouring down his cheeks.

"Oh," she said. "Something happened to Rowdy . . . I better go sit down. I'm sorry, Elmore. Colonel Snow. Oh, my. Maybe you guys need to go get yourselves some coffee in the kitchen. I just made some. Oh, my . . . I need to sit down . . ."

As her knees suddenly buckled, Elmore took the girl in his arms and hugged her close and tight and wept with her like a father would with his daughter who had just learned that her young husband had died in the war.

"Oh, Brenda Kay," Elmore said, swallowing hard. "The Lord took him in an instant. Rowdy never felt a thing. He just went to Heaven."

"Oh," was all she could say, and she held on to this man she had known as a hometown hero when she was just a little girl and Rowdy was a little boy. Then she cried hard, "My poor Rowdy . . ."

"I'm calling Rowdy's folks, then I'll call your mama and daddy, here in a few minutes," Elmore said. "I wanted to tell you first, then the folks back home. A Marine out of the Denver recruiting district office is already on his way to make the casualty call to Rowdy's momma and daddy in person, but we'll let them know first, sweetie. Unless you want me to wait. I've already got all their plane tickets bought. They'll be here tonight. June will follow up with your momma and Rowdy's, taking on that load of getting things coordinated for them, so they'll get here without trouble.

"Right now, I'm going to help you pack your clothes, and you'll come stay at my house through all of this, you hear me?"

She nodded yes, sobbing.

"Your momma and daddy and Rowdy's folks will all be at my house together for as long as it takes. I'm taking care of everything, don't you worry," Colonel Snow went on. "I got lots of room, and we're like family. We all came from the same well out there in Wyoming. This is what we do. You understand?"

"Yes," she said, her face against his chest, soaking his uniform with her tears.

Elmore tilted her face up and looked in her wet eyes. Then he kissed her forehead. "Honey. I am so, so sorry. I just don't know what else to say."

"I know, Elmore." Brenda Kay wept. "I'm fresh out of words, too."

— 8 —

Red-eyed and feeling totally shitty, Liberty dropped her overstuffed kit duffel and her tightly packed personal travel bag at the entrance of her cubicle. Letting out a breath, ready to just collapse in the chair at her desk, her eyes caught a yellow Post-It note taped on her nameplate on the left side of the doorway. It read, "See me, ASAP," and had her boss's JK initials circled at the bottom.

"Shit," she said, taking the note, wadding it up, and dropping it in the trash as she left her bags by her desk and dragged ass down the hall to Supervisory Special Agent Jason Kendrick's office. He headed the Enhanced Tactical Operations Division that Liberty now called home.

Two knocks followed by a gruff "Enter" led Liberty Cruz inside the very well-ordered office of her boss. FBI awards and Marine Corps memorabilia decorated one entire wall. Autographed photos of Kendrick with President George W. Bush; Chairman of the Joint Chiefs of Staff, Marine General Pete Pace; and two commandants of the Marine Corps, General Mike Hagee and General Al Gray, dominated the center of the collection of walnut and brass. Next to them, hanging at near-equal prominence, an autographed shot of Kendrick with former Assistant Director in Charge of the FBI, New York Division, Jim Kallstrom, recently taken at the Marine Corps Law Enforcement Foundation gala in New York City. A fellow Marine, Kallstrom headed the FBI and Marine Corps organization that provided education scholarships to the widows and children of Marines and federal law-enforcement officers killed in the line of duty.

As a young blade, Kendrick had served with Kallstrom on the FBI special operations task force that took apart the so-called Pizza Connection, working closely with undercover operative, FBI Special Agent Joe Pistone, known to the Bonanno crime family as Donnie Brasco. A few years later, the more experienced Agent Kendrick helped Kallstrom and the team get the goods on the "Teflon Don," Gambino crime-family boss, John Gotti. Kendrick had followed Jim Kallstrom through the bathroom window of the infamous Ravenite Social Club in Little Italy and planted electronic-surveillance devices there, and in the upstairs apartment that Gotti used for Mafia meetings. Recordings of those conversations put Gotti behind bars for life and broke the wheels off the Gambino gravy train. As such, Jason Kendrick and legendary agents like him and Jim Kallstrom were Liberty's real heroes. They did what she wanted to do.

"Hell of a good job, Agent Cruz. Top rung at sniper school and at SERE school both. Most impressive," Kendrick said, putting the final touches on an email, his eyes focused on the computer screen.

"Would you have accepted anything less, sir?" Liberty

said, standing at attention, centered six inches in front of the supervisory special agent's desk.

He looked at her and smiled. "Not one bit less, Agent Cruz."

She smiled, still at attention. "You left a note on my cubicle, sir."

"That I did," Kendrick said, and pointed to a chair. "Have a seat."

"Thank you, sir," Liberty said, and sat, trying hard not to expose her fatigue.

Kendrick slid a manila folder trimmed in red, marked TOP SECRET across his desk. "Take your time reading through the brief; however, the folder does not leave this office."

Liberty nodded as she began working her way through the pages, and Kendrick went back to typing more emails on his computer.

When Liberty Cruz looked up from the folder, after reading the last page of the briefing, she saw Agent Kendrick leaned back in his desk chair, sipping coffee, waiting for her.

"What do ya think?" he asked her.

"Pretty mind-boggling, to be honest, sir. I had no idea," she said, and slid the top secret folder back across her boss's desk. "We have acts of cold-blooded murder, kidnapping, human trafficking, drug trafficking, major theft. Instance after instance. And nothing done to these thugs? Seriously?"

"One of those things you don't realize until after you've gone to war," Kendrick said. "All of it pretty much outside our legal jurisdiction, as it now stands with our current status of forces agreements and treaties with the struggling and still-forming governments of Iraq and Afghanistan. But, yes, as you say, pretty mind-boggling."

"A Baghdad cab driver shot by a security-contractor supervisor, purely for sport? A delivery driver murdered by this same creep the same day. Killed them both for the fun of it? Because he was going home the next day and had not killed anyone during his year in Iraq? Seriously, sir? There's literally no rule of law governing the conduct of these government contractors in Iraq or Afghanistan?" Liberty said, amazed.

"Only the host nations' rules of law, which are basically nonexistent right now, considering the war and all," Kendrick said. "State Department pays off the injured families and closes the book. The criminals go scot-free. That's why the Senate investigation, and the president directing the FBI to look into things. We have to make a recommendation before anything truly disastrous happens."

"Like mass murder," Liberty offered.

"Or a host of other really scary possibilities, including press coverage, once you think about it," Kendrick added. "On one side we have Virginia Senator Jim Wells, a fellow jarhead with the Navy Cross and two Silver Stars from his Vietnam service, wanting some sort of ruling authority in Defense or State Departments, or both, overseeing the contractors, and prosecuting all criminal acts. More or less, pulling government contractors under the umbrella of federal jurisdiction, pretty much the same kinds of rules that the military operates under. Which I think is pretty sane and long overdue, if you wanted to hear my opinion.

"Then on the other side, we have Nevada Senator Cooper Carlson championing the status quo and his special interests. Which I think are probably pretty shady but we have no evidence to prove it, just me suspecting it. And him saying the contractors ought to have every freedom to operate as any other American business does in any other foreign nation. The United States should not try to extend its jurisdiction into other nations."

"And what does all of this have to do with me?" Liberty asked.

"Your kit packed?" Kendrick asked.

"Yes, always, but I have a bunch of dirty laundry," Cruz answered.

"Wash it or change it," Kendrick said. "You've got a helicopter to catch at 1400. You'll launch from here with three other tactical agents who make up your team, and chop to Dover Air Force Base, where you'll depart via C-17 Globemaster for Baghdad tonight."

"My team?" Liberty smiled.

"Don't feel so flattered just yet," Kendrick said. "Your mission is no picnic. Not so much gunslinging, but finding facts, gathering intelligence, and verifying witness claims, so the director and the attorney general can make a solid recommendation to the president. All undercover and highly classified. That's the hard part. Keeping your cover locked tight. I warn you, any gunplay had better stand righteous and well justified."

"But, my team, sir?" she asked, still smiling.

"Yes, your team. I've got faith in your moxie," Kendrick said. "But it's your ass if anything goes awry."

Kendrick pulled a thick folder from a stack of wire

baskets on his credenza and slid it across his desk for Liberty to take.

"You might tuck that someplace safe," he said. "Travel orders, vouchers, authorizations for weapons, points of contact, clearances, letters of access and authorization signed by the director, should you hit any snags."

"And what if some people don't want to honor these documents?" Liberty asked.

"You have my mobile number. Call me twenty-four/seven," Kendrick said. "I have the director's mobile number, twenty-four/seven, and he has the hotline to the president."

Kendrick pointed his finger at her. "Don't take shit from anybody, especially that weasel running Malone-Leyva who you had your little one-nighter with some time back."

Liberty's eyes opened wide. "You're watching me?"

"We're watching him," Kendrick said.

"I am so embarrassed," Liberty said. "We met at that security industry party at the Washingtonian. So long ago, I had almost forgotten it. Cesare Alosi, what a scumbag. I caught him going through my laptop and reading my email. I threw him out and never spoke to him again."

"He's got your picture on his desk in Baghdad," Kendrick said.

Liberty's eyes got bigger. "Sir! I had no idea he even had a picture of me! I have nothing to do with him!"

Kendrick laughed. "Relax. We know. We checked. You passed muster. But you might use his attraction to you to our advantage."

"I'm not going to bed with that guy if that's what

you're suggesting," Liberty snapped. "Don't ever consider using me in any kind of romantic relationship with him or anyone else. I'm not that person. Frankly, sir, I'm offended that you would even suggest it."

"Look, Agent Cruz," Kendrick said. "I'm not suggesting anything of the sort. Your familiarity with him is an intelligence advantage, that's all. Use his fondness for you as a tool, or don't use it. I wouldn't dare go there, to suggest you compromise your integrity, and you ought to know it. However, Mr. Alosi does have your picture on his desk, and obviously has an attraction to you. Use that fact at your discretion. I'm just saying, it may open doors."

"Judging by what I've learned about Cesare after the fact, some very dangerous doors," Liberty added.

"Very dangerous indeed," Kendrick agreed. "That's why you have a three-man enhanced tactical team assigned to provide you high cover at all times. Cesare Alosi and his boss, Victor Malone, the company's owner, won't hesitate to eliminate any threat. And I mean with extreme prejudice."

Liberty gave him a look, reality soaking in.

Kendrick made a motion to his coffeepot and cups, and Liberty took him up on the invitation.

As he filled both cups, Kendrick continued, "We also have three undercover intelligence operators working on the inside at Malone-Leyva. Just so you're aware. In addition to your high cover, we've got these guys, who are amply capable to step up if you need help."

"You think Cesare might try to kill me?" Liberty asked, a pang of anxiety hitting her.

"Definitely if he regards you as a threat," Kendrick said, going back to his desk and Liberty returning to her seat. "Here's a little story, and we're still looking at this pretty close.

"A month ago, a Marine Scout-Sniper died in Wisconsin. Seems he and his wife had gone home on leave and went out dancing with friends. The Marine went to the bar to refill their beer pitcher and never came back.

"In a little while, sirens and cops outside brought out the crowd. The Marine had apparently wandered onto the highway, supposedly in a drunken stupor. A passing motorist, a fellow from China who spoke little to no English, had hit the Marine, stopped, and reported the accident.

"Now, interestingly, the wife and friends all emphatically say that the Marine was not drunk when he left to get the beer. Not even tipsy. They had danced more than drank, so it makes me wonder, too.

"Anyway, not much of an investigation followed. Country sheriff in the middle of Wisconsin and all. Naval Criminal Investigative Service wrote it off as just another alcohol-related fatality. The lad was put to rest and the books closed on his death. However, the Commandant of the Marine Corps doesn't like how the case smells and asked us to take a look, especially with the background behind this guy.

"You read about the security supervisor who sport shot the two Iraqi civilians?"

Liberty nodded yes. "Taxi driver in Baghdad and later that day near the airport a delivery-van driver."

"This Marine staff sergeant had gotten out of the

Marine Corps and went to work for Malone-Leyva, knocking down five hundred dollars a day. He's one of three eyewitnesses who saw the supervisor murder the cab driver and the delivery driver. He and his partner, a former Army Ranger, reported the incident to their boss, Cesare Alosi, and he fired them all, including the supervisor who committed the murders. Swept everything under the rug.

"So, the Marine and the Ranger launch a wrongful-termination lawsuit against Malone-Leyva. Their only option to bring the murders into the light of day. Iraq isn't investigating and doesn't care. State Department won't touch it, and Defense Department doesn't want anything to do with it, either. So, the civil lawsuit is their only route to justice for the murders. That drags on, you know the legal-paper drills, and the boy needs a paycheck, so he returns to Marine Corps active duty. He had kept his Marine Corps Reserve options open, you see. Just in case things didn't work at Malone-Leyva. Smart boy.

"The Marine also shared the details of all this with a Marine Scout-Sniper officer friend of his, along with a few other Marines in the sniper community. This officer is a close pal of Senator Jim Wells, and brings all this information to the senator's attention. This raises the hackles of Malone-Leyva, they go after the Marine officer with a few legal endplays in federal court that don't work. So they illegally tap the Marine officer's phone lines and data stream and intercept the communications between him and Senator Wells. Private communications between a citizen and a United States Senator. Yes, very illegal. And the Marine officer's attorney, who successfully defends his client's privacy against Malone-Leyva, uncovered this skullduggery, informing his client of it, the judge, and Senator Wells, who is livid to this day.

"At any rate, last month, when the Marine staff sergeant and his wife go home to Wisconsin for some family time, he ends up dead. Likewise, any other witnesses to the purported murders also clam up, and everything goes away, except for the one very pissed-off United States senator who would love to run up and disk Malone-Leyva."

Liberty let out a deep breath. "Very convenient accident."

"Very convenient indeed," Kendrick said. "Alosi and Victor Malone are smart, but invariably the bad guys always leave something stupid behind. Some little splinter, and it takes them down. But in the meantime, you need to keep your head on a swivel and take no chances. Like Senator Wells and the commandant, I believe Malone and Alosi iced the staff sergeant, and they will not hesitate to do you, too."

"Don't worry, sir," Liberty said. "Alosi's smart but not that smart, and he's a bit of a gunslinger, impulsive."

"True, Alosi's careful, but you're right. He does get a little impulsive when his buttons get pushed." Kendrick nodded. "Victor Malone, on the other hand, he's much more cautious and never impulsive. He'd make it look like an accident. I suspect he personally arranged our Marine's death in Wisconsin. But would they kill you, an FBI agent? Yes. Especially Malone. His wife is Enrique Leyva's sister."

"Enrique Leyva? I'm not familiar with him," Liberty said.

"At first glance, a well-respected Mexican businessman on the outside, but behind that front, he heads a drug cartel based in Matamoros, Mexico, that extends along the border to Nuevo Laredo and down to Monterey," Kendrick said. "Along with far-reaching relationships with powerful Mexican leaders, Leyva has strong ties with the likes of El Chapo Guzman and his Sinaloa organization, and Los Zetas."

"I've heard my mother talk serious stuff about Sinaloa and Los Zetas both," Liberty said. "She's spent nearly all her DEA career at El Paso Intelligence Center. She's told some really terrible stories about the Zetas, especially in the past few years."

"Bloody sons of bitches, excuse my French," Kendrick said. "They contract out to other cartels as enforcer death squads from Juarez to the Gulf Coast."

"So I've heard," Liberty said.

"At any rate," Kendrick said, "Victor Malone lives in a castle outside McAllen, Texas. I mean it is literally a castle. They say he's got a full body mount of an African bull elephant in his den, along with mounts of every other kind of dangerous or exotic animal. Polar bears, cheetahs, you name it. Literally a castle filled with dead animals. I'm a hunter, but I was taught to kill for food. To shoot a living creature to make a wall decoration? I'm sorry, but that takes a very inadequately equipped human being, if you get my drift."

Liberty laughed. "Oh, yes, sir. The guy with the big truck and little boots."

Kendrick laughed. "Well, yeah. Then I do drive a big black Ford Super Duty diesel four-by-four."

"Sir, you've got some very big boots." Liberty smiled. "We do have exceptions."

"Yes, we do." Kendrick smiled. "However, my point about Victor Malone stands. He's a very dangerous, very wealthy man who holds no boundaries and zero ethics. And he has some extremely dangerous in-laws south of the border."

"Then, sir. If you don't mind me asking. How did he land a government security contract?" Liberty asked.

"Like the rest of these scumbag mercenary contractors," Kendrick said. "Victor Malone makes big campaign contributions to members of Congress, and even the president. For too many politicians, all money's green."

"I better get my laundry done," Liberty said, leaving her coffee cup on the side table and checking her watch. "Back here for a 1400 launch?"

"Yes, but I want to see you and your team at 1330," Kendrick said. "I've got your guys drawing your weapons and gear right now. You just need to get yourself back here pronto, ready to travel."

"Yes, sir," Liberty said, heading for the door.

"By the way, Agent Cruz. That boyfriend of yours, Gunnery Sergeant Jack Valentine," Kendrick said.

Liberty stopped. "I didn't think you were watching me."

Kendrick shrugged. "I do keep tabs on my people. Are you surprised, or offended?"

Liberty smiled. "No, sir. Neither surprised nor offended. Very much expected. I'd do the same thing. It's nice to be loved, sir."

Kendrick smiled back. "Well, I do honestly care about you and every agent in my command. However, let's keep any mission talk out of your conversations with Gunny Valentine or anyone else outside your team. For the Gunny's protection, more than anything. He's got enough on his plate without worrying about you. And I sure as hell don't want him mixing it up with people should you get your, ah, shirttail in a wringer."

"My tit in a wringer, you mean?" Liberty laughed.

"Your Marine Corps influence is telling." Kendrick chuckled. "At any rate, when you get to Baghdad, act normal. See your gunny when mission allows. Stick to your cover story at all costs. You're there on an administrative audit. Let him and anyone else there believe this is purely a rookie jaunt for an up-and-coming agent to test her wings. Nothing tactical or special operations. Make out like you won a trip to Baghdad as a prize for doing so well in school. Got it?"

"Yes, sir," Liberty said, and left.

Afternoon sun cut long shadows across the Baghdad airfield as Gunnery Sergeant Jack Valentine and seven of his MARSOC operators trailed out to mount a waiting US Army Black Hawk. The chopper would fly the patrol from LZ Victory to a no-name crop-of-rocks insertion point known only by grid coordinates in the al-Anbar wastelands, north of Hit.

Two local cops and a clutch of Iraqi security force soldiers, gaggling within smelling distance by their trucks, gawked at the unholy tribe, festooned with long guns and made up for war. The Iraqis' surly looks told what their minds said. None of it good.

Each Marine sported his own devil's face, painted with different menacing designs of brown, tan, and black camouflage. Bold dark stripes slanted evilly across their foreheads, tilting above their eyes. Accent lines off the sides and under their eyes joined wide streaks of black and brown that angled down their cheeks. Some men had totally blackened circles covering their eyes, and black-smudged triangles in the hollows under the ridges of their cheeks. They also drew teethlike lines over their lips, so that their war-painted faces resembled the classic death's-head. Other faces, like Jack's, resembled a demonic tiger.

Each of the Marines wore an embroidered black ace-of-spades patch with a Punisher skull in its center, trimmed in red, and a pair of black-and-white dice showing snake eyes on the fronts of their Kevlar operator's vests. The team logo that Jack had designed. He had a Jacksonville ball cap and T-shirt shop crank out three hundred of the embroidered patches along with a five-foot flag of the same logo design that now adorned the HOG Wallow wall behind his desk. On the men's backs, they each had painted a red-trimmed black crusader's Templar cross. Another Jack Valentine novelty to set his tribe of Spartan warriors apart.

Jack heard one cop gag out in a disgusted Arabic voice, *"Shayatin mukali."*

He recognized the colloquial Arabic phrase for "painted devils," a name the Hajis had given American snipers, so he stopped his crew and smiled at the men.

His black-over-brown tiger-striped face, slanting bold lines above and around his eyes and down his cheeks, evil and dark beneath the shade of his flop hat, contrasted by his flashing white teeth, startled the Iraqi security crew.

Then a soldier wearing two gold stars on green epaulettes, the lieutenant in charge of the Iraqi detail, pointed at Valentine, recognizing him, and said, *"Ash'abah al-Anbar! Ash'abah al-Anbar!"*

The other men mumbled the words, too, eyes glaring, faces frowning, as if they had just seen old *Iblis* himself.

"Yeah, baby, I'm back! The Ghost of Anbar," Jack bellowed out, and let go a wicked laugh. "Old *Shabah* the bogeyman himself has returned to haunt your bloody lands. Beware! Beware! My *shayatin* and me, we're out there in the darkness, killing your cousins and devouring their souls."

"Dude." Cotton Martin laughed. "So much for winning the affections of our local hosts."

"I know," Jack said, striding to the helicopter. "Elmore will be proud of us when he hears about it."

"Yeah, Gunny V. That's what I'm afraid of. Just like the spades and skulls you got going on in the hooch. And that freaking black wall," Sergeant Clarence "Cochise" Quinlan said, stepping fast behind them. His old pal from Ninth Marines, Sergeant Sammy LaSage, marched with him.

"Don't forget the Templar cross, Cochise." Jack smiled.

"Oh, Heaven forbid!" Quinlan let out. "It's like we painted these big-ass targets on our backs. First we piss off the Hajis like we're back for round two of the Crusades, then we all wear massive indicators to give them something to aim at."

"You worry too much, Cochise," Jaws said, hot on his heels with Bronco Starr.

Corporal Randy Powell, whom Jack had named Chico because he considered Randy a name for a male cheerleader, and Corporal Petey Preston brought up the rear.

When they reached the Black Hawk, Jack shook hands with the crew chief and machine gunner, both Army sergeants. They still had the rotor tied down, and the front seats sat empty.

"You two hard chargers going to drive this ship?" Jack asked with a grin.

"Naw," the crew chief grumbled, "Captain Foulks is still in the ready room doing chalk talk, and I think Lieutenant Snyderman's in the latrine changing her tampon or taking a shit."

Gunny Valentine took a gander back at the buildings that sat at the edge of the flight line and thought for a moment.

"So we've got a female copilot?" he asked.

"And pilot," the crew chief said, and licked the load of Copenhagen out of his lower lip and spit it to the side, careful not to splatter the brown suede on Jack's Desert RAT boots or his own.

"Women drivers," Valentine said, feeling the guy out.

"Good pilots," the crew chief came back. "Can't fault their flying or lack of balls. They'll dust you in a hot LZ and not blink. But they are a royal pain in the ass."

"Attention to orders, and micromanaging the shit out of everything we do," the door gunner chimed in.

"Them against the male-dominated world," the crew chief concluded. "Busting the shit out of the glass ceiling."

"We'll keep that in mind when we meet them," Jack said, and looked around at his crew. "Don't be fucking around with your wise shit. Got it? We're just going to ride and jump off. That's all."

All seven of his team nodded.

Jack reached in his cargo pocket, took out a clear-vinyl-covered tactical map section, and unfolded it.

"Gather round, children," he said, and put his finger at their insertion point. "You should have this down pat, so tell me where I have my finger, and don't say up my ass or on the end of my hand."

Bronco said, "Departure point. From there we spread the two teams in a line and work our way toward the road, then move parallel to it north."

"Roger," Jack said, and looked at LaSage. "Sage, what's our intervals?"

"Team one and team two spaced by seven hundred meters, and each interior two-man team split by two hundred meters," LaSage answered.

"Coordination, Jaws?" Valentine asked the strong silent one.

"We're up on covered net, we'll have visual reference by infrared and night optics, and our reporting points," Alex answered.

"Be sure we know where each team is at any given moment. Vital to survival and success," Gunny Valentine stressed. "Staff Sergeant Martin will ride the inboard flank for team one. I will ride the inboard flank of team two, across that seven-hundred-meter divide, opposite him."

"Why such a big gap down the middle?" Bronco asked. "I never understood that part of it. Why not two hundred meters like between the two-man teams?"

"What happens if team one somehow gets seen, or engages enemy fire?" Jack asked. "Hajis will move on them, without likely seeing us, too, or vice versa. When they go after Cotton, Sage, Chico, and Petey, then we can pivot on their flank and light 'em up, just like an ambush."

It still didn't make any sense to Jesse Cortez, so he just smiled like he bought it.

"What is our final objective, Cochise?" Gunny Valentine asked.

"Besides hopefully snatching a prisoner or two we can take home to grill? Personally, I like mine smoked with sweet barbecue sauce," Quinlan said with a chuckle, but bought nothing but groans from the team.

"After our night of sweeping north," he continued, "we end up establishing blocking positions at both ends of the trestle over the Euphrates about a klick and a half south of Haqlaniyah. On the east side, half of us set up at the railway crossing with Alternate Supply Route Phoenix, also known as Iraqi Highway 19. Our other half sets up at the railroad crossing on Main Supply Route Bronze, known locally as Iraqi Highway 12, on the west side of the river.

"We shoot anything with guns coming up any roads anyplace or trying to sneak up the river. We definitely take out anybody running ahead of the sweep that one-five's commencing up MSR Bronze along the west side of the river, and ASR Phoenix on the east side of the river at first light. We remain in position until relieved at about 0900, if we're lucky, early enough that we can make it to Al Asad Air Base for one-five's command brief of Two MEF, and get hot noon air-winger chow if we play our cards right."

"Right. Good job, Cochise." Jack nodded and looked at his team. "Any questions?"

No one said anything.

"Double-check your gear, one last time," Jack said, then he looked at Cotton Martin. "Us eight on the final lift leaves three back at the fort to cover what comes in the door. Billy-C in the saddle, and he's got our number."

Cotton nodded. "Too bad we couldn't bring him along and employ a rear-echelon commando to cover the phones."

"Lame as Billy is? He'd just be deadweight," Jack said, and took a bite out of a Snickers bar he had melting in his pocket, and went to sucking chocolate off his fingers. "Claybaugh limping around with his ass in a sling. Think about it. Besides, Billy or not, I want Drzewiecki and Rasputin with us, fixing guns. The entire crew aboard on this operation, there's absolutely no reason to leave any capable man at the rear. Smedley excluded."

"Goes without saying," Cotton said. "By the way, Sergeant Romyantsev doesn't like you calling him Rasputin."

"He tell you that?" Jack asked, licking more chocolate and finishing the messy candy bar.

Cotton shook his head. "No, Drzewiecki did."

"He serious?" Jack said. "I rather like Rasputin. If he doesn't want to be called Rasputin, then you guys can call me Rasputin. Rasputin the fucking He-Devil. It fits right in. Hell of a lot better name than Romyantsev. How did we end up with alphabet soup as our armorers anyway?"

"You got a point," Cotton said, and checked the setting sun. "Getting late. The other teams should already be deployed. Mob Squad up at the lake, and Sergeant Durant, Hub, Hot Sauce, Jewfro, and Ironhead running rear guard behind one-five headquarters element for now."

"Right," Jack answered, and looked at his watch.

"And what about this flat hat you know at one-five, running this sweep? An old friend you say?" Cotton asked.

"A dear old friend. From my days down in Colombia with Elmore," Jack said, showing a big smile. "Lieutenant Colonel Edward Bartholomew Black Bart Roberts."

"A descendant of Black Bart the pirate, so they say," Cotton said. "I heard the boys talking about him."

"That's right," Jack said. "He's got your old running mate Tim Sutherby with him, too, leading First Battalion, Fifth Marines sniper platoon."

"Sutherby? Really?" Cotton smiled. "Thought he was in Afghanistan."

"Came over to one-five when I MEF came in country from Pendleton. Found out today when I did some final checking on one-five," Jack said. "They'd had him busy around Ramadi. Black Bart heard he was down there and snatched him up."

"He's been here all along?" Cotton asked.

"Apparently so," Jack said. "I knew they had a new team working Ramadi, but I didn't know it was Sutherby."

"He's one badass gunslinger," Cotton said. "Makes me kind of feel sorry for the Hajis."

"Only about a second?" Jack smiled.

"Not even." Cotton grinned. "Like maybe an interval of Planck time."

Jack grinned, remembering their discussion of the first instant of the creation of the universe with Elmore Snow, and Cotton's explanation of how the physicist Max Planck had divided the first second of creation into intervals based on the time it takes the speed of light to travel one meter.

"At any rate, I knew one-five had their hands full, so much area to cover," Jack went on. "So I told Colonel Roberts I'd like to bring out a team or two, from time to time, if he could clear it with the powers that be. Next thing I know, we got this full-blown operation plan. Good opportunity to put some of our guys to meaningful work."

"Yeah, but the whole fucking herd?" Cotton said.

"I'm not leaving any able-bodied operators back there to get saddled with more bullshit escort duty," Jack said. "We lose another Scout-Sniper, it's going to be for a better reason than protecting a can of beans."

"Black Bart cleared all this with Elmore before he departed for Lejeune?" Cotton asked.

"Sure. Mostly," Jack said, not knowing for certain how much Colonel Snow really knew beyond what he had told him. Then he considered. "Well, the colonel may not know about the entire MARSOC detachment coming along. That's me making a command decision, and not giving Captain Burkehart room to back out. But I'm sure the colonel's cool with it. Black Bart and Elmore are tight. No way Colonel Snow would ever turn down his asshole buddy from Medellín."

"Elmore see your hooch decorations before he left?" Cotton asked.

Cochise Quinlan looked up. "Gunny kept all that dark shit in the box until the colonel got on the plane."

"Going to be a welcome-home surprise." Jack smiled.

"What's Elmore going to say?" Martin asked.

"He'll love it!" Jack answered. "Besides. Shit didn't come in until the day Elmore left, and he saw the boxes. I even gave him his patches. Not like I'm hiding it."

"Punisher skulls, snake-eye dice, and Templar cross gunwale to gunwale might look a bit rabid to him," Cotton offered. "You know, his strong Christian values, and how he never says motherfucker unless he's really pissed off."

Jack grinned. "I got Christian values, too. Only difference, I'm a sinner that don't care to hide his shit."

Cotton Martin rolled his eyes. "One day, lightning will come out of the clear blue and strike you dead."

"Colonel Snow's cool with it. Promise," Jack assured his staff sergeant.

Cochise Quinlan and the rest of the team gave Jack a look, not so sure about their gunny's confidence.

Captain Margaret Foulks and First Lieutenant Cynthia Snyderman walked toward the helicopter, helmets under their arms and their short-cropped hair fluttering in the hot wind. Both women looked trim, shapely, and fit real well in their flight suits.

"Dude, check it. They're hot!" Bronco Starr let slip.

"Like you had a prayer," Jaws grumbled.

"That's your trouble, Alex," Cortez came back. "No optimism."

Suck on it," the blindfolded girl heard the stinking man say, inhaling his foul breath in her face as he grunted out the Arabic words in a thick Palestinian accent. Then she felt the muzzle of his Makarov PMM nine-millimeter pistol press against her lips.

Terrified, she obediently opened her mouth, and he shoved his gun inside it, the oily steel cutting her tongue and lips against her teeth. Simultaneously, he pressed his stiff cock inside her vagina, carelessly tearing her hymen, and immediately began fucking her rough, fast, and hard.

Helpless, the young virgin, more child than woman, lay tied naked, spread-eagle on a filthy cotton ticking mattress atop rusty wire springs on a wrought-iron bed in a house in the far countryside west of Haditha. The gun pushed to the back of her throat gagged her, muffling her cries. She prayed as tears flooded from her eyes, soaking the blindfold, asking God to please take her life without delay.

On the other side of a blanket nailed over the otherwise-open doorway to the room where the man raped the girl, Giti Sadiq and her two fellow Christian slaves taken from Al-Shirqat huddled on the floor, against the wall. Holding tight to each other, they shut their eyes and prayed for God's mercy, hearing the grunting of the man and the whimpers of his victim as the metal bed banged and squeaked.

Giti and her captive sisters had met the child only briefly in the kitchen an hour earlier, a thirteen-year-old Greek Orthodox girl kidnapped in the Syrian city of Deir az-Zur and spirited to Iraq with one of Abu Musab al-Zarqawi's al-Qaeda Iraq recruiting teams. Her captors had taken this girl, who had introduced herself to Giti as Lina, along with five others. The terrorist soldiers had raped and killed four of them during their journey to Haditha but had saved the barely teen virgin, Lina, as a gift for their leader.

The sixth Syrian girl, a heavyset sixteen-year-old Alawi Shia called Sabeen, who happened to be in the wrong place at the wrong time in Deir az-Zur, had somehow survived repeated raping and now worked as a kitchen maid between rounds of abuse. She prayed with Giti and the other two Christian slaves, and asked Jesus to save her, too, even if she was a Muslim.

"That is Zarqawi in there raping Lina," the sister called Amira whispered to Giti. "I saw him. It is Zarqawi."

Giti put her hands over Amira's mouth. "Do not say this. Not to anyone. Never again. They will kill you. We cannot know such things, or we, too, will surely die."

Then came the gunshot. A single pop.

All three girls flinched at the bang. Giti blinked at Amira, and their third sister, Miriam. At the same time, dishes crashed in the kitchen, followed by Sabeen's shrieks, then unrelenting sobbing for her young friend Lina.

Giti and her slave sisters huddled together, holding each other tight, crying and praying, terrified. "Perhaps Jesus has blessed poor Lina," Giti thought, "taking her from this evil place. Perhaps that is how He will take me, too."

"Get in here! Clean this mess!" the old graybeard Abu Omar Bakr al-Nasser bellowed from the doorway at the three frightened girls. Men quickly hustled out the body of little Lina and left the mess of brains and blood for the maids.

"You!" Abu Omar said, pointing at Giti. "Get in the kitchen and help that mindless fat fool clean up the broken plates she dropped. We have important guests dining with us tonight, so you make sure this meal is fit for them."

Giti bowed low and gladly hurried from the murder room and its bloody mess, which Amira and Miriam had to clean up.

Cesare Alosi had waited late for his executive assistant, Irene, to leave for the day before he took the stolen First Battalion, Fifth Marine Regiment operation plan from its hiding place, between the pages of the *New York Times* newspaper that he had carried in the office that morning and laid on the bookshelf behind his desk. He ate his lunch in the office, just to make sure that Irene did not snoop through his stuff, as he suspected that she often did when he was out.

Irene acted suspicious when she left because Cesare never stayed late. She always locked up. Reluctantly, she finally left, irritatingly curious, asking all sorts of questions but trying to sound casual asking them.

Tempted to rush Irene out the door, Cesare bided his time and painfully let the clock tick. He sat at his desk, feet up, sipping a Coke, thumbing through a Sergeant Grit catalog, his nerves gnawing through every second.

When she had finally gone, he huddled over the combination color printer, scanner, and copy machine, carefully making both a paper duplicate and digital scan of the operation plan without removing the staples and not creasing any pages. He took the paper copy, fastened the pages together, and put it in his desk's locking file drawer. He then bumped off the PDF scan to a thumb drive and secured the little USB data-storage device with the paper copy. Last, he wiped all traces of the document from the scanner and computer tied to it.

He took the original operation plan in its top secret envelope, tucked the package back between the pages of his *New York Times*, folded so that the crossword puzzle showed on the outside, and drove to Baghdad International Airport. A daily visitor there morning and evening, Cesare slid right past the US and Iraqi security forces' checkpoints leading into and through Camp Victory with the newspaper lying casually on his Escalade's front passenger seat.

Inside the busy compound, he drove to the operations building, where he made his regular morning and evening visits, parked, and walked toward the guarded entrance with the newspaper under his arm. A quartet of US Army sentries at the door watched him as he stopped at a trash barrel, took the *Times* from under his arm, dropped it in the can, and walked away. A few steps toward the door, he stopped as if he had changed his mind, went back to the trash, and retrieved his newspaper, but slid the top secret operation plan out and buried it under a collection of odd paper, candy wrappers, lunch sacks, soda cups, and drink bottles.

As he walked through the secure entrance, a familiar face to the men who stood guard, he smiled as he handed the sentry his identification. "You know, I almost tossed out my *Times* without doing the crossword puzzle. Can you imagine? It's the best part of the paper!" And showed the soldiers the page with the squares left blank. He laughed. "It's been one of those days."

All four soldiers smiled and nodded politely, as if they gave a rat's ass, while the sergeant in charge logged Mr. Alosi in the building and sent him on his way.

Cesare made his evening rounds with his usual joint forces operations, intelligence, and security liaisons, and departed a little more than an hour later. He raised no eyebrows, just another step in his mundane daily routine.

As he drove out the gate and headed to his apartment, he felt proud of himself. Got rid of the incriminating evidence right under their noses. With them watching!

At his apartment, he dialed Victor Malone's private line on his secure company sat-link phone.

"You took care of it?" Malone said without even saying hello but going straight to the point as he answered the call.

"Done," Cesare said.

"Good work on grabbing that CIA contract," Malone said. Then asked, "This help us lock down that DOD security deal?"

"Closed it right after I sent out our CIA contract team," Alosi said. "Very fortunate timing. Literally doubled our business with two strokes of the pen."

"You didn't do anything bonehead, like make copies, did you?" Malone asked.

"Of course not." Cesare laughed.

When Jack Valentine and his seven Marines dropped on the secluded landing zone in the sprawling desert, several miles east of the Euphrates River and south of Haditha, the sun lay blood orange on the western horizon. By the time they reached their first reporting point, darkness had engulfed the world.

After checking in by covered net radio with one-five's operations chief, Jack and his Scout-Snipers gathered in a circle, guns pointed outward, eating their evening meal on a hill of hard earth that hadn't seen rain in recent memory.

"Dryer than a popcorn fart," Sammy LaSage commented while working on a cold Meals Ready to Eat package of Smoky Franks that Marines had nicknamed the Five Fingers of Death.

"What would make people want to inhabit such a brutal land?" Cotton Martin asked Jack, as they ate their own mystery meals, and looked at the distant twinkling lights of Haditha on the west side of the river and Barwana on the east side, far to the northwest, and Haqlaniyah closer to the northwest, across the river. Somewhere ahead of them, Iraqi Highway 19, known on military maps as Alternate Supply Route Phoenix, running north from Hit, along the east side of the Euphrates, then just south of Haditha, across the river from Haqlaniyah, turning northeast across country to Baiji, on the Tigris River, lay hidden in the darkness.

Jack thought about it, started to say something cute, but thought some more. "I used to ask the same question about the shit-hole places around El Paso when I was growing up. You know? Fuck if I know . . ."

"Elmore says it's the Garden of Eden," Cotton added.

"Elmore says a lot of shit like that," Jack said.

"Hard to imagine," Cotton added, gazing into the darkness and at the distant lights. "A good land gone bad."

"There's no good land gone bad, Cotton," Jack said. "People gone bad. Not the land."

Cotton smiled. "Elmore tell you that?"

"Naw." Jack grinned. "I'm capable of coming up with a pearl of wisdom on my own, now and then."

They finished their food, and Jack gave Martin a nudge.

"Look here, brother," he said in a low voice, careful to be sure that only Cotton heard him. "Anything happens to me this trip, or down the road, I want you to step up and take over."

"What about Billy?" Cotton asked, taken off guard.

"Oh, he's my pard and all, don't get me wrong," Jack said. "I trust him with my life. He's capable. But dude, when it comes to smarts, you run circles around him. Me, too, sometimes, I think. I expect to see you wearing bars on your collars before long. Besides, don't you hold rank over him?"

"A month in grade," Cotton said. "But, Jack, you and Billy got a long history. Fallujah Two, a tour up here a year ago. Billy and Elmore go back, too. Don't you think Billy would expect to step up? Besides, won't Elmore pick him anyway?"

"I already had this talk with the colonel, a while back. He respects my choices. Like Billy or not, it boils down to one thing: You don't do stupid shit," Jack said. "Billy does stupid shit. Me, too, for that matter. Something happens to me, you tell Elmore I said you're my replacement."

"Whatever," Cotton said, and sat quiet for a while, watching the lights and picking up the movement of a truck driving along Highway 19 far to the south. "You see that?"

"Yeah," Jack said, binoculars up. "Long way off."

The headlights stopped and went out.

"Reckon it's an IED team?" Cotton said, still looking through his binoculars.

"Lights on, probably not. Then, you never know," Jack said. "It keeps working up our way, we might just find out."

"What brought up this business of something happening to you, anyway?" Cotton said, again talking low.

"Those guys at the airport," Jack said. "That one recognizing me. Called me *Ash'abah al-Anbar*, the Ghost of Anbar."

"So what?" Cotton shrugged.

"They know me. Know I'm here. Saw us leave. Zar-qawi's going to make it a point to come after me," Jack said.

"And?" Cotton said. "Just makes our hunting him easier."

"They might get me," Jack said. "Catch me unaware."

"They might get us all," Cotton said. "We're eight Marines sitting by ourselves in their desert. Nobody friendly even remotely close."

"But we're badass dudes with badass guns." Jack grinned.

"That's right, brother," Cotton said.

"One thing for certain," Jack said in a low whisper. "They won't take me prisoner. Not alive. I'm still breathing, I'm still shooting."

"Same here," Cotton said. "I'm pretty sure that goes for every man in the outfit."

"Prisoners get their heads chopped off on YouTube," Jack said. "Balls, too, most likely."

"They chop off my head, I don't think I'd be worrying too much about my balls." Cotton laughed.

"Unless they chop balls first." Jack grinned.

"Yeah, that would hurt." Cotton laughed.

"Anyway, I'm going down in a fucking blaze of glory, or I won't go down." Jack smiled.

"Brother," Cotton said, "you're not going down. None of us are. But we're going to take down a whole shitload of their sorry Haji asses."

"Fuckin' A," Jack said, and put out his knuckles.

"Fuckin' A," Cotton said, and bumped Jack's fist.

———

Giti Sadiq carefully placed a serving board layered with sliced roast goat in the center of the dining table for the men. Amira followed with a platter of khubz and pita breads in one hand, and in the other she balanced a tray loaded with dishes filled with hummus, tahini, fattoush, and rolled, pickled grape leaves stuffed with cheese.

Miriam put hot plates of sliced, steamed vegetables on the table after Amira had set down her cargo. Giti returned with two pitchers of cold water with lemon slices floating in them.

The men at the table, each a regional chieftain who supported the efforts of Jamaat Ansar al-Sunnah and al-Qaeda Iraq, drank coffee and chai as they waited for the last two guests to arrive, now embarrassingly tardy.

Abu Omar looked at his watch, then at Abu Musab al-Zarqawi. "I cannot imagine what has delayed them."

Zarqawi said nothing but began eating. The others at the table followed suit.

One of Omar's men came in the room a few minutes later and whispered in the old graybeard's ear.

"Juba and Hasan just passed our eastern checkpoint, coming from Haditha," Abu Omar told Zarqawi.

The boss of al-Qaeda Iraq gave Omar a nod.

Twenty minutes later, Dzhamal Umarov and Khasan Shishani hurried into the dining room, bowing and apologizing.

"We were delayed in Haditha this evening because of something marvelous!" Juba said in French, reaching inside a satchel and withdrawing a copy of the First Battalion, Fifth Marine Regiment's top secret operation plan. He took the document to Zarqawi, who stopped eating and began thumbing through the pages.

His eyes lit up as he read the words TOP SECRET on the cover.

Each of the pages was printed from photographs of the original operation plan shot by a cell-phone camera. Although rough and crude, tilted at one angle and another, the pages all read well enough for al-Qaeda Iraq to make some quick plans of their own.

Zarqawi smiled at Juba. "Top secret?"

"Yes, brother, top secret," Davet replied. "A most wonderful piece of luck."

"From your spy in Baghdad?" Zarqawi asked.

"A devoted agent," Juba answered, "dedicated life and limb to the Jihad."

"God is great!" Zarqawi smiled.

"Yes, brother," Umarov said, "God is great!"

Sweat oozed into the corners of Jack Valentine's eyes, burning them as he crouched in the blackness of a storm culvert, near a spot along the Euphrates called Alaleya, squinting into the hot Iraqi night. He blinked, reacting to the sting, and with his knuckle, wiped clear the trickles, smearing the black-over-brown camouflage tiger stripes surrounding his eyes and lined down his cheeks.

The four-foot-diameter water chute, where Jack hid, ran beneath a desolate stretch of Highway 19, the hardtop main roadway on the east side of the Euphrates River that ran from Hit through Haqlaniyah north to Barwana and Haditha. He and his seven painted devils had hunted without success since they left the rocky hillock where they had eaten their supper. Now they searched the farmlands and road area as they moved along the river, eyes open for likely suspects to bring home alive for interrogation.

As they came nearer to the river and its fertile valley, with farms scattered one after another, up and down both sides of its length, they anticipated that their luck might change. More people, more potential. Likewise, more risk. Especially if they triggered the local dog population to start barking.

If dogs began barking, they would have to head back east, out into the desert, and wait for them to go quiet. Then move north to another area, where the neighborhood alert system had not sent the bad guys back in their holes.

They worked toward the night's objective and morning extraction point, the train tracks and bridge over the Euphrates, southeast of Haqlaniyah, and west of where the railway crossed ASR Phoenix on the east side of the river. Jack hoped to present something more to Black Bart Roberts than empty hands and ghost stories, at the very least a few worthwhile skulls. But so far the patrol offered no prospects, and he badly wanted a live prisoner singing about the latest enemy happenings in the hoods around Haditha and those areas south, along the river where al-Qaeda and its allies seemed forever fruitful.

Peering from the dark hole with his night-vision optics, Jack focused on the slow-moving, ghostlike figures of his men drifting across the open ground, on the east side of the road, ahead of him. One after another, they moved swiftly and silently.

The two teams of MARSOC operators that slipped across the open terrain ahead of the gunny, cloaked by the moonless night, had broken into their two-man teams, working in parallel, as they had planned, searching for bombers and gunmen as they zigzagged northward.

With his last man now passing a point marked by three plate-sized flat rocks piled together by the first four-man team out, making a small, discreet pyramid, indicating the distance he had traveled from the culvert during his initial five-minute interval, Jack Valentine pressed the stem of his fat, black wristwatch, lighting the green luminance of its face, showing him the time. He estimated that he had three full hours of good darkness left before the moon would rise. A risen moon always caused the fish to stop biting and al-Qaeda gunmen to go into hiding. "Plenty of time to get set before that happens," he thought.

Bronco Starr and Jaws had made the initial departures, always-impatient Corporal Cortez first and, after five minutes, Jaws came across. Cochise Quinlan then followed the first pair. Jack had teamed with Cochise since they both shot the same zero.

On this mission, in addition to his support gun, Jaws took along an M82A3 SASR, Special Applications Scoped Rifle: a .50 caliber sniper rifle fed by a ten-round box magazine, designed and built by big-bore-gun guru Ronnie Barrett at his shop in Murfreesboro, Tennessee. Because of the two-thousand-meter distance that the SASR could fire its 660-grain bullets, and the tremendous power that it carried from muzzle to impact, Jack's snipers had come to call the big gun's round, Whispering Death. The Hajis never heard it coming before it took one of them out with devastating force. All an enemy would ever see was the red spray of blood in the air and the scattered remains where his suddenly dead cohort had previously stood.

With its wide variety of .50 caliber ammunition, ranging from incendiary rounds to Raufoss penetrators and depleted-uranium-tipped projectiles, the Barrett .50 could shoot through walls, cars, buses, engine blocks, and buildings. Qaeda could run, but they couldn't hide. And like Jaws liked to say, "If they run, they just die tired."

As he watched Corporal Gomez disappear into a dip that provided the first team a slight defilade for concealment, Jack eased himself out of the big storm pipe and gave one last look up and down Highway 19 above him.

Just as Gunny Valentine put his head up to look down the roadway toward Hit, he heard the sounds of fast-moving engines and noticed the silhouettes of two vans stirring a cloud of dust as they raced toward him with their lights turned off. Quickly, he put the night-vision scope to his eye to get a better look, and immediately knew these Hajis were an IED or sabotage team, most likely moderately armed but carrying a sizeable cache of explosives.

Bronco Starr heard the sound of the two vans' engines, then spotted the vehicles. He had just taken his place next to Jaws, when he drew bead on them through his scope.

Cortez gripped his sniper rifle with his right hand, finger next to the trigger, and wrapped his left arm under his grip, taking aim, loaded and ready. Jaws hurried to off-load his backpack and unstrap the SASR.

Since Sergeant Quinlan lay in the open, easily seen by the Hajis if he moved, when he heard the two vans approaching, he stopped crawling and lay flat on his stomach, his rifle tucked by his face. Calmly, the sniper slipped out of his backpack, tucked it at his side, and unrolled a camouflage cover that he kept stashed for occasions like this. He had made it like his Ghillie suit, decorated in frayed-out brown-and-tan-burlap strips. Quickly, he got into firing position with his rifle aimed toward the oncoming traffic, and covered up.

When Cochise Quinlan slipped beneath the sheet, he virtually disappeared. Even if someone looked right at him from the roadway with an infrared scope or other night optic, he would remain invisible, as long as he didn't move.

Carefully, Cochise snuggled into his rifle and took aim at the roadway above the culvert where Gunny Valentine had frozen in place, and waited for the two unlighted, speeding vehicles to come within range.

"They slowing down?" Bronco whispered to Alex Gomez as he focused his night-vision spotting scope on the lead van.

Jaws said nothing but sighted through the illuminated optics of the Schmidt and Bender scope mounted on the rail atop his .50 caliber rifle, trying to settle the crosshairs on the driver of the first vehicle. As he twisted the telescopic sight's zoom ring back from twelve to six power, giving him a wider and steadier field of view, the two vans slowed, then stopped.

The corporal from South Central LA took his eye from the gunsight and looked at his partner, whose mouth had dropped open in reaction to what he saw, and under his breath said, "Oh shit."

"Oh shit!" Jack Valentine shouted in his mind as he heard the two vans halt directly above his head. When he heard four doors slam almost simultaneously, and the sound of heavy footsteps crunch toward him on the road, he drew his Lippard 1911A2, .45 caliber, Close Quarters Battle Pistol. With it held next to his face, a 950-feet-per-second plus-performance hardball round locked in the chamber and the hammer cocked to the rear, the gunny hoped that he would not have to use it.

All too quickly, the gunny realized the four insurgents who had gotten out of the vans had no clue about his team's presence. The al-Qaeda quartet laughed and played grab ass as they chattered at each other in Arabic and began dragging what sounded like heavy metal containers from the back of the vehicles.

"No shit," Jack whispered on his intercom to Cotton Martin. "A storm culvert's a good place to pack full of high explosives. In two shakes, they'll be in here with me."

"Sit tight and cover up," Cotton came back. "We're set up. You just say when."

"Roger that," Jack whispered.

Locked in place with his back to the roadway, crouched just inside the culvert, but hearing these four turds shooting the breeze with such nonchalance, laughing and talking as they worked, the gunny leaned his head back and tilted his eyes upward to try to catch a glimpse of the men and get an idea of what they were doing.

Just as he looked upward, one of the Haji bombers stepped to the edge of the road, straddling the storm culvert, and began pissing, directly above Gunny Valentine.

"Is he taking a leak on the gunny?" Bronco whispered on the intercom, and muffled his laugh in his sleeve.

"Better be pissed off than pissed on, and right now, I think Gunny's both." Cotton Martin laughed and moved his night-vision spotting scope to an al-Qaeda insurgent carrying a large satchel that the staff sergeant guessed was odds-on stuffed tight with explosive detonators and probably C4 bricks to set off the main charges in the fifty-five-gallon steel drums.

"Jaws, you got the guy with the big sack?" the staff sergeant asked on the covered net intercom.

"Roger," Jaws said. "Crosshairs on him. Say when."

"Fire," Cotton replied.

With urine and mud splattering in his face, Jack Valentine squeezed off his first shot straight up, sending his high-velocity .45 caliber round directly into the pissing man's crotch. With the shot, a second Qaeda leaped into the ditch, and before he could blink, the gunny blew him off his feet.

As he killed the second man, Gunny Valentine rolled into the culvert for cover.

At the sound of the two rapid shots, Jaws squeezed the trigger of the Barrett and sent 660 grains of screaming death straight into the explosive-stuffed bag and the man who had his arms wrapped around it, trying to run.

As the .50 caliber round from Alex Gomez's rifle blew apart the man with the satchel, it set off a chain reaction of deafening explosions.

Orange flames boiled into black clouds of smoke as the gasoline in the two vans ignited and lighted the darkness for a hundred yards surrounding the wreckage. The echoing thunder from the explosions and the fire that now leaped fifty feet into the night sky drew attention from every farmhouse window within miles on both sides of the river.

With metal debris and vehicle parts tumbling from above and bouncing across the ground, Gunny Valentine held tight inside the shelter of the culvert. Then, with the last loud clank of truck parts hitting the ground, Jack grabbed his rifle and dashed straight down the shallow wash where his men had crawled, and nearly fell over Cochise Quinlan as he ran past him.

Seeing his shooting partner hotfooting it away from the remnants of the two burning vans, Sergeant Quinlan shouldered his pack, snatched his camouflage net in one hand and his rifle in the other, and followed the gunny.

"What now, boss?" Cotton said with a smile, as the gunny flopped on the ground next to him and looked back at the gasoline-fed flames that boiled high in the night sky.

"Score four." Jack grinned, blowing out a deep breath. "That son of a bitch pissed right over my head! You see that shit?"

"Looked like you put a hardball straight up his tailpipe for it." Bronco laughed.

"First time I ever seen a guy get his head blown off shot up the ass," Jaws said as he tied his Barrett back on his pack. "Might be a good idea if we put a move on this motherfucker, though. That weenie roast on the road will draw a crowd sure as shit."

"Hopefully, it will take them a while to figure out what happened, and we can be long gone," the gunny answered, then looked into the darkness where they needed to travel. "Maybe by then we can get regrouped on up north. Maybe find us a prisoner to snatch. Totally fucked up this area."

"Strange way to start a hunt," Cotton said, "but on the plus side, we did light up four."

"I ain't complaining. We ain't the ones lying scattered up there like roadkill," Sergeant Quinlan said as he departed into the night, leading the way.

After Liberty Cruz had checked into her Green Zone contractor and press corps hotel efficiency apartment, one of four similar rooms assigned to her and her team by the State Department facilities officer, she headed downstairs to meet her crew in the all-ranks service club for a late dinner and a few rounds of whatever flavor beer they served. For the simple advantage of having freedom of movement and less close scrutiny, and against the wishes of the embassy security officer, she and the team had turned down the white trailers with blast-proof roofs and reinforced walls, located within the compound gates, an old Saddam Hussein palace converted to the US embassy, Baghdad.

Construction on a new embassy facility had recently begun on the more than one hundred acres of the US compound grounds, overlooking the banks of the Tigris River. At the end of the day, the new embassy would cost taxpayers more than $600 million atop the $150 million already spent establishing the current US embassy, Baghdad. With cranes raised high in the air, the construction site made the growing structures a noticeable part of the city skyline and a hard-to-miss target. Liberty didn't want to be sleeping close to that bomb magnet, either.

Even dressed in military-style tan 5.11 cargo pants and matching blouse, sleeves rolled up and buttons open over a black T-shirt, and a black baseball cap with no markings, her long black hair tied in a bun and tucked under the cap, Liberty Cruz still stopped traffic. When she stepped through the zigzag entrance of the service club, hoping to not draw attention, all dozen or so late-night patrons, an all-male crowd, locked eyes on her.

Pointless now to try keeping a low profile, the long cool woman from the FBI took off her baseball cap, shook loose her hair, so that it fell around her shoulders, and beamed a big smile at the gawking crowd of horny men.

"Hello, boys," she called out in her best Mae West imitation. "I'm so glad you could see me."

Everyone hooted and laughed, including the FBI tactical team waiting for her.

Amidst the cheers, she sashayed across the room to where her three-man crew sat, grinning ear to ear.

The whole place sent up more cheers and whistles as she sat down.

Before she or her men could say another word, a pitcher

of Amstel beer slid across the table in front of her, along with five clean glasses. A good-looking blond-haired man with a well-trimmed moustache had brought them.

"Aren't you the bold one?" she said to the stranger.

"I never got anywhere just watching," he said, and extended his hand to all four at the table. "Chris Gray, CIA Operations. I believe you're the FBI team from DC I heard landed this evening?"

"No kept secrets in Baghdad, I see," Liberty said, shaking Gray's hand. "Should we make introductions, or do you already know our names?"

"I have them." Gray smiled, finishing the round of handshakes. "Jason Kendrick and I go back a ways. He gave me a heads-up. Asked me to assist on the down low, anywhere you needed. Keep a back door open and all."

Liberty smiled. "And where do you and Jason go back?"

Gray put his forearm on the table so that they could see his Marine Corps tattoo.

"It's like a Mafia family." Gray smiled back.

"Oh, don't I know. Once a Marine, always a Marine," Liberty said, and nodded at her team, the three of them Marines, too.

"Yes, I know," Gray said, and began pouring beer. "Semper Fi, brothers. You too, sister. Even though you're like an illegitimate stepchild to us Marines."

Liberty smirked at him and drew grins from her crew.

A tired and disgruntled waiter came to the table, impatiently tapping his notepad to take the orders.

"What's good?" Liberty asked him.

"Nothing here, but it's all safe to eat. You won't get

sick from it," he said in a strong Brooklyn accent. "Probably the shepherd's pie's your best bet. If you like Irish. I pretty much live on it and Mulligan stew."

The four new people all raised their eyebrows, fully expecting to hear an Iraqi accent to go with the waiter's dark hair, complexion, and need for a shave.

"You're American?" Liberty asked.

The waiter nodded. "I run the place. Name's Kelly. That's my twin brother Henry behind the bar, and my younger brother Jim does the cooking out back. We got a subcontract from Kellogg, Brown and Root. Seemed like a good idea at the time."

"Regrets?" she asked.

"We're making good money but hating life," Kelly said.

Liberty searched the table. "I don't see a menu."

"Behind the bar." Kelly pointed with his pencil.

After looking at the short list of mostly soup, stew, and potpie, she said, "No chicken breasts or fish fillets?"

Chris Gray laughed, then stopped himself.

Kelly smiled and shook his head. "Like I said, lady. What you eat here is safe. We make sure the meat is fresh and untainted. Vegetables likewise. Everything kept clean and cold until we cook it. Unfortunately, if we went to adding chicken or fish, we run some risks. Beef just costs too much to offer. We'd love to serve hamburgers, but keeping it in supply is hit-and-miss. Once in a while, we get some beef chuck and make stew. We're at the mercy of what KBR puts in the pipeline. For some reason we have an abundance of lamb, so we make it work. Our mom gave us some of her good home-cooked Irish recipes. We do our best, and don't hear complaints. And nobody gets sick. We run a clean, safe place."

Liberty eyed her crew and got nods back. "Looks like shepherd's pie all around."

"You too, Chris?" Kelly said, glancing down at the CIA operator.

"Yeah, why not," Gray said.

When Kelly had left, Liberty looked at Chris Gray for a long time, watching him get uncomfortable.

"What?" he finally said.

"Tell me more about your association with my boss," she answered. "I don't see how you and Jason could have served in the Marine Corps together. You're so much younger."

"Not that young," he answered. "I served in Second Force Recon in the Gulf War, back in '91, first time we came over here. Did four years, graduated college, came back to the Marine Corps as a lieutenant but got lured off by the CIA. My partner in crime here, another Marine, former captain and EA-6B Prowler pilot named Speedy Espinoza, recruited me."

"And Jason Kendrick?" Liberty asked.

"New York, just after the Gulf War," Gray said. "I finished out my tour there working on an intelligence mission with Jason and Jim Kallstrom. Also did some ninja training with their tactical agents. We roped down onto rooftops in the Bronx from black helicopters in the middle of the night. Counterterrorist and hostage-rescue stuff."

Liberty laughed. "Oh, I've heard a lot of stories about Jason's life in New York with that bunch."

"Some of the best people who ever walked this earth, in my opinion," Chris Gray said. "When I worked with them, both Kallstrom and Kendrick were legends."

"I agree!" Liberty said. "They still are legends."

Just then, Kelly brought a tray with large bowls of shepherd's pie stacked on it. Each shepherd's pie had a golden crust baked on top of it.

"Wow!" Special Agent Bob Hartley exclaimed. "I hope it tastes as good as it looks."

"We try," Kelly said, setting out the meals.

Hartley was the senior agent on Liberty's team. The other two agents were Casey Runyan and Clifford Towler, both of them junior to Liberty. Though Hartley was senior, he and his men had the single mission of supporting Liberty Cruz.

Hartley dug into his pie as soon as Kelly had slid it across the table to him. Likewise, Towler and Runyan plowed into their bowls, forks blazing. The aroma of the lamb, potatoes, onions, and carrots in thick brown gravy, with just the right amount of spice, filled the air.

Kelly set down a basket filled with fresh-baked Irish soda bread, warm from the oven, and a bowl of butter with it. Then he watched the people react to the food.

Liberty put her spoon through the crust as Chris Gray watched, then took a cautious bite.

"Wow!" she exclaimed, and looked at Kelly, who was all smiles. "I thought you said nothing here was good."

"Compared to the way my mother cooks, it's not good at all," Kelly said, smiling. "Yet, it is like I said. Nobody complains."

"This is delicious!" Liberty said.

"I live on it, like anyone else working here with half a brain," Gray said. "Irish home cooking. Hard to beat."

Kelly brought a fresh pitcher of beer and left while the five customers inhaled their dinner.

As they scraped the bottoms of their bowls, Liberty looked at Chris Gray once again.

"Now what?" he said.

"I have a friend who was in Second Force Recon about the time you said you were there," she said. "He also went to the Gulf War with Second Force Recon. You wouldn't happen to know Jack Valentine?"

"Oh yeah." Gray laughed. "As lance corporals we were hooch mates. Then Elmore Snow grabbed him for that corral of snake eaters that he runs. I never saw him again until this week. We're involved in a battalion operation with one-five out in the Denver Area of Operations. Speedy and I will be working with Jack and his MARSOC crew, on the intelligence side of the house. Small world."

"Has Jack already gone?" Liberty asked. "I was hoping to surprise him. He's someone special to me."

"I have no idea if he's left yet, but you'd better hurry if you want to catch him. Otherwise, I expect you won't see him for two weeks or so," Chris said, then sighed with a smile. "Someone special, huh?"

Liberty smiled back, her eyes saying everything.

"Now I'm envious of that worthless bastard." Gray laughed.

"You don't happen to know Cesare Alosi?" Bob Hartley interrupted, moving the discussion to business.

"I know of him." Gray nodded back to the agent. "Never met him, though. He cut a deal with my boss yesterday and got a crew of his security operators assigned to support our intelligence mission. I didn't object because they're three of Elmore Snow's old guys from back in the drug-interdiction-program days. Guy named Hacksaw in charge. You know him?"

"Hacksaw Gillespie?" Liberty asked.

"Yeah, that's him," Gray said. "He has a gold grill that puts most rappers to shame."

"Oh yes. I heard Jack tell many unflattering tales about him," Liberty said.

"How about Kermit and Habu?" Gray asked.

"Them, too." Liberty smiled. "Jack speaks highly of all of them. Anyone Elmore Snow has under his command, you don't need to worry about."

"Yeah, probably so," Gray said. "These boys seemed pretty dependable. Rough around the edges, but a cut way above any other security contractors I see wandering around these parts."

"How much did Mr. Kendrick share with you about my operation?" Liberty asked in a low voice so no one could hear beyond the table.

"No more than I needed to know, and that's the way I want it," Gray said. "I know you're on something all cloak-and-dagger, very hush-hush and shush-shush. Jason asked me to watch your back, should any security contractors or other hinky sportsmen come sniffing your trail. And my secret-agent stash of gee-whiz double-oh-seven stuff, and anything else among my resources you need are yours for the asking. You've got an open ticket, no questions."

Liberty smiled. "Thanks. And thanks for not asking to know more about our operation."

"Some kind of administrative assessment?" Gray smiled.

"That's the story, an admin audit." Liberty shrugged.

"Works for me," Gray said. "These jamokes will buy it without a blink. Guys like your friend Alosi might be a different story. He's a little too crafty for his own good, and he's hooked up with all sorts of people I don't like. His boss, Victor Malone, and a couple of French dudes that get around just a little too easy in a country that's supposed to be in the midst of a bloody war."

"What do you mean, my friend?" Liberty asked, suspicious of how Chris Gray had phrased it.

"Your picture sits on Cesare's desk, all framed and looking like you're more than mere acquaintances," the CIA operator answered.

"I thought you said you had never met Alosi," Liberty fired back, a little hot. She had started liking Chris, and this misstep in what he knew and didn't know put her off.

"I've never met the guy," Gray answered. "I never said I haven't been in his office. Like I said, he's a snake. And I apologize if he's your friend, but that doesn't change his status as a reptile."

"Oh, I'm no friend!" Liberty huffed. "I met him at a party at the Washingtonian Hotel in DC a while back. He seemed nice at first glance. Then I got to know him. He is definitely a snake."

"So, I guess Alosi has a few toys in the attic when it comes to women and relationships?" Gray commented.

"I'd say he has a lot of toys in the attic, and in a lot of other departments, too," Liberty said.

"I guess we'll keep this conversation just among us girls then," Gray said, looking around at the crew.

"Good idea." Bob Hartley nodded.

"Do a lot of contractors frequent this club?" Liberty said, sizing up the crowd.

"Naw," Gray said. "This bunch here is mostly State Department housekeeping guys. A couple in here work in the security office. Once in a while, a security contractor or two, like Hacksaw and his team, they'll come here for the cooking and good beer. For the most part, the hard-core mercenary types head up the International Zone to a little hideout called the Baghdad Country Club. Sex, imported hard liquor, Iraqi moonshine, if that's your bag, and every kind of nose candy and steroid you want. British guy that runs it, former SAS officer, seems a good sort, but a lot of stuff that gets exchanged in the surrounding gardens, I won't hang on him. It's the sorry clientele."

"We'd like to go to this Baghdad Country Club," Liberty told Gray.

Chris eyeballed Casey Runyan, then Clifford Towler, and finished with Bob Hartley. They all gave him a nod.

"It's not a place for a pretty girl like you to come through the door playing Mae West," Gray cautioned Liberty. "Gunplay is not unusual, and those animals lying in that den have teeth. They kill people for breakfast. You go in there; you'd better be well-heeled. And I don't mean the spiky ones on your feet that go with your evening gown."

"Can you set it up?" Liberty asked, impatient.

"Sure," Gray answered, still not liking it.

"Chris," Liberty said, firmness in her voice. "I'm a third-degree black belt, and an expert with a rifle and a pistol. I finished first in sniper school and SERE school both. I can handle myself."

"Oh, I know all about you," Chris said. "These guys are all experts at that shit, too. That's why they got hired to come over here and kill people. After a while, the killing becomes second nature. Like blinking your eyes. Way too many of these guys get jazzed on heavy steroids and stay high on meth and cocaine. Hell, they go drink vodka just to calm down. I don't care if you're Batman and Robin, you go in that cage with these animals, you could easily end up dead for just farting too loud. Or not loud enough."

"We'll keep that in mind," Bob Hartley said.

Jack Valentine checked his watch. Two thirty in the morning.

After the big blowup, the eight Marines had pushed hard and fast to the east, disappearing in the desert. Then they double-timed it north several miles. Far enough to feel confident that sleepers in the farms along the Euphrates River had not heard the explosions nor seen the fire.

The eight Marines spread out into their planned intervals of two-man teams and began moving westward, back toward the river and the rural population that lived along its banks.

Bronco and Jaws had taken position on the south end of the line with Cochise and Jack just up two hundred yards from them. Alex loved the Barrett SASR, so he had it out instead of his Vigilance .338 Lapua Magnum to support Jesse with the .338 magnum caliber M40A3 bolt-action sniper rifle.

"Before you go to shooting that big motherfucker, you make sure I got behind you, bro," Bronco Starr griped at his buddy. "That last shot you took, when you blew those motherfuckers up, dusted my ass. I got so much shit up my snot locker, I'll be digging out adobe bricks for a week."

"You talk too much, Hombre," Jaws said, and lay behind his rifle's scope. As he looked through it, he thought he picked up movement by a farmhouse in the bottomland by the river. "I think I saw something."

"Let me set up the night scope and take a look," Cortez said, hurrying to assemble the spotting scope with night-vision optics. "And before you shoot any motherfuckers, I want the video camera rolling. So keep your finger out of that trigger guard until I get set."

"Hurry the fuck up," Jaws said. "We got somebody in the kitchen. I saw a light go on and off."

Jack saw the light go on and off, and put his rifle on the farmhouse, too.

"No shooting until I give you a cleared to fire," Jack said, watching the man slip out the back door of his house. "He could be just some farmer with a case of the midnight shits. We need to see weapons. And if we could capture the bastard, that would be best."

"Whatever," Jaws grumbled.

Bronco had the digital video recorder set on the spotting-scope lens, and watched through a monitor while he lay back into his A3 sniper rifle.

As he watched the green shadows on the monitor, Jesse wrinkled his nose. "What's that guy doing? Is that a donkey?"

"Burro," Jaws said.

"They got burros in Mexico, dude," Cortez came back. "Fucking Iraq has donkeys and asses, asshole."

"Same motherfucking thing, you shitwad," Jaws snapped.

"Okay," Bronco said. "But what's he doing with it? You think he might be fixing to load it up with explosives and go plant a bomb?"

"Very possible," Jack answered on the intercom.

"Maybe I need to go ahead and shoot him," Jaws added.

"He's sure as shit tying that donkey to the fence rail, like he's going to put a pack saddle on it," Cochise Quinlan chimed in, watching through his night-vision spotting scope.

The farmer hung a feed box on the fence under the donkey and poured some grain in it. Then he walked back into the barn and carried out a wooden box about a foot tall and a foot and a half long and a foot wide.

"What's he got in that box? Explosives maybe?" Jaws said. "How about I take the shot, Gunny."

"If he's al-Qaeda, I want to try and get him alive," Jack said. Then asked Martin, "Cotton, you hearing this?"

"Roger that," the staff sergeant answered. "We're already in movement. Me, Sage, Petey, and Chico can slip in and surprise him. You guys keep him in your gunsights."

"Sounds like a plan," Jack said. "Just don't get yourselves blown up."

"Fuck," Jaws retorted, looking over at Bronco Starr.

"If we have to shoot him, you can shoot him, Alex," Jack said.

Jaws smiled, going back on his rifle scope. "That'll work."

Bronco looked close at the little green rectangular picture on the palm-size monitor and recorder connected by digital cable to the night-vision spotting scope.

"He set that box behind the donkey," Cortez said.

"Maybe he's going to stand on it," Jaws added.

"Why would he stand on it?" Bronco asked.

"Watch and find out," Jaws said, and began chuckling.

Jesse Cortez looked through the lens of his sniper-rifle scope, then looked closer at the green screen on the small monitor and video recorder.

The farmer looked over both shoulders and stepped up on the box behind the donkey. Then he let down his baggy pants and pulled up his shirt. His overly large penis got everyone's attention.

"Dude," Jaws said. "That guy's got a donkey dick."

"Good for him," Jack said, laughing.

"Dude! He's fucking that donkey!" Bronco said.

"No shit, Sherlock." Jaws laughed.

"You getting that on video, Bronco?" Cochise said.

"Fuckin' A, dude. Recorder rolling," Cortez said. "I'm posting it on YouTube when we get back."

"I didn't hear that," Jack said, then called Cotton Martin and his three snipers. "You and the boys come on back. It's just a farmer out for some late-night romance."

"Roger," the staff sergeant responded. "When we heard Bronco and Jaws chattering, we already made the U-turn."

"Good," Jack said.

"That a girl donkey or a boy donkey?" Bronco asked over the intercom.

"What the fuck difference does it make, ass-wipe," Jaws said.

"I don't know," Bronco said. "Maybe if the guy's like homosexual for donkeys or just regular, you know?"

"Fucking homosexual for donkeys? Are you serious?" Sammy LaSage let go. "The asshole's all fucked up from the get-go, fucking a fucking donkey in the first place. For crying out loud, dude."

"I don't know, but it looks like the donkey's enjoying it," Jack said. "She quit eating and has her upper lip pointed out."

"Gotta be a girl donkey," Bronco said. "A boy donkey wouldn't enjoy that big dick up his ass. Besides, this guy's a Muslim, and he wouldn't fuck a boy donkey. Right?"

"Unless it's a gay donkey," Jaws offered.

The more they discussed it, the more the donkey seemed to enjoy it. She now had her head raised and upper lip fully pointed like camel lips.

"That's one fucked-up freak show," Jack said.

"So, what do you want to do, boss?" Cotton asked.

"Leave the fucker alone," the gunny answered. "He's

probably a pillar of the community. We wouldn't want to upset that balance. Let's move north. We got three hours before daylight, and still no prospects."

"We got four dead motherfucking IED motherfuckers back up the road," Quinlan said on the intercom. "Fuck the prospects. I say we had a very productive night."

_ 9 _

First crack after morning Colors, Liberty Cruz ditty bopped up the company street of MARSOC Detachment, Iraq. She had on her nice-fitting desert-tan 5.11-brand combat pants and a matching cargo blouse that she wore like a jacket, unbuttoned and the sleeves rolled up Marine style. Beneath it, she wore a black Under Armour Tech Tank undershirt, and a set of dog tags on a ball chain dangling from her neck, bouncing over her ample breasts. Laced on her feet, Marine Corps Desert RAT boots, the ones that Jack had bought her.

In a long-drop holster suspended from her black-nylon-web operator's belt and Velcro strapped to the middle of her thigh, gunslinger style, right where her hand naturally fell, the FBI agent carried a flat black Lippard 1911A2 Combat NCO .45 caliber pistol. Another gift from Jack, and she liked it better than if he had spent the $3,500 it cost on jewelry. The .45 was, after all, the best handgun ever made, at any price. It carried an unconditional lifetime guarantee, even against willful abuse. With it, she could hold a six-foot cone of suppression fire on the enemy at six hundred yards and lay down accurate kill shots with it, open sights, at four hundred yards. A set of diamond earrings, for her, had nowhere near the dazzle of her Lippard, nor the firepower. She wore it religiously, and used it well.

White buds hung in both of Liberty's ears, connected to an iPod tucked in a handy pocket on her sports bra. As she walked down the street, she bounced off her toes with each step, keeping time with the music playing in her head from the just-released album *Best of Chris Isaak* and the song "Baby Did a Bad Bad Thing."

The rockabilly blues grind had the long cool woman from the FBI cruising low and happy, going to see her man, and absentmindedly singing with her jams as Smedley Butler came out the headquarters office door, headed to pick up mail. The look of such a fine piece of ass high stepping down his boulevard stopped the boy dead in his tracks.

"Can I help you, ma'am?" Corporal Butler called out.

Liberty never heard a thing and kept on walking.

Smedley ran to her, stopped in front, and took off his Marine-Pattern flop hat. "Can I help you, ma'am?"

Agent Cruz smiled large at the lad, pulled the buds from her ears, and chirped, "Hi there!" She looked at the rank on his desert MARPAT uniform collars, then the name over his right slanted breast pocket. "Corporal Butler."

She smiled more and Ralph Mouth blushed bright red.

"Yes, ma'am." He gulped, blinking, stunned from this tall, golden-skinned, black-haired beauty that looked like she had just stepped off a cloud straight out of Heaven.

"Can you tell me where I can find Gunnery Sergeant

John Arthur Valentine's office?" Liberty said, and put her hand on the young corporal's right biceps as she asked, and gave it a nice squeeze.

Reflexively, Ralph Butler tensed his whole body.

"My! You're like a rock!" Liberty flirted.

"Uh, Gunny Valentine's office is just down there," Smedley stammered, pointing to the operations hooch, feeling like he might pass out at any second. "He's got the big-boss desk right under the massive skull on the black wall. You can't miss it."

"I wouldn't think so. Thank you so much, Corporal Butler," Liberty said. "By the way, I'm FBI Special Agent Melita Cruz, should you need to put that in your duty log."

"Oh, yes, ma'am," Butler said, and immediately put on his hat and snapped a salute. The old adage, when in doubt, salute, kicking in.

"I am so flattered, Corporal Butler," Liberty said, "but I don't rate a salute. I'm like a police officer."

"Yes, ma'am," Smedley said, now rubbing his hand on his trousers leg as if it would clear the mistake.

"Thanks, Corporal Butler. Have yourself a glorious day!" Liberty said, and stepped away, heading to the operations hooch. As she left, she put the buds back in her ears, again bouncing to the rockabilly.

"Ma'am . . ." Smedley called out, the afterthought hitting him. "Gunny's not here! He's out in the Anbar with the rest of the detachment!"

She never heard a word, but kept bopping to Chris Isaak. "Two Hearts" came on the iPod, and it put her in the right mood as she came near the operations-hooch front door. She looked down at the HOG WALLOW–FORWARD sign and smiled. It had all the earmarks of Jack's artistic craftsmanship.

Liberty wanted Jack's surprise of her arrival in Baghdad to be perfect. Seductive and unforgettable. So she stopped outside the door, took off her blouse and her black ball cap, and let her long black hair unfurl over her bare shoulders. Holding her cap and blouse in her left hand, she looked around for anything that might show a reflection, so she could double-check her look, but found nothing. With no glass anywhere, she gave herself a quick up and down, straightened her sports bra and silky black tank top, took hold of the door, and stepped inside.

Cruz looked around and saw only one person in the operations hooch, him seated with his back to her at the big desk under the giant Punisher skull and Templar cross looming on the black wall above him. A flop hat covering his head, he sat humped over, his face about a foot from his computer screen. So Liberty loosened up and began a sexy swagger to him.

Billy Claybaugh rocked back and forth at Valentine's desk with Jack's personal laptop open, showing full screen a photograph that the gunny took on Onslow Beach of Liberty Cruz holding a volleyball. In it she wore a snug little black bikini with gold rings pressed against her bare hips, holding together the tiny patch of cloth in front to the one in back. Similar gold rings held together the small triangular patches of thin, silky black swimsuit material covering what it could of her breasts. That day, a cool breeze had come off the water, raising goose bumps on

Liberty's skin and hardening her nipples. The water beads and sand on her flesh, glistening with her smile had Billy-C living in another land, far, far away.

The unsuspecting visitor eased up a few steps behind the staff sergeant she mistook for her lover, and in her sexiest buttery voice, Liberty breathed out, "Instead of staring at the menu, why don't you just dive into the main course, Marine?"

Staff Sergeant Claybaugh let out a squeal and spun in Jack's swivel chair, his trousers unbuckled and his hand still inside. In that same second, he jumped to his feet and turned his back to Liberty, buckling up.

"Oh fuck," he let out as he turned back around to see the woman in the picture, who had dominated his sex fantasy, now standing three feet from him. Then he glanced back at the desk and slammed the lid of Jack's laptop shut.

For the next several seconds Liberty and Billy-C simply stood eye-locked at each other, awkward and completely speechless. Finally, Liberty cleared her throat and grew more and more angry as she thought more and more about what she had just encountered.

"Where's Jack?" she snapped, at the same time putting on her blouse, buttoning it up, and twisting her hair back into a bun and pinning it.

Billy hung his head, gasping hard. "He deployed evening before last, Liberty. Out in the Anbar. Western part of AO Denver. Won't be back for two weeks."

"Does he know you look at his personal pictures on his computer?" Liberty asked.

"Yes, but he doesn't like it," Billy offered.

"What kind of answer is that? Yes, but he doesn't like it?" Liberty said.

"In case something happens, I got his passwords, lock combinations, all that," Billy explained. "In case something happens to me, Jack's got my passwords and same. Cotton Martin's got both mine and Jack's, and we both have his."

Liberty didn't like hearing anything that suggested that Jack could get killed, and this made her wince.

"Why?" she asked but pretty much knew all the reasons.

"All of us do it, Miz Cruz," Billy said. "Makes sure the family can get into whatever they need to. Don't get locked out. You know. Helps them."

"And lets you little twirps clean up his bullshit so the bereaved family doesn't see all the perverted crap," Liberty let go.

"Well, yeah. That, too," Billy admitted. "But Jack don't have perverted crap on his computer. Maybe some sick shit, like we all do. Combat video, but nothing perverted."

"Oh, people getting blown to shit isn't perverted?" Liberty said, then wished she hadn't.

Billy just looked at her, a bit hurt.

"I get why you have Jack's password," Liberty went on, anger softening. "But he knows you look at his pictures?"

"He don't want me and Cotton looking at them, but we do," Billy said. "Now, we don't read his email or anything like that. We only look at the pictures of you. That's all. And it pisses Jack the fuck off!"

"It pisses me the fuck off, Billy," she added. "I had a better opinion of you than some pervy little nutsack pocket squirrel doing whatever it was you were doing while leering at a picture of me. You were doing what I think you were doing, weren't you Staff Sergeant Claybaugh?"

"I'd rather not say," Billy said as his eyes dropped straight at his toes.

Liberty let out a long breath. "I guess I ought to be flattered that you boys find me attractive. But I'm not!"

"Miz Cruz. Liberty. I'm sorry," Billy offered, and added with a wince. "Do we need to tell Jack about this?"

"Fuck no!" Liberty shot back. Then she sat down on the chair by Jack's desk, and Billy sat down, too. After thinking for a minute, she said, "When Jack checks in, tell him that I dropped by the office and wanted to surprise him. I'll be here in Iraq for a couple of months, working out of the embassy. We'll get together when he gets back."

"Is there anything else? Anything you need?" Billy asked, hoping to make up for lost ground.

"I guess not," Liberty said. She tapped her fingers on the top of Jack's desk and looked around the office. "This Gunny Valentine's idea of office decor?"

"Totally." Billy smiled, like it was a compliment of Jack's good taste. "We got ball caps and vest patches, too. I helped a little designing them."

"This is right up there with that Nazi-looking SS crap you boys had going on at Lejeune," she said.

"Our Scout-Sniper rune?" Billy said, defending it. "We got an arrow pointing north right through the middle of it. Nazis didn't have that. Besides, our SS looks different."

"I gotta go," Liberty said, getting to her feet and snugging on her baseball cap. As she started to leave, she looked back at Claybaugh. "You guys don't have any interactions with these security contractors, do you?"

"No more than we have to," Billy said. "Had a few run-ins. Nothing to write home about. Watched three drugged-out fools burn up an armored Cadillac Escalade a while back. That was entertaining. They're mostly scumbags living too close to the edge. You know, sex, drugs, rock and roll."

"You don't know anything about this hangout of theirs, Baghdad Country Club?" she added.

"Bloody bucket rod-and-gun club, what I hear. Off-limits. But that don't mean some military dudes don't show up there now and then. Mostly TOC-Roaches and Fobbits. You know the dudes that don't venture past the wire at the Tactical Operations Centers and Forward Operating Bases but want to look like they play rough?" Billy said. Then added, "Of course, that's all based from what I hear. I have no firsthand knowledge."

"Of course not. Thanks for the intel, Billy," Liberty said, and headed for the door.

When she got outside, she took out her mobile phone and punched in Chris Gray's number.

He answered, and she started talking.

"Chris," Liberty said. "Take me on a date tonight."

"I had planned to chop out to Hit this afternoon," the CIA operator began. He paused a few seconds, thinking, then added, "Since Speedy's already there, and we got the three contractors out there with him, I suppose I could put it off another day, for a good reason."

"I want you to take me dancing," Liberty said.

"Really? In war-torn Iraq? Let me guess where," Gray said, a sarcastic tone in his voice. "Baghdad Country Club."

"You're so intuitive!" Liberty said with equal sarcasm.

"It's a really bad idea," the CIA operator added.

"My tactical team will chaperone," she said.

"Oh, I see. Just like in ninth grade," Gray said.

"Eighth grade." She laughed.

"We will take separate cars, though, and your three lads will sit at a different table," Gray added. "I at least want it to feel like a date. Plus our cover's better if it looks like it's just us two."

"Of course," Liberty said. "And we'll have fun."

"By all means. Loads and loads." Gray laughed.

Jack Valentine squatted on his haunches in the dirt like an out-of-work tradesman outside a factory fence during the Great Depression. Six of his team squatted in a circle with him at Al Asad Air Base, finishing up paper plates of hot chow and red Kool-Aid "bug juice" they had gotten at the Air Force dining facility. Cotton Martin had hit the can with a copy of *Sports Illustrated* that he had borrowed from the battalion S-3 chief right after Lieutenant Colonel Black Bart Roberts's operational briefing and official launch of Quick Strike Vengeance.

Roberts and his planners had named the operation after Operation Quick Strike the prior year, in honor of the twenty-one Marines, including seven Marine Scout-Snipers and their Navy corpsman, killed outside Haditha.

Jack had mixed feelings about the name. Way too close to home, and perhaps signaling a bad omen.

Everyone among the MARSOC detachment had made the command briefing. Mob Squad had grabbed quick chow and caught a northbound Osprey headed back to Haditha Dam. Sergeant Bobby "Snake" Durant had caught a truck caravan headed north, up ASR Phoenix on the east side of the Euphrates River. He and Ironhead Heyward along with Hot Sauce McIllhenny, Jewfro Clingman, and Hub Biggs would carry out fringe operations, augmenting the Fifth Marines sniper platoon headed by Jack's old friend Gunny Tim Sutherby.

Staff Sergeant Drzewiecki and Sergeant Romyantsev had made themselves at home in the headquarters company with the battalion armorers. They went to work helping the Fifth Marines crew get caught up on broke-gun repairs, a point that Colonel Roberts had brought up in the command briefing, and he had graciously thanked Gunny Valentine and the MARSOC crew for pitching in.

Although he did not bring in prisoners, the colonel had made note of the IED team that Jack's crew took out and the big hole left in the highway up the east side of the river. That came right after thanking Jack for his help, and concluded with, "Better to be pissed off than pissed on."

Gunny Valentine grew tired of hearing it but politely laughed and took a bow for the colonel, nonetheless. The politic thing to do, rather than flipping him the finger.

"You boys look like a sorry lot," First Sergeant Alvin

Barkley said as he ambled up to the circle of snipers. He adjusted his big knife as he squatted by Jack.

"Still carrying that pig sticker," Jack said, shaking hands with him. "How's life been since I last saw you, Al?"

"Good all around," Barkley said. "Had I known you headed up the MARSOC detachment, I would have given you a nod hello when I dropped off the op plan the other day."

"No sweat, GI," Jack said. "How's Iceman and the Mob Squad working out for you?"

"It's just business." The first sergeant laughed.

Jack laughed, hearing the line. "Oh yeah. I've heard that a time or two from them. What'd they do?"

"Took out a baker's dozen Hajis laying in an ambush ahead of one of my rifle squads," Barkley said. "First throw out of the hat, Pizza Man and another fella. Nose?"

"Yeah." Jack chuckled. "Nick the Nose Falzone. That's Corporal Principato's shooting partner."

"So Sal the Pizza Man and Nick the Nose set up a high hide and see these Haji yo-yos setting up the ambush," the first sergeant continued. "They call my squad leader and have him alter his movement and run a flank attack on the insurgent position. As the enemy fighters try to maneuver on the attack, Sal and Nick take out a Haji every time one of them tries to run for it. Those two young corporals killed all fourteen."

"And when you go to compliment them, you get the standard Mob Squad line?" Jack grinned.

"It's just business. Nothing personal," they both said together.

Jack looked a few yards behind First Sergeant Barkley, where a Marine tossed an odd-shaped rubber toy and a dark brindle Belgian Malinois working dog chased after it. The Marine would give the dog commands, and when he executed, he tossed the toy as a reward.

"That yours?" Valentine said, nodding at them.

"Sergeant Padilla and Rattler, doing the Kong," Barkley said. "Yeah, I commandeered them from the MP company down at Camp Ramadi. Wasting away down there. That dog's real handy on a roadblock, or clearing houses. Notice the titanium teeth?"

"Yeah!" Jack said. "I did notice a sparkle in that dog's smile. That's quite the look."

"He shreds tin cans," Alvin said. "You should see it."

"Wouldn't want that big brute after me," Jack said.

"I almost feel sorry for the Hajis when Padilla sics old Rattler on them." Barkley chuckled. "Don't say 'Hot Sauce' around him. That's his attack cue."

"I've got a sniper named Hot Sauce," Jack said.

"Disaster waiting to happen," Barkley said, and thought a moment.

"Fallujah One," he went on. "I guess that's the last time we sat on our heels together and shot the shit in the dirt. Nasty-ass place. Your boy, Corporal Place, hiding a week in that trash pile, cutting off a section of the city from enemy movement. He stacked bodies like cordwood in the streets. Took ammo off machine gun belts to keep working."

"Took out a carload of Hajis with AKs trying to run the blockade. Two weeks' time he killed thirty-two enemy fighters. Got the Silver Star medal," Jack said. "Well earned."

"We finally got that shit pile cleaned out in Fallujah Two six months later," Barkley said. "That's when I gutted me a second Haji with my Bowie knife. Not as spectacular as Afghanistan, but no less a close call. Gun jammed and all."

"I recall it." Jack nodded. "Legendary piece of work, my friend."

"Fallujah. That's when the Hajis started calling you, what was it? Ghost of Anbar?" Alvin said.

"Ash'abah al-Anbar," Jack said.

"Right." Barkley smiled. "What was it, two thousand enemy dead at the end of it, all told?"

"Something like it. I thought more. Us hunting Zarqawi," Jack added. "A real zombie land."

"That rat bastard's smart-ass mouth," Barkley said. "I hear he's up here somewhere."

"We've had a standing mission to find and kill the motherfucker," Jack said.

"Good luck with that," Alvin said. "He's downright elusive. One asshole says he's up by Mosul. Another one says Ramadi and Fallujah. Now, we got some raghead goat fucker saying he saw Zarqawi at an al-Qaeda pow-wow out east of Haditha."

"My bet, out west of Haditha," Jack said.

"I guess you can find out. From what I read in the op plan, you're headed that way?" Barkley said.

"When Colonel Roberts drafted things up, he asked me where I thought we might find Zarqawi," Jack said. "I told him on the opposite side of the river from the main body of the operation. If we sweep the east side, he'll go on the west side. And vice versa."

"Cheating motherfucker, we'll hit both sides. See what he does," the first sergeant said, and spit in the dirt.

"Zarqawi might not even be in Iraq," Jack said. "One of the intel wizards who's supposed to know this shit says Zarqawi likely operates in and out of Syria. Him being Palestinian, he's got lots of cousins out there."

Jack squinted his eyes and looked again. In the distance, toward the landing area, through a boiling mirage, he watched a gigantic human being ambling toward them.

"I think that's about the biggest Marine I've ever seen," Jack commented, and pointed toward the man.

Barkley looked over his shoulder.

"My staff sergeant, who's still in the shitter," Jack went on, then with an interrupting thought, looked at Cochise Quinlan, who had stretched out on the dirt. "Sergeant Quinlan, come to think of it, you might check on Cotton."

Then he looked back at First Sergeant Barkley. "Like I said, my staff sergeant, Cotton Martin, stands six-foot-six, but that dude's got to be pushing seven feet."

"Staff Sergeant Marcellus Jupiter," Alvin Barkley said.

"No shit?" Jack said. "Like Marcus Claudius Marcellus, the Consul of Rome? One of the greatest military leaders to ever live?"

"Shit, I guess so," Barkley said. "I wouldn't have a clue. You're always full of oddball information."

"I got my bachelor of arts degree in humanities," Jack said. "Art, history, government, languages, philosophy. All that nonessential school-teacher-type bullshit."

"Hey, a college degree's a college degree, dude," Barkley said. "I've done good to get my associate degree in business."

"Better than most Marine knuckleheads," Jack commented.

"With that BA, why aren't you an officer?" Alvin asked. "That or running for Congress."

Both Marines laughed.

"I did put in for warrant officer," Jack said. "Selection board should announce the list in a few weeks."

"I thought they wanted younger guys than you and me," Barkley said. "You know, like closer to ten years in service than pushing twenty."

"They do," Jack said. "Colonel Snow has nagged me for the past five or six years to get it done, he says, before it's too late. You think anyone in their right mind would pick an outlaw with my reputation to put on the gentleman's green suit and lipstick lieutenant bars?"

Barkley laughed. "You never know. Some of the guys on that board are gunners and generals. Those old crusty dudes tend to like a little outlaw in a guy. They just might pick you. Best wipe your feet and wash your face. That tiger-stripe recon war paint won't let you in the officers' club."

"Fuck!" Jack said, looking up at Staff Sergeant Marcellus Jupiter towering over him. "This dude's even bigger up close. Like Shaquille O'Neal in MARPAT brown."

The massive dark green Marine didn't smile. He'd heard the jokes before, especially the Shaq comparisons. In fact, he did greatly favor the NBA All-Star now playing for the Miami Heat.

"I thought there was like a height limit in the Marine Corps," Jack said. "Something like six-foot-seven, because Cotton, my staff sergeant, said he just slipped under the wire at six-six."

"Read the regs, Marine Corps Order 6110," Staff Sergeant Jupiter spoke up, before First Sergeant Barkley could say anything. "The height-weight chart stops at eighty inches tall. The order itself does not specify a limit. It says that height and weight must fit the appropriate ratio and body mass index, and present a positive appearance in uniform. I have nearly zero body fat, and I max the physical fitness test. Gunny, my personal appearance ratios are just fine."

"You got that down pat, staff sergeant." Jack laughed, and Barkley just grinned.

"Every new officer I run into quizzes me on the appearance regulations," Jupiter said. "I stay well versed, Gunny. A guy big as me? It's survival."

"Don't I know it," Cotton Martin said, walking up to the big man and shaking his hand.

Cochise Quinlan squatted in the dirt and looked up at the Shaq look-alike.

"Fuck, you're big!" the sergeant said without thinking.

"So they tell me," Jupiter responded.

"Staff Sergeant Jupiter is a machine gunner in my company," Barkley said.

"That makes sense," Jaws said, getting to his feet after snoozing, and lifting his Barrett .50 sniper rifle. "Big guys get big guns."

"Got big dicks, too," Bronco said, standing up and chiming in.

Sammy LaSage, Petey Preston, and Randy Powell got to their feet, too, seeing the team about ready to leave.

Jaws looked at Bronco Starr. "And sawed-off little fuckers like you got stumps."

"But thick stumps," Bronco came back, laughing. "Length don't matter, it's the girth that brings on the moans."

Marcellus Jupiter had enough of it and gave both Bronco and Jaws a look that would sour milk.

"First Sergeant," he said, "I came over to let you know that we'll be launching as soon as we finish loading the Osprey. Pilot asked me to convey to the MARSOC team that he will take a couple of vectors along the river, per your instructions, drop low, and travel west to your tactical point of departure, drop you off, vector south, then east, across the river, then move north to the dam. Probably a good idea to beat feet over to the LZ."

"Since my reinforced rifle company's operating units will probably be your closest friendly forces, up by the dam," the first sergeant added, "we'll be the ones come running if you hit the shit. I've got your rally points, reporting points, targets, and patrol route on my maps."

"Cool," Jack said, falling in along the left side of Alvin Barkley. "You guys really are tight. Glad to have you covering our six. Hopefully, we won't need you, except when maybe we haul ass at the end of the hunt."

"That's the way we want it," Barkley said.

Bronco and Jaws walked behind Jack and the first sergeant. Preston, Powell, Quinlan, and Sage followed them. Staff Sergeant Jupiter led the way, ahead of the group, with Cotton Martin alongside him, talking basketball.

"Those dudes are big as fuck," Bronco said.

"Maybe to you," Jaws said.

"I bet Jupiter's dick's so big he scares horses," Bronco

said, and laughed. "Probably carries two machine guns. One in each pocket."

"Shut the fuck up," Jaws grumbled.

"Alex," Cortez complained. "You're one unhappy soul. Did your mother hate you as a child? Make you stay inside and practice the accordion while the other boys played baseball? Did your daddy piss in your Post Toasties?"

"Keep it up, you little shit," Gomez said, his big .50 caliber rifle riding over his shoulder while a semiautomatic Vigilance .338 Lapua Magnum support rifle rocked atop his hundred-pound pack, stuffed mostly full of ammo.

Each of the other Marine Scout-Snipers carried similar kits on their backs, loaded for a long-range patrol, facing a virtually unknown enemy, miles from any friendly support or rescue. While all four two-man teams used the Marine Corps M40A3 sniper rifle as their primary bolt guns, they carried models chambered to .338 Lapua Magnum, so that it shot the same ammo as the highly accurate EDM-Vigilance semiautomatic support gun that also doubled as a backup sniper rifle.

Besides the Barrett and its .50 caliber sniper rounds that Jaws carried, everyone fired the hard-hitting, far-reaching .338 Lapua Magnum as this mission's primary round. Additionally, Jack and Cotton each carried an M249 light machine gun or SAW, along with as many canisters of 5.56-millimeter Black Hills seventy-seven-grain ammo for them as they and their sniper-team partners could haul in their packs, along with ample supplies of primary sniper rounds.

"And you'll do what, Jaws?" Bronco Starr sassed.

"I'll stuff your short ass under a rock and stand on it."

Jaws laughed. Then he put his hand on his partner's shoulder and gave him a gentle push.

Cochise Quinlan nudged his fellow sergeant, Sammy LaSage, as he smiled and shook his head at the two clowns ahead of them.

"Ever notice how a sniper team that's worked together a good while acts like an old married couple?" he asked Sage.

"Good teams do, sure," LaSage agreed.

"You're fucking gay," Chico Powell crowed from behind. "Both you guys. Fruity-Loopy as three-dollar bills."

Sage lifted his leg and farted. "Ah, that felt so good. I wish I could do more."

"Dude!" Petey said, catching a full gust of the sour sausage gas.

"That's why they call those dogs I ate last night the Five Fingers of Death." Sergeant LaSage laughed.

Cochise Quinlan sniffed the air and caught a whiff. "Gunny V," he called ahead, "you remember Blewis and Coop?"

"Right," Jack answered. "Lewis and Cooper? Great sniper team."

"Yeah, Blewis and Coop. Didn't one of them like to eat Smoky Franks and chili dogs with lots of onions and shit like Sage does?" Cochise said.

"I don't have a clue," Jack answered. "I know that Coop loves fishing. But chili dogs and smoky franks? Cochise, I think you've got them, and me, mixed up with someone who might give a shit."

Jaws laughed. "Right on, Gunny V. Burned your ass, didn't he, Clarence."

"Fuck you, Jaws," Quinlan said, as they walked under the wing of the V-22 tiltrotor aircraft.

As his Marines climbed aboard, Jack stopped and gave a last look at the First Battalion, Fifth Marine Regiment's air base setup. All the comforts of home. For the next two weeks, he and his boys would live in the dirt and take turns sleeping on rocks in four-hour shifts.

Deep in his gut, he had a bad feeling. Couldn't shake it. Nagging, nagging, nagging.

"Let me ask you something," Jack said to Alvin Barkley, who waited to board the plane with him.

"Sure," the first sergeant said.

"We hit that IED team a day before anyone should have known that heavy military traffic would be coming up MSR Bronze or ASR Phoenix," Valentine said. "In the briefing, EOD said they took out two more on MSR Bronze, near the same spot on the other side of the river."

Alvin thought and nodded. "Yeah, that's right."

"Doesn't that bother you?" Jack asked.

"Now that you mention it." Alvin nodded, his brow wrinkled in thought, and he bit his lip. "Like they got word we'd come up the road."

"Could have been that they had eyes on the battalion and saw the movement ahead of the operation," Jack rationalized, trying hard to explain it.

"Yeah, but both sides of the river? Up there in the same place? From where we set up, we could have gone anywhere. No. That didn't tip them. Total crapshoot, unless they knew our plans," Barkley said.

"Does seem like I recall in the logistics section of the

operations plan, we've got big convoys pushing up both supply routes on day one," Jack said.

Barkley added, "I can see the MSR, frequent military traffic. But they knew to set bombs over there, on that side of the river, in that culvert, where normally it's mostly civilian traffic, when there's traffic at all. Somebody told them, or they got a copy of the op plan."

"That bothers me," Jack said.

"Me, too," Barkley agreed.

"Lucky we got 'em," Jack said, getting on the Osprey.

"Real lucky," Alvin Barkley said, following him.

When Chris Gray knocked on the door of Liberty Cruz's apartment, he checked his breath. She must have been standing right behind it, because when she opened up the CIA operator still had his hand cupped in front of his mouth.

Liberty laughed. "Checking just in case, huh?"

"Old habits." Gray shrugged.

"Wishful thinking. However, I do appreciate clean breath." Liberty smiled and gave him a peck on the cheek.

"Well!" Gray brightened.

"Come on, cowboy," the good-looking woman dressed for casual war laughed, and took off, strutting her stuff down the hallway. "Let's have fun."

Chris Gray couldn't help but admire the show of swaying long hair, shapely boobs, and swinging hips as he walked alongside her.

"Work, work, work. Work, work, work. Work, work, work. Hello boys, have a good night's rest? I missed you . . ." Gray said, mimicking Mel Brooks's lecherous character from *Blazing Saddles*, Governor William J. Lepetomane.

Liberty flipped him the bird as she turned the corner and started down the stairwell.

"Oh, you know that old movie," Gray said, jogging the steps with her, enjoying the view and not hiding it.

She smiled at Gray as she quickstepped. "Jack's favorite Western. His most repeated line? 'Mongo straight.'"

Chris Gray laughed. "I'll keep that one in mind."

Half an hour later, the two agents walked through the outer garden gates that hid the popular mercenary and media nightspot from the street, and went to the front door of the blue-stucco building with the big picture window that had the blue neon sign lit in it, BAGHDAD COUNTRY CLUB.

Casey Runyan, Cliff Towler, and Bob Hartley had arrived long ago, and had already made a circle of friends, betting on how many bull's-eyes Towler could hit on the dart board before missing. An old curved-top, neon-lit Wurlitzer jukebox filled with several hundred 45-rpm records blared out Little Eva singing "Loco Motion."

Blue light from the neon in the front window mixed with the red, blue, green, and yellow Christmas lights wrapping the shelves above the bar. Recessed orange lights hidden in deep sockets illuminated the mirror behind the bar, where all sorts of liquor stood on mirror-covered stair-step shelves, and gave the place that cheap dive look. All they needed was a handful of Eleventh Avenue hookers, and they'd have the total package, Liberty thought as she sized up the joint.

"Meet your expectations?" Chris Gray asked the lady as he led her to a table that an anxious Iraqi barkeep hurriedly wiped clean for them.

Every eye in the place caught sight of the striking woman and followed her as she and her CIA escort sat down.

"Your usual, Chris?" their waiter asked in excellent English with a British lilt to it.

"Sure thing, Ajax," Gray answered. "James in tonight?"

"He's gone on a jaunt with Ahmed. Down to the coast at Basrah," Ajax replied.

"Supplies?" Chris asked.

Ajax smiled and shrugged his shoulders.

Gray looked at Liberty. "What's your poison?"

"You got Jack Daniel's?" she asked the waiter.

"Yes, ma'am," Ajax said. "Maker's Mark if you prefer good Kentucky bourbon."

"Sure. Make it a double. Straight up. Neat," she said.

Gray looked at Ajax, and the Iraqi barkeep smiled back.

Then Liberty reached inside the front slanted pocket of her 5.11 blouse and took out a four-tube leather case of cigars. She drew out a panatela, took a scissors-like gold clipper from a sheath on the side of the pack, and snipped off the tip.

With the cigar clenched lightly in her teeth, Liberty smiled at the CIA man and his friend Ajax, both of them watching her with great fascination.

She asked Chris as she lit up, "Care for a smoke, cowboy?"

"Don't mind if I do, ma'am," Gray drawled out, taking a cigar from her case as she offered it, and clipped it with her nippers. He looked at the brown band on it and raised his eyebrows as he drew the roll of tobacco under his nose and sniffed. "*Monte Cristo Especiales Numero Dos.* Made in Havana. Not your run-of-the-mill Dominican replica, but the genuine article."

"My father, a defense lawyer in El Paso, has an old client in Juarez who keeps me supplied," she explained, as the fragrance of her smoke spread in the barroom and drew more looks and a few wise-ass comments about coming rain because pigs had sticks in their mouths. Her disruption not only saw Cliff Towler miss the bull's-eye, but he missed the dartboard entirely.

The laughs and the losing bet brought attention back to the game. Forking over a handful of bills, Bob Hartley then enticed their circle of gamblers into a game of Five-Oh-One, the FBI tactical trio's intention all along.

Cliff Towler had served as a Marine liaison captain with the British Royal Marines, and had learned darts the hard way. After having his clock cleaned along with his wallet, the American sharpened his skills on Five-Oh-One and Three-Oh-One, and learned the bull's-eye betting hustle from the British Marines as well.

Suddenly, a woman's wail after a hard thud and the crash of breaking glass drew everyone's attention to the far corner. Ray-Dean Blevins stood over Francoise after having given her a hard whack to the chops. She tried to crawl away, but he put the toe of his boot in her ass, delivering a cruel blow.

Liberty came straight up out of her seat, blazing, and before anyone else could do a thing, she had laid the inside of her forearm, the point just below her elbow, flat across Ray-Dean Blevins's face.

Blood sprayed as his nose exploded, and Cooder-with-a-D tumbled backwards into the booth where he and Francoise had sat.

When Chris Gray got there, Agent Cruz had already helped the French reporter to her feet.

Instead of a thank-you, however, enraged Francoise pulled her arm from Liberty's grasp and let loose a slur of French words, first at Ray-Dean Blevins, then at the woman who had come to her aid.

"You Americans!" Francoise screamed. "All alike! You think you can solve the problems of the world, but all you do is destroy and kill. You come to this country, so big and proud of yourselves. You know all the answers, don't you? Putting in your puppet regime. Always getting your way. You care nothing for the people you murder. Go to hell, American fuckers! All of you!"

With that, Francoise spit a glob of blood on the floor and tromped across the bar and out the door in her click-clack glittery shoes and snatch-hugging tight pants.

Liberty blinked at Chris Gray and her three men, who now stood with him among a crowd of mercenary contractors from around the planet. Then she looked down at Ray-Dean Blevins, slumped back in his seat with a wad of napkins crammed in his nose.

"Only a weak-assed coward of a man hits a woman!" she fired at Cooder-with-a-D.

Blevins just blinked.

The angry woman then pushed her way through the

wall of men, parting them like Moses, and went back to her table, where she picked up her whiskey and threw it into the back of her throat. She looked at the barkeep, and roared, "Ajax, bring me a triple!"

Every man in the place, except for Ray-Dean Blevins, began clapping.

Chris Gray sat back down and relit Liberty's cigar, then his own.

"I think that went remarkably well, don't you?" He smiled. "We certainly have their attention now."

"I'm sorry," Liberty said. "I lost it when that asshole kicked that poor woman. Slugging her wasn't bad enough, he had to put his boot in her ass."

"That new best friend you just made over there, nursing his broken nose, is Cesare Alosi's gofer boy, Ray-Dean Blevins," Gray said. "Grade A slime, and capable of anything, including cold-blooded murder. You'll need to watch your back with him now. That elbow smash on the hooter you gave him, in front of all these admirers? He'll definitely want revenge."

"Am I supposed to be scared?" Liberty asked, as Ajax delivered her a glass and a full bottle of Maker's Mark.

"Not scared, but you do need to be cautious," the bartender said before Gray could respond. Then he added, "Everything tonight's on the house. I can't count the times that scumbag has beat that poor woman. No one has ever stepped in until you did. Nobody wants trouble with him. Like most cowards, he'll never face you head-on but will shoot you in the back."

Liberty gave Blevins another glance as he sat in his booth alone, napkins stuffed in his nose, glaring at her.

"I'll keep that in mind, Ajax," she said.

"Welcome to my world, Miz Cruz." Gray smiled.

She looked at Chris. "What's the story on the woman?"

"Francoise Theuriau, so her passport reads," Gray began. "She works freelance out of the London bureau of the *Massachusetts Democrat and Morning News*, a progressive left fish wrapper in Boston. As you'd expect, they're critical of the war, Congress, the president, American Constitutionalism, and democracy in general.

"We ran deep background on her because she still has my terrorism antennas vibrating. She hails from Marseilles, but her French passport home address is in Avignon, where she also went to college at *Université d'Avignon*."

"Oh, he speaks French," Liberty said, and smiled at the way Chris rolled out the university's name with its French pronunciation.

"I did the Rosetta Stone course that State Department puts out," Gray said.

"So did Jack," Liberty said. "He's quite good with languages. He grew up speaking Spanish, from his mother, but then learned Castellón and Andalusian dialects, because of her classical Spanish background. That branched into Portuguese and French. Italian is next on his list, because I speak Italian and want to live in Milan someday, after I make my millions," she finished with a little laugh.

"Now I feel inadequate," Gray said. "How about Japanese? Jack Valentine master that, too?"

"I think he has the barroom pickup lines down pat, from his time in Okinawa," Liberty said.

"Yeah, me, too," Gray said. "Okinawa, Philippines, and South Korea gave me, like most Marines, a good foundation of international barroom and taxi language skills."

"I get so tickled when you Marines go into your bargirl routines." Liberty laughed. "You should hear Jack. What is it? Hello, GI. You buy me drink? Payday come, I love you big-time. Come on, I so horny. We go boom-boom."

"I love you long time. Make boom-boom all night. You want short time, that okay, too." Gray laughed. "Take me stateside, I love you plenty. Buy me Honda. Get me green card. Take me big PX."

"Oh, yeah." She laughed. "Do they really say all that silly crap?"

"That and more. We don't just make this shit up." The CIA operator smiled. "I think it's an acquired art form. Young privates and lance corporals, hitting the rock for the first time? They call them *chiisai sakana*, little fish. A sergeant or a young lieutenant, they're *ookii sakana*, big fish. The bar girls reel them in and drag them to the altar, *tak'san* and *sukoshi* alike."

"Jack calls it going native," Liberty said.

"I have friends who have good marriages to some of these girls," Gray said. "But most cases, it's hookers doing what hookers do."

"So this French reporter?" Liberty asked. "She doesn't strike me as a hooker trying for a brass ring."

Gray nodded. "Naw, just a slut reporter. But then, the great spy Mata Hari was a slut, too. Francoise definitely makes my intel nose itch."

"You put her under surveillance?" Cruz said.

"Sparingly and very carefully," Gray said. "Don't forget, she is a news reporter, a member of the press corps, covering the war for an American newspaper. Even if the rag unabashedly hates everything about the government and what we're doing. We get caught watching her, we're screwed."

"Politics." Liberty sighed. Then she looked around the room. It had settled back into darts and drinking. Ray-Dean Blevins had joined two other American contractors at a different booth. She nodded in their direction. "And how about those guys?"

"Frank-n-Stein," Gray said.

"Which one is that?" Cruz said, trying to not get caught watching them.

"Blevins's security team," Chris said. "Gary Frank. Squirrely guy sitting next to Ray-Dean. Former Marine Corps public-affairs sergeant. Malone-Leyva's press-relations man and a bed wetter. He's got a reputation of not holding his liquor and it running down his leg when he gets excited."

"And the guy across the table I suppose is something or other Stein?" Liberty asked, way ahead of Gray.

"You got it," Chris answered. "Fred Stein. Former Army Ranger, hard-stripe sergeant. He's a real special case of steroids and earwax. Obviously hated his father and loved his mother. Really loved his mother."

Liberty laughed, then added, "The opposite of the blonde with daddy issues?"

"Freddie likes them old and no teeth," Chris said. "I

have several stories of him in the villages, committing rape of women well past childbearing years."

"Disgusting!" Liberty shuddered.

"You want to dredge up the dirt on Alosi and Malone-Leyva, these are your boys," Gray said. "I've got a notebook full of interesting reading on that crew."

"I'd like to see it," she said. "Seriously."

"Sure," Gray said. "I'll drop it by your place."

"And nobody does anything about them?" Cruz asked.

"They're outside most jurisdictions, as you well know, and the law that matters doesn't care about the likes of them. Bad politics to the hand that feeds," Gray said.

"You should be in the FBI," Liberty said. "Jason Kendrick would put you to work, knowing you and all."

"My job." Gray smiled. "I don't worry about jurisdictions or Miranda rights. I get to kill the low-life motherfuckers."

Liberty lifted her glass. "Here's to that."

Ray-Dean Blevins's nose had already swollen double in size, and both nostrils had shut. When he talked, it came out muted and whiny. He held a cold beer bottle against his throbbing head as Freddie Stein and Gary Frank kept looking at Liberty Cruz sitting and laughing with the CIA operator.

"That's her, dude," Gary said, and snapped his glance away as the woman looked at him. "Definitely the bitch in the picture."

"You think Cesare knows she's in town?" Fred Stein asked Ray-Dean.

Blevins looked at her and sneered. "Fuck Alosi, and fuck her."

"I'd like to," Stein came back. "Her that is. Not Cesare. I don't swing that direction."

"You suck dick and take it up the ass, Freddie. Admit it," Gary Frank said, trying to sound tough to his buddies.

"I'll show you how to suck dick when I feed you mine," Ray-Dean said. "I'll hold your hands while Freddie jams his cock balls-deep up your ass."

"And you'll love it." Stein smirked.

"I'm not queer, you guys!" Gary Frank sang back.

"You're always talking about sucking dick and butt fucking," Ray-Dean said.

"Guilty dogs bark loudest," Freddie piled on.

"Dude," Ray-Dean said. "Gay's okay. Hell, you might come in handy. I'm sure as shit not getting any pussy off Francoise anytime soon."

"What was that shit about, anyway?" Stein asked. "You thumping her ass?"

"I had some stuff at my place. Bonus material I copped over at MARSOC headquarters, to win me some points with Cesare. You know, worth a few coins?" Ray-Dean explained. "Filthy cunt had pictures of my shit on her cell phone. I sat here and started thumbing through her crap, and up comes pictures of my shit. Fucking cunt! She must have took them when I was sleeping."

"She's working for Alosi, I bet. Getting it from you for free so he doesn't have to pony up," Gary Frank said.

Ray-Dean nodded. "My guess, too. That's Alosi's style. He's tight with her. I don't trust that motherfucker whatsoever."

"And we're sure that's Cesare's girlfriend over there?"

Gary Frank said, unsure with this as he was with everything.

"Fuckin' A, dude," Freddie said. "You said it yourself. That's her. Same bitch in the fucking picture he has sitting on his desk."

"Fuckin' A," Ray-Dean said. "Now I owe the cunt big-time. Break my nose with a sucker punch? Shit, I never saw it coming. Humiliate me like that? She's fucking dead."

Freddie, Gary, and Ray-Dean all nodded as they looked at Liberty Cruz and Chris Gray.

"You picking up on those three yo-yos' body language?" Bob Hartley mumbled to Cliff Towler and Casey Runyan, leaning against the bar, drinking Amstel Light in bottles.

"She really shouldn't have gotten involved with that fool. Let someone else be the hero," Towler said, and the other two FBI tactical operators nodded, agreeing.

"I don't fault her for much," Bob Hartley said. "She's a solid operator, but her one failing is that big heart tied right to her hot button. Emotional knee-jerking, even if it's justified, will get us killed."

"Fucking funny, though," Casey said. "The way she laid out that piece of shit. One shot, and bang! He's done!"

"What do you suppose those fools are plotting?" Hartley asked his team, and took another look at the whiskey level of the quart bottle with the red-wax-covered top sitting on the table between Liberty Cruz and Chris Gray.

"We need to clear her out," Towler said.

"Yeah," Hartley said. "She's sucked down a good third

of that quart bottle by herself. I don't think Gray took more than one or two hits. But the lady can put it away. I'm getting buzzed just watching."

"What if we start something with those three assholes?" Runyan suggested. "A little delay action to give her a chance to disappear."

"Probably not a bad idea," Bob agreed. "Keep those shitheads pinned down. They get out of here ahead of us, I'm betting they'll try an ambush before she can get two blocks down the street."

"That or follow her to the apartment and do something after she's turned in," Towler said.

"I wish she hadn't fucked around with that asshole." Hartley sighed.

"Yeah, that's what I said when my wife divorced me last year and married her boss." Casey Runyan chuckled.

"Alright, guys," Hartley said. "I'll play the drunk. You come fetch me out of trouble. If we're lucky, we won't kill them."

Liberty noticed that Bob Hartley had turned his baseball cap sideways as he came staggering toward them.

"You okay?" she said, as he ran into her table and knocked over the bottle of whiskey.

Chris Gray saw the wink and took Liberty's hand.

"Why don't we get out of here?" he suggested.

"You sure?" Liberty asked, not seeing Hartley motioning his eyes to the door but Gray getting the message.

"I'm sure," Chris said. "We need to go. Right now."

Then Liberty saw Bob Hartley making a beeline toward the booth where Ray-Dean and his boys sat, sucking on Heinekens.

"Right," she said, and got to her feet.

As the couple hurried out the Baghdad Country Club's front door, the long cool woman from the FBI could hear the commotion. Tables crashed. Glass broke. Two blasts of a shotgun. Then quiet.

Liberty turned, started to go back, worried about her boys, but she stopped as Ajax came out the door with a smoking Mossberg pump-action folding-stock alley sweeper in his hands. He looked around, making sure more trouble wasn't headed his way, and saw Liberty.

"It's okay!" he said, giving her an assuring smile. "We're all friends again."

When the Osprey had dropped Jack Valentine and his seven Marines far in the desert, west of the Euphrates, the team immediately pushed even farther west, following a dusty ravine to a rocky outcrop that gave them good cover until dark. They rested there and filled their stomachs until night, taking turns on security, with two men always on lookout.

With moonrise six hours away, blackest darkness shrouded them well as they pushed north, staying parallel with the Euphrates River's direction. Full combat kits strapped on their backs, loaded heavy with extra water and ammunition, testing their endurance, the eight men route-stepped ten miles into their hunting territory, west of Haditha and Haqlaniyah, and north of a dry wadi called Ashwa. To the south of them, at a camp called Wolf, a battery of American artillery with a list of on-call targets sat available for Jack and his Marines if they needed it.

Twenty miles northeast, First Sergeant Alvin Barkley kept a sergeant in his radio section tuned to Jack's team's frequency, paying attention to their reporting points, as they came in, and making sure the operations gunny had the eight-man MARSOC team's positions and activities updated on his map. At the same time, the S2 recorded all the reconnaissance sightings that Jack and his Marines reported. Should shit hit the fan, a react team stood ready to respond and hopefully extract the eight Scout-Snipers intact if they could get to them in time.

Jack's plan of going deep into the western desert and angling through the back door into their hunting grounds, on foot from the southwest, far from even remote populations, had effectively eliminated nearly every chance of barking dogs giving them away or watching eyes detecting them. No helicopters. No trucks. No Ospreys. No noise or flashing lights. They had slipped silently into the heart of these badlands as ghosts.

A golden moon rose over the eastern horizon as Jack and his boys settled into a line of hides that extended more than two miles along a rocky ridge above a dry rill that ran southeast, passing beneath MSR Bronze, where it ended at a bend on the Euphrates between Haqlaniyah and Haditha. Meandering parallel to this hardly noticeable rise of rocks and hard earth that followed the dry stream, a dirt road, crisscrossing other desert trails, likewise extended toward Syria, coming from the southeast, where it converged with other goat tracks networking the farms on the west side of the ancient Euphrates River, and extending from where the Marines lay to the northwest desert's oblivion.

If Jack and the boys had to make a run for it, they planned to double-time down the dry streambed that gave them good footing and overhead cover while a straight shot to MSR Bronze and the river, some miles away. It would be a haul, running with a hundred pounds of gear on each man's back, but it would have to do. Hopefully, Alvin Barkley and his reaction force would get to them in time if the proverbial shit hit the fan.

Scratched out of this cruel earth west of the Euphrates, all the way to Syria, over the centuries, little outposts had emerged at spots in the desert where sporadic and random deep wellsprings tapped into underground water and sustained life in this otherwise-lifeless place. For generations, dirt-poor families survived on these dirty plots, caretaking the precious water sources. Caravans going to and from Babylon to Damascus and the seaports of Beirut and Tyre or up to Homs and Aleppo, over thousands of years, camped at these waypoints, where a caretaker and his family provided refreshment and rest to weary travelers.

With the war, many of these families abandoned their poor existence, leaving their ancestral lands and precious water to belligerent strangers. Because of their far-flung obscurity, the outposts gave Abu Omar Bakr al-Nasser and his Jamaat Ansar al-Sunnah fighters excellent refuge in the midst of their surrounding American and Iraqi enemy forces. They lived much like the Apache and Comanche war bands did 150 years ago, fighting Texas Rangers, pioneer militias, and United States Cavalry in the American West.

The old graybeard Abu Omar had set up a number of

garrison outposts in these deserted farms. In them he bunkered caches of arms and ammunition, far off the beaten path, and quartered in them his eclectic army of migrant jihadists who drifted here from all parts of the world.

Typically, these old places had large and often complex underground storage chambers and living quarters, dug and tunneled over the centuries. What might look above-ground like just a simple, stone-and-adobe enclave with a few meager animal shelters could in truth have a great area of underground facilities. They provided Abu Omar's fighters a place of temperate comfort even in the harshest winters and most broiling summers.

Such was the outpost where Abu Omar and Zarqawi had dined a few nights ago, entertaining their war chiefs, and where Giti Sadiq and her Christian sisters, Amira and Miriam, and the Shia Muslim girl kidnapped in Syria, Sabeen, now labored in their slavery. Ironically, Jack Valentine and his crew had put themselves in a good position to see the various traffic routes going to and from this particular hole-in-the-wall enemy garrison.

Because she was Christian, Omar's henchmen had not bothered to bury the body of the young formerly virgin girl, Lina, after Zarqawi had raped and murdered her. They just tossed her corpse in a ditch a hundred yards downwind from the house and barns, where they also dumped other rotting garbage. Now the scavenging rooks and ravens and jackals picked the flesh off her sad bones.

Two miles south of this house and the ditch where the dead girl, Lina, lay rotting, Gunny Valentine and Sergeant

Quinlan made their hide. It sat at the far western end of the MARSOC team's two-mile picket of four hides. If the wind blew just right, Jack and Cochise could catch a faint whiff of the scent of Lina's decaying body. Yet in Iraq, the stench of death lay just about everywhere. To not smell death would get a man's attention.

Bronco Starr and Jaws held a spot five hundred yards down the line, east, from the gunny and Cochise. After a wide gap, in the next hide, Sergeant Sammy LaSage ran the primary sniper gun and Corporal Petey Preston took his turn spotting. Cotton Martin held command at the other end of their line, with Chico Powell taking first turn on their bolt rifle while the staff sergeant manned the team's Vigilance .338 Lapua Magnum semiautomatic support rifle.

Both Cotton and Jack had set up their light machine guns at arm's reach, should the enemy discover their positions and make a run at them. They planned to defend and hold ground, calling in the artillery and the reaction force. However, if the Hajis came at them in large numbers, they would bug out, call artillery on their abandoned positions, and run like hell.

"It's a plan full of holes and what-ifs," Jack had admitted to Black Bart Roberts, who had reluctantly approved the idea. Gunny Valentine had assured him that the worst-case scenario could never happen. He and his Marine Scout-Snipers were just too good to get caught.

The reward, on the other hand, he had told Roberts, was worth the risk. The crisscrossing patchwork of camel trails and the caravan hideaways scattered across the vast badlands could offer his team a target-rich environment, and maybe a high-value kill, the gunny had speculated.

"If I'm the bad guys, this is where I'm disappearing," Jack pitched. "They know we don't have manpower to roll over every rock. And drones and planes don't see everything. Me and my boys can. We'll be fine, sir. Trust me."

_ 10 _

At dawn, Jack took his first shot. A Haji on a Honda.

All night, the sniper teams had heard the sounds of car engines and truck engines and a lot of motorcycle engines. Vehicles moving far to the west of them, going north, then turning east, just beyond the horizon. The dead man with the rifle, riding the motorcycle, represented the net result of all their efforts.

Gunny Valentine had anticipated that with the busy crosshatch of camel trails, roads, and cross-country tracks across their killing zone, the night would have proven much busier. Prime real estate, he thought, given the busy road a mile to their south called T1, a straight shot out of Haqlaniyah westward to the south side of the town of al-Qa'im on the Syrian border, and the even busier MSR Bronze, Iraqi Highway 12, that ran several miles to their east and turned north, running along the Euphrates, also to Qa'im and Syria, entering the town on its north side.

When the Haji on the Honda broke over the horizon, he had blazed across the desert full-out, racing straight across their frontage, a thousand yards out, like a duck in a shooting gallery.

"Nice," Cochise Quinlan said, as Valentine's shot with the .338 Lapua Magnum chambered M40A3 bolt rifle lifted the man off the bike and put him in a series of cartwheels while the motorcycle tumbled end over end like a tin can.

All eight of the snipers had an angle on the man, but the gunny shot first, since the gunman crossed Jack's lane first.

"How do you feel about that shot?" Cotton Martin asked on the intercom.

"Something ain't right, you know?" Jack said.

"Roger that," Martin answered. "Like he's bait."

"Want we should slide out there and check him out?" Bronco asked, wanting to help.

"No," Jack said. "Let him lie. Everyone stay quiet and put your heads on swivels. If this guy is some kind of bait, they'll jiggle the fishing line."

Juba and Hasan lay hidden among rocks on a small rise in the desert, and watched the young volunteer ride the motorcycle as fast as he could make it travel across the empty landscape, racing it eastward. They waited as the rider shrank smaller and smaller, until they could only see the plume of dust behind his bike.

Then came the echoing report of the heavy rifle, a throaty boom that rolled across the desert, telling anyone with the understanding of such things that a sniper had just made a kill. The dust stopped, and they waited, now looking through their American military field glasses, trying to spot movement.

No one had told the young lad that he was bait. An attempt to draw out the snipers, or at least approximate their location. Abu Omar had given the kid from Amman, Jordan, who had ridden his Honda motorcycle overnight to join the jihad of Jamaat Ansar al-Sunnah with so many other enthused young men of late, a canvas dispatch case filled with meaningless papers. He told him to ride as fast as he could to Haqlaniyah, and to cut across country, away from the roads, so that the advancing Americans would not see him.

With a worn-out Russian AK rifle strapped across his back, and one magazine with six rounds of ammunition, Omar sent the boy flying.

"A very important dispatch to our brothers in the south," the old graybeard had told the boy, giving him the traditional hug and kiss on both cheeks. Then cried out as the boy rode away, "*Allahu Akbar*, God is great!"

The boy raised his fist high in resolve as he drove away, his rear tire chewing through the dirt, sending a brown plume skyward.

First he rode south a mile, then turned eastward and twisted the throttle full open, his AK rifle riding sideways across his back and the canvas pouch tied against his chest.

Juba and Hasan watched him make his turn toward the east and waited, watching to locate exactly where along the ridge above the shallow wadi the American snipers hid. The two jihadi snipers had all but given up when Jack finally took the one shot and killed the boy.

"Much farther to the east than we had estimated from their operation plan," Dzhamal Umarov told Khasan Shishani, watching through the field glasses and seeing nothing.

"What shall we do now?" Hasan responded, speaking in their native Chechen dialect of the Nakho-Dagestanian tongue of their Caucasian homeland.

Speaking in their language of birth made both men feel free. Around the Iraqis, as Juba and Hasan, they had to use a pigeon mix of French and Arabic. In Baghdad, as business partners from Avignon, Davet Taché and Jean René Decoux had to speak English with graceful southern French accents.

"The body and the wrecked motorcycle gives us an approximation," Dzhamal explained, pondering the situation. As a skilled sniper, he knew that the Marines would not needlessly expose themselves to kick around and check the pockets of a dead victim. They would wait and see who comes looking for the rider.

He scanned the horizon from his left to his right and pondered some more. Then he looked again at the small rise of the land that followed the dry streambed that extended to the east.

"Do you see, Khasan," Umarov said, pointing at the subtle rise in the landscape. "That little ridge follows the wadi miles and miles to the river. That is where our Marines wait to see who comes to collect the dead."

"May we now go home to Baghdad?" Shishani asked, hopeful. "We are days late on our return."

Dzhamal smiled at his partner, who had stood with him through thick and thin, through the demise of the

Soviet Union, who as a very young man had helped him build a successful business in France.

"We can do no one further good here, and certainly not if we are killed in a senseless battle, wasting a thousand good lives just to rave at our enemy," he said, still smiling. "Yes, it is time we return to Baghdad, or at least back to the Tigris, where people expect to see us."

"When?" Khasan Shishani asked, hopeful.

"We will make our report and go at once," Umarov said. "When Abu Omar and his army stir the bees, their stings will follow with severity. We do not want to be here when the bees swarm. While they fight, and provide a diversion, we will go north with Brother Zarqawi and cross back to Baiji while the enemy busies himself here."

"Dude, it's been two hours," Bronco Starr complained on his MICH helmet's hands-free headset.

"Patience," Jack answered.

"If anyone was coming, they'd have come by now, boss," Cochise piled on. "Seriously. Sometimes you draw a fold hand. No shame in it. We can pack up, move on, draw new cards. What you say?"

"You rolled the dice, Jack. Sometimes you get snake eyes," Cotton agreed. "Not much shaking in these weeds. Maybe we should swing back toward the highway and the river, where more people live. Closer to the operation, maybe they'll stir some business."

"We stick it out, according to the op plan, until nightfall," Jack said. "You heard that traffic running all night until daylight. If we move, I think we need to go in the direction of all that activity."

"True," Cotton said. "Nobody heading to see grandma at four in the morning. So let's move west when it gets dark."

"That's a plan," the gunny said.

"Fuck," Bronco let out with a big breath. "I'm cooked in my own juice. And I need to take a shit. Do you mind?"

"Drop down in the wadi and let fly," Jaws said. "Ain't shit happening but your shit."

"This really sucks, you know?" Bronco added while he slid to the rear and got in the wash, where he could squat.

"Suffer patiently and patiently suffer," Sage said, reminding Bronco of one of their sniper-school ethos.

Bronco moaned, and Jaws laughed.

"Sage," the corporal came back, "that's right up there with one shot, one kill, and the deadliest thing on the battlefield is one well-aimed shot. Give me a break with the Hathcock bumper sticker bullshit. I need to concentrate on cutting this turd."

"Suffer quietly and quietly suffer, Bronco," Jack said.

Walter Gillespie had taken an admin run to Baghdad for Speedy Espinoza, departing on the return flight of the same Osprey that had brought out Chris Gray. The two intelligence field officers had set up shop with the First Battalion, Fifth Marines S2 section, working in concert with them on Operation Quick Strike Vengeance.

Hacksaw, Kermit Alexander, and Cory Webster had

proven themselves valuable and trustworthy to Espinoza in the few days it took to unload the CIA boxes and plug in their computers. They acted like Marines, old Corps Marines. He quickly came to like them.

When Gillespie got to his apartment, a pile of mail and dirty magazines lay on the floor outside his door. He pushed it with his boot toe, then bent over and picked it up.

Before he put the key in his lock, he looked up at the inside top edge of the doorjamb, where he had pressed a little piece of Scotch Magic mending tape. It had broken.

Then he lay flat on the hallway and looked through the narrow space under his door, and used one of the pieces of mail to feel for any sort of wire or triggering device. Nothing else out of place, he slipped his key in the lock and gently turned it, standing at the side of the door.

With his back to the wall, next to the entry, he turned the knob and gave a push.

"No bombs," he said to himself as he went inside, clutching the stack of mail in his hand. He looked at the side table next to the door. Nothing out of place there, so he set down the letters and magazines.

For several minutes, he stood at the entrance and studied every inch of his apartment. Nothing moved. Nothing visibly taken.

"Why would anybody come in here except to steal my shit?" he asked himself.

Still he didn't move. Old habits kicked in. He studied everything more carefully, and thought.

In bad places, Hacksaw knew survival depended on

paying attention to the little things, like the tiny piece of tape he had stuck on the top of the door and doorjamb where no one would notice it, but it would tell him if someone had been inside. No one just opens a door when you're not home without doing something, usually bad.

"What the fuck were they after?" he asked himself, and pulled out his cell phone. He dialed Cory Webster's number.

"Webster," the voice answered.

"Habu," Hacksaw said. "You see those two CIA boys?"

"Yeah. Why?" he said.

"Ask them both if they had any reasons to have someone snoop my apartment," Gillespie said. "And before you ask, study their faces. When you ask, watch how they react and tell me."

"Roger," Habu said. Then turned to the two agents. "Yo, Chris. Speedy."

Both men gave Webster blank looks.

"What?" Gray said, as Hacksaw listened to them.

"Would you have any reason to have people snooping in Walter's apartment?" Webster asked, watching their reactions.

Both men raised their eyebrows, showing expressions of genuine surprise. Then frowns appeared.

"What's going on?" Chris Gray asked, stepping close to Habu. "That Hacksaw on the horn?"

"Yeah," Webster said.

Gray took the phone.

"Walter, what's up?" he asked.

"I'm standing inside my door," he said. "Someone opened up my apartment, obviously to come inside, but

I can't figure out why. Nothing missing. Nothing out of place."

"Maintenance maybe?" Gray suggested.

"They leave a note on the door, and I always know beforehand," Hacksaw said. "If it wasn't you guys, checking out my shit, which wouldn't piss me off at all, you're welcome anytime, then it was some ass-wipe up to no good."

"If they didn't take anything, then what?" Gray said. And thought a moment. "How about leaving something?"

"I'll check around," Hacksaw said.

"Let me know," Gray said, and clicked off the phone.

Walter Gillespie walked to the refrigerator and got a beer. Then he went to his silverware drawer and got the bottle opener. As he looked down at the array of knives, forks, spoons, and other utensils, a small black object in the back of the drawer, jammed behind the knife, fork, spoon, and other crap organizer, caught his eye.

"What the fuck's that?" he said, gulping a swallow of Amstel and taking hold of the thing. When he got it out, he recognized what it was. "A thumb drive? Why would anyone put a thumb drive in my silverware drawer?"

He set down the beer bottle and pulled out the silverware divider. Beneath it he found a copy of one-five's top secret operation plan. The one that Cesare Alosi had secretly made.

"Who the fuck?" Gillespie said, and it didn't take long for him to line up his prime candidates for the villainy. "Alosi and Blevins, those motherfuckers."

"What the fuck do I do?" he then asked himself as he considered the possibilities, and the impossibility of him explaining his innocence.

Just then, his phone rang. Chris Gray.

"Anything?" the CIA agent asked as soon as Hacksaw pushed the green button.

"A little misplaced humor by my boss and his scumbag," Gillespie answered.

"Alosi and Blevins," Gray said.

"Yeah," Hacksaw said.

"Like what?" Gray asked.

"A dead rat in my silverware drawer," Gillespie said.

"They break in for that?" Gray said, not believing it.

Gillespie waited, thinking, wanting to tell him the truth but knowing that the first thing to happen would be him investigated for possible spying, possible treason, definitely violating the National Security Act. Would anyone believe that he had really found the op plan and thumb drive, obviously with more damning evidence on it? More likely his frame-job accusers had their play backed up with more bullshit.

"Hang on a second," Gillespie said. "I got some asshole rattling my door."

He put the phone down, went to the door, and said to no one, "Oh, no, pal. He's got the room down the hall."

It gave him a moment more to think. "Do I trust Gray with the truth? He is a fellow Marine. So is Ray-Dean shit-for-brains." Then he thought about what would happen to people like Jack Valentine and his Marines if he said nothing. How in the hell had Ray-Dean or Alosi or both of the sons of bitches gotten their hands on the top secret plan in the first place? More importantly, what all had they done with it? Who else got copies from them?

"Look, dude," he said to Gray. "I'm real scared. You seem like a stand-up Marine. Speedy, too. I'm going to come clean with you."

"Dead rat in the silverware was creative, but I wasn't buying it," Gray said.

"Really? I thought it was pretty believable," Hacksaw said, a little bit hurt that his goofy excuse didn't wash.

"Alosi and Blevins are killers, not high school sophomores," Gray said.

"Right," Hacksaw said. "They wouldn't do stupid shit like that. They'd set me up to get killed. Or put in prison the rest of my life."

"Exactly," Gray said. "What'd they do?"

"Rat in the silverware drawer turns out to be a copy of the top secret one-five op plan and a thumb drive that has no telling what kind of bullshit on it," Gillespie said, and it felt awfully good to say it. "You need to warn Black Bart immediately. No telling who those assholes shared it with."

"You sure it's Alosi that done it?" Gray asked.

"Who else?" Hacksaw asked. "That slimy waste of skin has wanted my ass from day one. Victor Malone thinks my shit don't stink, so Cesare has his hands tied. This is exactly the kind of crap he pulls to cut off people's nuts, unless he has them murdered."

"Like the Marine in Wisconsin?" Gray said.

"Exactly that one," Hacksaw answered.

Gray looked at Speedy Espinoza, who stood next to

him, listening to the call. "You need to get Black Bart and his counterintelligence people here right now."

Then back on the phone to Hacksaw. "Listen, Walter. I need to make a call to an FBI investigator and send her to your place. Get everything verified."

"That would be Liberty Cruz," Hacksaw said.

Chris Gray hesitated, clearly disturbed. "What would you know about her? What does Alosi know?"

"Alosi knows jack shit," Gillespie said. "I gotta come clean on some more shit, Chris."

"It's getting pretty deep at this point, Hacksaw," Gray said, a little anger getting into his voice.

"What I say to you can't go beyond you. Me and my boys' lives depend on it," Gillespie said.

"Okay," Gray said. "My word."

"Your word as a Marine," Hacksaw said.

"My word as a Marine," the CIA agent said.

"About a year ago, Jason Kendrick approached me in Washington. I had just landed home from my first rotation with Malone-Leyva, started my supervisory training at our DC headquarters, getting to know Cesare Alosi real well. That's when I brought in Kermit and Habu as my team, got Victor Malone to hire them, and guaranteed he'd never regret it.

"Kendrick found me and said he was looking for someone with my credentials to work for the FBI as an inside man at Malone-Leyva. I didn't like the idea because I didn't know better. So, he took me to his office, showed me all the underworld connections with Victor Malone. Granted, I kind of liked Malone, still do, and he definitely liked me. So it was a tough business, me seeing that man's dark side. How people have disappeared who've crossed him. They don't just wind up dead, but literally evaporated. Something to do with hydrochloric acid reducing the body to liquid protein and flushed down the river.

"I told Kendrick that I wanted my boys, Alexander and Webster, brought aboard, and I would do it. We've been over here, this whole tour, reporting back to Kendrick."

Gray smiled. "Jason and I are old friends. I knew he had some people at Malone-Leyva undercover, but I didn't know who. The way Alosi hates you makes sense."

"Right. We don't do his sleazy crap, and that pisses him the fuck off," Hacksaw said. "Ray-Dean Blevins, on the other hand. Totally compromised."

"Your cover may be blown," Gray said, considering what he had just learned. "Alosi wouldn't take a big chance, violating national security, setting you up, just because he doesn't like you."

"My feelings exactly," Hacksaw said. "You can verify everything with my boys."

"They're right here by my side, nodding their heads," Gray said. "What about Liberty Cruz?"

"She doesn't know shit," Gillespie said. "Kendrick may have told her that he had some people here undercover, but I am certain he would not have told even her about us. It's a great risk even your knowing."

"Maybe we need to take a different approach," Gray said. "An open investigation for an NSA violation is likely the thing Alosi wants to see happen. It literally takes you and your team out of play."

"Roger that," Hacksaw said.

"I'll go to Baghdad and discuss this with Liberty,"

Gray said. "Gives me an excuse to take her to dinner again."

"She's Jack Valentine's girl, I guess you know," Gillespie said, looking out for his old friend.

"Painfully aware of it," Gray said.

"You have any ideas about this classified crap hidden under my silverware tray?" Hacksaw asked.

"A couple," Gray said. "I know what I'd like to do."

"What's that?" Walter asked, smiling. "Maybe you're thinking what I'm thinking? Some CIA-type dirty shit? Like, put all this back on Alosi?"

"Be nice," Gray said. "At least bust him up some."

"I got an idea," Hacksaw said.

"Something to do with his stooge, Blevins?" Gray said.

Hacksaw grinned. "His room's just a few doors down. Only question is how to put the spotlight on Cooder so he gets his room tossed by Liberty and the crew."

"I'll work on it," Gray said. "Meanwhile, put the smoking gun someplace Blevins won't find it but the FBI team will. Call me when it's done."

First thing Jack Valentine saw was the rooster tail of dust climbing in the air. Then he saw the blue Toyota pickup truck racing straight at him. As the vehicle got closer, Valentine could see the Haji behind the machine gun, lying over the top of the cab, locked into the headache rack.

"You on the SASR, Jaws?" Jack said on the intercom.

"Roger, boss," Alex Gomez said. "Locked and loaded, crosshairs on the motherfucker with the machine gun."

"Drop it down on the driver," Valentine said. "Everybody else, keep your sights on him but stand by. Jaws will take the shot. You ready, Corporal?"

"Fuckin' A," Jaws responded. "Got a range of fourteen hundred meters and closing straight at us at high speed. Wind is light, quartering left to right at two miles per hour. Aiming down at the wipers and letting him drive into my crosshairs."

"Light him up," Jack said.

The shot hit the windshield a few inches higher than Gomez had planned. It split the driver's head at the top, exploding it from his nose up. The impact of the MK 211 Raufoss round set off its internal high-explosive charge and sent glass and fragments into the two other occupants of the pickup cab. The tungsten-carbide penetrator not only took off the top of the driver's head, but also went through the cab and got the machine gunner square in the crotch.

Jaws's single shot scored four killed. The tumbling truck was merely the aftermath, scattering their bodies across the desert not far from the remains of the Haji on the Honda.

"Fuck!" Bronco exclaimed. "Might as well have hit those fuckers with a 198. Dude, nice shot. You fucked up their shit!"

"That's our job." Jaws grinned. "We fuck shit up!"

"We get back to Lejeune, I'm putting that on a T-shirt." Bronco laughed.

Then, together, they both chimed, "We fuck shit up!"

Jack had stayed on his spotting scope and tuned the focus far in the distance on their left flank. He didn't like what he saw. Not just another rooster tail of dust, but a whole line of them. Headed at them from the side.

"Eyes left, gentlemen," Valentine said. Now he understood how Custer must have felt when he saw the line of Sioux warriors coming over the rise at the Little Bighorn.

"Maybe we should pack our shit and head east," Cotton said, already gathering his kit, getting ready to run.

"Fuck, dude, I'm packed," Bronco Starr said, shouldering his gear.

Jaws was right with him, pack on his back and big gun in his hands. That's when incoming shots began dancing off the sand along the ridge.

Both Scout-Snipers hit the deck and dropped into the dry wadi. Over their heads, the ridge came alive with incoming fire.

"Corporal Butler! Get your ass in here! Now!" Captain Mike Burkehart yelled as loud as his voice could carry.

No answer.

Burkehart stood over the open classified-documents-file safe; the green government logbook open in his hands. He yelled again, "Butler!"

Still no answer.

He slammed the drawer shut hard and went to his desk and picked up the phone, punching in the number for the MARSOC operations boss.

"Staff Sergeant Claybaugh," Billy-C answered.

"Butler there with you?" Burkehart snapped, his words so sharp they could bite the heads off live kittens.

"Yes, sir," Claybaugh answered. "He's watching a training video, sir. Part of his NCO school."

"Put it on pause and both of you get over here, standing tall before I can hang up this phone. That clear?" Burkehart commanded.

"Aye, aye, sir!" the staff sergeant responded.

In thirty-six seconds flat, both Staff Sergeant Billy Claybaugh and Corporal Ralph Butler burst through the front doors of MARSOC Detachment, Iraq Headquarters, Billy-C limping as he ran, his crutches in his hands.

"Sir! Staff Sergeant Claybaugh and Corporal Butler reporting as ordered!" Billy-C said, snapped at attention with Smedley tight at his left side.

The captain got in their faces. "One simple question. The one-five operation plan. Where is it?"

Both Marines looked scared. They didn't have a clue.

"What?" Billy said.

The captain took a deep breath. "Two weeks or so ago, First Sergeant Alvin Barkley personally hand carried our copy of that top secret operation order to this office and put it in my hands. I signed his classified documents logbook and accepted possession for the detachment. I placed that envelope on Colonel Snow's desk.

"Corporal Butler, when you cleared the incoming correspondence and documents from his desk, you should have logged in that operation plan along with the other classified materials. Until that was done, you were under strict orders not to leave this office until all classified materials were secure. Am I correct?"

"Yes, sir, Captain Burkehart," Corporal Butler said, his face dead pale and his heart about to stop.

"Then why can't I find the one-five op plan in our classified files, and an entry in the logbook stating that it was placed in our files?" Burkehart said, steamrolling.

"I have no idea, sir," Butler said. "I logged in everything. I swear, sir. I don't read the stuff, I just log in the documents. Sir, I'm at a complete loss."

"I received a flash message just a few minutes ago, urgent fucking on fire," Burkehart said. He looked at his two dumbfounded Marines, and added, "At ease."

"What happened, sir?" Billy asked, now frightened.

"CIA intelligence reports that the operation plan's security has been compromised. Information from it, if not the entire bloody plan, may have fallen into enemy hands," the captain told the two Marines. "All recipients of the operation plan have been ordered to inventory their classified files and account for all copies of it."

He took a deep breath. "Gentlemen. We have a problem."

"Sir, Jack and the team have a lot bigger problem," Billy said. "Did you read their portion of the operation plan? They're out in the middle of no-man's-land, on patrol with no immediate support. You've got to figure that if the enemy has this plan, they also know all the contingencies and have them addressed."

The captain hung his head. "Keenly aware, Billy. That's why Colonel Roberts has ordered a halt to the operation and a redeployment of forces. More or less they're going to do a little hip shooting, hoping to catch the Hajis trying to catch us."

"But what about Gunny Valentine and the team?" Butler asked.

"Hopefully, he's got our people dispersed and they're getting the word to fall back and regroup, too," Burkehart said. "But back to the burning question. How did that operation order disappear from our hands? Who's been in our office?"

"There was that drop-dead-gorgeous FBI agent looking for Gunny Valentine. Then those three guys from Malone-Leyva," Smedley offered off the top of his head.

"Liberty Cruz, the gunny's better half," Billy-C said. "Very unlikely candidate. Did she even go in the headquarters office?"

Ralph shook his head no.

"Hacksaw Gillespie and those other two guys from Malone-Leyva, Kermit and Habu, they're old friends of Jack's. Marines from the old days," Billy said.

"I know Top Gillespie, and both Kermit Alexander and Cory Webster," Captain Burkehart said. "Back in the old days, when I was a young buck sergeant. They're rough as a cob but straight-arrow. Besides, I was in the office the whole time when they stopped by on their way out to Hit, wanting to see Jack. They're contracted to the CIA. All three hold top secret clearances."

"Then again, sir," Billy offered. "You never know about a guy. Not the first time good guys went bad."

"For a price," the captain added. "Money brings out the evil, that's for sure."

Corporal Butler began searching around like a dog in a round room looking for a corner, like he suddenly had to take a shit.

Captain Burkehart looked at him and gave him a nod to run to the head. Smedley took off, and the captain looked at Billy-C. "Poor kid has like a spastic colon. Gets the drizzles at a drop of a hat. Nerves mostly. Especially bad when he gets excited. He's the guy that can get the shit scared out of him. Literally."

Billy laughed. "Sorry, sir. Smedley's a good Marine, but spastic colon is not something I want by me in a hide."

"That's why he's our admin clerk and supply NCO," Burkehart said. "He wants to be a super trooper so bad he can taste it. I really feel for the guy."

"Yeah," Billy said. "We still let him wear the haircut and suit. Definitely, he's one of ours."

As the captain nodded agreement, Corporal Butler hurried back from the head.

"Sir, I know who stole that operations plan," he said. "I had to take a shit. Like just now. He's a Marine, so I asked him to watch the phone for five minutes. Not even five. He must have taken it. I'm pretty sure he came the same day that you had that big pile on Colonel Snow's desk."

"Marine?" Billy asked.

"Who was it?" Captain Burkehart followed.

"I made an entry in the duty NCO log, when he left," Smedley said, and went to his desk for the ledger. He thumbed through several pages, found it, and smiled. "Ray-Dean Blevins. He works for Malone-Leyva."

Walter Gillespie used a set of picklocks to get in Ray-Dean Blevins's apartment door. He had carried the burglar tools in a zipper case ever since he bought them in Medellín, Colombia, on his last drug-interdiction tour with Elmore Snow, Mutt Ambrose, Kermit, Habu, and Jack Valentine.

The smell of dirty clothes and a filthy, sex-stained bed stopped him for at least two steps.

"We get free maid service. Why doesn't he use it?" Hacksaw said, looking around the efficiency kitchenette hotel room.

He didn't even want to see what went on in the bathroom. The living room that doubled as a bedroom was a disaster, so he went in the kitchen. He smiled as he pulled out the silverware drawer.

"Perfect," he said, as he looked in it and saw the same kind of white-plastic organizer that he had in his own apartment kitchen's utensil drawer.

Walter took the paper copy of the operation plan, which he had carried in the back of his pants waist, under his shirt, and put it beneath the silverware organizer. Then he took the thumb drive, wiped clean of fingerprints, and dropped it in the back left corner of the drawer, exactly like Alosi or Blevins or both of them had hidden it in his apartment.

When he walked out of the flat, and locked the door behind himself, he called Chris Gray.

"It's done," Hacksaw said.

"Good," Gray said. "Too bad we didn't know yesterday."

"Why's that?" Gillespie asked.

"I just heard on the net that Gunny Valentine and his seven Marines got in some serious shit," Gray said. "Heavy fire from three sides."

"Ghost One, Corsair Three. React team notified," one-five's operations chief told Jack Valentine on the crypto secure command and control voice network.

As he said it, Alvin Barkley and a fifty-man strike team already knelt at the edge of their landing zone, waiting for air lift to arrive to take them to the endangered Marines. With them was Jack's Mob Squad. The first sergeant knew he couldn't keep Iceman, Nick the Nose, Pizza Man, and Momo out of the fight. He didn't even try, but called them first. Besides, the four MARSOC Marines had a kitful of Fleet Anti-terrorism Security Team training. They'd be handy.

Sergeant Jorge Padilla and the big brindle Malinois with titanium canines, Rattler, knelt close to First Sergeant Barkley and listened to the voice exchanges coming from the handset on the radio strapped to the communications Marine squatting on the other side of the strike-force leader with the big knife. Next to him, all four members of the Mob Squad listened, too.

With every tick of the second hand on Jack's wristwatch, the fire intensified and focused as the enemy force maneuvered closer to the low ridge over the shallow dry streambed where Valentine and his seven Marines lay.

"Gunny," Cotton called over his intercom. "Them closing on three sides, leaving a door wide open to the east for our retreat means only one thing."

"Copy that," Jack said. "We gotta go that way regardless. Trap or no trap. We move in wide intervals and amp up situational awareness. To our advantage, they'll want us all in the kill zone when they open fire, and we won't do it. Put Petey and Chico on point."

"You copy that? Petey? Chico?" Cotton said.

"Roger, copy all," Corporal Preston answered.

"Roger," Randy Powell said.

"You two hold your position for now," Cotton said. "Sage and I are coming to you with the SAW. You take fire, open up across their front. Move to lateral cover and the rest of us will come on flank with you."

"Good. Thanks," Petey Preston said, his voice jangled with intense nerves.

"Chico, Petey," Jack said. "You can do this. Trust your training. Put those nerves in your locker. You hear me?"

"Roger, Gunny," Petey answered, and took a deep breath.

Jack knew that was almost certainly a death sentence for his two corporals, but he had no choice. Someone had to hit the trap first. He hoped that the two young Scout-Snipers would see the danger area before stepping too deep into it. He hoped that the M249 light machine gun, formerly known as the squad automatic weapon or SAW, would give them the intensive suppression fire they needed to move out of the kill zone and find a covered firing position.

"Cotton, you and Sage hold on to your SAW," Jack said after thinking about it. "We'll huddle up before we run. I'm giving Petey and Chico the other SAW me and Cochise have. I want both machine guns on that end, now that I think about it. One behind the other. Bronco and Jaws? Any cans of five-five-six you're carrying, make sure they get with the two machine guns. You copy?"

"Roger, Guns," Jaws said. "I got four cans in the pack. Bronco has a couple, too."

As Jack looked over the top of the ridge, he saw a line of six or eight Toyota pickup trucks curved from the north side around to the east side, gunmen atop the vehicles firing machine guns. And more trucks behind them. A cloud of dust rose high along the horizon, and curved from north, across the west to the south. At their flanks, Hajis on foot ran a charge a thousand yards out.

"Let's move!" Jack yelled to his team. Then he pushed a button and called out on the command radio.

"Corsair, Ghost One. We gotta bug out now," Jack reported over his hands-free Telex Stinger 700 headset plugged into the Modular Integrated Communications Helmet he wore, a radio-equipped K-pot that all of the MARSOC Marines wore. "Our position not viable! We wait? We're dead. Ghost Team One taking a run for it down the wadi."

A moment of silence. Then Lieutenant Colonel Black Bart Roberts came on the net. "Roger, Ghost One. Corsair Actual here. Deploy to your rally point marked Whiskey Tango Foxtrot. Copy?"

"Roger. Last-resort extraction point." Jack laughed, bullets thudding and blasting through the dirt overhead. "Copy, Whiskey Tango Foxtrot. Departing now."

"Wolf commencing salvos on your position in three mikes," Black Bart said. "Can you be sufficiently clear?"

"Roger, Corsair," Jack said, running hard behind Cochise Quinlan. "Ample time. Three mikes our old position will be overrun. Hajis advancing fast in Toyotas and on foot."

Cotton Martin, Sage, Bronco, Jaws, Petey, and Chico ran ahead at a slower pace, waiting on Cochise, Jack, and the SAW exchange. Jesse and Alex had already passed forward their cans of M249 ammo, in running-relay fashion. Once they had huddled on the move and gotten the guns and ammunition passed off, they would spread again to wide intervals.

"Ghost One, Corsair. Can you give us an enemy estimate?" Black Bart asked.

"All of them!" Jack gasped, running for his life.

Black Bart took Jack's response meaning more enemy than he could count and closing fast in a crescent that wrapped around the eight Marines' north, west, and south flanks. He called the Tenth Marine Regiment's battery commander at Wolf, and ordered him to fire for effect on the MARSOC team's position, and paint the fire in an arc of steel and high explosives from north to south to a half mile west, and at last follow the wadi east a half a mile.

For the next twenty minutes, the gunners from Tenth Marines pounded the ground inside and around the arc a half mile in every direction. The rain of steel killed half the ground soldiers but none of those in the trucks. They managed to fall back before the incoming artillery landed. They joined the force of a thousand gunmen who lay back with their graybeard boss, Abu Omar Bakr al-Nasser, waiting for the barrage to end. Then they would go after the Marines.

Abu Omar and his captains watched the salvos at a safe distance and listened to the Marines' secure command and control voice traffic on four of six captured American radios, lost in action six months ago, which did not have their internal self-destruct codes executed.

The absconded operation order from First Battalion, Fifth Marine Regiment had given them all the discrete frequencies to monitor and stay one step ahead of the Marines. They knew to fall back after they flushed the MARSOC team, and trusted that their duo of ambush teams, equipped with the other two American radios, would intercept the Americans.

Jack Valentine and his seven Marines ran hard, loaded with their heavy packs and rifles. They managed to clear nearly a half mile from where they had lain when the first shell from the one-ninety-eights landed.

Cochise Quinlan glanced back when the first round shook the earth under his feet.

"Shit!" he said, and ran harder because the explosion felt like it had hit right on his heels. "Fuck, I hate being on the receiving end of artillery."

"Don't worry about the shit behind us," Jack gasped, charging hard. "Stay focused up front. Situational awareness, Cochise! Situational awareness!"

"Gunny," Cochise huffed, breathing hard. "I'm so situationally aware right now, I think I might shit my pants. Fuck, I'm scared."

"Me, too, Cochise," Jack said. "Me, too!"

Ray-Dean Blevins felt like shit. Looked it, too, as he and Freddie Stein and Gary Frank took lead on an executive escort from the embassy to the airport. Already, news spread that one-five had suffered a security compromise and had Marines under fire because of it. Bad news spreads fast, and worse news spreads like lightning in a thunderstorm over Florida flatlands.

Marines who now worked for Malone-Leyva talked it up on the company network. That news with the hangover from last night and from his vodka lunch break and a line of meth up the snot locker for dessert had Cooder-with-a-D flying high and mad. He knew that Cesare Alosi had capitalized on his treachery to get a CIA contract and a Defense Department contract, seeing the open needs that the plan made visible, and Malone-Leyva jumped first in line, grabbing the business away from all competition.

But that didn't bother Ray-Dean so much as his gut feeling that the man with no soul had probably sold the operation plan to the enemy, too, or worse yet, given it to the Hajis so that the Marines would look like losers and allow Malone-Leyva another chance to shine.

"You want a hit?" Ray-Dean said to Gary Frank, driving the armored Cadillac.

"Sure," the lout answered, and took the pint bottle of vodka and turned it up, taking a gulp. Then he let out a Rebel yell after swallowing the firewater, wiped the tears out of his eyes, and passed the bottle back.

"How about you, Freddie?" Blevins called toward the rear seat, where the third member of the low-life crew stood through an open sunroof, a Heckler and Koch HK417 automatic .30 caliber battle rifle in his hands. Rather than the M4 carbine or any other of the lighter-caliber 5.56-millimeter variants of the M16 platform, all Malone-Leyva operators carried the hard-hitting, longer-reaching HK black gun that fired the 7.62-by-51-millimeter NATO round.

"Does a nun have a cunt?" he said, dropping down and taking the bottle.

"Fuck if I know," Cooder said, after Fred Stein took his shot of clear hard liquor.

"Well they do, and I'd fuck one," Freddie said, and looked behind their Escalade to see the low-ranking State Department's US Agency for International Development, USAID, civilians and their suitcases, heading to the airport for the night flight back to the world. "Looks like we're about ready to rumble."

"Yeah," Ray-Dean said, and gave Gary Frank a tap on the shoulder. "Let's move out."

Two other Malone-Leyva armored stretch Escalades with full crews and two State Department security specialists fell in behind Ray-Dean and his boys. Another Malone-Leyva gun wagon manned with three machine-gun-wielding contract operators followed at the tail end, providing rear guard.

The street outside the embassy gates had filled with afternoon traffic, and the sidewalks were jammed with shoppers in the relative safety of the International Zone, where stores operated and life seemed nearly normal, except for the occasional car bomb and sniping.

Down the street, a taxi had pulled to the curb and had its hood up. The driver had the breather filter off the air intake, trying to adjust the mixture. He had the engine running, sputtering and coughing.

As he increased the airflow, the engine began to

smooth out, until he went too far. Then he quickly reversed the adjustment, enriching the mixture, and a loud pop came from the tailpipe.

"You hear that?" Freddie said, shouldering his rifle as they started down the street. People on the sidewalks had stopped in their tracks, reacting to the first loud pop.

Then the taxi driver turned the mixture again and caused two more loud backfires, one after the other.

"We're under siege!" Ray-Dean yelled, and instead of hitting the gas, Gary Frank hit the brakes.

Freddie Stein didn't wait for orders, but opened fire and emptied his first magazine before Cooder-with-a-D could get his door open and start firing, too.

"Light 'em up!" Ray-Dean yelled, tripping out the car door, and started hosing people on the streets with his HK417 assault rifle.

Like clockwork, Gary Frank pissed his pants and soaked the driver's seat with urine reeking of Prednisone and other cooked-up steroids he'd been taking, trying to bulk up with the boys.

Behind the lead vehicle, guns went out and operators searched for targets but found none. No one had shot at the convoy. A taxi backfired three times and the net result left thirty-five dead civilians on the streets of Baghdad.

Ray-Dean and Freddie never stopped shooting until a heroic State Department security officer maneuvered behind the lead Escalade and took the rifle out of Blevins's hands.

He pointed the black gun up at Fred Stein, and yelled, "Stop shooting, you idiot! Do you see any incoming bullet marks on anything?"

"They're shooting!" Freddie insisted. "I heard three shots!"

"Me, too," Gary Frank chimed in, now out of the car, his pants dripping wet. "I was inside driving."

Ray-Dean took out his bottle of vodka and finished it, in front of everyone.

_ 11 _

With the revelations of the First Battalion, Fifth Marines' operation plan to the forces of al-Qaeda Iraq, Abu Musab al-Zarqawi and Abu Omar Bakr al-Nasser sent word far and wide, urging jihadi faithful from all corners of the earth to come, join them in a great victory over the American infidels. Men and women, even boys and girls, from Europe, Asia, North Africa, and other nations of the Middle East, saw the messages on the al-Qaeda Web sites, and flocked to Syria and southwest Turkey. Day by day, sympathetic zealots filled the insurgents' ranks; many of them had never before seen war or had even held a rifle. Al-Qaeda Iraq's numbers grew by thousands overnight.

Twenty-six gunmen, some seasoned and some green recruits to Omar Bakr al-Nasser's army of Jamaat Ansar al-Sunnah lay waiting for the eight Marine Scout-Snipers to round the long turn in the dry streambed that ran eastward to rally point Whiskey Tango Foxtrot, another mile away.

Behind them and outside their flanks, another twenty-six al-Sunnah, al-Qaeda fighters waited in reserve, as reinforcements, should the American strike force land early. Before the reinforced ambush could slaughter the eight Marines running into their grist mill, then depart intact. It all boiled down to timing, and that depended on how fleet of foot were the approaching lambs.

Jamal al-Hakim, captain in command of the overall fifty-two-man force, hid in a nest of rocks and earth mounds just behind his ambushing force's left-flank machine gun, listening to the American command channel. He could not monitor the Marines' covered intercom because that frequency did not appear on the operation plan. Elmore Snow had long ago decided that internal intercom should be exactly that, internal. He didn't want anyone outside his unit hearing the often-colorful chatter among his operators.

Hakim had five machine guns. Three he had placed at each end and in the apex of his ambush. The other two waited in reserve, ready to move up, should he need them. He had planted the ambush along a gentle curve of the wadi, giving his center machine gun a clear field of fire a hundred yards down the streambed. The captain's right-flank gun had the shortest field of fire but covered the dead space at the other end of the curve. His left-flank gun covered nearly the same long kill zone as the center gun.

A pair of Claymore mines at the head of the ambush, just beneath his machine guns, ensured that once the Marines had filled the kill zone, death would come to them sudden and sure. The antipersonnel explosives made certain that no one penetrated their line, should the Americans turn into the center of fire and charge at them.

Jamal's only regret was that he did not have more than the two Claymores. Ideally, he would have had two more at the tail end of his kill zone. A deadly door he could close.

Lined shoulder to shoulder between the machine guns, fighters with Russian assault rifles waited hungrily. Captain Hakim had told them to exercise great patience because the Marines would likely spread their intervals. Even if the lead members of the team moved past them in the primary kill zone, the reserves could kill those few. He wanted all eight inside the lane before anyone opened fire.

Lying with the center machine gun, a jihadi with a small digital video camera focused his lens on the kill zone. Just as they had done last year, they would post this triumph over these *shayatin mukali*, painted devils, on the World Wide Web for all of sympathetic Islam to see.

Two men down, an especially anxious gunman called Ismail, a Sunni boy of seventeen from a village on the south side of Karbala, listened to the man with the camera chanting *Allahu Akbar* on the sound track as he rolled video, hearing the Marines approach. Ismail began chanting, too.

As Ismail blinked, staring down his gunsights, he saw the first Marine running fast into the kill zone. At that instant, the voices filling his heart with *Allahu Akbar* and visions of Paradise, the young man forgot everything his captain had stressed about waiting.

"Allahu Akbar!" Ismail cried as his pounding heart sent blood surging through his brain, and he opened fire.

Two shots struck Petey Preston before he knew what hit him. His body armor caught most of the bullets' energy, but he still went down hard. Hurt. Bleeding from shallow wounds and broken ribs, he gasped for air. Not fatal but painful.

Chico Powell ran thirty yards behind Corporal Preston and saw him bite the dirt. Instead of going lateral and opening fire with his support rifle, he ran to his buddy, who lay wailing, kicking his feet something awful.

Four shots hit Chico before he could reach Petey. One nailed his night optics on the front of his MACH helmet, parted his hair, and knocked him out cold. The other three buried in his armored vest's Kevlar, not putting holes in his body but also breaking ribs. He looked dead.

Petey quit yelling when he saw his bro go down, blood pouring over his face from the head wound. He thought the Hajis had killed his pard.

Instead of pissing and moaning, blinding pain aside, Preston rolled onto his light machine gun and opened fire into the nest of Jamaat Ansar al-Sunnah jihadis. He swept the entire frontage with grazing fire and put all of the ambushing gunmen behind the rocks and earth mounds at the turn in the wadi where they had laid the ambush.

Petey thought, so close but so far away. Just behind the bastards, east another mile, lay rally point Whiskey Tango Foxtrot and hopeful extraction. How did these bastards know to put their ambush here?

As he suppressed the enemy with his machine gun, Petey moved backwards, past the motionless body of Chico Powell, and found good cover at another turn in the wadi that he reckoned sat just outside the Hajis' kill zone. He tried to call the gang on his intercom but he couldn't catch his breath. He tasted blood in his mouth and knew he probably had a piece of bone stuck in his lungs.

"Petey! Chico!" Jack Valentine yelled on his helmet headset. No answer, but Corporal Preston did manage to find his radio button and sent an S-O-S with clicks.

Then Petey coughed, and that carried on his hands-free microphone.

With the one corporal apparently dead and the other behind cover, the enemy stopped firing and waited.

"Who shot?" Jamal al-Hakim shouted in Arabic, standing without thinking. "What fool shot! You didn't hear my orders? Hold fire until we have them all! Now look!"

All of his men sank behind their weapons, and Ismail emotionally melted into the ground.

"Me, sir," Ismail answered his commander, raising his hand. "I was overwhelmed." And the boy began to weep.

The cameraman glanced at the boy and shook his head.

Petey Preston held his fire, saving his ammo. He looked sadly at his pard, Randy. Dead. Facedown and bleeding in the sand. Then he saw Chico move his foot, coming to.

"Stay still, bro," Petey said on his intercom, his broken ribs stabbing his lungs as he breathed the words. Then he saw the subtle thumb on Corporal Powell's left hand point up and go back down.

Cotton Martin came alongside Petey. Sammy La-Sage, too.

"What's the damage?" Martin asked.

"I'm fucked unless I can get out of here pretty quick," Preston answered. "Kevlar took away the penetration. I got two bullets just inside somewhere. But I got broken ribs on both sides, and a slow leak in my right lung."

He spit blood to show the staff sergeant.

"And Randy?" Cotton asked, seeing the other Marine lying facedown, blood on the sand, his helmet still strapped tight under his chin but the night optics and front of the K-pot messed up from the bullet.

"Alive," Petey said. "Can't say how bad, but alive. He gave me a thumbs-up, and I told him to lie still. They won't waste ammo on a dead body."

"Back about fifty feet, there's that little turn that will let us set up a SAW on the other side of the wadi, and we can get an angle on their right flank," Cotton said, assessing their available cover and possible firing points.

Bronco and Jaws showed up with Jack and Cochise hot on their tails. In two minutes, all seven Marines snuggled close to the embankment, behind the cover of the elbow.

"From this turn, we can cover everything from center to left flank," Jack said, unhitching his pack.

"That elbow, back about fifty feet"—Cotton pointed—"gives us coverage of the center to right flank."

"You and Sage set up the other machine gun there," Jack said, and began looking high on the wash sides above the streambed. "We got a couple of good spots at higher angles. We'll put those Vigilance guns up there."

He looked at his Marines. "No scattered shots. All the ammo we got is what we got. Make it count. If we can't bust out of here, those Hajis the artillery missed will be running up our ass soon enough, and she'll be all over. So don't go to loving this place too much. We gotta grab Chico and get the hell out of Dodge."

"Love to go right now, boss," Bronco said.

"Tell me about it," Jack said, and gave Cortez a smile.

"You got a plan?" Cotton asked.

"Yeah," Jack said. "But you won't like it."

"Does that matter?" Martin smiled.

"No." Jack grinned back.

"Why ain't they shooting?" Sage asked, using his spotting scope to sneak a peek over the top of the embankment and try to pick out the enemy gun placements. "We got fifteen or twenty rifle barrels and Haji heads between what looks like three machine guns on bipod mounts. What do you suppose they're waiting on?"

"Us, I'd imagine," Jaws said.

"I think they're wanting to hold us here and take us alive," Jack said. "They figure we'll surrender when all those Hajis behind us arrive."

"Some people might do that," Cotton said. "But we know better, don't we."

"Fuckin' A, dude," Jaws said. "Nobody sawing my head off on YouTube."

"What about your plan I won't like?" Martin asked Jack.

"About a hundred yards back, I saw a little feeder gully coming in this draw from the south. Leads right out of this shit stream," Valentine said.

"Yeah, I saw it, too." Cotton nodded.

"We set up a base of fire here. Suppress the shit out of them," Jack began. "Grab Chico. Get back here. Bury me with a SAW and a sniper gun. I keep them in place while you seven run for it to that gully and head south. Sweep a big circle around to the rally point."

"Why don't we just set up a base of fire," Cotton said. "And use fire and movement tactics to get all eight of us out of here? Isn't that a better idea?"

"No," Jack said. "I thought about fire and movement first. They'll just chase us down when we move out. If they're on us, the minute we cross open terrain, we're all dead."

"We could fucking attack them!" Cochise Quinlan said, fire in his throat. "Bust out on both their flanks and kill the shit out of them. Worst that happens, we all go down in blazes of glory. But they sure the fuck don't capture us and cut off our heads on YouTube."

"Yeah, well," Bronco said. "Trouble with your plan, Cochise? We all fucking die. What about the tribe coming up our asses right now? You think about that?"

Quinlan shook his head and gave Bronco the finger.

"They'll vent all guns soon as we go for Chico," Jack said. "We tie them up in an exchange. Everybody falls back to the gully and exits except one man running a SAW back there, and me running mine up here.

"Cotton, I want you to lead the herd, so that leaves Sage to run the other machine gun. Once you guys disappear up the gully, he'll pull his gun and fly, too. I'll keep 'em busy. They won't know you've gone until you're well away.

"While we're resting, dig me a good deep hide in the bank, right behind this gun. I'll roll in it and you cover me with rocks and crap. Hide me good. If I live or die depends on how well you cover me."

Jack pointed to a platter-sized, flat-faced stone that had fallen off the bank wall the last time a flash flood had washed the wadi.

"That big rock?" he said. "Put it in front of my hide. When I quit shooting, I pull it over the front of my hole."

Cotton nodded okay, and the rest of the Marines looked at Gunny Valentine as if he'd lost his mind.

"I'm betting that with all our dirt work, improving our firing positions here," Jack explained, "they'll never consider that you buried me here. Who in their right mind would? Right? They'll chase after your tracks out of here."

"And why do you think that Quinlan's idea isn't viable?" Cotton asked. "The Hajis coming up behind us may not get here before we can kill this bunch and depart, and even get to the rally point. Strike force lands, we're home free. We've got six healthy Marines trained to the teeth in special warfare, and what do they have?"

"Six of us beats twenty of them hands down," Cochise chimed in. "I say we go for it!"

"I figure they got twenty or thirty people up ahead in that primary ambush," Jack explained. "Consider that they knew we would head this way because in their attack they left this avenue of retreat open to us. They got inside information. Just like last year when they killed those guys from Cleveland. They probably got the rally point staked out, too. So, besides this ambush, I am betting they're holding another thirty guns on the flanks and rear in reserve."

"They're counting on us charging them before their cavalry gets here. The obvious," Cotton said, understanding exactly what Gunny Valentine envisioned.

"They're prepared," Jack added. "Someone on their end in that ambush got trigger-happy and hit Petey and Chico at the mouth of their kill zone. That little fuckup gave us a chance. Otherwise, we'd be dead ducks."

"They'll never anticipate us leaving anyone behind. So we hide the gunny good, he's got a chance," Jaws said. "We could draw straws to see who stays."

"Bullshit!" Jack said. "I make the decisions, not you. I stay. You go. If anybody dies, it's me, and I'm not planning on dying. Got it?"

Bronco gave Gunny Valentine a look that said it all. A lot like the look that the Apostle John must have had on his face when he watched the Roman soldiers nail Jesus Christ to the cross. What do you say to a man who is sacrificing his life so that you can live?

Just then a voice came on the command channel.

"Ghost One, Corsair Actual."

"Corsair Actual, Ghost One," Jack said. "Go ahead."

"Ghost One, position report and casualties, over," Black Bart said.

"Stand by, Corsair," Jack said, pulling out his GPS and taking a reading. "Uploading grid coordinates now."

"Ghost One, Corsair Actual. Copy. Coordinates received," Colonel Roberts said. "Can you give us a casualty report?"

"Negative at this time," Jack responded. "We will need medevac at rally point, over."

"Ghost One, Corsair Actual," Roberts continued. "Be advised that operation plan security has been compromised."

"Not surprised," Jack said. "They had our number from the get-go. Definitely we're compromised."

"Roger that, Ghost One," Bart Roberts said. "Per that compromise, revise all references and points to Plan B. Repeat. Revise your references and points to Plan B, per final operation briefing discussion. Do you copy? Over."

Jack thought a moment and recalled Colonel Roberts telling all commanders and key noncommissioned officers at the final briefing that should there be a reason, they would institute a general Plan B to the operation. Basically, all extraction and insertion points moved five clicks south. Likewise, all frequencies moved down channel five clicks.

"Roger, Corsair." Jack smiled. "Plan B. Thank you!"

Cotton smiled, too. So did Sammy LaSage, Bronco, Jaws, Cochise, and even Petey, now wheezing as his lung filled with blood.

"How about it, Chico? You up for Plan B?" Jack said on the intercom.

Randy Powell answered back, still playing dead, "Plan B? Works for me. Don't that put Whiskey Tango Foxtrot out of this fucking riverbed and closer to our position anyway?"

"Yes, it does," Jack said, suddenly feeling the love of God shining on them. "If they got people waiting a mile east of us? We'll be five kilometers south. That also gives Alvin Barkley and his strike force ample opportunity to kill the shit out of these guys."

"So, Gunny. Does that alter your plan any?" Cochise asked, hoping that Jack would give up his suicide idea and run down the gully with them.

"Makes it a lot more likely you'll survive, but changes nothing on my end. I still have to hold here so you guys can exit," Jack said. "Don't worry. It'll just be a long walk for me, unless Alvin Barkley brings a hell of a lot of Marines, and you guys come after me."

"That'd be wonderful!" Bronco said. "Can't we do that? Land Barkley and his guys here instead?"

"We'll be dead before they can get here," Jack said.

"At best, they won't swoop in for another twenty minutes. We don't have five."

"Right. We need to beat feet now," Cotton said.

Jaws and Cochise moved to the high positions. Jack got behind the SAW while Bronco, Sage, and Cotton worked fast, digging holes, pulling rocks, getting a deep trench for Jack to slide in.

Quickly, they had the gunny covered to his head.

"Bronco, you stick with Jaws, feed him and me ammo," Jack said. "When you bug out, one under each arm on Petey and run your asses off. Do not look back."

Cochise glanced down from his firing point. "Gunny, I ain't leaving. We never left anyone behind, and I'm not starting now. I'll cover up, too."

"Sergeant," Jack said in his gunny voice. "You will leave. Survival of the team depends on your gun. We've got two wounded. That means two carry two, plus our gear. Your gun is important. Am I clear?"

"Yes, sir," Quinlan said, his voice choking.

Just then someone shouted from down the dry riverbed.

"Hey, Marines," Jamal al-Hakim called out. "Ghost One. That would be *Ash'abah al-Anbar*, the Ghost of Anbar. We have been expecting you! Gunnery Sergeant Jack Valentine!"

"Fuck you!" Cochise Quinlan yelled back. "Valentine ain't here."

"Oh, I think he is," Jamal responded.

Jaws yelled, "He's a pussy! Hiding in the rear with the gear at Al Asad with all the FOB-rats and TOC-roaches."

"Ghost One is Jack Valentine!" Jamal insisted. "We

hear you loud and clear. Everything you say. Surrender. No one has to die. Not today."

"Kiss my ass," Jack shouted. "I'm Ghost One, and that ain't Jack Valentine. Not anymore. He's pushing pencils."

"That is too bad," Jamal said. "We had a special day planned for *Ash'abah al-Anbar*. A celebration with him as guest of honor. Now you must go to the party without him."

"Stick your head up and say that, you donkey-fucking son of a bitch," Cochise yelled. "That's right, we got you on video going balls-deep."

A spike of anger and prolonged impatience sent the captain up, out of his rocky nest. He, like all of his comrades, believed that the fatal authority of God dealt in all things. God's will even determined the flip of a coin. It was God's will that he was here killing these Marines.

Just as Jamal rose to his knees, to dare the insulting Marine to go ahead and take his shot, Cochise Quinlan lit him up. Three quick rounds from his Vigilance support rifle splashed home. The Haji captain never knew what hit him.

As Cochise fired, so did the entire team.

Sammy LaSage and Jaws ran out, under the suppression fire and grabbed Randy Powell, and dragged him to the far side, where Cotton ran the SAW.

"I'm going back for Petey and the boys, and we'll beat feet," Jaws said.

"Do it!" Cotton Martin said, dropping a spent can from the light machine gun and locking in a full one.

Cotton then switched guns with Sage, patted him on the helmet, and headed for the gully, with Corporal Powell running at his side, his arm on Martin's shoulder.

Ahead of them, Bronco and Jaws carried Petey the same way. However, Cochise Quinlan kept firing above Jack.

"Move out, Marine!" Jack yelled.

"I can't leave, Gunny!" Sergeant Quinlan cried out. Tears streamed from his eyes. "I can't see you die!"

"Those Marines need you, Sergeant!" Jack snarled. "Do your fucking job!"

The words stung, but the stocky, stubborn sergeant knew the gunny was right. Two more shots, one more dead Haji, and Cochise dropped to his knees. He pushed the big rock right by Jack's face and checked the rest of his concealment.

"It's a good hide, Gunny," Cochise said. "Is it okay for a guy to love a guy?"

"Sure it is, Cochise," Jack answered, shooting the machine gun. "Just don't fuck me."

Cochise laughed. "I love you, Gunny Valentine. More than just a brother. All of us, we're like all part of each other. Does that make sense?"

"Absolutely," Jack said, and put his hand on the sergeant's boot toe and gave it a pat.

Cochise looked at the gunny. "Don't fucking die!"

"I'm not!" Jack said, and changed cans while Cochise opened again with his Vigilance rifle. That's when he saw Petey's M40A3 sniper rifle lying on the embankment.

"I'm leaving this Vigilance for you, Gunny," Cochise said, and quickly buried his rifle and Petey Preston's satchel full of ammunition, which he had pulled from the Marine's discarded backpack. "Rifle and ammo at arm's reach, to your right. It's buried good."

"Get the fuck out of here!" Jack yelled, and Sergeant

Quinlan got to his feet. Heavy fire returning from the three machine guns and a dozen rifles chewed up the dirt above and around both Marines.

"Don't fucking die!" Cochise yelled as he stood to run.

"I won't," Jack shouted back, bullets flying.

"Promise?" Cochise strained, his voice breaking up.

"I promise!" Jack said, working the machine gun.

With that, Sergeant Clarence Quinlan disappeared.

Jack Valentine shot out the six cans of SAW ammo that he had. When he popped the last bullet downrange, he slid deep in his hole, tossed the machine gun aside, and pulled the rock in front of his face. He prayed that he hadn't knocked away any camouflage. With that last round spent, Jack felt more alone now than he had ever known in his life.

Jack waited and prayed. He knew that if Jamal, the al-Sunnah captain, had known to call him Ghost One, he no doubt had monitored the command and control encrypted radio channels. To do that, the enemy had to have the working crypto receivers and call frequencies.

However, he didn't think that the Hajis had ears on the MARSOC team's discrete intercom band or frequencies since they had never acted on any information that they should have obtained if they could monitor them. Such as the fact that Randy Powell had played dead and gotten away with it. Had they known he was alive in the open, they would have finished him with their machine guns.

For this, the gunny was thankful for Elmore Snow's insistence that his teams not carry one radio with all channels, but two different devices with different radio bandwidths. One for the command communications and the other for internal voice chatter. Both connected with their helmet headsets, as if one radio, but command could not hear the cross talk among the team. The colonel had told his Marines that once small unit leaders began giving that kind of access and direct control to higher headquarters staff, soon bean counters and even the president would be sitting in lounge chairs, sipping cocktails and quarterbacking special operations missions. Something that must never happen. "Micromanagement kills Marines," Elmore had said.

Carefully, Jack reached inside his vest and felt his command radio. He wanted to turn it off and save the battery. When he gripped hold of it, however, he felt it sizzle and smelled faint electrical smoke. He checked his GPS position locator transmitter receiver; it too had died.

He had heard nothing of his Marines over the intercom since they left. With the two other radios gone, that worried him. Of course, on the move, dodging an aggressive enemy, they would spare words.

"Cotton, you copy?" Jack whispered over the handsfree, looking up the dry riverbed from a small hole by the rock. He hugged his M40A3 sniper rifle that he had in his hide with him, along with his pack full of .338 Lapua Magnum ammunition and four canteens of water that his team had left in addition to his own four bottles, plus two bags of dehydrated food. They had packed food and water for a couple of days, so Jack knew he would have to make every drop of water count and stretch every crumb of food.

While Cochise Quinlan had buried Petey Preston's Vigilance semiautomatic support rifle and his satchel full of .338 magnum ammunition, he had tossed aside Corporal Preston's backpack and what was left in it. Simply too much nonessential crap to carry in addition to his own pack. Plus it offered a distraction to the enemy. However, the emotional sergeant had unintentionally left behind his entrenching tool, stuck in the sand by an empty hole. It reminded Jack of a grave marker. All it needed was an empty helmet hung on top of it and empty boots at its base.

To help disguise the gunny's hide, the team had dug several other shallow fighting holes and made sure they all had ample spent brass in and around them. They also left plenty of tracks running every direction, on their way out, to draw the enemy away from Jack.

"Cotton," Gunny Valentine called again. No answer.

For a minute or two, which seemed like an eternity, the world fell silent. Jack felt his heart pound in his ears, and he held his breath.

Then all hell broke loose.

Machine gun fire swept up and down the dry riverbed, sending bullets into every aspect and angle.

"Here's where I die," Jack told himself, anticipating a burst hitting him where he lay. The dirt and rocks on top of him would do little to repel .30 caliber hot lead.

Somehow, God must have heard his prayers. Bullets landed around him but not in him. Then, moments later, a dozen-plus Hajis came charging into Jack's position, shooting up the world even more. A gang of them walked directly on top of him several times. One gunman even stood in the middle of Valentine's back, searching for clues.

One man picked up Corporal Preston's backpack and dumped out all the contents. Socks, two douche-bag dinners, water bottles, some empty spare ammunition magazines for the Vigilance, a pair of binoculars, a bottle of Cholula chili sauce. But no ammunition or much else of real value.

The Haji threw the pack in the dirt and kicked one of the MRE bags like a soccer ball off the side of his foot at another gunman who kicked it back. Then the two men began playing football with the brown-plastic pack of dehydrated food. Jack smiled.

"This just might work," he told himself.

Another enemy gunman took Cochise's forgotten entrenching tool, gave it a good look, started to keep it but decided it would be in his way. So, he stabbed it in the ground next to the rock hiding Gunny Valentine's face. The little shovel blade just missed his head.

A voice in the wadi, far behind the gunny, yelled something in Arabic, and other voices approaching in the wadi from the west answered. Then everyone took off running and jabbering to each other.

Moments later, pickup trucks rumbled along the top of the dry riverbed, running along both sides. Several other Toyotas rolled up, stopped, and took on passengers. Then all of them sped off. Jack supposed they went in chase of his Marines, following their tracks.

"Cotton!" Jack said above a whisper, gambling that no one waited behind.

"You're alive!" Staff Sergeant Martin answered, breathless, still shouldering Chico Powell as he ran hard.

"Yeah," Valentine responded. "They're mounted in trucks, hot on your six."

"We're a hundred yards out of our rally point," Cotton said. "We'll set up defensive positions in those rocks and fight it out there."

"I can hear Ospreys," the gunny said, to give his brother hope.

Cotton stopped and listened, and he did in fact hear the beating propellers of the V-22 tiltrotor planes growing louder, approaching him.

"I hear them, too!" Martin came back, and Jack was surprised, because in truth he had not heard a thing.

"Take cover, bro. Kill as many as you can," Jack said, just as he heard gunfire open up to the south.

"Fuck! Those guys are fast!" Cotton said, taking fire from several dozen pursuing al-Sunnah gunmen riding in the fleet of pickup trucks.

"Gunny!" Cochise Quinlan shouted on the intercom. "Soon as we get these guys killed out, we're coming to get you. Sit your ass tight."

"No can do," Jack said, pulling himself out of his hide. "I got to move out while I have the chance. All you guys hear me?"

"Yup. All of us hear you loud and clear," Cotton said, helping feed ammo to Sammy LaSage's light machine gun, chopping away at the Hajis that had now leaped from the trucks and scattered behind rocks and mounds.

"I'm heading west, back up this wadi about twenty kilometers, maybe thirty," Valentine told them as he gathered up Petey's discarded meals and water. He left the backpack because his own was enough to haul. But he did grab Cochise Quinlan's entrenching tool.

"Then I'm going to make a big-ass circle north, arc back around east, and I'll head to Haditha Dam, following parallel to MSR Bronze," Jack told them as he did a quick look around the area and headed out. "You copy that?"

"That's one big-ass circle," Cochise said. "Why not go straight east from where you are? We'll have people out looking for you, air and ground. Be where we can find you."

"Hajis will be looking for me to go east, direct to friendly lines, or south toward Wolf. If they know I'm left behind," Jack explained. "I'm hoping they don't figure that out. But if they do, they'll be turning over every rock searching for me. I want them where I'm not. The long way is the best way. I got food and water. I'll be fine."

"Roger that," Cotton said, talking and shooting.

"Make sure that no one says anything on the command net about me out here," Jack said.

"Why's that?" Martin asked.

"I think the Hajis captured some crypto radios and have our command frequencies monitored. That guy calling me Ghost One. A dead giveaway," Jack said.

"You know," Cotton said. "I did a double take on that, too. They had to be listening. Think they have this net?"

"No," Jack answered. "They would have killed Chico if they'd heard us talking to him playing dead."

"Makes sense," Cotton said.

"But keep word of me off the net," Jack said. "If they don't know I'm here, that's best."

"They'll figure that out pretty quick, though, after you kill a few of them," Cotton said. "I don't see how you can go that distance without running into a Haji or ten."

"I don't plan on their seeing me," Jack said, jogging west with the pack on his back, his M40A3 rifle slung across one shoulder and the Vigilance rifle in his hands.

"Well, Gunny, you know how that always seems to work out," Cochise said.

"Yeah, unfortunately, I do," Jack said, huffing along, his signal getting scratchy and weak.

"We get in the Ospreys, what's to keep us from swinging out where you are and grabbing you?" Cotton said.

"That'd be great if I didn't have my world crawling with Hajis, and if I had a working GPS so I could give out coordinates," Jack said. "It's dead as a mackerel along with my command radio. Fried like bacon. Don't know what did it, but they're toast. All I got is this weak-ass intercom, and it's about out of range. So good luck finding me."

"We can give it a try anyway. Take a run or two up the wadi," Martin said.

"Oh, definitely do it," Jack said. "If you can get them to swing out here. I'm beating feet west, fast as I can haul ass. But I also have to keep off the skyline, and that makes me a little difficult to spot from the air."

A few minutes later, he had run out of range. All he heard now was static, so he shut off the intercom radio to save his battery.

More than a hundred of Abu Omar's Jamaat Ansar al-Sunnah jihadi fighters converged on Cotton Martin and the six MARSOC Marines huddled in the cluster of rocks at the alternate rally point they called Whiskey Tango Foxtrot, Plan B.

"I'm down to my last magazine," Jaws said, now working his Vigilance support rifle, having already depleted his .50 calibers and set aside the Barrett Mark-82.

Sergeant Sammy LaSage went to work with his bolt-action sniper rifle, after setting aside the SAW, having spent its last can.

Bronco had run out of all his rounds and huddled next to Jaws with his pistol out, and two .45 magazines handy to reload. Chico Powell and Petey Preston had nothing but short guns left, either.

Cotton Martin tossed his next-to-last rifle magazine to Jaws and kept the last one for himself. That's when he looked up and saw the first of two Super Cobras swing low and open fire on the jihadis, putting two rockets and several acres of 20-millimeter gunfire into their midst. Hajis scattered in every direction, running for their lives.

Hot on the attack helicopters' tails, three Ospreys set down and dropped their ramps. Sixty strike-force Marines poured out of the aircrafts' bellies, shooting and snarling, with Alvin Barkley at the lead, his big knife on his leg, charging out of the first bird to set down, Sergeant Jorge Padilla and Rattler hot on his heels. Staff Sergeant Marcellus Jupiter brought the last twenty men out of the third V-22 aircraft, the Mob Squad among them.

It didn't take long, and they had the Hajis scattered and mostly dead. Anything that even remotely resembled a Toyota truck got blown to pieces. Toyota wreckage and enemy bodies littered the desert.

After loading the seven Marines and the strike force, the trio of Ospreys launched to the north and turned west, following the dry wadi where Jack had fled. They made three low passes, going well beyond a distance any human on foot could have run.

Jack had to hug the ground in a clump of rocks and dirt. As the planes flew overhead three times, he could do nothing. He couldn't breathe a word. Just yards ahead of him, he watched a dozen al-Sunnah gunmen also hiding from the aircraft.

He had no clue whether the Hajis had come in search of him or just happened to be crossing the desert plains. Regardless, he decided to hold tight a few hours until full nightfall. They'd be gone by then, and he could move out.

While he waited, well hidden, he checked his gear. Curious about the dead radios, and hoping he might revive them, Valentine carefully and quietly slipped them out of his operator's vest.

As he looked closely at both radios, he saw the trouble. A shred of copper bullet fragment had somehow gone down his Kevlar vest, ripped through the back of the command radio, and struck the top of the GPS, where it lodged.

"Crap," he breathed to himself and checked to see if his intercom radio had taken a hit, too. It seemed okay as he examined the case, then he remembered turning it off to save the battery. He looked at the sky as the dozen Hajis departed out of the wadi, and he wished that the planes would now make a fourth pass. But they didn't.

"I should have taken the chance and called them down!" Jack said to himself, and shrank into his hiding place. A sense of loss and utter frustration suddenly drained him.

Then he took a deep breath, stuffed the radios back in their pouches, and told himself, "Suck it up, Jack. You'll be fine."

Ray-Dean Blevins leaned against the passenger-side front fender of the Escalade, a sneer on his face, belching bad gas, watching State Department security officers and US Agency for International Development workers helping Iraqi police and Red Crescent attendants tend to the wounded. He considered it a waste of time. His face and posture visibly projected his surly attitude.

Freddie Stein sat in the backseat of the Cadillac, brooding, while Gary Frank stood on the other side of the car, trying to shake dry his pissed-wet pants and blubbering incoherently to anyone who had the misfortune of coming near him that he had nothing to do with the shooting.

"I was just driving!" he whined. "I followed orders."

It didn't take long for Cesare Alosi to roll onto the scene in his Cadillac behind a second car with a three-man crew of pipe-hitting shaved heads who looked like he had recruited them from a California prison. One even had a face tattoo. Spiderwebs across his cheek. A black widow by his eye. He and his partner, a guy with Nazi SS lightning bolts on his neck, both had UDT Freddy the Frogman inked on their forearms but wore navy blue ball caps with gold SEAL eagle, anchor, pistol, and trident emblems embroidered on them.

"SEAL, huh?" Ray-Dean said to the oversized thug with the face tattoo.

The guy touched his ball cap, and said, "Oh yeah."

"What team? Six?" Cooder asked.

"Right, me and George," the face-tattoo guy said, nodding toward his ugly partner.

"Seems like every guy I ever met with a shaved head and Navy tattoos was in SEAL Team Six. Kind of like Marine Snipers," Blevins said. "George there your swim partner?"

"Naw. What do you mean, swim partner? I worked alone. Special missions," he said, and George gave Cooder a look.

"All top secret, huh?" Ray-Dean said, nodding.

"Yeah," the face-tattoo guy said.

"What was your class?" Blevins asked, his bullshit meter pinging. Even a slimeball Marine like Cooder has one.

"What do you mean, class?" George said, and he turned his SEAL cap around backwards.

"BUD/S class, dude. What class?" Ray-Dean asked, now having fun with the two phony apes, probably biker-gang dropouts. Maybe not even that.

"You know, that was quite a few years back," George said. "What was it, Ken?"

"We went to SEALs straight from Army Green Berets," Ken said. "They gave us a pass since we was already trained. We went to UDT school at Pensacola."

"I never knew SEALs or even UDT had a school at Pensacola," Blevins said.

"What were you, some kind of know-it-all jarhead?" Ken with the face tattoo said.

"Yeah, that's me," Cooder said.

"You assholes don't know shit, so shut the fuck up," George grumbled.

"I guess all your other team guys are dead, too? Some badass operation in Somalia?" Ray-Dean smiled. "All missions top secret and that bullshit?"

"Yeah," George said, getting more pissed.

"What kind of medals you two collect? I bet you got a chest full. Those top secret missions and all. Lots of bragging rights, huh?" Blevins grinned even bigger.

"Fucking Navy Cross, and Ken has four, count 'em, four Silver Stars, shit stick," George came back.

"Oh! Badass!" Ray-Dean exclaimed, half-drunk and smelling like shit.

"Keep up your wise-ass shit and we'll show you bad-ass," Ken with the face tattoo growled.

"Just curious," Ray-Dean said. "No disrespect, dude. What about Freddy the Frogman on your arm there? You UDT and SEAL both?"

"Fuckin' A," George said. "What the fuck did you ever do besides chop down all these unarmed civilians?"

"Shit, dude," Blevins said. "Like I said, Marine Corps. All I got is an honorable discharge. I'm a pure piece of shit, and I know it. But hey, dude, I don't claim to be someone I'm not."

"What you saying?" George snarled, his hand going on his Glock strapped in a rig across his chest.

"Not a thing." Blevins shrugged. "You got it, you wear it. I know a couple guys on SEAL Team Three, down at Ramadi, and a guy on their new Team Seven. I think he's back at Coronado. I just never met anybody really from Team Six. That's all. Until I met you two."

"Shows what you fucking know," Ken with the face tattoo said, and walked to the front of the Escalade, where Cesare Alosi busily talked with both hands to the US embassy chief of security.

"Yeah. I know shit. Fucking posers," Ray-Dean grumbled, watching George walk to the front, too, and join the important people in conversation. Like he and his asshole buddy belonged in charge, too.

The embassy security boss shook his finger in Alosi's face, and that made Ray-Dean grin, feeling a great deal of satisfaction, seeing the slick asshole getting a taste of shit put back in his mouth for once. Then Cesare glared at Blevins and came to him as the human waste leaned on the Cadillac's fender looking narrow-eyed back at his master.

"You and these two idiots you call a crew, go pack your trash. You're leaving Iraq," the Malone-Leyva boss told Ray-Dean. "I'm booking you on the next flight out of Baghdad that has three open seats. Cargo or first class, it doesn't matter. You're out of here. I've had it."

"Where to, sir?" Freddie Stein chirped, standing up through the sunroof. He had quietly put down the Escalade passenger window so he could hear what the boss had to say.

"Anyplace. I don't give a shit. As long as you're gone from my life," Alosi answered. "Get as far from me as possible. You three are finished. Terminated. Fired. Let payroll know where to send your checks after we deduct today's damages."

Cesare took two steps away and stopped, looking at the Escalade. "Blevins, when I get you booked on a flight, drive that piece of shit to the airport. Leave the keys at our liaison desk. Don't let me ever see you again. You copy?"

"Fuck you," Ray-Dean said.

"Mr. Alosi, sir," Gary Frank pled, hurrying around the car, his pants pissed wet, smelling harsh, and getting under Cesare's nose, wreaking of steroid urine. "I just drove! I never fired a shot! Why are you canning me?"

Cesare looked at the sad sack with his urinated trousers. He didn't know what to say, so he just walked away with the phony SEALs, George and Ken, and the other tattooed shaved head who drove their armored Escalade.

He told George, "Round up these passengers and get this caravan to the airport. Then see me at my office."

"Tonight?" George asked, like it would interrupt his other important plans.

"That would be helpful," Alosi said, and walked back to his car.

"Fuck him and the horse he rode in on," Ray-Dean said, and slid in the driver's seat, his ass squishing in the urine that filled the foam under the upholstery. He looked at Gary Frank. "Get the fuck in and shut the fuck up."

Cooder looked in the back, and Freddie Stein still stood in the open sunroof, whimpering. "Sit the fuck down!"

Blevins then pulled the shifter into low D and smoked the tires as he left.

"I guess you got the word," Liberty Cruz said on her mobile phone to Chris Gray, who sat in his temporary office in the one-five command center at Al Asad Air Base.

"What's that?" Gray, the seasoned intelligence officer

answered, having several options for an answer to which word he got.

"Malone-Leyva. They screwed the pooch," Liberty said, and bubbled some laughter as she said it.

"I heard chatter about a shoot-out in front of the embassy today. Somebody lit up a bunch of shoppers. That it?" Gray said.

"Our boy, Ray-Dean Blevins and his Frank-n-Stein A-team mowed down thirty-five unarmed Iraqi civilians, shopping on a leisurely Saturday afternoon," Liberty gloated. "It's that runaway train we saw coming. It's finally crashed."

Chris Gray began laughing.

"So, what's the joke?" Liberty asked, and she felt a little dirty laughing, too, in the midst of such a tragedy. She ought to feel terrible but didn't. Yet Chris Gray's laughing had brought it all home.

"I'm laughing about Blevins, not the killings. That's terrible," Gray explained. "It's just that of all people. Cooder Blevins and his crew of nitwits. The poetic justice is a little too perfect. Can you tie Alosi into it?"

"Of course not," Liberty said. "However, this incident may well dump the whole applecart for all these mercenary contractors. Put them under somebody's jurisdiction. I just got off the phone with Jason Kendrick. They got the flash-message traffic from State Department, and Senator Jim Wells is on the warpath. They're subpoenaing Victor Malone."

Gray laughed hard. "Oh, that's too good. Malone will love that limelight."

Then the CIA operator cleared his throat, and asked Liberty, "How about some more interesting news?"

"Like what?" Cruz said.

"Some of our intelligence leads tell us that our boy Ray-Dean Blevins may have illegally gotten his hands on a copy of the First Battalion, Fifth Marines' highly classified operations plan, and it possibly ties to Cesare Alosi using some inside information to land a couple of fat contracts," Gray went on. "Just guessing, but Malone-Leyva did show up at the head of the line and nailed down some very nice contracts before anyone else had a shot."

"Where did he get the document?" Liberty asked, taken totally off guard with the news.

"We're just now looking into it," Gray said. "MAR-SOC reported to higher headquarters this afternoon that their copy of the operation plan is missing from their classified-documents safe. Ray-Dean Blevins was a visitor to their office at that same time."

"Oh, that does point an ugly finger at him, doesn't it," Liberty said. "What about the people at MARSOC? Are they in trouble?"

"Captain Mike Burkehart, the detachment officer in charge, has his tit in the wringer over it," Gray said. "He received the document from First Sergeant Alvin Barkley, who hand carried it to him, and the skipper signed for it. He said he put it on the desk for the admin corporal to log in, and from there it disappeared. I've known Mike for a long time. A good man, but he won't see promotion to major. He does have his twenty in, so he'll gracefully disappear."

"What a shame," Liberty said. "Fucking Blevins. That figures. Alosi had to have sent him after it."

"You'd think," Gray said. "But as far as any real evidence goes, we got jack shit. Just coincidental happenstance at this point. I don't even know that Ray-Dean really has the plan or how much of this is true or just bullshit. You need to get your FBI team busy. Definitely get yourself officially in his apartment with some kind of warrant and start tossing over the furniture."

"Oh, that's a given," Liberty said. "I'll have to get State Department to arrange with Iraqi officials to give us jurisdiction cooperation. That shouldn't take long, given their attitudes about security breaches."

"Another interesting twist," Chris Gray said. "Cooder's girlfriend, Francoise Theuriau. You remember her? The mouthy little dog-faced French reporter in the tight pants he was thumping on at the Baghdad Country Club? She's flown into the wind."

"Really," Liberty said.

"We put a tail on her this morning, and she went to an office in the International Zone belonging to a couple of other frogs from Avignon," Gray said. "They're suspicious because they seem to go anyplace with no trouble at all. Like the bad guys gave them a hall pass."

"Hum," Liberty mumbled, and said, "spies maybe?"

"France and al-Qaeda don't make a lot of sense, but you can never tell about rabid socialists like Francoise," Gray said. "This Davet Taché and Jean René Decoux materialized in Avignon some years ago, coincidentally with the collapse of the Soviet Union. We find them as students, at the same university with Francoise Theuriau.

Early life? Nonexistent. But they claim French citizenship by birth in Paris. Parents all dead. No living relatives. Very stinky."

"Passports?" Liberty asked.

"Sure. All quite legal, and the French say the two men are solid citizens. Philanthropists and patrons of the arts," Gray said. "Wealthy men of position and influence in Avignon, and a bit of pull even at our own embassy. The State Department folks I queried on these two jokers got downright defensive when I started prying into the closet."

"Pull them in. Have a talk," Liberty said.

"I would, but no one has seen these clowns for a couple of weeks," Gray said. "They went up north to Baiji, buying antiquities. Nobody at the hotel they checked in has seen either man or their drivers and bodyguards since that first day. They checked in at the hotel and vanished. Their cars are still parked in the hotel garage. Not a scratch on them."

"What about Francoise?" Liberty asked.

"Oh, Miss Theuriau." Chris laughed. "Our eyes watch her go in the frogs' trading company office, and she doesn't come out. One of our Iraqi agents goes inside and talks to the receptionist. She says Francoise went to the restroom, then left. She didn't come out front or back, so I'm betting they have underground that leads to al-Qaeda."

"Wow," Liberty said. "You think that Blevins could be committing espionage in cooperation with her?"

"For a pile of money? Yes," Gray said. "I think that Ray-Dean Blevins and Cesare Alosi both would cut their own mothers' throats for a price. I don't put treason past either one of them."

"I'll keep this in mind while we investigate the shooting today," Liberty said.

"That shooting is the perfect door opener," Gray said. "Just don't let them see you coming. Especially Alosi."

"Oh, I'm keenly aware," Liberty said.

"By the way," Gray said, his voice casual. "A little bird offered a tip on Blevins. Check close in the kitchen. You know, dump out the drawers. Apparently, Cooder likes to hide his drugs and stuff there. So, look under stuff, not just inside the obvious. No telling what you might find."

"Very interesting. We'll do that. I'll let you know what we find," Liberty said. Then added, "So, you've had yourself a busy few days."

"Yes, I have," Chris said. "Now I also have some particularly disturbing news. Especially for you. I saved it for last because it is that bad."

"What's that?" Liberty said, a jolt of adrenaline hitting her like a brick.

"Gunnery Sergeant Valentine's team got way in over their heads earlier today," Gray said.

"Is Jack alright?" She gasped, fighting back the urge to scream at him.

"Two of his men wounded, not bad. Broken ribs and a few bullet holes," Gray said.

"And Jack! What about Jack?" Liberty wailed, her voice straining with fear.

"Their last communication with him, he was fine," Gray said. "He's on his own, however. Out in the badlands."

Liberty groaned on the phone, unable to speak.

"Look, Liberty," Gray offered, "Colonel Roberts has

pulled out all stops to find him and get him out. He's an old friend of Jack and Colonel Snow. So, it's more than just a Marine MIA. Which is bad enough. It's also very personal for him."

"How did it happen?" Liberty choked out in a broken voice.

"Jack being Jack, sacrificed himself to give his Marines a chance to escape," Chris told her. "They got entrapped. The enemy knew where the Marines were operating and set up an elaborate ambush. Somehow, the gunny and his men avoided getting caught in the middle. Jack set up a base of fire with his machine gun, kept the bad guys busy while his boys ran out the back door."

"Oh! That's Jack Valentine alright!" Liberty said, a surge of anger in her voice. "He thinks he's bulletproof!"

"Well, there's a little more bad news," Gray added.

"Why not! If I don't have enough bad news, just pile it on," Liberty let out, her voice cracking, and now she broke into full-fledged tears. "When Jack gets in the shit, it's not just bad, it is always really terrible. There's no half stepping with Gunnery Sergeant Valentine."

"The enemy has mobilized a major force on the desert," Gray went on. "Large numbers pouring in from Syria and the north. Looks like a major offensive by Zarqawi and several insurgent affiliate groups. My opinion? They got that operation plan, and formed a counterplan of their own.

"Colonel Roberts has shifted everything to a counter-offensive posture. All positions and camps on high alert. I'm afraid they've got their hands full. Finding Jack in the midst of this? Well, it doesn't look good. I'm sorry."

"Oh no!" Liberty moaned, crying hard. "Oh my God!"

"Liberty, listen to me," Chris Gray said. "It is very, very important that this conversation remains between you and me. Jack's life depends on secrecy. Al-Qaeda may not even know that we have someone missing. However, if they realize that Jack Valentine is lost in their desert, they'll pull out all stops to find him. He would be a prize."

Liberty could say nothing more. She just cried.

_ 12 _

Jack walked all night. Judging from his normal pace, about three and a half miles in an hour, given his rest stops, he estimated that he traveled twenty miles. He angled slightly southwest from the wadi, and crossed the T1 roadway sometime after midnight. He decided to go parallel to it as a means of keeping his direction from veering too far right or left. He chose walking on the south side of the highway because of increasing cross-country traffic he heard north.

All he had to steer by was his little bubble compass on the side of his watchband. It worked well for establishing directions, but serious navigation across open wastelands for long stretches, trying to follow an azimuth, required something with more guts. With his radio and GPS position locator sat link dead, he wished that he had gone ahead and stuck his old trusty Silva Ranger in his vest pocket.

He always carried the timeworn compass, just in case. Only this trip, Billy Claybaugh had called him OCD for always packing it and never needing it. So to show the staff sergeant he wasn't OCD, and didn't need a security blanket, nor would he need to suck his thumb without it, Jack dropped the Silva compass in the flat middle drawer of his desk.

"I guess I showed Billy." Jack had laughed to himself.

The reason he veered south, rather than remain on the closer, north side of the T1 road, was that all night long he kept hearing trucks and cars with bad mufflers driving fast across the wastelands to his north, coming from the west and heading east. The elevated highway gave him a slight buffer as well as a known landmark to use for orientation.

Half a day more walking west, and Jack planned to arc northward, before he drew too close to the city of al-Qa'im, which lay just off the Syrian border. Another ten miles from where he called it a night and stopped to rest through the next day. He would make his turn well before T1 made its bend north and intersected MSR Bronze, Iraqi Highway 12, outside the town of al-Obaidy, a farming community on the south banks of the Euphrates River, just east of al-Qa'im. A busy place for al-Qaeda.

Jack decided that when he reached the point that he could see MSR Bronze on the horizon, he would turn his course eastward. Remaining well in the wild lands, he'd move parallel to that highway at a distance, as it took him homeward, bending toward the south and Haditha.

Once he got close enough to Haditha Dam, he'd turn on his MARSOC short-range intercom and start calling. One or all of his four-man Mob Squad, Iceman, Sal the Pizza Man, Nick the Nose, and Momo, standing duty with Alvin Barkley and his Marines, would surely have their ears on, listening. Undoubtedly, they would also have the S2 and S3 cued up on the channel. He absolutely didn't want to approach their base unannounced.

In a matter of days, Jack could grow a healthy dark beard. With his tanned complexion, inherited from his Latina mother, he knew he would look way too much like an Arab. On the run, he considered, that might be a good thing. But hiking toward the forward operating base at Haditha Dam, the look could get him killed.

As Gunny Valentine tucked himself into a cozy hide that he dug with Sergeant Quinlan's entrenching tool among a bunch of rocks and a crop of two-foot-tall Alhagi camelthorn bushes, just before sunrise, he heard the coursing sound of diving jets followed by the rolling thunder of their bomb loads delivered on targets far to his east. He wished badly that he had some way to talk to those guys. He'd direct them on the trucks and cars rumbling all night to his north.

An hour before morning Colors, an over-capacity number of military officers and ranking enlisted Marines stuffed the briefing room at Al Asad Air Base. Cesare Alosi had caught a ride on the Osprey out of Baghdad carrying the headquarters contingent of so-called security experts and intelligence analysts and other big thinkers.

First seat he grabbed belonged to the Marine Expeditionary Force chief of staff, at the end of the conference table, just to the right of the commanding general. To his right, the regimental landing-team commander had his seat. The battalion sergeant major caught the blundering civilian before the bosses entered the room. He promptly hustled Alosi out of the colonel's chair and pointed at the seats along the wall, in the rear.

"I need to be at the table," Cesare argued.

"I need to see documentation of your top secret security clearance," the sergeant major answered.

"Do you know who I am?" the Malone-Leyva boss huffed. "I have the same rank and privileges as an oh-six colonel!"

"I need to see that clearance, or you're not staying in here at all," the sergeant major responded, and tagged at the end, "sir."

Alosi reached in his breast pocket and took out his passport. Folded inside, he kept a copy of his clearance document. He wagged it under the Marine's nose.

The sergeant major took it, checked his name, and looked at a list of invited guests on a clipboard, found Alosi's name, checked it, then handed him back his clearance.

"Nothing that anyone says or anything that you see goes outside this room," the sergeant major told Cesare. "Your seat is back there, not at this table. According to the list, you're only a guest, here in purely a consulting capacity. If someone asks you a question, you answer it. Otherwise, you remain silent. Do you understand? Sir."

Alosi glared at the Marine, found a chair at the very back of the room, against the wall. On his way to it, however, he stopped at the coffee urn on a side table and poured himself a steaming cup of the general's brew.

The room quickly filled, and Lieutenant Colonel Edward Bartholomew Roberts took his place at the lectern on the right side of a large rear-projection screen in the front of the room. Seconds later, everyone stood, and the MEF commander and his chief of staff entered and sat down.

Alosi juggled his coffee getting to his feet. When he sat, he spilled a third of the hot joe down his trousers leg and on his shoe. It splashed on the boots of the major sitting next to him, too, and drew a frown.

"As you no doubt know, gentlemen," Black Bart began, "we have shifted from an overall offensive posture in Operation Quick Strike Vengeance to more counter-offensive actions. This is due to a breach of security that is under investigation, and the resulting enemy buildup of forces. Before we had a handle on this, our units suffered a series of surprise ambushes along MSR Bronze and ASR Phoenix.

"We managed to thwart one action of particular note that was directed at a Marine Special Operations team, and rescued seven of their eight members. Two of those men suffered non-life-threatening wounds. One Marine remains missing in action.

"Estimated enemy dead stand at three hundred, in that one action alone."

"Three hundred against eight Marines? Very impressive," the general remarked.

"Many more escaped, sir," the colonel said. "When I asked the team leader for an estimate of enemy force, his response was 'All of them.'"

"That many, huh?" the chief of staff said.

"And more coming into Denver Area of Operations daily," the colonel added.

"For now, our forces from Haditha Dam south to Hit

have altered our original sweep plan to one of search and destroy," the battalion commander continued. "We send out probes with quick-response reinforcements backing them up. The probe encounters fire, they hold as we bring the hammer to bear on the anvil."

"How's that working out, Colonel Roberts?" the chief of staff asked.

"Quite good," Black Bart answered. "We now use our operation plan as a guide to establish where we think the enemy force will be lying in wait."

"What about the missing Marine?" the chief followed.

"We suspect that the enemy is not aware he is out there," Roberts responded. "Gunnery Sergeant Jack Valentine is one of the best special operators in the Marine Corps. He is a survival expert, master of field crafts, as well as possessing the full pack of Force Reconnaissance training. Unfortunately, he has no functioning communications except a short-range ultrahigh-frequency intercom that may or may not still be working."

"You have searchers looking for him?" the general asked.

"Absolutely, sir," Roberts answered. "Drones and aircraft making zigzag passes along the desert area north of T1 and within that area. No sign of him. However, each of the sorties has scored impressive strikes on enemy forces transiting the area in trucks, cars, and on motorcycles.

"With the increased Haji movement and apparent gathering of forces we've encountered, Gunny Valentine, no doubt, has set his profile extremely low. He'll be next to impossible for us or the enemy to spot.

"Valentine's senior assistant team leader, Staff Sergeant Terrence Martin, who is here in the room, said that the gunny is hiking a big circle, west, north, then east, and will end up at Haditha Dam. Given his skills, one of our top Scout-Sniper instructors, we won't likely see him until he pops his head up at the final objective. We thoroughly briefed our Marines up there on the situation, and they have their ears and eyes wide open."

"Do you think it's possible that the enemy may have killed him or has him prisoner?" the chief of staff asked.

"Given who he is, the enemy would definitely make a big deal of it," Roberts said. "Only other possibility is that he died in the desert, unknown to anyone. Not a prospect I like to consider. As I said, he is equipped for survival and well trained. I expect him at Haditha Dam in coming days."

"His name again?" the general asked, jotting notes.

"Gunnery Sergeant John Arthur Valentine," the battalion commander answered. "He goes by Jack."

The regimental landing-team commander leaned forward and told the general and chief of staff, "Valentine's last tour here, the Hajis pinned him with the name *Ash'abah al-Anbar*. The Ghost of Anbar. He scored a pallet of high-value kills around Fallujah, then a bunch up here, too, augmenting Twenty-fifth Marines. Very creative fellow. He put phony guns in fake sniper hides on rooftops, had guys go to and from them, as if they were manned. Then, when gangs of Hajis moved on the positions, he killed them from afar with his team's direct sniper fire and took out their support crews with light artillery. Very creative man.

"Needless to say, the Hajis don't like the gunny one bit. Sir, if they got Jack Valentine, dead or alive, we'd definitely know it. He would be a highly publicized prize."

"What they don't know won't hurt them then," the general said. "Gunny Valentine's identity and the fact he's missing in action stays under tight wraps. That clear?"

"That's what I prefer, sir, and Colonel Roberts strongly concurs," the regimental boss said. "Valentine's best chance is total secrecy. If the enemy realizes we have a Marine missing, they'll go to great efforts to find him. If they learn it's *Ash'abah al-Anbar*, they'll put every dog they have between Baghdad and Damascus on the hunt."

"No doubt," the general said. "That also means that search and rescue efforts have to remain secret. Keep them looking like search and destroy. We sure as hell don't want to tip the bastards by flying grid search patterns."

"Correct, sir," Roberts said. "My opinion, Gunny Valentine's got to pretty much get himself out of the desert. We go fishing for him? It could get him killed."

Cesare Alosi sipped what was left of his coffee and could not help smiling, imagining all the possibilities.

"What crawled up your ass?" the major sitting by him said, seeing the man sparkle.

"Oh," Cesare said, "I'm just thrilled that Gunny Valentine has got a real chance. He could well make it."

No sooner had the briefing ended than Alosi hurried with the gaggle of straphangers and horse-holders back to the tarmac for their ride home to Baghdad, and he began digging through the address book in his smartphone. United States Senator Cooper Carlson. Perfect payback. As he got on the Osprey, he brought up the phone number.

When the aircraft landed a few minutes later, Cesare couldn't wait until he got to his Cadillac. As soon as he closed the car door, he punched his phone's GO button.

An aide answered, then put Alosi straight through.

"You still in Iraq?" Cooper Carlson said, standing in a black-silk robe by a floor-to-ceiling bank of windows in his penthouse apartment atop a Las Vegas hotel, held by the blind trust that his big-money cronies had set up for the senator's share of their partnership in several high-end gambling resort properties.

"Yes, sir," Alosi said.

"Why, you sound like you're just down the street," Carlson said. "I'm about to turn in for the evening, and Henry says you're on the phone. Finally got a night off from campaigning. The wife's gone to Los Angeles for the week, so I have a sweet young thing on her way up to make me sleepy."

"Oh, I envy you, sir," Cesare said. "A blonde?"

"With big tits." Carlson laughed.

"How would you like a little tidbit of anonymous information that if you play right will put you on the front pages on both coasts, and on CNN and Fox News?" Alosi said.

"What on earth do you have? Saddam's fabled weapons of mass destruction?" Carlson bubbled.

"Not that, but something that might work even better. Something that will make you the glowing champion of the little man, truth, and the American people's right to know," Cesare offered.

"Out with it!" Carlson said.

"How about a serviceman missing in action?" Alosi teased. "How about a military cover-up of it, too?"

"They got a soldier missing in action, and they're covering it up?" Carlson said, and smiled like a greedy cat in a roomful of fat mice. "That ought to take the pressure off your shooting fiasco of those thirty-five dead Iraqis."

"This isn't just any serviceman," Alosi said. "He's one of their best Special Operations Marines. In fact, he's the senior Scout-Sniper instructor in the Marine Corps, and the top operator in the Marine Corps' answer to Delta Force and SEALs, Marine Special Operations Command."

"Henry!" Carlson bellowed. "Get on the extension and start writing this stuff down."

The aide grabbed the phone at the desk. "Here, sir."

"What's this guy's name? And give Henry all the dirty details," Carlson said.

"This information is strictly confidential, sir. Classified top secret," Alosi said, covering his ass.

"They'll never know you told me a thing," Carlson said.

"And, do you have a special reward for me? You know, me thinking of you and your campaign," Cesare said, smiling.

"Name it. It's yours," Carlson said. "Now I've got a blonde with big tits that wants some of my cock meat. You and Henry take care of this business, while I take care of the monkey business." He laughed and so did Cesare.

"What was that guy's name again?" the senator said, getting off the line. "You listening, Henry?"

"Yes, sir," Henry said.

"Valentine," Alosi said. "Gunnery Sergeant John Arthur Valentine. They call him Jack."

A North Carolina gust off a thunderstorm caught the door behind June Snow and banged it against the house as she struggled her way into the Camp Lejeune officer-quarters kitchen, lugging sacks of groceries. Just back, they had flown home to Wyoming for Rowdy Yates's funeral at the Veterans' Cemetery on the northeast side of Casper.

June and Elmore had gotten home late last night. The colonel had gone to work early, feeling bad, so the missus decided to cook a stew for dinner, and they would turn in early. She made a run to the Camp Lejeune commissary, bought groceries, and when she got home, Elmore's car sat in the driveway. Way too early for him to be home for the day.

With the wind giving her fits at the door, she thought surely her husband would come running to help. So, when he didn't, she set the bags in the kitchen and went upstairs to find him.

As she pushed open the bedroom door, she saw Elmore on his knees at the side of their bed, praying like a child. His green military Val-A-Pack suitcase sat bulging, packed full, by the closet door. A canvas special operations kit bag, likewise stuffed, lay next to it.

June Snow knew without asking that a whole new wave of bad news had come home. Elmore never had to mention that he would fly back to Iraq tonight from Cherry Point. The longtime military wife knew it without asking.

"What happened?" she said softly, after she knelt by her husband and bowed her head with him.

He looked at her. "Jack Valentine's missing in action."

She let out a breath, took her husband's hand, and began praying, too.

After Elmore finished his talk with God, he waited for June. Then he lifted her to her feet and gave her a long kiss, filled with his years of love for the hometown girl he romanced in the wild lands where Headgate Draw meets Crazy Woman Creek.

"Mike Burkehart called me," he told her. She said nothing, and Elmore went on, "His career's finished. They lost a classified document. Some character, a former Marine from one of those bloody security companies, apparently snatched it when Corporal Ralph Butler had his head turned."

"What was it?" June Snow asked.

"The top secret plan for the operation that Jack and our detachment supported," Elmore said.

"And?" June added.

"And, the information in that operation plan apparently fell into enemy hands, compromised the whole battalion, including the eight-man patrol that Jack led. The enemy lay in ambush for them. They estimate fifty enemy at least, and hundreds more behind them. By God's hand, and Gunny Valentine's courage, all seven of our boys got out alive, but Jack stayed behind."

"Jack Valentine sacrificed himself to save his Marines," June said, and sounded a bit perturbed in her tone.

"I hope he didn't sacrifice himself," Elmore said, and pinched his wife on the cheek. "Jack provided cover for his men to escape. That's what a leader does. I would have done it and expect no less from any of my Marines."

"Oh, I know," June breathed out, "but it is just so Jack. You know what I mean. He loves a good show."

"I doubt that Jack is very pleased right now," Elmore responded. "Captain Burkehart said that the gunny had successfully evaded capture. Now, our boy has a long, lonely walk in the dark, working his way to Haditha Dam by way of the western desert in Anbar Governance."

"I'll call the chapel's prayer chain," June said, starting to leave.

Elmore took her arm. "No. You can't say anything to anyone. It's top secret. We're banking that al-Qaeda doesn't know a Marine has gone missing. We absolutely don't want them to know it's Jack. Our prayers will have to be sufficient."

June kissed her man. "What time does your plane leave?"

Nothing hurts worse than snagging a little toe on the leg of a coffee table. Cesare Alosi thought he had broken his off when he ran sock-footed to grab his ringing phone.

"Shit!" he screamed, dancing on one foot as he pushed the green button while the lightning bolt from his toe struck home. "Hold on! For crying out loud!" he wailed, falling in his chair and catching his breath.

"What!" he blared. "I think I just broke my toe!"

"Oh, poor you!" Liberty Cruz sang back and laughed.

"Miss Cruz? That you?" Cesare said, and spread a big smile. The pain suddenly worth the run for the phone.

"In the flesh, Mr. Alosi," she said.

"Cesare, please." He smiled and looked at her picture on his desk. "Someone told me you had come to Baghdad, but I could not believe it. What on earth for?"

"Oh," Liberty sighed, sounding exasperated. "I graduate SERE School, report to Washington, and what do I get? Typical female shitty little job, like they're doing me a favor. An administrative audit of the Baghdad FBI station."

"It's a man's world," Cesare said, and meant it. "Women come into it, they have to expect shitty little jobs. That's life in big-boy pants. Get used to it."

"I know," she said, trying to sound agreeable but already pissed off at Alosi's man's-world idealism. Some people who are assholes simply can't help being the assholes that they are. But Liberty didn't say anything of what she thought, only what she considered Cesare wanted to hear.

"I hate to ask you," she said, "but our FBI team in Baghdad is now investigating the shooting of the Iraqi civilians. We need to locate Ray-Dean Blevins and his crew. Can you help? I told them I knew you and that you would."

"I fired the three of them on the spot," Cesare said. "They're awaiting transportation back stateside. I have not talked to any of them since the shooting of those poor people. Frankly, I hope I never speak to that crew again."

"Can't blame you there, Cesare," Liberty said. "You wouldn't know where we could find them? Any ideas will help."

"I'd start at his apartment," Alosi said, trying to sound casual, but now worrying about what Cooder-with-a-D might say to the FBI if he had a little pressure put on him.

"You know," Liberty said, "I happen to be standing

in Ray-Dean's kitchen right now. He's nowhere around. And let me tell you, this boy lives like a pig."

"How did you get in his apartment?" Cesare said, and had to work at sounding calm. "You have no jurisdiction."

"Well . . ." Liberty said, letting the word stretch into almost a whine. "Iraqi police have taken jurisdiction on the killings. They opened full cooperation with the FBI in the investigation. Also, we have a little matter of some highly classified materials that we found hidden under the organizer tray in Mr. Blevins's silverware drawer. You wouldn't know about that, would you? Espionage and violation of the National Security Act of 1947? It opens a whole world of jurisdiction for the FBI. The Iraqi government is bending over backwards to help us, too. They're very upset at the security compromise. It is their country after all."

"I had no idea!" Cesare exclaimed, really scared. "What sort of classified documents we talking about? I should know about these things. It's a reflection on our company."

"Oh, I'm sorry. All I can share is the fact that the material we discovered in Mr. Blevins's apartment is highly classified," Liberty said. "Your man and his conspirators face serious charges. A capital offense."

"Death penalty?" Alosi gasped. "Seriously?"

"Treason is a capital crime," Liberty said.

"But nobody's been put to death," Alosi argued.

"You ever hear of Julius and Ethel Rosenberg?" the FBI agent said, trying really hard to suppress the tone in her voice that gave away the elation she felt, driving a dagger into the slimeball's heart.

"That was like the 1950s. The McCarthy Red Scare," Cesare scoffed. "America wouldn't do that now."

"Don't bet on it. If the espionage costs American lives? You better believe we'll fry the sons of bitches," Liberty fired back. Bob Hartley, Casey Runyan, and Cliff Towler stood close to her now, listening on the smartphone's speaker. Hartley had a big grin going on.

"Well, those sons of bitches deserve what they get!" Cesare said, trying to now sound supportive. "You can count on Malone-Leyva pulling out all stops to assist the FBI in bringing the scumbags to swift justice. Let the chips fall where they may. Just rest assured that no one in this company had any idea that Blevins or those other two fools on his team had anything like espionage going on."

"Count on a thorough investigation, Cesare," Liberty said. "We appreciate your cooperation. Now, how about any ideas you may have on Blevins and his crew's location?"

"If he's not at his apartment, there's only one other place I'd look," Alosi said.

"Baghdad Country Club?" Liberty said.

"Oh! You know the place?" Cesare said, trying to sound surprised.

"Of course you know I do." Liberty smiled. "I would be disappointed if your agents had not reported seeing me there with Chris Gray just after I arrived in Baghdad."

"They mentioned this beautiful woman with long black hair smoking a cigar," Alosi answered. "I thought it might be you, but no one said your name."

"Of course not," Liberty said.

"You heading there now?" Cesare asked.

"Closing up Ray-Dean's apartment as we speak," Liberty said. "We've got what we need for now."

"Look, I'll head to·the club myself," Cesare said.

"Oh, I think we have it covered," Liberty said. "But if you really want to help. By all means. Join us."

"Thirty minutes?" Cesare said.

"Probably less," Liberty said.

High in a window overlooking the Baghdad Country Club a block away, Ken with the face tattoo lay on a table atop a Remington model 700 custom sniper rifle chambered to shoot the standard Russian 7.62-by-54-millimeter rimmed Dragunov sniper-rifle round. George sat in a chair by the table, watching the front door of the saloon where Ray-Dean Blevins, Freddie Stein, and Gary Frank had gone two hours ago, getting snot-slinging, commode-hugging drunk.

When the phone rang, George with the Nazi SS neck tattoo answered, "Yeah."

"You remember what we talked about at my office?" Cesare Alosi said.

The big guy with the shaved head wiped sweat off of it and had to think.

Ken looked away from the scope on the sniper rifle, and said, "Come on, George. You know. After we took those civilians to the airport. We went to the office and talked about stuff."

"Oh yeah," George said. "That?"

"Yeah," Cesare said. Then added, "Are you where you said you'd be?"

"Were we supposed to be someplace else?" George said.

"Look," Cesare said, "I have no doubt that right now our communications are anything but private, much less even resembling secure. Do you understand?"

"So, we shouldn't talk about what we talked about?" George asked.

"Not even," Ken grumbled, rolling on his side on the table. "You're dumber than a fucking lamp, George."

He grabbed the cell phone from his partner.

"Boss," Ken said. "The mission's a go?"

"Yes!" Cesare said, relieved. "Be quick. You have less than twenty minutes."

"It's all good, boss," Ken said. "We did a little prep work, just in case it was a go. You know?"

"Very good," Alosi said, smiling. "Very good indeed. You've got the green light on the mission."

Chris Gray had listened to Alosi's phone calls for days, and to his henchmen just now. He grabbed his driver at the CIA office in the embassy and headed out. On the run to Baghdad Country Club, he called Liberty Cruz.

"Two hours ago, I got a call from Ajax. Blevins and his crew arrived at the club, drinking hard," Gray said. "Just now, I'm monitoring Alosi's phone, and he gives a crew of enforcers a green light on executing a mission they'd talked about shortly after the civilian shootings.

Fair warning. Ears up, eyes open. Something's going down."

"We're nearly there now," Liberty said, Bob Hartley zigging and zagging through Green Zone traffic, the female agent in the backseat of a government GMC Denali, hidden by black, bullet-resistant glass. "You think they'll try something against us? Surely not!"

"Actually, I was thinking old Cooder and the boys," Gray said. "If Alosi's guilty, I'm betting that Blevins and Frank-n-Stein can nail him. Especially now that you recovered the missing copy of the op plan and the thumb drive. Dead men tell no tales."

"About that missing copy," Liberty said. "The one we found in Blevins's apartment is a copy of the missing original. Made on a machine you find in any office here."

"Maybe Cooder passed off the original, for the cash. Kept a copy as a backup to sell to the next bidder," Gray said.

"Who knows?" Cruz said. "It's not the original, but it's incriminating for Blevins. I want to hear what he says."

"You better step on it then," Gray said. "I've got a hunch that Cooder and his boys may not live much longer."

"We're five minutes out," Liberty said.

"Look in the mirror," Gray said. "Right behind you."

Cesare kept punching the speed dial on his built-in car phone as he raced to the Baghdad Country Club. "Come on, Blevins! Answer!" he yelled, dodging between traffic.

Just then, a slurry Ray-Dean finally got tired of hearing

his smartphone buzz on the saloon table and picked it up. "What the fuck now? You piece of shit!"

"Thank God!" Alosi said. "We've had our differences, Ray, but I'm warning you. Get out of there now! I'll explain later. You have to leave right this second!"

"What the fuck are you babbling about, you greasy maggot," Ray-Dean said.

"Yeah, you're a fucking piece of shit off the bottom of the shit pond, Alosi," a good and drunk Fred Stein added.

Gary Frank sat there silent. He thought he might wangle his job back. After all, he persisted on telling everyone, he had only followed orders. Just drove the car. He never fired a shot.

"You've got a crew of FBI agents maybe three minutes from the club!" Cesare yelled on his speaker as he drove his Escalade several cars behind Liberty and Gray, spotting them now and keeping them both in sight.

"What for?" Ray-Dean said.

"To arrest your dumb ass!" Cesare shouted, his face beet red and the blood veins bulging on his forehead.

"They got no jurisdiction," Blevins argued.

"They do for treason," Alosi came back.

Freddie Stein heard the word "treason," and it sent him running out of the club. He jumped in the backseat of their team's Escalade and locked the doors.

"Let me in!" Gary Frank screamed outside, yanking on the door handle. He had bolted on Stein's heels. Then he saw the FBI Denali jump the curb outside the outer garden that surrounded the Baghdad Country Club and watched it slide sideways on the edge of the parking lot.

Chris Gray came in behind them, skidding to a stop, too.

Cesare Alosi guided his Cadillac carefully over the curb and parked behind the two embassy cars, well away from where Ray-Dean had left the Malone-Leyva Escalade, just a few feet from the blue-stucco building with the big darkened plate-glass picture window and blue neon sign in it.

Gary Frank took off running, heading for the trees and hedges that hid Baghdad Country Club from the Islamic society offices next door.

Ray-Dean made a dash for his car but had only made two steps out of the country club's front door when his Escalade exploded in a mushroom of orange-and-white fire.

Car doors flew two directions, and the roof went straight up. The hood was torn off its hinges and sailed through the blue-stucco building's picture window, destroying the blue neon sign and taking out most of the tables and chairs across the center of the nightclub.

Luckily, no one inside died. They had all hit the floor when Freddie and Gary tore out of the room and on their heels Ray-Dean screamed on the phone at Alosi, "You double-crossing son of a bitch! I'll make you pay!"

When Ray-Dean had run out of the bar, he caught a faceful of energy from the explosion, blowing him off his feet and sending him skidding across the gravel parking area.

Gary Frank had made it to the trees, successfully pissed his pants, then instantly died when the first sniper shot split his head in half.

Ray-Dean staggered to his feet, saw Cesare Alosi running

toward him, behind Liberty Cruz and Chris Gray. He tried to run to them as well, but Ken with the face tattoo put a Russian-made bullet into his heart.

His third and fourth shots just missed Cesare, Chris, and Liberty. They ran for cover while George and Ken gathered their gear and left the rimmed Russian sniper-rifle shell casings behind.

Midafternoon, Jack awoke, stewing in his own sweat. The camouflage sheet he had spread over his hiding hole, blending him with the rocks and the Alhagi camel-thorns, made him invisible unless a person walked directly over him, but it also trapped the heat. Not a breath of a breeze stirred in the sweltering afternoon, and that just made things worse.

He took out his second bottle of water since he had lain down and emptied it in his mouth.

"I hope I don't end up having to drink my own piss," he said to himself, saving the empty bottle with two others.

Jack knew not to starve himself on food or water. He needed to keep his energy and vitality at a high peak if he expected to survive the long walk through the desert. When people trying to survive limit their water and food intake to below minimums, they fall weak and die. One thing he learned in survival training, focus on finding food and water at all times while pressing onward to the objective. He counted on finding water and food sources along the trek and taking what he needed from them. They were out here. He just had to see them. If the travelers of old could do it, so could Jack Valentine.

Just as he had started to pull out some food to nibble from an open package of Meals Ready to Eat, Jack heard the roar of a truck engine. When he raised his head to see, a tire spun by his face, and the greasy underbody of a Toyota pickup truck went flying over his head.

"Shit!" he said, putting his head out to see if the passing vehicle simply had run past him or its riders had seen him.

A quarter mile away, the blue pickup truck with a gunman in the back, carrying an AK rifle, made a spinning donut turn, shooting dirt sky-high as he came back around.

"They saw me," Jack grumbled to himself, taking his Vigilance rifle and putting the crosshairs on the driver, now bearing down on him. "I shouldn't have looked. They saw me when I stuck my head out. They were going away, and dumb-ass me, I had to look."

At a hundred yards and closing, Jack's shot killed the driver, and the truck turned sideways. It shot up in the air, flipping like a football kicked for a field goal. The passenger managed to stay inside, but the rider in the back went bouncing across the world, his arms and legs snapping and his head twisted on his neck like a rag.

The tumbling wreck came straight at Jack, and he lay flat in his hole as it passed overhead and stopped rolling fifty feet behind him.

Somehow, the passenger inside managed to survive it all. He crawled from the wreck moaning. Then he saw Gunny Valentine standing, his hand reaching down his leg for the pistol strapped there.

The Haji had a broken leg. When he tried to stand and

aim his AK rifle at the Marine, the bone folded below the knee. He went down hard but still kept going for his gun.

"Fuck, dude," Jack said, pulling out his Lippard .45 and taking aim. He squeezed off a 230-grain flat-nose hardball into the guy's head. "It just ain't your day."

_ 13 _

"You're free to go," Liberty Cruz told a haggard, disheveled, stinking-body-odor, dirty-underwear, ragged-out Cesare Alosi as she took manacles from his hands and feet that chained him to a chair bolted to the gray-concrete floor with a curious drain in the center. There were no water faucets in here, nor a showerhead.

Chris Gray typed in the unlock code on the keypad outside that opened the steel door to the secure interview room at Camp Liberty, on the north side of Camp Victory joint military headquarters, letting Cesare walk out with Liberty and Bob Hartley behind him. Tucked among rows of hundreds of similar nondescript block-shaped white modular buildings, the CIA took interesting people here for long, often persuasive periods of discussion about all they knew.

A tight-lipped secret, the place had no flags or signs nor anything else to set the CIA annex apart from all the other hundreds of identical refrigerator-like modules, except for the number stenciled in black paint on each corner, and some bombproof steel doors with special locks. The Camp Liberty complex provided Chris Gray and Speedy Espinoza a snug place outside prying eyes and ears to do their dirty work and prepare for other dark jobs. Their CIA teams could also come here unnoticed, store gear, shower, hit the rack in the dozen adjoining sleeping modules, watch television, relax, or drink a beer or two undisturbed. Iraqi counterparts could also bring clients here with black bags on their heads, and no one paid attention or cared.

For the FBI special-weapons-and-tactics team, and their leader, Agent Cruz, it provided the perfect spot to turn a few screws, if needed, plot and plan, and not have to tell a soul about it. Gray extended the invitation to use the facility right after he concluded that Liberty Cruz and her boys could play hardball on anybody's team.

The compound's location also gave Liberty the added benefit of being close to the joint-military-command headquarters, where she daily checked on the status of Jack Valentine. There, she could speak directly with Black Bart Roberts over the resecured command voice network, getting his reassuring updates. Gunny Valentine was his friend, too, in the way that colonels and gunnery sergeants can be professional and share a strong, long-lasting friendship.

Liberty had wanted to tell Jack's mom and dad about him missing, and tell her parents, too. But Roberts forbade it.

"We will only worry them with our not knowing a thing," the colonel explained. "More importantly, anxious parents who fear that the enemy has their sons often try to reach out to them on their own, and appeal for mercy via the news media, who are all too enthusiastic to help, for their own selfish interests. Jack's life greatly depends on the enemy's not knowing he's out there."

"I understand," Liberty agreed. So she bit her tongue and did not discuss Jack Valentine with anyone, not her team and not even with Chris Gray, her new best friend.

Work and focus on Cesare Alosi took her mind off her missing Marine. She spent day and night at the CIA modular offices. So did her crew. They liked it here better than the Green Zone apartments in town.

They had spirited Cesare to Camp Liberty right after Ray-Dean and his boys got theirs, under the guise of protective custody, should anyone up the chain ask questions. If what Alosi had claimed was true, that al-Qaeda or the Iraqi police, or both, wanted retribution for the slaughter of the thirty-five civilians in the protected International Zone, and that's why they killed the men responsible, then the killers might also want to get even with the dead men's boss.

Cesare could do nothing but cooperate.

Bob Hartley took agents Runyan and Towler to the airport right after the shootings and car bombing at Baghdad Country Club, looking for George and Ken, where Cesare said he had sent them. He had supposedly given them a green light to hunt a sniper outside the KBR terminal at Camp Fallujah.

The FBI agents did in fact find the two skinheads, rifles and kits with them, mounting a Malone-Leyva black Jet Ranger helicopter with the silver M-L and Scorpion logo on its side, about to depart for Fallujah. The agents inspected their weapons. Nothing dirty, all clean, oiled, ready for service. Both men freshly washed, too.

Runyan got on the phone with the dispatcher at the KBR terminal and he confirmed that Malone-Leyva had contracted with their company to take care of security, and the ongoing sniper problem that not only took its toll on trucks and drivers but took an increasing number of Marines and soldiers patrolling from Camp Fallujah and Camp Ramadi, too. He complained about their delay. Hartley disconnected the call in midsentence of the KBR dispatcher's rant.

Liberty slapped a set of handcuffs on Alosi as soon as he opened his mouth to whine. Poor Ray-Dean Blevins and bed-wetting Gary Frank still quivered in the dirt, as Freddie Stein lay scattered in pieces with the car. Cesare immediately sang his song about the Iraqis wanting to get even, and that's why they must have murdered the crew.

"Bullshit!" Liberty said as she clamped the bracelets as hard as she could squeeze them on Alosi's wrists.

"You put them on too tight! That hurts!" Cesare wailed.

"That's because they're new," Liberty popped back. "Wear them awhile. They'll stretch out."

Chris Gray took Miz Cruz aside while Bob Hartley shoved the squirmy little dirtbag into the backseat of the CIA Denali, so they could head to the airport and before Iraqi security forces got there to make things more difficult.

"You have no jurisdiction," Gray reminded her, taking Liberty aside. "Have you thought about what you're going to do with him? And what about Jason Kendrick?"

"No!" Liberty said. "And jurisdiction can kiss my ass.

You know and I know he had those guys murdered before I had a chance to talk to them or protect them. Fuck the rules. Fuck Kendrick. I want Alosi's head on a pike!"

"In Iraq, we do things differently," the CIA operator said. "No jurisdiction? No court to back you up? No problem. In the States, no evidence, as in our case, you let him go. Here, the CIA can take any asshole off the street for any phony-baloney reason we hatch up. Hold him as long as we need or until we get bored, or the son of a bitch dies. Worst case, we at least make Cesare sweat his balls off."

"What do you have in mind?" Liberty asked.

"I've got his conversations with his people, ordering the hit, recorded," Gray said. "We can let him listen to himself giving the green light for a while, until it sinks in good and deep. Then we let him listen to the recording of him calling Ray-Dean on his car phone. He didn't think we had that number. But I'm the CIA. I got your number. Maybe we scare him. Say we'll give him to the Iraqi national security cops."

Liberty smiled and looked at Alosi sitting smugly on his hands in the backseat of the Denali. "Even though we can't really give him to the Iraqis, I'd enjoy pressing the sneaky bastard. Watch him squirm."

She looked back at Gray. "Honestly, though? I don't think he's going to say a thing. He's getting away with espionage, murder, the whole thing, and he knows it."

"So, we have a few days' fun torturing the smug little motherfucker. See how he likes the taste of his own shit," Gray said. "Junkyard justice."

Liberty laughed and looked back at Alosi. "Fuck yeah."

For the next four days, they pressed Alosi. Let him sit it out in the little white room with the one-way glass window. They cooked him to stew the first twenty-four hours with the heat up and no restroom privileges until he finally went to the corner and urinated on the wall. When he took a shit there, they locked him to the hard bottom metal chair bolted to the floor, where he slept sitting up, if he slept. No restroom privileges.

Chris Gray played a repeating loop of his recorded telephone conversations with his pipe-hitting enforcers and with Ray-Dean Blevins on an overhead sound system. During breaks, Liberty came in the room with Hartley or Towler or Runyan at her side and questioned him. He sat cuffed to his chair, glared at her, and said zilch.

Then Cesare spent the next day in total silence, with bare fluorescent tubes overhead burning a pale dismal green hue against the white walls and gray floor. Bob Hartley brought him a meal of bread and water. Alosi ate it, drank the water, and smiled defiantly.

After that, Chris Gray turned on thirty straight hours of Norwegian black metal rock over the room's embedded surround-sound system. Tsjuder, Mayhem, and Immortal roared out their apocalyptic rage, mixed with random selections from Marilyn Manson, turned up full blast. A nonstop loop with the lights shut off. The sealed room, blacked out, left Alosi in utter darkness, smelling his shit and hearing without relief the raspy voices of what Satan and his demons must sound like.

Alosi endured it all and still said nothing. Not one word. He felt proud, powerful. Fouled drawers and all. He showed them.

Then on the fourth day, CNN reported the findings of the Iraqi police that the Americans guilty of killing the thirty-five civilians had died from an al-Qaeda attack. Zarqawi had issued a statement: Retribution for the innocent lives the Americans took. He gave credit for the bombing and sharpshooting to none other than the legendary Phantom of Baghdad, Juba the sniper, and his sidekick, Hasan.

Two Russian sniper rifle rimmed shell casings were conveniently found in an open floor of a nearby building, and the ballistics on the bullets taken from the bodies matched, proving that they were fired from a Dragunov rifle. American and Iraqi bomb experts also determined that the bomb had all the earmarks of al-Qaeda Iraq.

"It was fun, Cesare," Liberty said, as the disheveled, red-eyed, and exhausted Alosi walked out of the small white room. "We'll have to do it again real soon."

"You fuckers," Cesare said as he gathered his cell phone, wallet, watch, pocket trinkets, and keys. "I won't forget this. You don't fuck with me and not get fucked back. I know people. You should have killed me. Your asses are mine now."

"We can always help you out there, ass-wipe," Bob Hartley said. "Got a black bag in the back, just your size."

"Fuck you!" Cesare snapped at the smiling FBI man. "Fuck all of you!"

Chris Gray took a lean against the wall by the outer door to the white modular building where they had worked over Alosi's mind for four and a half days. Runyan and Towler sat out front in the FBI Denali, waiting to take the Malone-Leyva boss to the airport, where a company gun crew and driver waited for him.

The CIA operator took out a green packet of Doublemint chewing gum, unwrapped a piece, and folded it in his mouth. Then he pushed out a piece toward Cesare as he departed.

"Go ahead. Take one." Gray smiled. "Helps the breath."

When Elmore Snow finally reached Baghdad, he found Captain Mike Burkehart dozing in an airport lobby chair with Corporal Ralph Butler zeed out beside him. They had waited in front of one of the lobby flat-screen televisions since eight o'clock that morning, four hours ago.

Elmore's flight leg from RAF Mildenhall, in Suffolk, England, to Baghdad had been delayed while US Air Force mechanics repaired a hydraulic-system issue. Something to do with the rear ramp fully closing on the C-17 Globemaster. He had caught a ride on a retiring C-141 Starlifter at Dover Air Force Base, making its final flight, after a choppy ride out of Cherry Point the day before on a Marine Corps UC-12W, known among the civilian world as a Beechcraft King Air 350 turboprop.

He had managed to sleep most of the transatlantic hop, two good nights in the BOQ at Mildenhall, then part of the way from England to Iraq. So when he arrived in Baghdad, he came off the plane well rested and ready to work.

The colonel gave Mike Burkehart a nudge on the toe, and the captain popped open a blood-red eye. Then he shot an elbow into Sleeping Beauty Butler that sent the kid bolting out of the seat.

"Sir!" the corporal stammered, snapping his heels together. Burkehart stood by him and reached a welcome handshake to Elmore Snow.

"Sorry about the delay," the colonel said. "You waited here the whole time?"

"Yes, sir, just this morning," Burkehart said. "Only information we could get was that your flight was delayed for a repair. We had no idea if it would be an hour or a day."

"How are you holding up, Mike?" Elmore asked, and gave Smedley a look, too. "And you, Corporal Butler?"

Smedley shook his head. "I don't know, sir. Pretty bad, I guess."

"Neither of us will go to jail." Burkehart smiled, and put his arm over the poor, sad corporal. "Smedley won't be reenlisting, and I'm retiring when we rotate out of here."

"I'm afraid it's all out of my hands," Elmore said. "I tried to intervene, but the general said we cannot make exceptions when it comes to national security. I have to agree. It is what it is."

"Sir, I know. There's no heartburn here with either of us," Burkehart said. "I should have logged in that op plan the minute First Sergeant Barkley handed it to me. When I signed his logbook, I just tossed it on the pile on your desk. I never thought about it again. A hectic day. Billy-C getting shot and all."

"How is Sir William Claybaugh?" Elmore smiled. "He sitting down okay?"

"Doing fine, sir," Burkehart said. "Out in the truck waiting for us." Then he turned and looked at Corporal

Butler. "If anyone took it in the shorts, it's Smedley. I didn't tell him about the op plan on your desk. Just too busy with the bullshit. You know how it gets."

"Sir," Butler said, hanging his head. "I should have looked. My job, keeping track. I let crap pile up. I'm the one who let that piece of shit Ray-Dean Blevins come in and make himself at home. I should have thrown his ass out!"

"What's the story on the filthy traitor?" Elmore asked.

"Got blown away," Burkehart said. "He and his crew. Their vehicle bombed, killed one guy. An al-Qaeda sniper, they say Juba, took out Blevins and the other guy."

"I heard tell that police recovered shell casings from a Dragunov and matched them to bullets they took out of the bodies, both Russian," Smedley added.

"So, it was an al-Qaeda hit," Elmore said.

"Who else?" Burkehart shrugged.

Elmore shrugged, too, then suddenly turned toward the television monitor overhead. He caught someone on CNN saying Jack Valentine's name.

"What did he say?" the colonel asked, and all three men watched the news broadcast.

Behind the news anchor was a boot-camp head-and-shoulders photograph of a very boyish Jack Valentine wearing dress blues with an American flag behind him. Across the bottom of the screen, a banner of red with white lettering announcing, BREAKING NEWS. AMERICAN MISSING IN ACTION.

A white-bearded news anchor said, "Marine Corps and Defense Department spokesmen have issued an official no comment on the report that Marine Special Operations

Gunnery Sergeant John Arthur Valentine is missing in action.

"United States Senator Cooper Carlson of Nevada had this to say about the official no comment from military leaders, following his announcement of the missing Marine."

The shot cut to Senator Carlson standing at a lectern on the grass outside the main entrance of Nellis Air Force Base, where he made a speech for campaign supporters and the national and Nevada news media. His staff had prepped the reporters before the event, letting them know that the senator would make an announcement of national importance. They had also rounded up every screaming bobblehead they could wrangle off the streets of Las Vegas to create the illusion for the press that the villagers had awakened, torches and pitchforks in hand, and now rallied around their champion, Cooper Carlson, for whom they chanted, "Coop," from his days playing college football at Princeton.

"I have railed against this abusive administration and its illegal war in Iraq," Carlson bellowed over the lectern at the cheering crowd. "Our servicemen and -women deserve better. They deserve diligent representation and attention, from a government that cares greatly for their lives! Not the cold and callous leadership that we have today! But impassioned, caring leaders like me! I have always stood up for our military people and fought hard for them."

The crowd erupted and chanted, "Coop! Coop! Coop!"

"Today, we have a heroic Marine missing in action, Gunnery Sergeant John Arthur Valentine, who selflessly sacrificed himself, saving his platoon. Allowing them to retreat to safety while he held off the enemy single-handedly," Carlson bellowed. "He deserves a medal and undying gratitude from his nation. Not the cold shoulder! Our military leadership cares so little about this one man that they turned their backs on him. Cut him adrift in the Iraqi desert. He wasn't even worth one airplane to search for him! As of this minute, we have no idea if Gunny Valentine is dead or alive, or worse yet, captured! Will we soon see him beheaded on video?"

The people cheered more, and the CNN cameras zoomed tight on the grandstanding politician.

"Now," Carlson shouted, his voice hoarse from yelling. "Our president and our military leaders have shut the door in our faces. No comment, they say. After we have found them out in this cover-up! What can they say?

"Well, here's what I say. One word for them: Busted!"

The whole crowd went crazy.

"We have reached out to Sergeant Valentine's mother and father in his hometown of El Paso, Texas, where he was a high school football star, loved by the whole city," the CNN news anchor said as the shot cut back to him in the Atlanta studios. "Here is our correspondent Gustav Cisneros with Harry and Elaine Valentine."

The shot cut to a father wearing a Vietnam veteran baseball cap, his face drawn, overwhelmed with sadness, and a mother in tears, holding a framed photograph of their missing son. While they talked, the camera took close-up shots of the many pictures of Jack Valentine, from his days in high school, in his football uniform, to a more recent shot of him with gunnery-sergeant stripes on his Marine Corps dress green uniform and a chest filled with ribbons topped with gold jump wings and a silver SCUBA/UBA head. A photo his mother had taken of him when he came home on leave following his tour in Iraq the prior year.

"Has anyone from the Marine Corps contacted you, Mr. Valentine?" the reporter asked.

"First thing we heard about Jackie missing was when that senator from Las Vegas called us last night," Harry Valentine said. "Nobody from the government has said a word to us, except for him."

Elaine Valentine held up the picture of Jack and pled in the camera, "Please, Mr. President. Go find our son! Bring our Jackie home."

"Do you think he may have been captured, and the government is just not saying anything?" Gustav Cisneros asked Harry Valentine.

"Jack Valentine will never be taken alive!" the gray-headed man snarled in the camera, his face red with anger. "I'll tell you this! He'll send one hell of a bunch of those al-Qaeda sons of bitches to hell with their seventy-two virgins before they kill him. They won't take my boy easy! Not my Jackie! No, sir!"

The camera panned to Elaine Valentine, who wailed and cried, "Please come home, *Mijo*!"

"So, Mr. Valentine, you think your son could be alive and not captured?" Cisneros asked, as the camera shot reversed to the reporter, then to Harry Valentine.

"I know my son's alive!" the old man said. "As smart as he is, I'll put money on him out there in that desert, avoiding capture and putting in the ground every al-Qaeda bastard that gets in his way."

Harry put his arms around his wife and hugged her. Then he said at the camera, "My boy's coming home. I'll put money on it! And he'll be real pissed that anybody had the nerve to make his mama cry."

"You think that the government has kept this a secret because they believe Sergeant Valentine is alive and avoiding capture?" the reporter followed up.

"Probably so. They've got their reasons," Harry said. "They could have told us about it, though. It wasn't right, us hearing about Jackie gone missing from some politician."

Cisneros looked at the camera. "Gustav Cisneros reporting from the Valentine home in El Paso, Texas. Back to you in Atlanta."

A scene of the shooting that took place outside the embassy came on the screen, and the news anchor said, "In other news from Iraq, Senator Jim Wells of Virginia has called for a full Senate investigation of the conduct of security contractors in Iraq, following the tragic gunfire that claimed the lives of thirty-five civilian bystanders. Wells is calling for the president to order that all contractor companies operating in any combat zone come under State Department and Department of Defense jurisdiction, in light of the deadly shooting by Malone-Leyva security agents on the street outside the United States embassy in Baghdad."

Then a picture of Ray-Dean Blevins in a Marine Corps uniform came on the screen. "The American contractor reported responsible for the shooting died just days later in a car bombing and sniper attack in Baghdad. Ray-Dean Blevins, a security supervisor for Malone-Leyva Executive Security and Investigations, along with his two-man crew, Frederick Stein and Gary Frank, were killed in an apparent attack by al-Qaeda Iraq in retaliation for the shootings of the civilians."

Elmore Snow looked at his two Marines. "I don't know why I bother even asking you two what's new. All I have to do these days is turn on CNN or Fox News."

Smedley Butler took Colonel Snow's luggage from his hands. "Let me get that, sir."

Captain Burkehart said as they headed for the Hummer, parked outside with Billy-C standing guard, "Colonel, to be honest. I'm ready to retire. My brother's got a gun shop in Loveland, Colorado. I'm going there to work. Fix guns. Teach people to shoot. Live the dream. I'm done with bullshit."

Liberty Cruz sat on the end of her bed in her Green Zone apartment, combing out her wet hair, crying. She had a small picture of her and Jack Valentine, taken during a lovers' weekend at Nags Head, on the Outer Banks of North Carolina, out front of Nestle's Nook, a little beachfront motel where they stayed. The owner, Herman Nestle, and his wife, Charlotte, ran the little place, each cottage personally decorated by Charlie, as they called Charlotte, who also baked key lime pies that drew nightly crowds that filled their little Cedar Post Barbecue Kitchen, where the motel office and front desk sat at one end.

She and Jack had planned to get married that weekend. But a fight took the air out of that balloon. Liberty wanted to wait on having children, until after they had accumulated some wealth and success, from the business that her attorney background and FBI training, experience, and connections would open, once she launched her own security and investigations company. Her lifelong dream. She wanted a summer villa in the mountains overlooking Milan, Italy, or near Saint Tropez, France. They could rent it out when they weren't using it, she had rationalized with Jack.

They would build their primary home someplace safe, away from the Mexican border. Perhaps Colorado, she suggested.

Jack, however, loved Mexico. His father had no family to speak of, a brother somewhere in Minnesota he hadn't seen in years. But his mother had a wonderful family down in the heart of beautiful mountains down south. Clear streams ran into crystal lakes teeming with fish. They could just disappear, he told Liberty. Live a simple, happy life with lots of children. His Marine Corps retired pay and money she could earn doing legal work for surrounding villages would have them living in style.

"It's Mexico, Jack!" Liberty blew up. "Drug cartels run the place nowadays. Don't you read the papers?"

"No." Jack shrugged. He could only remember the beautiful times he spent with his parents, visiting his mother's family. How he and his father had spent peaceful, beautiful days sitting in a small boat on Lake Santa Maria, looking in the clear water and catching more fish than they could ever eat.

Liberty cried more as she thought of Jack, alone in the

desert. Iraqi insurgents wanting to kill him. She cried more, too, because she knew that neither of them could commit nor compromise to the other's vision of what a good life would be for them together.

She wanted nice homes, wealth, and luxury, and Jack wanted simplicity. Money never interested him. He got a Bachelor of Arts degree in Literature and Art, for crying out loud. He didn't pursue something that would enable him to climb a ladder of success. He read Victor Hugo and Herman Melville, and dreamed of a world painted by Salvador Dali. Completely unrealistic!

"Oh, Jack!" she wept, and kissed the picture, just as someone knocked on her door.

Her cheeks streaked with tears and her hair hanging straight and wet. Not a smudge of makeup on her face, she started not to answer it, but then the voice outside changed her mind.

"Liberty!" he said. "It's Elmore. I know you're in there, so open up."

She ran to the door, and opened it. When Colonel Snow started to step inside, she threw her arms around him and kissed his cheek.

"Finally!" she cried. "Someone who loves me! Elmore, I need a hug so bad!"

The bristly gray old warrior smiled and gave her a big, long hug, and kissed her cheeks, tasting her tears. Then he looked into her eyes. "I'm so sorry about everything. I spoke to Jason Kendrick and he told me what happened. What he had to do. Girl, what got into your head?"

"Oh, Elmore," Liberty said, and closed the door behind her dear friend. "I don't care about all that."

"Jason told me he had relegated you to security over the copy machine and supply closet," Elmore said. "After the stunt you and the CIA pulled with that Malone-Leyva boss, what's his name?"

Liberty laughed. "I should have gone ahead and killed the bastard. I planned on resigning from the FBI in a year or two anyway. Opening my own contracting business. Investigations, legal digging. Corporate intelligence. Some security work. That's always been my goal, even before I went to law school. What Malone-Leyva proves to me, what I've always thought, is that a person with the right tools and contacts can get filthy rich in this business. I made some lasting friends with the CIA, and my contacts with DEA go way back. I'm ready to sprout wings and soar with the eagles."

"So getting more or less canned is no big deal?" Elmore said.

"Not at all." Liberty smiled. "It opened my cage and lets me fly."

"To be honest," Elmore said, "Kendrick had a good laugh about how you put that boy through the wringer. Satanic rock music in the dark? What did you hope to gain?"

"Satisfaction." Liberty smiled again. "I just wanted to fuck him up."

"Then why the tears?" Elmore asked.

"For a Marine colonel and a man married to one of the classiest women I have ever known, you're not very smart," Liberty said. Then Elmore noticed the little framed snapshot of her and Jack, lying on the bed.

"You know, I travel with a small framed picture of June

and me," Elmore said, picking up the photograph and looking at the couple, smiling in front of the motel sign. "Our tenth anniversary. Niagara Falls, of course. We stayed in a beautiful stone three-story bed-and-breakfast on the other side of the river, in Canada. Why haven't you and Jack gotten married? He'll never love anyone but you, and I know you won't have anyone but him. What's the holdup?"

"That's part of why I was crying, the holdup," Liberty said. "The biggest reason is my utter frustration with that asshole Senator Cooper Carlson. What could possess anyone, let alone a half-wit politician, to announce to the world and al-Qaeda that we have a Marine missing in the desert?"

"And tell them it's one of their greatest enemies, on top of that?" Elmore added. "It's one thing to tell them it's a Marine, but to let them know it's Jack Valentine, their so-called Ghost of Anbar? Carlson ought to be indicted for murder if they get their hands on Jack now."

"I want to know who the hell told him!" Liberty fired back. "That's the son of a bitch I want to lay hands on. What we did to Cesare Alosi is child's play compared to what I want to do to the bastard that tipped off Carlson. Cut off his ears and fingers and feed them to the dog while he watches. Then cut off his dick and balls and stuff them down his throat."

Elmore took a step back. "Your beauty is only exceeded by your wrath. What if I told you that Colonel Roberts suspects that the man responsible for tipping off Carlson is the same man you had in your torture chamber?"

"How's that?" Liberty said, backing up, her eyes big.

"His S3, Major Rick Stepien, sat next to Mr. Alosi during the secret briefing about the redeployment of one-five's forces, and Jack's situation," Elmore said. "Alosi spilled coffee on Rick's trousers leg and boots. He said that the so-and-so lit right up when the colonel announced Jack's name and said he was missing. The NSA's investigating, but Carlson won't cooperate. He insists that he received the information through legal channels and warns against any witch-hunting."

"If Cesare was there, he told Carlson," Liberty said. "They're tight as Frick and Frack. Nobody else in Iraq would have done it. I wish I had known this while I had him chained to a chair in the CIA's inquisition room."

"I think it's probably lucky for you that you didn't know it," Elmore said.

"Who in the hell else besides Alosi does Carlson propose could give him the information, legally?" Liberty asked, her arms folded and a frown on her face that would ice a lake.

"Carlson says that he receives legal information from constituents serving in Iraq daily," Elmore said. "People who were not in that classified briefing and not constrained by the National Security Act, per se, but who knew of Jack's missing in action and were compelled to ask their senator to put pressure on the president to rescue the man. Then Carlson goes on his rhetorical tirade about representing the truth and protecting the low-ranking people in uniform who suffer at the whims of the elite commanders."

"Oh, what a crock of shit!" Liberty said.

"We had a lot of Marines on that reaction force that rescued my seven operators," Elmore said. "They knew that Jack had stayed behind, and I am sure that was the talk of the teepee when they got back to base. Any number of people who heard the tale could have called the senator."

"And Cesare Alosi skates again," Liberty growled. "He is made of Teflon. Gets away with murder and sharing classified information with the enemy, and now this, too."

"One day, God will judge him," Elmore said, offering her consolation. "We have to forgive those who hurt us and pray for those who hate us."

Liberty looked at him, pursed her lips, and replied, "Let God forgive him. I want to punish the slimy bastard."

Elmore smiled at her. "You never answered my question."

"What's that? Marriage?" Liberty said, and laughed. "The short answer, Jack is just so Jack!"

Elmore laughed. "Yeah. That describes everything about Mr. Valentine. Jack is just so Jack. No other words can explain it. He is unique."

"He paints pictures, pens poetry, writes literary-fiction short stories." Liberty sighed. "He thinks that Harper Lee hung the moon. He keeps looking for her to publish a next novel. A sequel of *To Kill a Mockingbird*."

"Don't forget J. D. Salinger," Elmore added.

"Oh, my goodness, yes! Jack Kerouac, too, but Salinger stole his heart." Liberty laughed. "Jack drew a charcoal picture of how he imagined Holden Caulfield looked. I had it framed because it looks so much like Jack!"

"Ah, the Catcher in the Rye, Jack Valentine." Elmore smiled.

"Why did you allow him to get that Bachelor of Arts degree?" Liberty asked. "Completely useless! What's he going to do? Teach? Read Henry Miller to the boys?"

"They might enjoy hearing the stories written by that nasty Bohemian." Elmore laughed.

"Seriously, Colonel Snow," Liberty said. "You had to approve his off-duty classes. Why art and literature?"

"Jack is a classically educated man. Brilliant. Gifted in so many ways," Elmore told her. "He's studied Shakespeare and the Holy Bible cover to cover. He knows a Henri Matisse from a Claude Monet by just glancing at the painting when most Marines wouldn't even know who they are. Jack feels the emotions of Pablo Picasso and Paul Cézanne when he shows you their works. He lights up! He laughs at the ridiculousness of life, seen in the works of Salvador Dali, and the lust of life shown to us in the works of such impressionists as Paul Gauguin and Vincent Van Gogh.

"How many Marines have you met who can paint your portrait, and make it look like you, and at the same time recite in entirety the wonderful speech made by Prince Harry to his men before battle in Shakespeare's *Henry V*?"

Liberty smiled and began to quote, "'We few, we happy few, we band of brothers. For he to-day that sheds his blood with me shall be my brother; be he ne'er so vile, this day shall gentle his condition. And gentlemen in England now a-bed shall think themselves accurs'd they were not here, and hold their manhoods cheap whiles any speaks that fought with us upon Saint Crispin's day.'

"Elmore, it's more than a speech. It's the love of my life's ethos. And it makes me cry when I think too much about it," Liberty said. "Jack is so Jack."

"The poet warrior," Elmore said. "He lifts my heart."

Then the old Marine snuffed back tears after he said it, rubbing away their wetness with his thumb knuckles.

He reached inside his back pocket and took out his wallet. He unfolded a piece of paper.

"Two years ago," Elmore said, clearing his throat, "Jack wrote a poem for me. He has this secret soft and loving side to him. He loves God. Never doubt that boy's faith, regardless of his foul mouth and rough exterior."

Liberty looked at him and wrinkled her forehead.

"I know that, too, Elmore," she said. "We went to Sunday School together. I saw him stop his car on a busy highway and rescue a stray puppy, when someone had dumped it in the country. And don't forget what got him in the Marine Corps. His best friend was gay. Jack didn't care. He loved Marco Gonzalez from the time they were little boys, and Jack risked ridicule from everyone by loving the boy. He didn't care. He didn't judge his friend. He loved him. It didn't make Jack gay. It made him a good Christian! And I love Jack, and I loved Marco, too! Because Jack taught me."

Elmore smiled. "You, too, know Jack's secret soft side. Out with the boys, he's just one of them. He keeps his faith in his heart and lives the honesty of the moment. Jack's foul mouth, rude behavior, and abject honesty hide a lot of that secret soft side and, unfortunately, his Christian faith."

"Not so secret if you know him, and not soft," Liberty told the colonel. "A real man! Real men don't worry about softness or what people think. They do what their hearts say. Kind of like a colonel I know, too."

"So." Elmore smiled. "That good-hearted man, a real man, he wrote this poem and gave it to me. I'm a Jesus guy, and Jack knew I'd like it. He calls the poem 'Somewhere Beneath the Rain.' Jack wrote under the title, 'A Lyric Inspired by the Holy Spirit.' I love that!"

Then the colonel began to read:

> *Somewhere, beneath the rain,*
> *a soul cries out for God to end his pain.*
>
> *Somewhere, inside the night,*
> *a soul cries for God to end his fight.*
>
> *But I am happy.*
> *I am saved.*
> *Christ has found me,*
> *He ended my pain.*
>
> *Yes, I am happy,*
> *I'm all-right.*
> *Christ has found me,*
> *He ended my fight.*
>
> *Somewhere, beneath the sky,*
> *a soul cries to God for answers why.*
>
> *Somewhere, on a city street,*
> *a soul cries out to God for comfort,*
> *for eternal peace.*

And where am I?
And where are we?
What have I done to bring Him to you?

Liberty threw her arms around the aging Marine's neck and hugged him hard.

"What will we do if Jack doesn't come home?" she cried, and a whole new flood of tears rained from her eyes as she held on to Elmore Snow.

_ 14 _

For three nights, Jack Valentine had walked with confidence. Moving after dark and going into hiding before sunrise to sleep through the day, he made good progress, unseen by anyone except the men in the truck he killed the second day, and a caracal that came sniffing just after sunrise the third day. The cat looked just like mountain lions he had seen as a youngster in the Guadalupe Mountains near El Paso, but stood half their size, and had long, black hair tufts coming off his ears like those on a lynx.

Jack lay still with his eyes open, blinking at the beautiful tawny cat with black muzzle and big, clear brown eyes. The animal came searching for rodents among the thornbushes where Jack had hidden to sleep through the day.

He had finished his last bottle of water with the end of his food when he had tucked himself to bed that morning, watching the nonaggressive cat nose around. Jack thought in another night's walk, he should see signs of Haditha, the dam, and, hopefully, his cohorts. He could do that with ease, well rested, hydrated, and fed.

After no luck the fourth day, no food nor water, his lips already swelling, mouth sticky with thirst, Jack realized he had mistaken a low, long-running ridge for Main Supply Route Bronze, and had turned east too soon. Now, for all the Marine knew, he could be walking in circles.

When he realized the mistake, he felt stupid. He had wondered why he heard no traffic on the highway, and it just didn't click in his tired brain. To make matters worse, the gunny had followed that long-running line of the higher ground rather than steering first by his little bubble compass on his watchband and using the land feature as a reference.

"Where the fuck am I," Jack reeled, searching the darkness in every direction with his night-vision optics. Panic struck him hard. His gut twisted as he considered how much greater his thirst and fatigue would now grow.

He had fallen victim to an increasingly complacent routine. With each passing day, his confidence had grown, trusting his sense of direction and the high ground rather than fundamental, disciplined land navigation, shooting an azimuth with his little bubble compass, finding landmarks along that line and walking to them. Too simple. Too stupid.

Now he faced bleak water options, too. He had to do something drastic simply to sustain his life. Digging holes under Alhagi outcrops might find moisture, but Jack also considered he could be digging a long time with a little shovel and no result. Like the mesquite and ocotillo of his native desert near El Paso, Alhagi roots can grow thirty feet deep underground before finding water.

"I've got to drink piss," he told himself, and filled one of the empty water bottles with it, rather than wasting the body fluid on the ground. Salty, foul-tasting, loaded with dangerous bacteria, the risk of illness easily won over his alternative, dying of dehydration and heat exhaustion.

"Piss drinking. It's a last resort. I'm not there yet," he said, scanning the horizon with his night-vision scope. "My best option now is to find a house. Deal with the inhabitants. Get food and water and press on."

When he took the night-vision scope from his eyes, and rested them in the darkness, he noticed from his side vision an area along the skyline brighter than others. If he looked right at it, the bright area disappeared. If he looked away, he saw it.

"Imagination," he thought at first, but remembered what a seasoned Force Recon Marine had taught him in Basic-Recon school about night fighting in Vietnam. They had no night-vision optics except the bulky Starlight Scope, and it was a piece of shit compared to the clarity of what every Marine had hanging on his helmet today. Instead of technology, those old war dogs had used their God-given night vision and mastered the darkness.

"Don't look right at something to see it in the night," the salt had taught Jack. "Look about ten or twenty degrees to the side. Let your rod vision go to work. Scotopic vision they call it. The center of your eye is filled with cones that see color and bright-lit objects. We're day creatures, so we rely on our cone vision more than rod vision. Cones dominate our eyesight. But we do have a good number of night-seeing rods, if we just learn to use them.

"Animals, like horses, have fewer cones and more rods in their eyes. They see better at night than purely day animals. Nocturnal creatures, like owls and cats, have nearly all rod vision and can see at night as if it were daytime.

"Your rods surround the outer area of the eye while cones fill the center area. So to see something in the dark, look slightly away from it."

Jack laughed, his thirst pronounced but heart uplifted. "Definitely a house there, just over the horizon."

He checked his little bubble compass, determined that the lights glowed just northeast of his location.

"I may even see Haditha when I reach this farm," Jack said to himself as he trudged toward the brightness.

Every tenth step that he took, he sidestepped to his left one step.

"Right leg stronger than the left leg," he reminded himself. "Compensate for the tendency to drift the direction of my dominant leg."

Little things from the introduction to land navigation course that he had taught his Scout-Snipers perked to the front of his consciousness as he pressed onward, checking his compass and keeping his bearing on the bright spot.

"Funny how life can suddenly depend on something so trivial as a dime-store compass," he said as he followed the little trinket that he put on the side of his watchband. He had bought it more for looks than function; however, now he appreciated how well it really worked.

With each step, the brightness that he had hardly noticed became brighter so that he could see it when he looked directly at it. He thought how easily he could have passed up noticing it, and would have continued walking in a circle to the south and, without a question, died.

"With the jackals and cats and rats out here, they might never have found my body," Jack said as he trudged.

"Elmore must have prayed for me. Definitely my mom. She's got a hotline to God."

An hour later, with the brightness getting more pronounced, Jack finally saw the house lights glowing.

"Thank you, God!" he said, and meant it.

He looked at the farmhouse and outbuildings with his sixty-power spotting scope. Three trucks sat outside, and two men with rifles walked guard duty while their brothers slept inside.

Jack prayed as he looked through his scope. "So far, so good, God. Your hand brought me this far, so I'll just have to trust You the rest of the way."

When he checked his watch, he realized he had less than an hour before sunrise. To the right of the house, he looked at the sky. Rather than black, it now shone gray, and the stars faded.

He looked for a place to hide. Very little offered relief to the flat landscape. Little patches of Alhagi and weeds that grow with them seemed his best option. Then way ahead, perhaps even too close to the farm, about a half mile from it, he noticed the hump. Rocks covered with windblown dirt. Alhagi growing around it. Perfect.

Twenty minutes later, Jack began digging in, building a hide for the day. He checked his range. Eight hundred seventy-two meters. That would work.

"I'll keep watch from here," he told himself. "When the bastards leave to go blow up some shit, I'll slip in and steal some food and fill my bottles with water. Haditha Dam can't be far from here if I just keep pressing northeast."

All around the outside of the house where Abu Omar Bakr al-Nasser made his headquarters, gunmen squatted, eating breakfast and drinking tea. Inside, the girls hurried getting food to all the men who still waited for their morning meals.

"Why do you just sit here and stuff your faces? We must find this devil before he escapes us!" Abu Omar bellowed, storming through the house and outside in the hard-baked dirt dooryard. Surrounding them, a fleet of rusted and filthy Toyota and Nissan compact pickup trucks waited with pipe racks on the beds, some bristling with machine guns, with belts of ammo draped from them.

Yasir al-Bayati, Abu Omar's aide-de-camp and general gofer, hurried behind the Jamaat Ansar al-Sunnah chieftain, carrying the old graybeard's satchel and rifle.

"They will be finished soon enough, master. Many have not yet eaten," Yasir reminded him, both men speaking the native Arabic of their Sunni faith. "We will get that dog today, without fail. It is God's will!"

The graybeard looked back at his most trusted servant and cracked a hint of a smile. "I know that. But they must fear my impatience or we waste our entire day here. We must scour the land for this filth, Valentine. What a prize he will be! Removing his head while the world watches us will bring our jihad great fame. It will put fear in the hearts of all who oppose us."

"Oh yes, master!" Yasir said, bowing and scraping. "God's will be done! God is great! God is great!"

Today, Omar wore his Russian Makarov nine-millimeter pistol in a leather shoulder holster, not that he knew how to use the gun much less hit anything with it, unless he put the muzzle against some poor bastard's head. But he thought he looked powerful wearing it, along with the Moorish-style sword with a ten-inch-long brass-leather-and-ivory-decorated handle, and a gleaming eighteen-inch-long curved chrome blade hanging on his belt. A gift for his birthday two weeks ago, he fancied cutting off Jack Valentine's head with it.

"The wadi to the south, I say," Omar fumed, looking across the broad lands twenty miles west of Haditha, where he had made his headquarters these past weeks. "We keep looking to the north and the west, and this *Ash'abah al-Anbar*, that the men so fearfully call him, slips ever closer to his rescue. He still waits in the south, I tell you, near where we last saw him and his Marines."

"Oh, you're right, master," Yasir said, watching the men finish their food. "No one can survive these lands long on their own, not without knowing the ways of them. Surely not some American. He will sit where he is and wait to be found. Just as you say."

"That is right, Yasir," Abu Omar said, and glared at his men. "Someone is helping him, or we would have found him by now. We must go house to house, everywhere he could have gone. As long as we see the Americans still searching, we know he is among us. Somewhere."

"We will find him!" Yasir said. "It is God's will. I know it is God's will."

"Perhaps." Omar nodded, looking west to the open

desert. "Certainly, Allah wants nothing to do with this son of a pig."

Suddenly, the old graybeard heard the rushing sounds of screaming jets overhead, and both men ducked for cover inside the doorway. Seconds later, the earth shook with bombs striking targets.

"As we increase numbers, hiding from the American planes grows most difficult," Yasir said.

"Let them bomb!" Omar said, defiance raising his voice. "Our numbers will increase nonetheless, and we will not fail in our jihad! Yasir, that truly is God's will! *Allahu Akbar!*"

"*Allahu Akbar!*" Yasir echoed.

Cotton Martin finished his breakfast early and took a seat in the blockhouse atop the hard, high wall that surrounded the camp at Haditha Dam, where Delta Company, First Battalion, Fifth Marines held the ground. Craig Ironhead Heyward and Bobby the Snake Durant sat with him.

Heyward from Dallas and Snake from Lawton, Oklahoma, both men loved the NFL Cowboys. They talked up the greatness of Coach Bill Parcells but missed Jimmy Johnson, and proffered how former New England Patriots quarterback Drew Bledsoe was yet another waste of time in a long list of wastes since Troy Aikman left the team, although last season the pokes managed nine wins above seven losses. Both Marines liked the Cowboys' new acquisition, controversial tight end, Terrell Owens.

"The man's got a mouth," Ironhead told Bobby the Snake, "but he backs up his trash."

"That he does," Snake agreed.

They both wondered about the undrafted free-agent backup quarterback, Tony Romo, whom the team picked up three seasons ago from Eastern Illinois University, and all they had done with him so far was sit his young ass on the bench.

"Six-two and two-thirty, he's got the body to be a great quarterback," Bobby Durant said. "I seen him in the preseason last year, and I like how he can scramble. Dude's got an arm, too."

"But where the hell is Eastern Illinois University?" Craig Heyward sang back. "Totally unheard-of non-drafted dude, how did he not get anybody's attention if he's any good? I didn't even know Eastern Illinois University existed, much less had a football team."

"Guys like Tony Romo come out of nowhere and become great," Snake said. "Don't judge him until there's something to judge."

"You got to figure that if Bill Parcells has kept Tony Romo around this season, he sees something worth having," Cotton Martin broke into the conversation. He, too, liked the Dallas Cowboys, and the Denver Broncos. A two-hat man. His American Football Conference team, the Broncos, and his National Conference team, the Cowboys.

"Fuckin' A, dude," Ironhead said, a total Cowboy hard-core devotee. "Coach Parcells is the best since Tom Landry, and nobody will ever be as great as Tom Landry."

All three Marines nodded reverently at the mention of the late Coach Landry's name. It was like speaking of Jesus.

"Now, if we could just find a way to fire Jerry Jones." Cotton laughed. Ironhead and Snake laughed, too, and nodded yes. Nobody liked the Dallas Cowboys owner. The man who had unceremoniously fired Tom Landry.

"God bless Tom Landry," Snake said.

"May he rest in peace," Ironhead added.

Then the three Marines got quiet and looked out of the blockhouse atop the high, hard wall, again searching the morning horizons for any sign of Jack Valentine.

With the gunny missing and the enemy alerted to his status thanks to CNN, Staff Sergeant Martin had moved the entire detachment of MARSOC Marines, including the armorers, to the lake area north of Haditha. Every man mattered now.

With one-five calling off the sweep operation, more or less falling back to Fort Apache and hunting renegades in the daylight on patrols that took no real-estate ownership but just hunted bad guys, he saw no further advantage in deploying the special operators among the battalion. Colonel Roberts agreed, and even sent two additional rifle platoons to Haditha Dam with Martin and the boys as reinforcements to support Company D overwatching the top end of AO Denver.

Martin planned to run multiple long-range patrols out to the west day and night, searching for Gunny Valentine. Captain Charlie Crenshaw, Delta Company, Fifth Marines commander, at Alvin Barkley's behest, assigned the first sergeant and fifty Marines to support the MARSOC detachment's efforts to find their missing man.

Speedy Espinoza had at first decided to send Hacksaw, Kermit, and Habu back to Baghdad, since the purpose for their augmenting his CIA staff had all but disappeared in Hit. Because they remained under contract with the CIA, he thought that Chris Gray might put the oddballs to work at their Camp Liberty complex, where their other assortment of off-center characters stayed away from the stiff collars that worked at the Baghdad embassy offices.

However, Walter Gillespie had different ideas. He had gone to Black Bart Roberts and given the man a good master-sergeant-to-lieutenant-colonel talking-to. Since his FBI cover was no longer viable with the Malone-Leyva intelligence mission, he had already called Jason Kendrick in DC and gotten his release from undercover duty, except as far as backup for Liberty Cruz and her team was concerned. Kendrick told Hacksaw that simply as Marines, he needed to uphold that side of the deal. No argument from Hacksaw but total agreement.

So when Hacksaw approached Speedy Espinoza with the idea of going up to Haditha Dam and pitching in on the search for his buddy, Jack Valentine, the CIA agent not only agreed but packed his trash, too. When he called Chris Gray to let him know the plan, Speedy learned that Elmore Snow and Staff Sergeant Billy Claybaugh had already departed for Haditha Dam and would welcome the crew there with open arms.

"Shit," Gillespie crowed. "Old Hammer will feel plumb left out of such a grand reunion of great Marines. Why, with our talent manning the ramparts, we'll have young Master Valentine home in no time."

"We may have to sleep in the ditch," Speedy said. "I talked to Captain Crenshaw, said we were coming, and he told me we'd better bring cots. He's fresh out, as well as a place to park them."

"Me, Kermit Alexander, and Cory Webster slept most of our Marine Corps careers down some hole filled with shit anyway," Hacksaw said, smiling with his impressive gold grill at the former Marine major and Prowler pilot turned CIA spook.

"Just saying, accommodations might be sparse." Espinoza shrugged. It didn't bother him much, either. He'd endured much worse, too. But it didn't make him like it any better.

"I don't plan on laying boots up in the barracks no ways," Gillespie said. "We're up there huntin' our boy Jack Valentine. Number one priority, Bubba. Get him out alive."

Morning sun and gentle breezes lifted Giti Sadiq's spirits as she finished hanging blankets on the clotheslines that stood between the back of the house on the Anbar desert where Abu Omar made his headquarters and the adjacent barns where they kept an ample supply of chickens and goats for milk, eggs, and meat. Today, all the men had gone hunting this Ghost of Anbar right after breakfast, led by the old graybeard himself. Now she sang freedom songs from her heart, loud and happy.

A few steps away, Miriam and Amira had already shucked off their clothes and thrown them in the wash pot filled with soapy water that heated over a hot hardwood fire they had built in the backyard right after breakfast. They chased each other in the sunshine and open world, naked, laughing like children at play. Washday baths. No men. A blessing from God.

Sabeen, the Shia girl from Syria, wrapped her shawl around herself as she took off her clothes and put them in the great black boiling cauldron. Chubby all of her life, ashamed of her fat, she hid her nakedness. The rolls on her belly, her large breasts, the fat around her buttocks, thighs, and ankles made her feel ugly, undesirable. Outcast.

The last blanket draped over the rope line carried out a twofold purpose: airing out the bedding of the al-Sunnah gunmen who lived at the ancient desert water stop with their general, and giving the girls a sense of privacy, should their watchdog, Yasir al-Bayati, return unannounced from his so-called hunting.

He had claimed to see a fabled white oryx, a rare and endangered animal, legendary in folklore, that once thrived across the Arabian deserts and Persia, and at one point not long ago had been declared extinct by world wildlife conservationists. No one had yet sighted the Arabian oryx in Iraq since their return from extinction to the endangered list, but some people now said that they had seen them in Jordan.

"Boosolah do not know borders. So why can't they be here in Iraq, too?" Yasir had argued with the other men who teased him and said they had seen unicorns grazing in the desert, too. They scoffed at his tale of seeing the big buck with a harem of three doe. Yet the old goatherd stubbornly insisted that the animal had magnificent ebony horns that curved over his shoulders like great black scimitars, a full meter long.

"You're a fool," the men had cackled at him. "Go back to the lovely goats that you use like a man does a wife."

The old Arab from Baiji, who had also known Giti's father and never liked the man because he had wealth, and Yasir had nothing, left the men, disgusted. He would hunt the mystical great white oryx. He would kill it and bring it back to the house, where he would butcher it for them and feed it to these fools. Then they would surely respect him.

Yasir had lived his entire life herding goats with his brothers on the open lands along the Tigris valley before the war. He joined Abu Omar's Jamaat Ansar al-Sunnah more out of emotion than common sense. His talents lay more with goats than fighting Americans.

In Baiji, he had witnessed Omar beheading Giti's father and brothers, and him shooting the mother and her baby girl in their heads. He was glad that the old graybeard had spared the pretty young girl, Giti, even as a slave. He felt bad for the Sadiq family, but they got what they deserved.

Rather than respected as a warrior, Yasir found himself relegated to last car. A personal servant. When anything needed doing, Omar took the men and left Yasir to mind the girls and the herd of goats and the chickens.

"I will show all of them, even Abu Omar," Yasir said to himself that morning. He struck out to hunt the white oryx buck that he called Boosolah, just after the men had departed. Yasir told the girls not to tell anyone. Why should they? If they did, Abu Omar would punish them as well as Yasir. So the old Arab trusted them.

He didn't worry about leaving them alone here, either.

Where could they go? If they tried to escape, they would surely die in the desert. And they knew that quite well. The remote headquarters on the Iraqi desert needed no walls to keep the girls from running away.

The man, now late in his forties and never married, treated the girls well. He had no meanness in him, but he did like watching the pretty females. He felt strange comfort hearing Giti sing her songs of Jesus. Abu Omar ordered him to punish any of the girls if they ever mentioned their Savior, Jesus Christ. But he didn't do it.

Yasir never said anything. He let their Christian faith remain their business. As long as they kept up Muslim appearances, wearing their hijabs and shawls, covering their heads and necks in the presence of the men, all was well.

"If we just lived and let live, we would have no war," Yasir had thought. "What does it hurt to sing a song? It is only a song."

Giti stripped bare and threw her clothes in the steaming cauldron full of soapy water. Then she jumped in the giant galvanized tub, near the wash pot, that they had filled with hot water for their baths. Miriam and Amira still played chase, not caring that Giti got in the tub first, and Sabeen stood clutching her shawl, legs pressed tight together, shivering.

"Too bad!" Giti sang out, giggling. "I get the clean water today."

Here in this bitter land, bathing was a luxury for the girls, rare and splendid in their lives of slavery. It refreshed their spirits as well as their bodies.

Miriam and Amira grabbed small pots and began dipping water, pouring it over Giti's naked body as she stood in the galvanized steel receptacle that would double to rinse the clothes after all four girls had bathed.

"Is that a baby bump?" Amira asked, surprised, pointing at Giti's growing belly.

Giti looked back at her, and the fear on her face said enough to Amira to let it drop. Miriam had already known, and she dreaded the day that Abu Omar discovered that his sex toy carried his child. It was a death sentence.

Doing her best not to think of her growing baby, trusting God to carry out His will, Giti smiled at Sabeen. The shy Syrian girl stood shivering nearby, wrapped tight, watching the girls and dreading her turn to stand openly naked while the others poured water over her.

"Come, get in with me!" Giti called to Sabeen, and extended her hand.

"I am modest," the Syrian girl replied, ready to cry.

"You are our sister, Sabeen," Giti told her. "We are the same. You just have more beauty than I do. Please, come. Get in the water, and we will wash away all your heartaches."

Miriam ran to the plump girl and gave her a hug. "Jesus loves you, Sabeen. Don't you know? We love you, too!"

"Jesus cannot love me, I am Muslim," Sabeen said.

"You are wrong," Giti said. "Let Jesus fill your heart! All your sadness will fly away. Here, we will pray for you."

Giti, Miriam, and Amira joined hands around Sabeen, closing her in a circle, and began to pray:

"Oh Father in Heaven, You are the great, loving God of all creation," Giti said, and Sabeen lowered her head, too.

"Lord Jesus, take the heart of Sabeen who does not yet know You but wants Your love," Miriam added.

Amira closed their prayers, "Take Sabeen into Your

eternal embrace, Lord Jesus. Let her know that You are her Savior, too."

Then all three said, "In the Name of Christ Jesus our Lord, our Savior, and Your only begotten Son we pray to You, oh Father in Heaven, amen."

"My Savior, too?" Sabeen asked. "What must I do for Jesus to save me?"

"Believe!" Giti laughed and embraced her.

All four girls hugged, and Sabeen dropped her shawl, and stepped into the washtub, her chubbiness exposed to the world. Giti stood in the water with her.

"God made you this way, just as He made us," Giti said, taking a bowl and pouring water over Sabeen's head, then over her own.

Amira took the soap and a cloth and began washing the Syrian girl's back, while Miriam washed Giti's.

While the four naked girls celebrated their momentary freedom, Yasir al-Bayati walked heavy-footed to the animal sheds and dropped a dead wild goat he had shot. No white oryx today, but a mostly white buck goat with a brown stripe down his back and a black mask over his face and tail. He had black horns barely a foot long.

"Wild goat tastes best," he said, hanging the carcass with bailing wire in the rafters, letting its blood drain in the shade.

When he first saw the animal, chewing on dry weeds, he thought it was the white oryx. Maybe his mind made it appear much bigger and with the long, curved black horns. So he shot. Then when he got to the dead animal, he cursed the goat's life as well as his own miserable existence.

"They will mock me now," Yasir said as he walked to

the water trough and washed his face. Then he heard the girls laughing. He looked toward the back of the house and saw the clotheslines draped with blankets, and smiled.

Quietly, the old Arab crept to the blankets and pulled a gap between them. All four of the naked girls in open display immediately excited him to rigid hardness.

He wanted to relieve himself as the girls washed each other, soap on their bodies, water sparkling on their skin. The fat one, Sabeen, caused him the greatest lust.

Yasir breathed hard and rubbed himself as he looked at the girl, the nest of wet black hair hiding that place of greatest ecstasy for a man. A thing he had not known in more than ten years.

Suddenly, a flash came over the man, and he stopped masturbating.

"What filth!" he fumed, disgusted with himself, and rubbed his hand on his shirt.

The vision that had come into his fantasy-filled mind was not having sex with the fat girl but of the men in their beds at night. Downstairs in the tunnels, hidden from light. They did things with each other that left Yasir filled with self-loathing.

One night, he had allowed one of the young boys to get in his bed, and he took Yasir in his mouth. It had felt so good, and he ejaculated stronger than ever in his life.

A few days later, one of the other men cut the young boy's throat. They tossed his body in the garbage with the dead girl. As a homosexual, doomed to hell, he deserved no respect, not from the self-righteous Muslim men, nor would he receive any mercy from Allah.

Yasir looked again, and knew he could not end the day

without relief, so he threw open the blankets and walked straight at the girls.

"Whores!" he shouted at them, his member still rigid and showing.

Four screaming girls suddenly huddled around each other, covering their breasts and crotches with their hands, crying. Giti ran to the wash pot and used the stirring stick to pull out clothes. It didn't matter whose or what, as long as the soaking-wet garments covered them.

She threw the steaming-hot white-cotton slips at her three sister slaves, and lastly took something for herself.

Rather than putting on the items, the terrified girls wrapped themselves with the wet underclothing, the hot water scalding their skin.

"You! Fat one!" Yasir said to Sabeen. "Come to me."

"What will you do with her, Yasir?" Giti pled.

"That is none of your business," the Arab goatherd retorted. "Best you and the others get dressed and forget everything about this today."

Giti ran to him, took him by the arm. "Please! Yasir. Master. Take me instead. You can kill me and I will be happy. Do not take Sabeen. She is innocent."

"She is a whore! All of the men have had her, coming back from Syria. Except me. Now I will have her, too," Yasir argued. Then he looked at Giti. The white wet cotton slip did not hide her breasts, her dark nipples, or the black hair covering her crotch. It made her nakedness look more lustful to him, hidden but not really hidden.

Sabeen looked at Giti. "No. Please. I will go with Yasir and give him what he needs. I am hardly innocent. As he said, I am a whore."

"Not in God's eyes!" Giti said, and began to cry. She feared that the Arab would take his pleasure with the girl, then kill her, out of his own fear of what Abu Omar might do to him if he learned of this breach of trust. Sabeen did not yet fully know Jesus, and Giti could not bear the idea of the girl's dying before she found salvation.

"Sabeen has no knowledge of lovemaking," Giti pled, as Yasir pulled the fat girl toward the barns. He snatched a blanket off the lines to use as a bed.

"I will teach her!" he muttered.

"You will have to kill all of us then!" Giti exclaimed, and the old Arab stopped.

"Why?" he said. Then he, too, realized that if he raped Sabeen, he would have to kill all the witnesses of his crime against his master.

"Take me," Giti said. "Let her go. We promise to say nothing to Abu Omar. You will not be raping me, but enjoying the pleasures that I freely give to you of my own accord."

"I can give him the same pleasure," Sabeen said, not wanting Giti to sacrifice for her.

"No!" Giti scolded her.

Then she came close to Sabeen, and whispered, "What if he leaves you with a baby? What will you do? What do you think Abu Omar will do?"

Sabeen realized that Giti already had a baby in her, and once she showed enough, Abu Omar would throw her to the men, who would rape her and kill her and toss her lifeless body on the other dead, with the garbage in the ditch.

"Please, Sabeen," Giti said, and looked at Yasir.

The old Arab suddenly felt ashamed and let her go.

He looked at Giti and hated himself.

"I am sorry," Yasir said, hanging his head. "I heard your laughter and saw the blankets hanging on the line. I looked behind them and saw you naked. My lust overwhelmed me. I am a despicable wretch. May Allah have mercy on me."

"Yasir," Giti said, and smiled at the shamed man. "I forgive you. God has forgiven you. Poor man, in so many ways you are a slave, too. Just like me, like Sabeen."

"I am truly sorry," the sad man said. "I have never done anything so terrible in my life. I am ashamed."

"I will go with you, Yasir. If you need a woman's attention," Giti said. "My own choice. You need love, too."

"No," he said. "I must atone. I must wash myself and pray that Allah shows mercy for my weakness. I also have a goat to butcher."

"You did not see the white oryx?" Giti asked him.

"Only a goat," he answered as he walked away, humbled, dejected.

"You will find him one day, Yasir," Giti said.

"God willing," the old Arab said.

"You are a good man, Yasir," Giti called to him, as he walked to the barn.

"No," Yasir said, not turning around. "But thank you for saying so."

Jack Valentine had fallen asleep watching the house, waiting for the gunmen in the Toyota pickups to leave. When he awoke, he thought he had dozed off for only a moment. When he looked at the house, the trucks were gone. He checked his watch, after eleven o'clock. Exhaustion, lack of food, dehydration had taken a toll on him.

The Marine's tongue felt thick and so dry that he could hardly swallow. Not a drop of saliva in his mouth. Just sticky goo that clogged on his tongue and throat. Jack's head throbbed from lack of water, his brain literally shrinking like a grape turning into a raisin.

Lips? Forget about it. They had dried out yesterday, now they cracked yellow and bled.

Gunny Valentine put his spotting scope up and studied the house for any sign of life. Nothing moved.

"Oh, I could use a drink of water about now," Jack said as he watched the place through the scope. He shifted the optics to the outbuildings, then behind them, behind the house, and back on the house. Nothing moved in the windows. Nothing moved around the house. The front door was closed. No vehicles were parked in the dooryard.

"Wouldn't it be wonderful if those guys have all gone, and nobody is home?" Jack said, and it hurt to smile, but his heart did lift.

Still, Jack watched. Cautious as a wild animal.

It took all of his willpower to wait a full hour, but after nothing moved, he began pulling himself with his elbows and toes in a low crawl.

He had slipped out of his backpack and put it with his bolt-action rifle in a drag bag that he pulled behind himself. Jack had also taken off his helmet and put it in the bag, too, and wore his flop hat, which allowed him more freedom of vision and a lower profile.

Before he had started, he took out his folding knife and cut a good assortment of camelthorns and weeds, festooning them on his drag bag and himself. His flop hat looked like a big clump of weeds as he pushed himself across the ground toward the house.

Moving with discipline and precision, Jack used the better part of another hour to cover the half mile from his hide to the off side of the barns, farthest away from the house, and the place anyone would least notice him as he rose from his belly to a crouch.

Squatting on his feet, Jack gathered his kit with his left arm, slung the Vigilance rifle on his right shoulder, drew his Lippard .45, and ran to the front door.

Then, standing to one side of the doorway, he quietly lifted pressure on the latch. It wasn't locked.

So, the gunny took a breath, lifted the latch once more, and pushed the door open from the side. Then he peeked around the jamb and saw an array of bedding rolled and stacked against the wall in the front room.

As he slipped inside, he pushed the door quietly shut behind him, easing the latch closed. While the front room was dark, the next room looked unusually bright. Too bright for sunlight.

He set down his kit by the door and walked, quiet as a cat, to the next room. Blinds were drawn shut; an electric lamp stood by a small chair and desk where someone had been reading and writing.

When Jack noticed the nearly empty tea glass and a smoldering cigarette in the ashtray, his hair stood up.

"Someone's home," he said in his mind. "Did he see me?"

Jack searched every direction and saw nothing moving. No sounds but a distant hum, like a small engine on a welder, or a light plant, but far away or well muffled.

A third chamber, much larger than even the front room, sat off the opposite side of the house. Quietly, Jack slipped to that doorway and peeked inside. An exceptionally clean room, it had a wood floor, as opposed to the tile-covered concrete elsewhere in the house. The room had nothing in it except several small rugs rolled up.

"Their little barracks chapel," he thought. Then he glanced back at the room where the cigarette smoldered with the lamp turned on at the desk. "Where did he go?"

Jack silently eased his way to the door in the center of the house that led into a kitchen, complete with propane range and an electric microwave and refrigerator. And indoor plumbing.

He went to the fridge and opened the door. Inside, jars of condiments and bowls of leftover Iraqi food. Even a jug of cold tea.

Then he looked at the sink and ran his tongue over his cracked, dry lips. Two steps and he hit the faucet handle. Out poured clear, clean, cool water from a deep well. He leaned over and put his mouth on the tap.

It was heaven! He could feel his parched skin absorbing the moisture. A cup sat on the counter next to the sink, and Jack grabbed it and started gulping down the fresh, cool, wonderful-tasting, life-giving liquid.

"Oh God, thank you!" he said, finishing his second cup. Then he drank a third and a fourth. He had never known anything so awesome as a simple drink of water until this day.

He sipped his fifth cup, and looked out the back window as he drank, and noticed the open back door.

"If he ran away, that's fine with me," Jack thought,

and felt more relaxed. "Obviously, this guy smoking the cigarette saw me run to the front of the house, and he slipped out the back. Good riddance, I say."

Jack went to the living room, brought his gear to the kitchen, and fished out water bottles. When he had them all filled, he began searching the cabinets and cupboards for food. Then he looked again in the yard behind the house and noticed several four-inch-diameter pipes coming up from the ground. Some had tin hats on them, and some were just open stacks. Just like vents coming off the roof of a house.

Jack looked around the kitchen and saw a side door. He opened it, expecting to see the inside of a broom closet, or hopefully a pantry full of canned goods, but instead he found a stairwell carved deep down into the earth. Each step made of stone, and the walls and ceiling of the passageway that led downward were lined with similar stones, as if in an ancient castle.

He had heard of the camel stops on the caravan routes, many of them thousands of years old. Their deep springwater sources fed from the snows on the tops of the Taurus Mountains of Turkey, far to the north. The same origins of the great rivers, the Tigris and the Euphrates.

As Jack entered the stairwell, he felt the cool stone walls rubbed smooth by countless hands over the millennia, people feeling their ways down the steps to cool chambers and the hidden wells beneath the house.

Down at the bottom of the stairs Jack saw more lights shining, and heard the rumble of a light plant engine.

"That's where they hide their generator," Jack said to

himself as he slowly and deliberately walked down the passage at the bottom of the stairs, careful to not make a sound. Then he smelled cigarette smoke. "And this is where our mysterious friend is hiding. Or maybe he's not even aware that I am here. That would be cool."

Jack pressed his back against the stone wall of the passageway at the bottom of the stairs and peeked into the large underground chamber beneath the house. Along the great room's walls he saw shelves filled with canned food and US military Meals Ready to Eat. More shelves held boxes and boxes of ammunition, and on the floor he saw steel cases filled with rocket-propelled grenades. Next to them sat racks of rifles and some mortar tubes and B-40 RPG launchers.

Then a door opened at the other end of the cavern, and the loudness of the electric generator filled the room. Out stepped a surprised, middle-aged Iraqi man, wiping his hands on a grease rag.

The fellow never had a chance to speak. Jack put two quick hardballs from his Lippard .45 square in the suddenly dead man's chest.

"Well, sometimes good shit happens," Jack said as he went to the food shelves and filled his arms and pockets with American-made douche-bag dinners. He knew what he could expect from them. Not worth risking life and bowels on canned local crap, possibly full of bugs and botulism.

As he was about to leave, his eye caught sight of a box of fragmentation grenades. He smiled, grabbed two, and jogged up the stairs to the kitchen. After tucking his food and water in his backpack, rolling up the drag bag and stuffing it in a side pocket on his pack, slinging his M40A3 sniper rifle on one side, strapping on his backpack, his helmet tied on it, his Vigilance rifle in hand, Gunny Valentine pulled the pins on the grenades, rolled them into the stairwell, and ran like hell out the back door.

Two muffled booms sent dirt rolling out of the house behind Jack. A second later, a more pronounced explosion, from the munitions in the underground chamber detonating, brought down the house. In seconds, it disappeared inside a boiling brown cloud, the ground collapsing beneath.

Jack Valentine smiled as if he had accomplished something genuinely great. He said in a loud voice, "What is it that we do? Oh yeah, that's right. We fuck shit up!"

The gunny laughed as he took a bearing with his handy compass on the side of his watchband, finding his northeast homebound bearing, and looked on the horizon for a landmark that he could use for steering across the wide, flat desert.

He squinted his eyes, trying to see a plume of dust, and reached in his operator's vest for his compact binoculars. As he put them to his eyes and focused, he saw what caused the spouting dirt. Three trucks loaded with a dozen al-Qaeda gunmen running straight at him.

"Fuck me to tears!" he said, and ran hard, looking for a place to hide. "I wonder if there was another dude back there? Maybe he had a radio and called for help."

Jack Valentine had cleared less than fifty good steps from the smoking house when he heard coursing sounds above him: the shrill cries of jets diving in attack. Heart pounding, he stopped and looked up, when he heard the screams of two large bombs headed his way.

Ahead of Jack a shower of rockets took out the three compact pickup trucks. When they blew skyward, Jack dove for the ground.

Behind the Marine, the whole world exploded.

Jack never saw or thought anything else after that. Not for a long time.

Severe, sharp pain like lightning bolts shooting up his spine brought the Marine gunny around to consciousness. His eyes blinked open, and the first thing that struck him was the terrible smell of urine and old shit, like the bottom of a dirty outhouse on a hot day.

As his senses returned, Jack realized that he lay naked on a dank, stone floor. A man with a gray beard and a black Muslim skullcap sat in a high-backed wooden rocking chair. He held a long, electric cattle prod in his hands and smiled.

"I told Yasir that a good jolt of juice up your rectum would bring you out of that coma," Abu Omar told the gunny. "He worried that it might kill you."

Omar laughed, showing his nasty brown teeth.

"No, I told Yasir. The Ghost of Anbar does not die so easily."

Jack tried to stand, but the chains wrapped tight around his ankles with his wrists padlocked to them kept him on the nasty floor.

"Fuck you!" Jack yelled at the old graybeard, and got

another dose of the cattle prod on his naked butt for his trouble. The voltage sent the Marine convulsing across the floor, and Abu Omar laughed out loud.

"Hurts like a motherfucker, doesn't it!"

Jack moaned, and shut his eyes while he caught his breath. His worst nightmare had come true.

"What shall we do with you, Gunnery Sergeant John Arthur Valentine? That is your name," Omar said. "Of course, we will execute you for the world to see. But before that. What shall we do with you? Do you have a suggestion?"

"How about I stick my foot up your ass," Jack snarled. "Take these chains off me. I'll show you what hurts like a motherfucker!"

"Oh, I am sure you would," Abu Omar said, rocking back in the chair. "You know, Jack . . . You don't mind that I call you Jack, do you? Certainly not.

"Anyway, I have to give you credit. You are an amazing man, surviving as you have done, such a long time in the desert. Resisting an entire army single-handedly, as you did to allow your men to escape. Commendable!"

"Kiss my ass," Jack said.

"Oh, Jack Valentine," Omar said. "In so many ways, it is a sad thing to see you die. But I assure you, it will be a glorious death. A tribute to you. A once-great warrior, defeated, humbled under a more powerful sword. My sword!"

"American jets took me down, asshole, not you," Jack said, looking at the man in the rocking chair holding the cattle prod across his lap. "That's the truth. You never had a chance at me until I had a run of bad luck. A few more steps, I'd be home free."

"Perhaps," Omar said. "But Allah handed you to me,

nonetheless. In a few days, you will surely die under my sword. That I promise you!"

"You know. You're a bunch of fucking cowards. Strip a man naked and chain him to the floor. How tough is that?" Jack said. "You're a fucktard. A fat-assed old goat fucker."

"Fucktard?" Omar laughed. "I have not heard that expression before. I shall remember it. As for your clothes? They shredded to rags from the bombs your planes dropped on you. I am amazed that you lived! Hardly a scratch on you! Most remarkable."

The old graybeard leaned back in the rocking chair, shaking his head.

"I do wish your equipment had fared better," Omar sighed. "I truly want one of your Remington model 700 rifles. I hoped I might obtain yours since you will no longer need it.

"The blast literally bent the barrel of the Marine sniper rifle you had on your shoulder. And the other one? The Vigilance rifle, another nice gun. It broke into three pieces! Can you believe it? Snapped in three pieces.

"Your backpack, and everything inside, confetti. Truly amazing that you live. Not even a broken arm or leg."

"Divine providence," Jack said, rolling onto his butt and managing to sit up with his hands between his ankles. He looked at Abu Omar on the level, eye to eye, and spoke in a soft, certain tone. "You won't cut my head off, either. I'm getting out of here, and I will kill you. That I promise!"

"Ha!" The al-Sunnah boss laughed and rocked back. "You are a bold man, Jack Valentine! I like you!

"I thought I would hate you, and I did hate you, but

now I like you. You have, as your Marines say, very large balls!"

Jack smiled at the old man in the rocking chair.

"I will walk out of here, and I will kill you."

Abu Omar laughed again. "I look forward to the coming days, Gunnery Sergeant Valentine. You are quite something. Your confidence. Your certainty, despite everything that surrounds you. A man in chains, in a dungeon, held prisoner by a thousand guns, and you boast of killing me. Amazing."

Then the graybeard shouted upstairs, "Giti! Miriam! Come tend to this filthy beast. Wash him, and put some clothes on him. We want the infamous and humbled *Ash'abah al-Anbar* presentable for our video cameras."

_ 15 _

The girls brought Jack Valentine a milking stool to sit on while they washed him. He said nothing but winced as Giti took a cloth soaked with iodine and disinfected the dozens of bad scrapes, cuts, and bruises across his back, butt, and legs.

"I am sorry if this burns, but you were cut to pieces along with everything you had on," the girl said, speaking English with almost a British accent.

Jack looked at her. "What happened to them? My clothes and my gear?"

"Your clothes?" Giti said. "We took what was left of them off your body. I do not know about any equipment."

"So the old goat with the filthy mouth told the truth. My kit and guns blown to shit," Jack said, and noticed that Miriam put her hand over her mouth and hid her laughter.

"What's so funny?" Jack said as both girls rubbed soap in his hair, on his face, chest, legs, butt, crotch, even the soles of his feet and palms of his hands. Almost a ritual-istic cleansing, as if preparing a body for the grave.

Giti smiled, and said softly, "Our husband, the old

goat with the filthy mouth. Miriam finds that amusing, because it is true. His mouth is repugnant."

"I thought he was your father," Jack said, looking at the young girls. "You're both his wives? You're just kids."

"Not by choice, and Abu Omar has two other wives in addition to Miriam and me," Giti answered in a low voice, so that no one outside the cell could hear what they said.

"You're like slaves then?" Jack said.

Giti nodded yes. "We are slaves. Truly."

"Your English," Jack said. "Where did you learn to speak it so well? You sound British, in fact."

"Miriam here, and our sister in Christ, Amira, and I studied English, along with French at the Presbyterian Christian School in Mosul. In addition to being a very good farmer, my father taught language at the school," Giti said.

"So you're not Muslim?" Jack asked, looking at the scarves that covered the girls' heads and necks, and the plain Muslim dresses they wore.

"We are Christians but have accepted the Muslim way, as our master, Abu Omar Bakr al-Nasser, requires of us," Miriam said, and looked at her sister. "Giti is with child, and our husband will soon disown her and give her to the men. They will rape her and kill her."

Miriam began to cry and lowered her face, taking a rag from the clear water and beginning to rinse the soap off Jack.

"That's true, Giti?" Jack said. "You are Christians, and your name is Giti?"

She nodded yes. "Giti Sadiq. We come from the village of al-Shirqat, halfway between Mosul to the north and Baiji to the south. Abu Omar murdered my father and brothers, cutting their heads at the throat with his long knife. Then because my mother and younger sister would not submit to Islam, he shot them both as they knelt at his feet.

"He murdered Miriam's father and mother and sister the same. Amira's parents and brothers, too. We were afraid to die, and Abu Omar found us attractive, so we put on the scarves of Muslim women and submit to him."

Miriam wept as she washed Jack. "I have prayed so much that Jesus will come and claim me. Take my life. I should have gone to Heaven with my mother."

Giti shot her elbow into Miriam. "Don't say such things. We did not deny Christ; we only put on these clothes. Do not forget that we still pray to our Savior, and the Holy Spirit of Jesus still takes care of us."

Jack let out a huff.

"You don't believe in Jesus?" Giti asked, genuinely surprised. "All Americans are Christians. You do not believe in our Lord Jesus?"

Jack laughed. "I guess I do. I did in Sunday School a long time ago. And I have my holier moments from time to time, feeling the spirit, so to speak. Mostly when I need God's help."

"But you do not take your faith seriously?" Giti asked.

"I guess no more than most people," Jack answered. "We have our exceptions. My colonel. Elmore Snow. He's a pretty serious Jesus guy."

Giti smiled. "Submitting to Christ, living for Him is all that we truly have in life. Don't you believe that?"

"Probably not," Jack said, being honest. "Most of the time, I don't live for Jesus; I live for myself. I expect I'm a source of disappointment for the Lord. I think if most people are honest, that's the truth about them, too."

"I am amazed!" Giti said. "I so want to go to America one day. A place where we can praise Jesus and worship God without worry, freely. And everyone there loves Him. Now you say this is a falsehood?"

"Hate to break your rose-colored glasses," Jack said.

"What does this mean?" Miriam said.

Jack shook his head. "America's pretty rotten these days. People shop and play on Sunday instead of going to church. Walmart open twenty-four/seven, porn on every corner, casinos, too. It's gone to hell in a handbasket."

"They no longer worship God on Sunday?" Giti asked.

"Lots of people still do," Jack said. "Don't get me wrong. My mom and dad, they're Christians, in church every Sunday. But these days, more Americans don't darken the chapel door except on maybe Christmas and Easter. Most people in America today? They worship money."

"That is so sad," Miriam said, using a dry cloth on Jack, rubbing the water from his hair.

"To have such liberty, and so many blessings of wealth as you Americans have. To not praise God for these things? For your freedom? It makes me want to cry," Giti said.

Jack thought a moment, and said, "We're pretty piggish, I guess."

"Yes you are," Giti agreed. "I would give anything just to stand on my feet on American ground. Even for only a day!"

Jack looked out the door and saw the old guy with the rifle guarding the entrance keeping his eye on them.

"What are you looking at?" Jack called to him.

The old guy didn't understand what Jack said but knew it wasn't anything he should like. So he just looked more, and Jack scowled.

"Don't mind him," Giti said. "That is Yasir, a Bedouin man who herded goats with his brothers for many years along the Tigris valley where I lived. My mother bought milk and cheese from him before the war. He is not a bad man. Yasir has a simple mind, so don't be rude to him."

"What about your husband?" Jack asked, as the girls finished drying him.

"Abu Omar?" Giti answered, as if there were anyone else.

"Right," Jack said. "What's his story?"

"Before the Americans overthrew President Saddam Hussein, Abu Omar was Colonel Omar Bakr, commandant of the Republican Guard in Baiji. He lived in a fine home, and was born in Saddam's hometown of Tikrit. Some say he is related to him.

"Colonel Bakr held great influence in the Arab Socialist Ba'ath Party. Then came the Americans three years ago. It seems an eternity now. He lost everything. Even his wife and children, who died in the bombing in Baghdad.

"Some men from Jordan and Syria joined Abu Omar and they formed the insurgent army, Jamaat Ansar al-Sunnah, a protector of their Arab faith. He is vicious and cruel."

"Help me escape," Jack whispered.

Giti reacted as if the American had jolted her with Abu Omar's cattle prod.

"You can come with me. You and your sisters," Jack told her. "I will get you to America. You and your sisters. I know people who can get it done. I promise!"

"Do not speak of this ever again!" Giti whispered. "You will die, and so will we."

"Miriam said he was going to kill you soon, because you're pregnant," Jack reminded her.

Giti glared at Miriam. "He will kill not only me but Miriam and Amira and our Syrian sister, Sabeen, too."

"Sabeen?" Jack asked, now considering the problems and advantages of four teenage girls. "Can she use a gun?"

"Certainly not!" Giti huffed back in a harsh whisper.

Miriam leaned close, and said, "She might be able to use a gun. She is from Syria, after all. You don't know. What is so hard? Point the gun and pull the trigger."

Jack smiled.

"What is all this whispering?" Yasir said in Arabic with a loud, commanding voice.

He looked at Jack. "Why have you not dressed him? Are you wicked girls admiring his manhood? Shame on you!"

Amira came in the door behind Yasir.

"Ah, there is Amira now with the clothes," Giti said in Arabic, and pointed at her sister.

Then she pointed at the keys on Yasir's belt. "You must unlock the chains, so that he can dress."

He looked at Jack and didn't like the odds. "I will get some help."

The old goatherd hurried upstairs to find backup, and Giti turned to Jack.

"What you suggest is utterly impossible!"

"Nothing's impossible," Jack said. "God has saved me many times over. He got me this far. He will not leave me to die here. Where's your faith?"

"Suddenly you have faith?" Giti said. "It is not something you can choose today and forget tomorrow."

"Does God require my faith to protect me?" Jack said. "People with great faith pray for me, and God hears them. We will get out of here. If you can't trust me, trust God."

"I cannot think of this!" Giti said.

Miriam and Amira both looked at her with big eyes and question marks.

"Why not?" Amira blurted. "If I die trying to leave this horrible place, it is better than living what is left of my life here."

Miriam reminded Giti, "Very soon, Abu Omar will notice your baby bump. Then what? Do you wish him to feed you to his lions?"

"We will talk of this later," Giti told them.

"We don't have time to talk it over," Jack reminded her, and made a cutting motion across his throat.

"Abu Omar will not kill you today," Giti told Jack. "They must wait for Abu Musab al-Zarqawi. He will want to be here, or he will have you brought to him."

"Zarqawi?" Jack asked.

"Yes," Miriam said. Giti looked at her as if she said something wrong, and Miriam shrugged back. "What?"

"We should not talk about these things," Giti said.

"We must!" Amira said. "God gives us courage and His blessings. We must do this!"

"Zarqawi. Do you know where he hides?" Jack asked.

"These days, he stays in a safe house in the country near the village of Hibhib," Amira said.

"I've never heard of the place," Jack said.

"Hibhib is a small community on Iraqi National Highway 2, maybe fifty kilometers north of Baghdad," Giti added. "Have you heard of Khalis and Baqubah?"

"Yeah, I think so. They sound familiar," Jack said, committing everything to memory, his Force Reconnaissance Marine self kicking into high gear.

"The village is maybe six kilometers west of Baqubah, as the bird flies," Giti said.

"As the crow flies," Jack corrected her.

"Yes, as the crow flies"—Giti nodded—"because there are no roads directly from Baqubah to Hibhib. You must drive ten kilometers up to Khalis, then down to Hibhib, another six kilometers. Or drive south, then up again, an even greater distance."

"How do you know this?" Jack asked the girls.

Amira smiled. "My grandfather and uncle live in Hibhib. I have many family there, so I know Hibhib exactly."

"No, I mean, how do you know that Zarqawi is in Hibhib?" Jack asked. "We have searched for him for years."

"Zarqawi was here only two weeks ago," Giti said. "Abu Omar offered him my family home at al-Shirqat, that he now uses, but Abu Musab said that was too far from Baghdad. Then he spoke of his house in Hibhib, a place he always goes to hide. No one looks there because it is quiet. Many of Saddam's people hide there, too. People protect them there."

"Do you know the house?" Jack asked.

"Amira knows it," Giti said.

"Can you draw me a map?" Jack asked.

Amira looked puzzled. "I am not good with drawing."

"Just directions to it from Hibhib," Jack said.

Amira smiled and nodded yes.

"Write them down on paper and hide it," Jack said. "When we escape, some of us may die. We must promise each other that we will make sure that the directions you write down go with one of us who makes it out alive."

All three girls looked scared. Fear and the sense of reality rushed upon them with the talk that some of them, or all of them, might really die.

"We will pray," Giti said, and gave Jack a stern look. "You, too, must pray. Jesus loves you. Love Him, and He will take care of you."

Jack smiled. "Yes, Jesus loves all the little children of the world." A hint of sarcasm showing.

Giti smiled. "Yes, and He loves their mommies and daddies, too."

"Even the bad ones?" Jack asked.

"They make Him weep," Giti said.

"I will say my prayers," Jack promised.

"Good," Giti said. "We must have a plan, if we do this. What shall we do?"

"Best time to escape is during the wee hours of the morning, when men standing guard can't keep their eyes open," Jack said.

"When we start our cooking, no one is awake, even the men outside keeping watch always have their eyes closed," Miriam said. "We can sneak away without them noticing?"

Giti smiled. "No one gets hurt. I like this."

"Sorry, but shit happens," Jack said, and the three girls frowned.

"It does!" Jack said.

"Yasir has the keys to the doors and to a truck that he uses to get supplies," Amira said.

"You swipe the keys, unlock me, we steal the truck, and run," Jack said. "Very simple."

Giti smiled.

"Simple plans work best," Jack said, "but we always hit a snag when the mouse tries to sneak past the cat. We need a distraction, and a way to take out the guards. Timing. We must pick a time when they are weakest."

The three girls looked puzzled. Impossible.

"Think about it," Jack said.

"We will come up with a plan of dealing with Yasir and his guards in the next day or two," Giti said.

Jack didn't like the idea of waiting. He wanted to leave now. But considering that the people that Omar had watching him would be on their toes this first night, and in a day or two they might then fall back into more comfortable, complacent routines, he told Giti, "Give it three days."

Giti looked at her sisters. "Three days?"

"Yes," Miriam said. "But no more than three. Abu Omar may decide to take matters in his own hands, especially if he does not want to share the fame as the one who captured and now executes this man they call the Ghost of Anbar."

"My name is Jack," the gunny said. "Jack Valentine."

"We never knew you by anything except *Ash'abah al-Anbar*, as the men call you," Giti said. "Valentine you say? Like the celebrated day of love?"

"That's me." Jack smiled.

"What about Sabeen?" Amira asked Giti.

"We must take her, too," Giti said.

"She is so slow and always afraid," Miriam cautioned.

"All the more reason she must come," Giti said.

"And Yasir?" Amira asked.

"I have an idea, and Sabeen can help," Giti said.

"So today's jihadi show is what?" Jack asked, looking at the blue medical scrubs that Amira had brought him.

"A display, I suspect," Giti said. "They want to draw attention to you, and themselves as such heroes, capturing the Ghost of Anbar. All the men upstairs are talking about you and how great they now are. They want the notoriety among the other factions."

"But what's to stop old Abu Omar from deciding to hog the show all to himself? Cut my head off in the morning, and as you say, not share fame and glory with Zarqawi."

"As you said"—Giti smiled at Jack—"we must trust God. He has brought you this far."

"Yeah, but I could have done without the part where I'm sitting naked in an ancient Persian dungeon with my wrists chained to my ankles," Jack said.

Voices grew louder as Yasir and two other gunmen came down the passageway to the cell where Jack sat chained, naked and freshly washed, with the blue medical scrubs folded on his lap.

"Good," Yasir told the girls as he walked in the room and saw them sitting quietly with their backs turned toward Jack, waiting for the guards. He gave Miriam a push with the toe of his boot, looking tough for the two younger al-Qaeda gunmen. "Go upstairs and get to work with Sabeen, cooking our dinner."

"What about food for him?" Giti asked, as she and the two other sisters hurried out the door, bowing their heads so that they did not make eye contact with any of the men.

"Abu Omar said nothing of feeding this snake," Yasir said, again in his commanding voice to impress his subordinate guards.

"Very good, master," Giti said, and that made Yasir smile. He liked the show of respect, especially in front of the men. "Get going! If I need you, I will call you."

Jack watched the girls hustle away, then looked at Yasir and the two young henchmen with him.

"You boys suck each other's dicks? Or do you prefer giving blow jobs to strangers?" Jack asked them with a smile, as if he had just complimented the three men.

Yasir and one young man cracked half smiles, taking the compliment that they did not understand. But the other gunman slapped Jack on the side of his face with the flat side of the wooden buttstock on his AK rifle.

"Americans speak such filth!" the young jihadi said.

"Two of you don't understand a word I say, but one does," Jack said, smiling bloody teeth at the angry guard.

"I should hit you again for provoking me," the one who understood English said.

"You should not react to bullshit prisoners say," Jack told the young man. "If you'd played dumb-ass with fucktard and dipshit here, I might have said something important, thinking you didn't understand me."

"Shut up," the Haji said.

"Don't say I never taught you anything." Jack smiled, nodding down at the locked chains.

The one who understood English told Yasir in Arabic, "Unlock the chains. If he moves, we will shoot him."

Then he looked at Jack, and said, "You will get dressed. If you raise a finger, as if you want to escape, I will shoot you in the head."

"Abu Omar won't like it." Jack smiled and spit a glob of blood on the floor between Yasir's toes as he went to unlock the padlock between the gunny's ankles. Then Jack looked back at the English-speaking Haji and smiled more. "I dare you to shoot me."

A range of mountains lay northwest of Haditha Dam and lake, and Elmore Snow looked at them with orange clouds from the sunset shrouding their distant peaks. Standing in the blockhouse atop the high hard wall, he thought of home, and of his wife, June, and his daughter, Katherine. The girl was growing up too fast. How sweet life would be right now, he thought, if he had already retired from the Marine Corps.

He thought of Rowdy Yates, lying at rest in the Evansville National Veterans Cemetery on the outskirts of Casper, Wyoming. He thought of Brenda Kay, now living at home with her family up Headgate Draw, and wondered how she would live her life without Rowdy, the new baby coming soon.

Elmore stared out at the sunset, the great flat desert and small hills, and thousands of empty square miles where Jack Valentine fought to stay alive, the proverbial needle in a haystack.

"Colonel Snow," Captain Charlie Crenshaw called from the ground on the inside of the high, hard wall. "Our CIA contingent has beamed up something on their computer that al-Qaeda sent to *Al Jazeera* about an hour ago, and they posted it to their Web site."

"Jack?" Elmore asked, as his heart crashed flat to his boots.

"Afraid so, sir," the Delta Company, Fifth Marines commanding officer answered.

"Did they kill him?" the colonel asked, his voice broken. He didn't know if he could handle losing another Marine he held so close to his heart.

"Not yet," Crenshaw said. "They got him dressed in a blue jumpsuit and threaten that they'll cut off his head unless America releases all the prisoners at Abu Ghraib."

"Motherfucker!" Elmore screamed into the empty desert from his high perch.

"Excuse me, sir?" the captain asked.

"I'm sorry, Captain Crenshaw," Elmore said, and headed down the ladder. "Something I say when I am really upset."

"I've heard tell," the skipper said, leading Lieutenant Colonel Snow to the blockhouses where Speedy Espinoza had set up his CIA intelligence shop with Hacksaw, Kermit, and Habu bunking there, too.

When they got inside, Espinoza clicked the PLAY button on the news agency's Web site.

Jack Valentine sat on a short milking stool in what appeared to be a room with stone walls. An al-Qaeda black flag draped the background, and two men with rifles, dressed in black outfits and their heads and faces wrapped in black, stood at each side of the Marine. A man directly behind Jack, also wearing a black ninja suit and mask, held a short Moorish sword with a broad, curved blade.

A gray beard peeked below the mask that the man with the sword wore, suggesting that he was older and probably a higher-ranking al-Qaeda Iraq boss.

The man bellowed his speech in Arabic for all the jihadi brethren, then spoke in very good English:

"We are the Army of God, Jamaat Ansar al-Sunnah, may Allah be praised. Today we have captured the American Marine, an evil assassin of the faithful, Gunnery Sergeant John Arthur Valentine, known to us as the minion of Satan, *Ash'abah al-Anbar.*

"It is God's will that America must release all of our faithful brothers from the prisons at Abu Ghraib and at Guantanamo, Cuba. American forces must also lay down their arms and the infidels depart Iraq and all the lands of the Levant. Unless this happens in the next seventy-two hours, I will execute Gunnery Sergeant John Arthur Valentine in the method of our faith. May Allah be praised!

"Allahu Akbar! Allahu Akbar!"

"And kiss my ass," Speedy Espinoza said, clicking off the video.

"Seventy-two hours," Elmore said.

"Probably about seventy hours by now," the CIA agent said, "given the time lost after *Al Jazeera* received it and that it took for them to post the video to their Web site."

"Less than three days." Elmore sighed.

"Fuck!" Bronco Starr said.

"We shouldn't have left him there!" Cochise Quinlan protested, and the colonel looked at him.

"He saved our lives, Colonel. All of us," Petey Preston said. "Me and Chico, we'd be dead if it wasn't for Gunny V."

Elmore Snow cocked his head to one side and gave Billy Claybaugh a look. Then he wrinkled his forehead at Cotton Martin and pointed his thumb at corporals Preston and Powell. "I thought those two went to Germany. To the hospital."

"Sir, Cotton didn't have a thing to do with it," Staff Sergeant Claybaugh spoke up.

"You knew about this?" Elmore said to Billy-C.

"Yes, sir," he answered.

"After the fact, sir," Chico Powell said.

"I busted 'em out, sir," Sergeant Cochise Quinlan said, stepping up to take full blame.

"You know, you guys are U-A," Elmore said to the two wounded corporals. "Do the hospital people even know you're missing?"

"Those Air Force dudes at Charlie Med?" Petey Preston smiled. "No, sir. They don't have a clue. Never will."

"Who has your record books?" Elmore asked. "Captain Burkehart sent those to the hospital when we transferred you out."

"We have them right here, sir," Cochise said, and the two Marines held up large envelopes that contained their enlisted Service Record Books and all their orders.

"Didn't I see this in a movie once?" Elmore said, and began to laugh.

"Sir, we ain't hurt bad," Preston said. "Couple of leaks here and there, a few broken ribs. Hey, you get dinged up worse than this playing high school football. We don't need to go to a hospital. They let Staff Sergeant Claybaugh stay at MARSOC on light duty. Why not us?"

"Yeah, and I see how that's working out, too," the colonel said, looking at Billy-C leaning on his crutches.

"I'm healing just fine, sir," Claybaugh said.

"We got our antibiotics and everything," Powell said. "Billy even got some extra refills for us, so we're fat. Way more than we need. Don't worry about anything, sir. We got all the bases covered."

"You know, a daughter in high school is less trouble," Elmore said, and let out a long breath of frustration. "I'll call Captain Burkehart and have him start fixing this."

"Sir, nobody's going anyplace without Gunny Valentine," Jaws piped up.

"That's the law, sir," Bronco chimed in.

"Whose law?" Elmore asked.

"Our fucking law, sir," Jaws said, deadpan and serious.

Six men sat at a table eating a late-night dinner, surrounded by two dozen gunmen in the al-Qaeda safe house near the village of Hibhib. At the head sat Abu Musab al-Zarqawi. Davet Taché stood by the door with Jean René Decoux and their female spy, French journalist Francoise Theuriau.

"Juba, Hasan, and the lovely Francoise," Zarqawi said, "always you make the stylishly late entrance. So very French of you."

Davet smiled, and said in French, "Fashionably late as always, sir. However, I rushed here from Baghdad as quickly as I could with wonderful news from Omar Bakr."

"Make them a place at the table," Zarqawi ordered the men who served their meal.

"Even the woman?" one of the gunmen asked, looking at Francoise.

"Certainly," Abu Musab huffed. "Do you know what this woman did for the jihad? She is the one who gave us the secret plans. It is our honor to sit with her tonight."

Francoise smiled as she made her way to a chair. She adjusted the dark blue hijab around her head and neck, making sure it remained properly tucked inside the top of her dress, hiding any hint of her breasts. Rather than click-clack high-heel slippers with open toes, now she wore plain brown shoes with socks, and a long brown dress and matching long blouse. Proper Muslim attire.

Davet Taché and Jean René Decoux wore fine Armani silk and wool-blend summer business suits. Davet's light gray with a thin blue pinstripe and Jean René's a dark tan.

"We have come to stay a few days if you don't mind," Davet said. "Things have become somewhat difficult in Baghdad. One of our American contacts has become a liability of late. While the FBI investigates him, we thought it best that we make ourselves unavailable."

"Juba, or it is today your French character, Davet," Zarqawi said. "You and Hasan, and this woman, may remain my guests for as long as you desire. Now, what news?"

"The one they call *Ash'abah al-Anbar*, the Ghost Sniper, Gunnery Sergeant John Arthur Valentine," Juba began.

"I heard that pig on CNN say his name some days ago," Zarqawi remarked. "What of him?"

"Abu Omar has him." Davet smiled, and looked all

around the table, and at the men standing guard. All of them aglow.

"Hah!" Zarqawi let out, and slammed the heel of his hand on the table, rattling the dishes. "Have him brought to me! I will saw off his head!"

"Abu Omar begs your indulgence," Davet interjected.

"Indulgence?" Zarqawi huffed. "I want that American here. Not at Haditha! Here!"

"Sir," Juba said. "He has already released a video to *Al Jazeera*, making demands. Omar will behead Gunnery Sergeant Valentine in three days."

"Insubordinate fool," Zarqawi grumbled. He sat thinking for a moment, angry. Took a breath and nodded.

"What's done is done. Three days it is," Abu Musab said. "I will do the beheading. It will take place here."

"Very good, sir," Davet Taché responded, still speaking with his eloquent French. "We will send word to Abu Omar."

Elmore Snow tossed on his cot for two hours, trying to force himself to get at least four hours' rest, a minimum he considered needed for any combat leader. He could not get the picture out of his mind of Jack Valentine sitting shackled in front of a camera and the black-suited terrorist with the Moorish sword going to work, cutting off his head.

He laced up his boots at 3 a.m. and went to the Company D communications module. The colonel gave the sergeant standing the watch a pat on the shoulder. "Got a line to Baghdad?"

"Yes, sir," the sergeant said, tired and staying awake with willpower and strong coffee.

"I need to call this number. MARSOC Detachment headquarters," Elmore said, and handed the Marine the information.

"Anybody even left back there?" The sergeant smiled at the colonel.

"Better be at least a captain and a corporal, and one of them had better be awake," he said.

Two rings and a groggy Ralph Butler answered, "MARSOC Detachment, Iraq. Corporal Butler speaking, sir or ma'am!"

"Skipper nearby?" Colonel Snow asked.

"He's with that good-looking FBI agent and the CIA spook, over in operations," Butler said.

"Patch me to them," Elmore said.

Two rings, and Mike Burkehart answered, "Operations, Captain Burkehart speaking."

"Mike, Colonel Snow here," Elmore said.

"Yes, sir," Burkehart said. "We saw the video of Jack if that's why you're calling."

"Yes, and there's more," Elmore said. "I figured you guys got the news. Speedy Espinoza said they have a team of CIA analysts working on that video in Baghdad, and a group at Langley, too, around the clock. They make anything of it?"

"Let me put Chris on," Burkehart said, and handed the phone to Gray.

"What have your people figured out, anything worthwhile?" Elmore asked.

Gray said, "Given that the people who have Jack claim

to be this bunch of Sunni insurgents calling themselves Jamaat Ansar al-Sunnah, Assembly of the Helpers of Sunnah, the teachings and writings of Muhammad, we have a very good idea who the guy with the big knife is."

"Abu Omar Bakr al-Nasser," Elmore said. "Way ahead of you. Got a couple of interrogator-translators and an S2 officer who doesn't sleep much at nights either, on account of him researching these monsters."

"How about Colonel Omar Bakr Abd al-Majid al-Tikriti?" Gray said.

"That's a new spin. Like putting a circle around his X, when a hillbilly checks into a Memphis hotel?" Elmore joked.

Gray laughed. "I had to think about that a minute, Colonel. Yes, sir, exactly like that.

"You got a deck of those Saddam Hussein bad-guy playing cards they used to hand out?"

"I guess I lost mine," Snow answered.

"You recall this one dude in there, former Iraqi interior minister, defense minister, Republican Guard general, chief of Saddam's intelligence service and all-around monster straight from hell, Ali Hassan Abd al-Majid al-Tikriti?"

"Chemical Ali. Of course," Elmore said. "He's the guy that gassed the Kurds."

"Roger that," Gray said. "Sitting in a Baghdad jail cell as we speak, awaiting the hangman's noose as his appeal winds its way slowly through the political system here."

"Let me guess," Elmore said. "Our guy, Abu Omar, is somehow tied to this creep."

"Oh yes," Gray said. "Like first cousins."

"Chemical Ali is a first cousin of Saddam Hussein," Elmore said.

"Give the colonel a gold star," Gray said.

"So this guy, Abu Omar, is Saddam's brother?" Elmore asked.

"Not quite," Gray said. "He's Saddam's other first cousin. Abu Omar shed the al-Majid al-Tikriti identifiers in exchange for the al-Nasser family and location device."

"Nasser. Isn't that like a royal family in Dubai?" Elmore asked. "One of the Arab Emirates?"

"More like Qatar, but, yes, a United Arab Emirate family," Gray said. "His mother's mother comes from Doha, and that bunch is very well fixed. Tied to that oil money."

"Why hang around Iraq?" Snow asked.

"He has designs on moving up and taking over here," Gray said. "Reestablishing the Sunni Ba'athist regime."

"Oh, how very ambitious of him," Snow said.

"He's got plans for guys like Zarqawi," Gray said. "And they ain't pretty."

"I wouldn't think so," Elmore said.

"As a little background," Gray continued, "Abu Omar had become Chemical Ali's go-to guy, before the war, and Saddam's favorite headsman, when it became necessary to move a rebellious underling out of office in the dark.

"Everything in Omar's life ran lined with silk and gold until that day of shock and awe in 2003, when President Bush's shit hit the Baghdad fan."

"Boys up here said something about Abu Omar losing

his family in the bombing, and that put him on the war-path," Elmore said.

"Yeah, that did happen," Gray said. "He sent them to Baghdad, checked them into the Ishtar Sheraton Hotel, where they'd be safe from the American bombs because that's where CNN slept. Except Omar didn't count on the mortar and rocket attacks that hit the hotel later. Killed his wife and four boys, stair-stepped down seventeen to three years old."

"I'm sorry to hear that," Elmore said. "He is a man like us, and losing his family is terrible."

"Don't waste your time weeping for this piece of shit, Colonel Snow," Gray said. "He's not worth one tear. He kept a whole raft of concubines his entire married life. His wife was nothing more than a money bag."

"I see," the colonel said.

"Abu Omar has a thing for young girls, you know," Gray continued. "The younger the treat, the better he likes them.

"But what drives his train is his ambition of one day ruling Iraq. Just like Saddam did. He's not so much the devout Muslim as he is the evil maniac hell-bent for power."

Elmore laughed. "Aren't they all? Especially Zarqawi."

"I'd say so," Gray agreed. "Even that fat-ass Iran-loving leader of the Mahdi Army puts on the devout show, but in our heart of hearts we all know he envisions himself running the show in Iraq as supreme leader of the faith and king of the nation. He draws that inspiration from his mentor, Grand Ayatollah Sayyid Ali Hosseini Khamenei, who rules the roost in Iran, stepping into the shoes of our favorite terrorism monger, Grand Ayatollah Sayyid Ruhollah Khomeini. You remember Ayatollah Khomeini, don't you? The bombing of our Marines in Beirut in 1983 ring a bell?"

"Who can forget?" Elmore said.

"These guys?" Chris Gray said. "All one lump of scum."

"You got pictures? Locations? Intel?" Elmore asked.

"Langley's pumping Speedy's computer full of good stuff as he sleeps," Gray said. "And how come you're not sawing a few logs yourself?"

"Who can sleep?" Elmore said.

"Yeah." Chris laughed. "We don't do that here, either. In fact, there's a pretty red-eyed lady from the FBI sitting in Jack's swivel chair, studying maps of al-Anbar and all that crap from Langley as we speak."

"I thought she was flying back home today," Elmore said. "Didn't Kendrick recall her since the lid blew off her investigation, and Alosi and his boss got subpoenaed to testify before that Senate committee?"

"She plied her wiles, Elmore. You know pretty women and gruff old men. Kendrick's just like the rest of us." Gray chuckled, then Liberty snatched the phone from him.

"Jason told me that I should stay here until we rescued Jack," Liberty told Colonel Snow. "He cares. He wants us to get Jack back alive. No plying of womanly wiles. Besides, Mr. Kendrick knew I'd be worthless back there, and I might even be a help here. So he told me to stay."

"How about your three boys?" Elmore asked.

"They took the flight home with Alosi," she said.

"You're welcome to the facilities there with Captain Burkehart and Smedley," Elmore told her.

"I've already moved in," Liberty followed.

"Jack's bunk?" Elmore laughed. "Or is that a dumb question?"

"You know me too well, Elmore," she answered.

"Stay close to the phone," the colonel said.

"I wish I could be there with you guys," she said.

"You'll do fine with the skipper and Smedley," Elmore said. "It would be problematic, even if you could manage to get up here. What would you do, anyway?"

"Go out and hunt Jack, with you guys," she said.

"Get some sleep, Liberty. I'll call you later," Elmore said, and hung up the phone.

He walked to the next module, where Speedy Espinoza had set up shop and pounded on the door.

"Wake up!" he bellowed, imitating his all-time hero, John Wayne. "You're wasting daylight."

"What the fuck?" Espinoza moaned, opening his eyes to total darkness. "What time is it?"

"Four thirty in the morning. Coffee's made," Elmore said in John Wayne character, as Speedy opened the door.

The colonel went to the three racks where Walter, Kermit, and Cory still snored, and started kicking cots.

"Top Gillespie, I'm surprised that you let this air winger beat you to breakfast," Snow growled.

"We're up, Colonel," Hacksaw grogged, rubbing his eyes.

The outside door swung open, and First Sergeant Alvin Barkley stepped through, helmet on and combat-ready.

"You boys ready to rock and roll?" He smiled, a big

old-fashioned metal canteen cup in his hand, steaming with hot coffee.

"Getting that way, First Sergeant," Snow answered. Then he looked at Espinoza. "Speedy, beam up your computer and open that big file that Langley sent while you rested."

The former Marine pilot had already sat in the chair and begun typing in his password. In seconds, he had a list of maps and pictures. He clicked on one and up came a photograph of Abu Omar in his Republican Guard uniform, no beard and a black moustache under his nose. He looked remarkably like his cousins, Saddam Hussein and Chemical Ali.

Next thing, CIA Agent Espinoza opened a file that had side-by-side portraits of Omar. One, a photograph of him in a business suit, bare chin and moustache, and the next, an artist's take on what he might look like with a beard and typical dress of an insurgent leader.

"I know that guy!" Barkley exclaimed the second he saw the graybeard with dirty teeth.

Espinoza gave him a look. "Oh do tell."

"Way back, when we first started setting up shop here," the first sergeant went on. "Abu Omar comes rolling up in this fucked-up Russian truck stacked to the sky with all kinds of vegetable produce. Boxes and boxes lashed to the cargo deck of this smoking piece of rusted shit. He has this real pretty young girl in the passenger seat, showing off a little titty for the Iraqi cops who checked them out.

"I had Sergeant Padilla with his killer dog, Rattler, smiling those titanium teeth of his at these scumbags, checking out the truck. Dog alerts, so I want to inspect the cargo. He's got something hidden under all those onions.

"Both the Iraqi police and the local army bosses stop us in our tracks. They say they know this old goat fucker and claim that he's harmless. Like ten seconds later, we get a call on the radio from our bosses, and State Department orders us to stand down. He's just a harmless old farmer from Baiji trucking his vegetables to Haditha.

"Harmless my ass! I'm chapped. So's Padilla."

Then the first sergeant stuck his head out the door, and yelled, "Jorge, get your ass in here with your dog. Give this goat fucker a look and tell me if you know him."

In ten seconds, Sergeant Padilla and Corporal Rattler stood front and center in front of the CIA computer. He took one look at the picture.

"Motherfucker!" Padilla said. "We had him in our hands! Those Iraqi cops. Fuck them! They let this asshole go!"

Elmore thought for a moment, and observed, "He's probably not far from Haditha then."

"I'd say within a twenty-mile radius," Barkley said.

"Let's get this show on the road!" Elmore said. "Instead of wandering up and down the MSR and side roads, we're going to fan out in a line and move west. I want a five-mile-wide sweep."

Espinoza sat pecking at his computer, and brought up a map. "There it is. Langley sent it, too. I've been searching for this map forever. Take a look."

"What is it?" Snow asked, looking at the screen and the first sergeant at his side, the room now crowded with a growing number of Marines who had begun stuffing themselves into the tight quarters.

"For two thousand years, probably more," Espinoza said, "camel caravans moved large tonnages of cargo from the seaports to Baghdad. These caravans traveled down south to ports by Kuwait, and those along the Mediterranean coast. Places like Tyre and Beirut. Crossing the desert to the west took doing. Once they intercepted the Euphrates flowing south at Haditha, they had it made, followed it to Baghdad. But getting across all this dry country?

"Scattered out here in the desert we see these places in the middle of nowhere. How can people survive out here? No water. Just sand and rocks. Right?"

"Water wells and underground facilities," Elmore said.

"Bingo!" Speedy laughed and pointed at the red dots on the map. "Each of these locations is an ancient caravan stop. See how they fall in a line that leads toward the Mediterranean seaports?"

Then he pointed at one forty miles southwest of Haditha. "This one here? You had a nest of Hajis based in it. We ran an air strike on it day before yesterday. Took out a trio of gun wagons running high speed cross-country, then we hit the house with two five-hundred-pounders.

"Pilots reported that they saw the place on fire before their bombs hit. Smoke plume drew them to the target. Could be Jack was nearby. Very possible that he set the place ablaze and got caught there?"

"Good guess," Elmore said.

"Should we check it out?" First Sergeant Barkley asked.

"No," Elmore said. "They won't be keeping Jack in a bombed-out camel stop."

"But they will have him in one that is still operational,"

Speedy said, pointing to seven more in a thirty-mile radius, along two lines west from Haditha.

"Flip a coin and shoot?" Elmore asked.

"I think start visiting them systematically," Speedy said. "We need to get rolling."

"How's that look, First Shirt?" Elmore asked Barkley.

"We're organizing gear, getting Marines suited up, loading ammo. It takes time," he said.

"Can we get moving by eight o'clock?" Elmore asked.

"By nine, anyway," Barkley said.

_ 16 _

Burning orange bleeding across the Iraqi desert from first light of a new day cast the Arabian oryx buck's white coat the same color as the blood-red dunes that surrounded him and his three doe. He stood munching a salad of low-growing green succulents that had found moisture somewhere deep beneath the sands, and gave life where none might otherwise exist.

The oryx had just risen from his bed on the side of a dune where his three mates continued to lie and watch him browse among the thorny plants. His magnificent ebony horns, which curved in graceful arcs like swords over his back, flashed in the morning light. They complemented the glossy black that covered his muzzle and bold jaws, and masked his eyes. Black hair also covered his legs and grew in long strands off the end of his white tail.

The antelope had made their beds on the sand dunes, where heat from the sun had absorbed deep during the previous day, and kept the animals warm during the cold desert night. Lying on the east side of the dune kept any chill from prevailing westerly breezes off their backs.

One of the doe carried a kid in her belly. The other

two had not yet cycled for this year's reproductive season. The buck stayed close to them, ready for their next heat, meanwhile fending away predators and rival bucks.

Some Bedouins who had herded goats and hunted the dry lands of Arabia and Persia centuries ago had thought the white oryx holy and magical. Even in their Muslim faith, they kept their superstitions and myths of the past much alive, even in these modern times.

Yasir Sayf al-Din ibn Abbas al-Bayati shared those Bedouin roots and mystical beliefs. Ever since he caught that one brief glimpse of the big buck and his three doe, he dreamed of them. In those visions, he marveled at the animals from afar, watching them graze on the succulents, obtaining vital moisture for their bodies from eating the plants, much like camels do.

As he dreamed, Yasir al-Bayati felt peace. No war. A calm and goodness filled him. He longed for those days to return, as he remembered life in his childhood.

A cough and a voice upstairs awoke Yasir, who lay on the cold stone floor of the passageway, wrapped in a blanket outside the dungeon door where Jack Valentine slept in chains and had no blanket.

The old Arab jumped to his feet, and grabbed his rifle, which he had leaned against the wall when he wrapped himself in the blanket to keep warm, but had also fallen asleep quickly afterward. He looked up the stone-lined tunnel where two other gunmen under his command were supposed to also stand guard, and they, too, had wrapped up in blankets and lay snoring on the floor.

"Wake up, you fools!" he ordered, kicking the men. Then he hurried back to the wooden door that kept the

Marine secure in his cell. He quietly unlocked the padlock put through a steel hasp above the old iron latch.

Carefully, Yasir pulled the door open barely a crack and peeked inside. The American lay curled in a fetal ball, his back to the door. All was well, and he sighed in relief.

"Fuck you!" Yasir heard the prisoner say, and shut the door, satisfied, despite his failure, first night as officer of the guard and chief jailer, slumbering on the job and allowing his men to fall asleep, too.

Then Yasir heard his master's voice, up early, arguing. He climbed to the top of the stairs and listened as the two guards under his command took posts by the dungeon door.

"Please, cousin," Abu Omar Bakr al-Nasser said to Abu Musab al-Zarqawi on his telephone, "I cannot travel to Baiji today. I must remain close to home because of the illness that has visited my household since yesterday. It is far too great a risk to everyone for me to venture such a distance. Why don't you visit me instead? We will meet at our uncle's house at al-Rawa."

Zarqawi felt like shouting but kept his calm. "I understand, dear cousin. May Allah rid you of this illness before it takes its toll on your household. I will come to you this time, but you must promise to follow my advice. To not follow what I advise you could mean that this grave illness claims you and all those you love."

"I will meet you at our uncle's home in al-Rawa tonight. I promise to hear what you say, but I have my own ideas of how to deal with this illness. May Allah give us wisdom to follow his will, and Allah keep our families safe from further illness." Abu Omar smiled, triumphant.

He knew he held the cards and the guns to get his way. Zarqawi knew it, too, or he would never have subordinated himself to risk traveling the day's journey to the little village on the Euphrates halfway between Haditha Dam and al-Qa'im.

Yasir nearly fell down the stairs as Giti Sadiq and slave sister Sabeen pushed their way past him, carrying breakfast for him and his guards downstairs, and a bowl of rice with beans sprinkled in for Jack, per Omar's order.

"Watch yourselves!" Yasir scolded them, regaining his footing, then following the two girls.

At the bottom of the steps, he pulled the cloth off the tray that Sabeen carried. "What do you have for us?"

"Hummus and cheese, pickled goat meat and dates, and warm bread with tea," Sabeen said, as Giti set their table.

"What about him?" Yasir asked, giving a nod at the closed wooden door.

"Rice with some beans, and a cup of water," Giti said, and lifted the cloth off the tray that she had carried.

"This is much better than the food the Americans give our brothers in their prison at Abu Ghraib," Yasir commented. "Abu Omar is far too kind to this son of a pig."

"Abu Omar has ordered this food for him," Giti said. "If you have issues with his feeding, you should discuss it with our master. I am happy to do as I am ordered."

"As you should," Yasir said, straightening up and speaking firmly to the girl.

"Will you unlock the door?" Giti asked.

Yasir took the ring clip of keys off his belt and found the one that fit the padlock. When he opened the lock, he smiled at Sabeen.

"Lovely Sabeen. How have you been this morning?" he asked the shy girl, and she turned her eyes down and blushed.

"Very good, sir," she answered.

Jack saw Giti and sat on his stool. She gave him the bowl with no spoon. He had to rake the rice and beans into his mouth with his fingers.

"Here, not so fast," she said in English, and gave Jack the cup of water. He gulped it down and wanted more.

"May he have more water?" Giti called to Yasir, speaking Arabic.

The Bedouin thought for a moment, came into the foul room, and took Jack's cup. In the hall, he dipped the cup into a jar filled with drinking water and came back.

"That is all for him today," he told Giti. "Unless he is alive to eat tonight."

Giti looked at Jack, and when Yasir went back in the hallway and began flirting with Sabeen, she said, "Take your time. Sip the water. It is all you may get today."

"Thanks," Jack said, finishing the rice and few beans.

The girl then checked over her shoulder and fished out a healthy strip of pickled goat meat and two dates.

"Do not let Yasir or anyone else see this food," she said. "Omar would kill me if he knew."

Jack palmed the food and slipped a date into his mouth.

As he chewed, he said, "Any news?"

"Perhaps good news," Giti whispered, as Jack pretended to eat more from the bowl and chewed the meat and dates.

Outside, Sabeen kept Yasir busy in the hallway, flirting

back, while his two minions ate their fill of breakfast and drank their tea.

"Abu Omar leaves for al-Rawa this morning for a meeting tonight," Giti said.

"Who with? Any idea?" Jack asked, swallowing the last of the meat and dates.

"I think with Zarqawi," she said. "He argued against meeting in Baiji, which is not far from Hibhib, and told his so-called cousin to meet at their uncle's house in Rawa."

"Anything else?" Jack asked.

"They are discussing an illness that befell the family yesterday," she said. "You are no doubt that illness. They both want to resolve this illness their own ways."

"Fighting over me. I should be flattered." Jack laughed. "Zarqawi wants the honor of cutting off my head. I nearly shot him less than a year ago, you know?"

"Why didn't you!" Giti said. "Our sister Lina would be alive. Zarqawi raped her, then shot her in the head with his pistol while he ejaculated inside her."

"Such a hero," Jack exclaimed. "I won't miss with my next shot. I'm Killing Abu Omar, then Zarqawi. That's a promise."

"I do not like talk of killing," Giti said.

"Get used to it, kiddo. It surrounds us," Jack said.

Giti shuddered and shook her head.

"So with Omar gone, that leaves who in charge here?" Jack asked, hopeful, feeling energy from the two dates.

"I suspect that Abu Omar will take most of his men with him to al-Rawa," she said. "He will not meet the lion without a means of killing him. But he will not leave you attended lightly, either."

"I'm hardly a threat locked in here," Jack said, pondering the what-ifs. "He'll post some good men here to make sure I don't pull anything funny. Put someone in charge who he trusts."

"That is what I believe, too," Giti said, then she smiled. "He will not anticipate the four little lambs of his harem fighting back, however. That is our advantage."

"Smart." Jack smiled. "You should join the Marines. I could use a wise apple like you."

"Wise apple?" she frowned. "Is that good?"

"Very good," Jack said.

Several of Abu Omar's gunmen sat on rocks beneath a grove of date palms that grew a hundred feet in front of the house. Their roots tapped into the water supply that also fed the well in the downstairs chamber and ran a trickle into stone troughs built in the midst of the trees, tamarack, and salt grass that lived off the overflow for the animals.

The men ate the sugary confection harvested from the trees and drank tea as they waited for Abu Omar to get mounted and depart for al-Rawa. Along the way, they would stop at two other similar oases, pick up more gunmen in Toyota and Nissan four-by-four war trucks.

Abu Omar preferred to drive his truck, a new blue one with big off-road tires, nerf bars, and matching chrome-pipe headache rack. Two Russian-made Kalashnikov PKMS machine guns gleamed on top, mounted at each corner above the cab.

When he stepped through the door, his men stopped talking and looked at their leader, amazed.

No longer did he wear the baggy clothes of an Iraqi peasant, with a scuffed pistol belt and bare sword stuck in it, but he had bathed, and even trimmed his beard short. He wore green military riding trousers and polished brown cavalry boots, laced at the top, up nearly to his knees. His breeches' legs were pegged tight inside the boots. On his waist he had tied a red-and-black sash with braided fringe ends that draped down his leg. No longer wearing his shoulder rig, a brown leather Sam Browne held his Makarov 9-by-18-millimeter PMM, packed in a polished brown-leather holster with a flap buttoned over the top. Matching leather magazine pouches rode next to it.

On the opposite side of the gun belt, Omar wore his ornate short Moorish ceremonial sword in a black-silk-covered scabbard. He wore red-velvet wraps with rank insignia of field marshal, a circle of five gold stars surrounding a winged Iraqi lion, a design of his own making, mounted on his brown uniform shirt's epaulets.

Crowning his head and tied behind his shoulders, Abu Omar wore a fine white-silk-and-wool-embroidered royal keffiyeh with a gold-and-red-braided agal making four rope circles around the headdress, and from it four long red-and-black-silk cords tipped with fringed tassels hanging down his back.

As he spoke, he slapped his leg with a black-leather riding crop.

"Today, our army of Helpers of the Sunnah will claim command of all Iraq governance states," he said. "Today is our day of honor.

"I intend to halt with blood the command of Abu

Musab al-Zarqawi once and for all. His dwindling forces, most of whom have already defected to our ranks, can join us or die with him today."

A long silence fell over the men. They didn't know if their leader had lost his mind, or if he truly had decided that their Jamaat Ansar al-Sunnah army now stood ready to dominate al-Qaeda Iraq.

"Hurrah! Hurrah!" shouted Yasir al-Bayati, and he began firing his AK rifle in the air.

That woke them up.

The men standing under the date palms raised their rifles skyward and fired them, too.

"Hurrah! Hurrah!" they began shouting, and soon the place had erupted to shouting and shooting.

Even underground, in the dungeon, Jack heard the shooting and hoped that the place had fallen under attack.

Abu Omar raised his hands, and the men cheered.

"Now, mount up," he yelled to them.

"Should I drive or will you?" Yasir asked his commander to go, too.

"My most trusted captain, Yasir Sayf al-Bayati," Abu Omar told the old goatherd. "You must remain here, in command of six men to guard our prisoner. Zarqawi may send men to steal him, so I put you in charge of my best men."

"You think he would come here?" Yasir asked, now frightened at the idea of standing off a swarm of al-Qaeda with just six men. Even the six best would never match a force of any size. Besides, Yasir had never killed a man. Not even fired a gun at another human being.

"It is very unlikely, to be truthful, my friend," he said,

putting his arm over Yasir's shoulders. "Yet it could happen. I anticipate that he will try to kill me in al-Rawa, hoping to turn my forces to his command. However, he fools himself to believe that Iraqi faithful will follow some Palestinian from Jordan posing as a kaliph of the Sunnah. I have it on good authority that his father is Shiite and his mother a bloody Catholic."

"Very good, sir," Yasir said, bowing his head low to his master with a courtly salute of fingers touching his forehead, saying, "*Adab*," showing his respect but feeling rejected once again.

"Mind the women," Omar said, looking at the four girls standing politely in a line behind Yasir. And to them he asked, "Am I not handsome today?"

All four girls bowed and curtsied to him.

As Giti stood back straight and forced a smile to Abu Omar, he looked at her more closely.

"Giti, you appear rosy today, almost blooming," the washed and pressed man still with brown teeth said, smiling. "And it appears that you've grown around your belly. Are you with child, daughter?"

"Oh, Abu Omar, master," she said, curtsying and bowing her head. "My glow comes from your magnificence today. I assure you, I am not with child. I know how that would distress you. A peasant slave girl with your child. It is my unclean time. That is all. I swell and bloat. I am having these horrid cramps!"

"No, no, no, no!" Abu Omar shouted, putting his hand out, in front of his face. "Do not speak of such things in my presence! Do not disgust me with talk of a woman and her unclean period. I forbid it!"

"Go inside! Never speak of such things to men! You have work!" Yasir scolded, and sent all four girls indoors. Then he apologized to his master. "Sir, she is a Christian, unaware of morality and decency. They walk among men with their heads uncovered, and their bare legs showing."

"Teach them to know better, Yasir," Omar said, and walked to his truck. He motioned to the gunman sitting behind the steering wheel to get out and go to the other side. "I shall drive."

Then, as he stepped in the cab, he stood on the side-bar step, and shouted to his men, "Follow me!"

A white Chinese-manufactured King Long nine-passenger minivan with dark-tinted back windows drove up the highway past Samarrah, on its way through Tikrit. If all seemed well at that point, it would turn onto Highway 19 just outside Baiji and cut across west to Haditha, then around to Rawa. If things did not appear safe that route, they would take the long ride, up to Mosul, across through Tel Afar, and then back south to Qa'im, and from there to Rawa. Five hundred miles rather than two hundred fifty.

Abu Musab al-Zarqawi sat far in the back with two bodyguards. Another bodyguard drove the air-conditioned minivan that had a compartment built in the floor where Zarqawi could hide, along with a small cache of weapons, at roadblocks. Three children sat in the middle seat, and a woman posing as their mother rode in the front passenger seat.

For soldiers and police at checkpoints, this looked like

any other typical Iraqi family traveling the highway. They had papers and stories for every contingency.

By the time they reached Tikrit, Abu Musab ordered the driver to find the next fuel stop and pull in. His stomach had begun rumbling shortly after breakfast. Now it had gotten unbearable. Possibly nerves. Possibly bad meat.

Al-Qaeda Iraq's leader could not get to the restroom fast enough. When he came out twenty minutes later, his face damp from washing it, he looked pasty pale and green under his eyes.

"We should turn back, master," his bodyguard who drove told him. "We can send word to the others who went ahead of us, and those behind us. Let Abu Omar have the American and enjoy his moment of praise. It remains our victory."

Zarqawi could only nod and walk back to the van.

"After Omar Bakr takes the head of the American," Zarqawi said, stretching out in the backseat, behind where the other two bodyguards sat, unbuttoning his trousers for his stomach to relax. "Take Omar's head, too. Send it to me in a white box."

"Very good, sir," the aide said. "Anything else?"

"A blue ribbon on it," Zarqawi said.

"On Abu Omar's head?" he asked.

"On the box," Zarqawi said, forcing a smile at the gunman as he released a long, foul-smelling fart.

"Very good, sir," the driver said, and turned to the woman and children who stood outside. "Get in. We will go back to Hibhib."

When the telephone rang in Abu Omar's office and bedroom, Yasir looked at the other men, not knowing quite what to do. All other times, the boss had left strict orders for everyone to leave things alone.

As the phone rang again and again without stopping, a guard posted by the front door gave Yasir a look and a shrug.

"Alright!" Yasir said, and went into the office.

He picked up the cellular telephone tied to a rooftop booster and antenna. "Yes?"

"Our cousin has fallen ill," the voice said. "He cannot travel to Rawa today. You should proceed as you have planned. We will get together later."

Then the caller hung up the phone.

Yasir looked at the handset and put it back on Abu Omar's desk.

"What is it?" the guard at the door asked.

"Abu Musab al-Zarqawi has fallen ill and will not come to Rawa today," Yasir said. "He says to proceed as planned."

"Very good!" the gunman said. "We should send someone immediately to tell Abu Omar. He will be very unhappy if he waits at al-Rawa tonight, and Zarqawi does not come."

"I know!" Yasir said, frustrated, worried, confused.

He was not good with decisions.

"I will go," Yasir finally told the man at the door.

The gunman shook his head no.

"I will take one man with me," he said. "You will have four men here, plus yourself and those four girls. Just do not unlock the door to the cell, and all will go well."

"I am in charge!" Yasir said. "I will decide who goes and who stays."

The gunman bowed and smiled at Yasir. "I only made a suggestion. Of course, you are in charge. What shall I do?"

"Take one man with you and inform Abu Omar that Abu Musab is ill, and will not be in Rawa," Yasir said.

"Very good, sir," the gunman said, and whistled to a cohort in the yard, standing watch. He pointed to a white Nissan pickup with a Kalashnikov PKM machine gun on top. "We go to Rawa to fetch Abu Omar home. Zarqawi is not coming."

Giti came running from the kitchen when she heard the truck leave. "What is wrong?"

"Get to work!" Yasir scolded her. Then Sabeen came to the door.

"Are you alright, Yasir?" she asked, smiling at him.

He smiled back at the hefty girl who lifted his heart when she gave him those looks, as if she desired him as much as he wanted her.

"All is fine, Sabeen," he said, and she came close to him and stood at his side, looking outside, watching the dust trail behind the departing truck. Yasir imagined that this must be how it felt to have a wife by one's side. He savored the moment.

Two other trucks sat beneath the cover of the date palms, and infrared-reflecting camouflage netting draped over them, where aircraft flying patrols overhead could not spot them.

Yasir had one truck's set of keys on the ring that he carried on his belt, his truck that he used for his errand runs to Haditha. It had no guns or mounting racks for automatic weapons. Just a rusty white pickup with rattling windows and a radio that buzzed when he played it.

The other truck had a headache rack on the back with a Russian PK machine gun mounted on it. Loaded and ready to run. One of the guards downstairs had those keys.

Elmore Snow, flanked by fifty-four Marines mounted in eighteen up-armored Hummers with machine guns on turrets, rolled online. Ahead of them, the first water stop on Speedy Espinoza's map of caravan routes.

As the flanking vehicles took up defensive positions, surrounding the ancient outpost, Colonel Snow and First Sergeant Barkley pulled their truck past a line of date palms, into the dooryard, scattering a hundred goats that roamed the place. A shaggy brown dog came running out of the house, and Rattler, who sat in the back of the Hummer with Sergeant Padilla, began growling.

"Keep your dog in the truck until we take care of this one," Elmore said as he stepped out, and Alvin Barkley set the brakes.

An Arab in a black-and-white-checked keffiyeh, khaki trousers, sandals, and a ragged white shirt came out of the house, behind the dog, waving his hands in the air and jabbering Arabic so fast that the interrogator-translator who got out of the next Humvee couldn't understand the old herdsman. He told him to stop his tirade and speak slowly.

"We are peaceful people here," the Bedouin said slowly in his native language. "We are poor and peaceful. We raise goats and feed travelers as our ancestors have done here since God made this land."

With each phrase, the translator told the colonel and the first sergeant what the man said.

"Who is here besides him?" Snow asked.

After a translation, the old man with the gray scruff growing on his cheeks and more empty gaps than he had left of his long yellow teeth, pointed at the house and started to cry as he spoke.

"My old wife and me, and our little granddaughter," he wailed, real tears blinking from his wrinkled eyes. "My sons have been taken, and their wives, too. All taken for the war and all dead. All that is left to carry my legacy is one little girl who is eight years old. She hides inside with her grandmother. Please do not harm us."

Alvin Barkley looked at the colonel and shook his head. "We need to check the basement. These guys can cry a good story. The Hajis will leave an old man and a woman and a little kid to sit on top of their explosives and guns."

The colonel looked at the translator. "Tell him we mean no one any harm, but he must put the dog in the barn and allow my men to search the house and the basement."

Before the translator had finished, the man began waving his arms in the air and protesting.

"See what I mean?" Barkley said. Then he looked at the translator. "Tell him to put the dog in the barn, or I will shoot it."

Then the first sergeant turned back to the Hummer. "Sergeant Padilla, you and Rattler do your thing."

The big brindle Belgian Malinois with the mostly black face, flashing his titanium smile, came bounding out of the Hummer. He gave two good barks at the old man pulling the dog to the barn and shot the gap to the house.

Before Sergeant Padilla could catch up, Rattler began barking and digging on the floorboards of the kitchen.

Cotton Martin with Cochise Quinlan at his side, backed up by Ironhead Heyward and Jewfro Clingman, guns drawn and cocked, stacked outside the doors and filtered into the house with Sergeant Padilla.

An old woman and little girl came running out the door when the dog ran inside. They ran screaming to the old man, who had finally gotten his dog shut away, and they clung to him for dear life.

"They know their shit has hit the fan," Barkley told the colonel.

"Yeah, but they don't have Jack here. I hate to waste precious time," Colonel Snow said.

"They got guns and ammo, and heaven knows what else hidden under their floors," Barkley said. "Could have a whole battalion of Hajis down in the caverns. Some of these places have quite a setup underground."

"Colonel," Staff Sergeant Martin shouted at the door. "You're going to want to see this."

Elmore gave a hand sign to Bobby Durant. "Snake, you take charge of those three civilians. Bronco and Jaws, go with him. Mob Squad, you four with Biggs and Hot Sauce, grab some of Barkley's boys and clear those barns.

Check under floorboards. Could have Hajis lying in there with guns."

Then he and Alvin Barkley headed into the house. Just as they got to the door, Elmore looked back at his men. "And be careful of that dog!"

Sal the Pizza Man had just cracked the barn door and got met with snarling. He took a step back, pulled his pistol, but the old man came running, pleading in Arabic.

"No, no!" he cried, and stepped inside the door. In a few seconds, he came out with the dog on a rope.

Elmore smiled. "Glad it went that way. A good herd dog like that probably cost the old Bedouin a passel of goats."

"I'd a shot the dog," Alvin said, stepping inside the house with the lieutenant colonel.

"We need to win the support of the people," Elmore said. "We don't win much, making them our enemy by killing the man's dog. Around these parts, he'd probably rather you killed his wife."

"I know." Barkley smiled. "And he loves his wife."

"You can't have justice without righteousness," Elmore said. "And you can't have mercy without love."

Barkley nodded. "Another wise saying from the colonel?"

"A wise saying from the Reverend Dr. Martin Luther King." Elmore smiled.

In the kitchen, Rattler clawed hard on the floorboards, leaving deep marks in the wood. Then Cotton opened a side door that looked like the entrance to a pantry but hid the passage to a world of underground chambers. The working dog bounded down the stairs, Sergeant Padilla hot on his tail, and began barking and snarling amidst a chorus of terrified human screams.

Colonel Snow and First Sergeant Barkley stepped into the kitchen with their guns in their hands, and found Staff Sergeant Martin waiting at the open door at the top of a stone-lined stairway. Below, Rattler barked and snarled while four men wailed loudly for mercy.

At the bottom of the stairs, Jorge Padilla held Rattler on a short lead. The black-faced shepherd with titanium teeth wanted nothing more than to finish chewing arms off four Hajis, now on their knees, bloody wrists zip-tied, Jewfro and Ironhead holding rifles on them.

Barkley called outside on his radio. "I need two fire teams in here to take charge of four prisoners, an interrogator-translator, and a corpsman."

Cotton Martin motioned for Elmore as he pushed open a door. "Come in here, sir. Take a look."

It opened into a long chamber filled with double-stack metal bunks, made up military style with US Army blankets tucked tight on the mattresses. Along the wall, a rack of fifty rifles. At the end of the barracks, a raft of Russian B-40 launchers and boxes stacked full of rocket-propelled grenades piled next to a hundred wooden boxes of Russian ammunition. Stenciled on the gun racks and ammo cases, the crest of Saddam Hussein's Republican Guard.

"How many of these places do you think are out here?" Elmore said. "It's like they're getting ready for newly arriving troops."

"Exactly," Martin said.

"Fuck!" Alvin Barkley said, walking into the long squad bay. "What is this? Marine Barracks al-Sunnah?"

"Mind-boggling, isn't it," Elmore said. "We need to go upstairs and have a heart-to-heart talk with the proprietor of this establishment."

An interrogator-translator squatted by the four prisoners, while a Navy Medical corpsman bound up their dog bites. The translator spoke to them in Farsi.

"These guys are Hezbollah, volunteers from southern Lebanon," the ITT Marine gunnery sergeant said. "They call themselves Sons of the Ummah. A radical Islamic community linked to all Muslim schools and sects worldwide, regardless of whether they be Shiite, Sunni, Khawarji, Sufis, Baha'is, Ahmadiyyas, Druze, Alevis, 'Alwis, or any other of a couple dozen more sects you might name. It's the old enemy-of-my-enemy thing going on with these guys."

"Palestinians?" Elmore said.

"Yes, sir. Just like Zarqawi," the Marine translator said. "Your basic Beirut bomber type, motivated by the sainted teachings of such ilk as Ayatollah Khomeini and Osama bin Laden. These four arrived here from Syria this morning, hell-bent on martyrdom."

"If they came here to die, why didn't they try just now?" Snow asked the translator.

"One look at that monster with metal teeth, him shredding their filthy hides." The Marine laughed. "All of a sudden, jihadi martyrdom didn't seem quite so appealing. They thought the devil had hold of them."

Sergeant Padilla had Rattler sitting at attention, watching the four prisoners. A slight, hardly noticeable slack off the lead and he went to snarling and barking at the men. Padilla laughed as the men wailed in fear.

"See what I mean, sir?" the translator said, as the dog handler took back his short lead and Rattler silenced, but still happy and smiling. Rattler thought of his Kong reward time with Jorge. He knew what he had earned.

"Good boy, Rattler," Padilla said, and patted the dog.

Outside, another translator from the four-man ITT crew had gone to work on the old man and his wife, quizzing them, as the Marines led the four Palestinian prisoners out of the house. They had zip-tied the Bedouin's hands behind his back and now put plastic handcuffs on his wife and even on the little eight-year-old granddaughter.

Seeing the zip ties going on the little girl, crying and afraid, the old Bedouin again broke into a jabbering tirade of pleas a hundred miles an hour.

Elmore came out and saw what was happening and wanted to stop it. He could not accept handcuffing the child, nor the old woman.

"It's a bluff, sir," First Sergeant Barkley said, taking the colonel by the arm before he could stop the show.

"The child doesn't know it," Snow said, seeing the terrified little girl.

"Sir, give these guys a chance," Barkley said.

Elmore bit his tongue, hating every second of what he saw, and listened to the old man spilling his guts.

The lieutenant in charge of the Interrogator Translator Team came to the colonel. "Abu Omar was here with a hundred men about two hours ago. A dozen guys based here went with him to al-Rawa for a meeting. The old man said he thought it was Zarqawi."

"Get on the horn to Captain Crenshaw, First Sergeant," Elmore said.

"Way ahead of you, sir," Barkley answered, talking on the command-channel radio. "Forces are deploying to Rawa as we speak."

"What about Gunny Valentine, Lieutenant?" Elmore asked. "Does he know anything?"

"He heard that Abu Omar had him in his dungeon," the Marine officer answered.

"Which dungeon?" Snow said, and walked to the old man. "Tell us which place! We have no time for games!"

The Marine speaking Arabic told the man what the colonel had said, and the goatherd pointed west. "There are three wells that direction and four wells that direction," pointing south. "Abu Omar moves from one to another. But all of them are his strongholds. I do not know in which fortress he keeps *Ash'abah al-Anbar*."

"What do we do?" Elmore asked the first sergeant and Staff Sergeant Martin, now surrounded by their men.

"Split up?" Cotton asked.

"Half go south and half go west?" Barkley agreed.

Elmore thought and shook his head no.

"We all go south," Elmore said. "That place that took the bombs the other day, pilots said the place was burning when they pickled a pair of mark 82s down the chimney. Jack was there. Had to be. He showed up on YouTube right after. Omar's headquarters can't be far."

Barkley took out a map section and spread it on the hood of his Hummer. "I marked all those locations that Espinoza had on his computer. Down here to the southwest is the oasis that got bombed, the place you believe Jack got snatched."

Three other red dots sat in close proximity to the bombed-out camel stop, and the first sergeant pointed to each one. "These two don't offer advantage, so we can hit them at the toss of a coin."

Then Barkley put his finger on the red dot about twenty miles west of the Euphrates River, halfway between Haditha and Haqlaniyah.

"See the wadi down south and another wadi just north, both running east, not that far to civilization?" he said. "They use those wadis like highways. Keeps them off the skyline, and if a plane flies by, they pile up next to the ravine wall."

Elmore looked at the topographical lines on the tactical map, studying the contours of the land. Then he looked to the southwest of the prime location and saw that Barkley had marked a red X there.

"What's that?" Snow asked, pointing at the X.

"Rally Point Whiskey Tango Foxtrot, Plan B," the first sergeant answered. "That's where we picked up your boys, and we killed a whole shitload of Hajis."

"Given the size of that squad bay here," Elmore said, looking at the red dots marked across the desert from Haditha and Hit to Syria and Jordan, "Abu Omar could house a force the size of a regimental landing team out there."

"Yes, sir, he sure could," Barkley said.

Elmore looked again at the red dot that Alvin Barkley had pointed out as the prime spot, not that far from Haditha.

"That's Abu Omar's headquarters," Colonel Snow concluded. "What is it, twenty or thirty miles southwest of here?"

"Maybe that, Colonel Snow," Barkley said. "But given the rough terrain, we go cross-country, it may take us two hours. We can shoot the gap soon as we get our Army counterparts and the Iraqis here to take charge of the prisoners and clear out the basement."

Elmore looked at the house and checked his watch. "We can't just blow it to hell and move on?"

"Sure, sir." Barkley smiled. "But what about the prisoners? We can't drag them along. How about we shoot them? Just like the Hajis do. Blow the shit out of the place and kill everybody."

"You made your point, First Sergeant," Elmore said, and let out a frustrated, deep breath. "We'll wait."

Then Colonel Snow looked at the poor old man and his family. They stood, huddled together, zip ties on their wrists, scared to death. The child tore at Elmore's heart. This was the part of war he hated worst. It ranked right behind losing men.

Elmore knew more than most the toll that war takes not only on the warrior but the people trapped between sides. They do what they must to survive. They have no politics, except family and living.

As Dr. King had taught, justice does not exist without righteousness, and mercy does not exist without love. Elmore believed to be righteous, to be just, to be honorable, a man must take every opportunity to show mercy. It might turn a heart and win a war.

"Have somebody take the zip ties off that fellow and his wife," Snow said. "And please get them off that little girl. They're not combatants. They just live here."

_ 17 _

"**C**ome and eat," Giti called to the four men standing guard, two outside the house and two inside, AK rifles slung on their shoulders. They leaned their weapons in a line against the wall by the doorway, handy but out of the way, and sat down on four chairs at the kitchen table.

Amira and Miriam put bowls of stewed vegetables on the table, and Sabeen served the four guards from a large, cast-iron skillet with slabs of sizzling wild goat steaks. She forked out the four she had fried in the heavy pan and put two fresh ones on the fire to cook for Yasir, since he had brought home the meat.

"A wild goat that Yasir hunted on the desert," Giti said, getting the tall pitcher of hot tea ready for the men. "You should thank him for this meal."

One of the gunmen laughed as he began cutting his steak with a table knife. "Oh yes, this goat must be his fabled Boosolah, the white oryx. We will have unicorn next week."

The other three laughed as Giti pressed the tea leaves, and got the beverage ready to pour in their cups.

"Here, let me," Sabeen said, and took the pitcher from Giti.

The Syrian girl took something from her apron, and Giti watched as she lifted the lid to the tea pitcher and poured something inside it.

Giti mouthed words to her, "What did you do?"

Sabeen then opened her hand and showed Giti a triangular-shaped, small plastic squeeze bottle that had contained thirty milliliters of eye drops. On the label she read, "Visine. Gets the Red Out."

"Eyedrops?" Giti mouthed, her eyebrows straight up, eyes peeled wide, her face expressing complete puzzlement.

Sabeen poured the tea, smiling, acting the hostess with the mostest. Then the heavyset girl shoved the pitcher into Giti's hands, seeing smoke rolling off the meat in the skillet. "Here, take this!" she exclaimed, and ran to rescue Yasir's steaks before they burned.

The guards got another laugh, seeing the fat girl hustle.

Sabeen wrapped a hot pad around the iron skillet handle and lifted it from the gas flames as she turned off the burner.

"Giti, take Yasir his plate of vegetables and the tea. I will follow you with the steaks," Sabeen said, holding the hot, heavy, cast-iron skillet with both hands.

She had it all figured out. The minute she found the eyedrops in Abu Omar's bedroom, sitting on his chest of drawers by his bottle of nasal spray. The desert heat and dry, dusty air played havoc on his sensitive eyes and nose.

As the girls went down the stairs, Giti whispered, "What have you done? What are we doing?"

"Escaping, silly," Sabeen whispered back. "Trust me."

Yasir sat on a stool with a rifle across his lap, by the big wooden door to the dungeon cell where Jack Valentine lay, waiting for his miracle, seriously praying that God would intervene somehow. Faith, at this point, was all the Marine had left.

It had been four hours since Abu Omar had departed with most of his men, and Jack expected the crew or a big part of them to come back soon. With each minute that he waited, his hopes sank, and the sincerity of his prayers grew stronger.

"We will not feed that man in there," Yasir said, seeing the two steaks sizzling in the skillet.

"Certainly not," Giti said. "It would be far too risky to open that door with so few of us here."

Yasir nodded. "Absolutely right! I am glad you see it this way. He will not starve. When Abu Omar returns, he will saw off the American's head," the Arab said, and drew his thumb across his throat, smiling at the girls.

"Killing is wrong," Giti said, setting Yasir's plate on a small side table that had two chairs with it, used by the guards posted at night. "Come, sit and eat."

He checked the ring of keys on his belt, gave the big door a good look, checked the lock, then went across the hallway and sat at the table. Sabeen stood behind him and put both slabs of steak on his plate, next to his ample helping of stewed vegetables.

"You get the most," Giti said, taking the pitcher of tea, about to pour it. "You are the hunter who brought home the meat."

Yasir smiled, looking at the wonderful plate filled with hot, fragrant food. "Yes, I did. The men should be grateful."

"They are eating and enjoying the wild goat steaks upstairs right now," Giti said. "Do you hear them laughing and talking with Amira and Miriam?"

"Yes, I did well, didn't I," Yasir said, and held his cup for Giti to fill with tea.

Just then there was a crash upstairs, as if the dining table had collapsed. Dishes shattered on the floor as the four guards fell from their chairs and began to yell and wail. Amira and Miriam screamed.

One man lunged for the rifles by the door, but rolled in a ball on the floor in the doorway and cried as he gagged and vomited. Another in the kitchen thrashed violently on the floor, suffering convulsions.

Miriam ran for their guns and grabbed two of them. Amira was right behind her, taking the other two. The girls ran outside and dropped the rifles in the yard. Then they came back inside, terrified, not knowing what they could do for the men or if they should do anything.

The reaction from the eyedrops struck slowly at first, the men feeling a bit of discomfort. They kept eating the good meal. Then suddenly the full force of the poison hit them. All four guards threw up everything they had eaten and gasped for air. Their body temperatures plummeted, along with their blood pressure. Their bronchial tubes constricted nearly closed. One man quickly lapsed into a coma, and another's system crashed so suddenly hard that he died.

"What?" Yasir said, and stood from his chair.

As he rose to his feet, Sabeen took a full baseball swing with the big, cast-iron skillet and whacked the old Arab across the back of the head. Bong! The force sent Yasir over the table, which collapsed into broken pieces.

He rolled on his back and quivered on the stone floor.

"You killed him!" Giti screamed.

"Oh, no! Yasir!" Sabeen cried, and knelt by him. Then she smiled up at Giti. "He still breathes!"

"Praise God," Giti said. "I should go upstairs to see what has happened!"

"No!" Sabeen cried out. She grabbed the keys off Yasir's belt and held them up for her sister slave. "Set the American free! I did this so we can escape! Hurry!"

Jack had heard the commotion and got on his milk stool as the door swung open. Giti rushed to him and fumbled with Yasir's keys, looking for the one that opened the padlock that held the chains wrapped tight on Jack's wrists and ankles.

"That one," Jack said, pointing at a small brass key.

When Giti had the lock opened, Jack removed the chains from his ankles and wrists.

"What the hell took you?" he asked Giti.

"I could not think of anything to distract the guards or get Yasir's keys," she answered.

"So you were just going to let me die?" Jack said.

"Everything seemed so impossible!" Giti cried, and she collapsed, overwhelmed by terror and panic.

Jack picked her up and gave the girl a strong hug. "Faith makes all things possible. You're a Christian, right? This is what Christians believe. Right?"

She nodded, and pointed at Sabeen, who still knelt by Yasir. "Our sister Sabeen came up with the idea, and did everything. I had no clue, except to do as she said."

"What was the idea?" Jack asked, now in the hall, getting Yasir's AK rifle and examining Yasir's key ring He looked for a set that fit a truck and found them.

"Eyedrops!" Sabeen said, and laughed.

"Eyedrops?" Jack responded, bewildered.

"At school in Damascus," she said, "a girl told me of putting two drops of Visine in a person's drink as a joke. It makes them have diarrhea. Uncontrollable diarrhea."

"And that works?" Jack said, slipping up the stairs, the rifle loaded and ready for action.

Giti followed him. "It created the disruption."

At the top of the stairs, Jack listened. Men gurgled and moaned and gasped for air.

Amira and Miriam stepped in front of the doorway, and Jack nearly pulled the trigger.

"Don't do that!" he said, and walked into the kitchen where two men lay on the floor, their faces in vomit and their skin ash gray.

"Did you poison them?" Amira cried.

"They tried for their weapons but could not stand up," Miriam said. "We took the guns outside."

Jack aimed the AK at one gasping man and shot.

"Why did you shoot him?" Giti screamed. "He was in pain."

"He'd get over it and kill us," Jack said, giving the other guy a push with his bare foot. "This one's dead."

"Eyedrops did this?" Giti asked, amazed. "Sabeen! It has poisoned these men!"

Sabeen ran up the stairs and looked.

Another gunman lay dead in the entrance to the living room. The fourth lay on the floor, snoring and moaning. His body had cooled to a dangerously low temperature, and his blood pressure had fallen so low that he had lost consciousness.

"The girl at school said two drops in a drink would make a person have diarrhea. That is all!" Sabeen cried. "So I put in the entire bottle. These were five men! I wanted to be sure it gave them the full effect! I am sorry!"

Sabeen took the empty Visine flask from her apron, threw it at Jack, and he caught it.

"Don't be sorry," Jack said, holding the bottle and reading the label. "Active ingredient, Tetrahydrozoline HCI zero point zero five percent, redness reliever. Inactive ingredients, benzalkonium chloride, boric acid, edetate disodium, purified water, sodium borate, sodium chloride.

"I recognize boric acid and sodium chloride, but I have no idea what the rest of this shit does. Obviously, it had a serious effect on these poor bastards."

Then Jack read the warning. "Keep out of reach of children. Serious injury can occur if swallowed, particularly in children. If swallowed, get medical help or contact a poison control center right away."

He looked around at the carnage. "I'll have to keep this in mind."

"What about that poor man in the living room?" Giti said. "What about Yasir downstairs?"

"You want to stay here and take care of them? Be my guest. I'm leaving," Jack said, looking around the house.

Seeing the door that led to Abu Omar's private bedroom and office, he headed that way.

In the corner, Omar had a large mahogany wardrobe closet. When Jack opened the double doors, he laughed.

"That lying son of a bitch!" Jack yelled, and took hold of his backpack, Advanced Operator vest, still stuffed with full ammo magazines, and helmet. There in the corner leaned both the M40A3 Marine sniper rifle and the EDM-Vigilance semiautomatic.

He slipped on the AO vest and pulled open the Velcro-closed pockets inside the liner.

"They didn't check this very well," Jack said, fishing out his command radio with the bullet fragment in it. Then he got out his GPS position locator, also ruined with a bullet fragment. Last, he reached deep, and smiled. "Still in here, too." And he pulled out his intercom radio.

He put the helmet on his head, and pushed the on-off switch on the little transceiver. In a second, he heard a faint hum in the helmet's ear pads.

"She still works." He smiled, then turned the little radio off. "Better save the battery until we get close enough to my boys to use it."

Then he rummaged through every drawer and box, threw things on the floor, searching. "Ah, here's my watch," he said, finding the timepiece, bubble compass still intact, in the bottom of Omar's dresser.

When the gunny dumped the last drawer on the floor he sighed, frustrated. "Where's my Lippard?"

"What is a Lippard?" Giti asked, standing behind him.

"My handgun," Jack said. "A Lippard 1911A2, MAR-

SOC Close Quarters Battle Pistol. A .45 pistol effective out to six hundred yards."

"This?" Sabeen said, and reached under her dress and withdrew the camouflage-painted firearm.

"Yes!" Gunny Valentine laughed.

"You will want this, too," Sabeen said, and reached again under her dress and unbuckled Jack's rigger's belt and long-drop holster she had strapped to her thigh and waist.

"What were you planning to do with that?" Jack asked.

"In case I had to shoot one of them, I could," Sabeen said, and smiled like a child.

"You are a gem, Sabeen." Jack laughed, and Giti hugged the large girl.

Jack glanced around the room. "I need my boots and some socks."

"Over here," Miriam said, pulling back the door. In the corner behind it stood Jack's RAT combat boots and his tan-wool socks draped over their tops. "They did not fit Abu Omar. Nor even Yasir. Much too big. Like everything, you Americans have large feet."

Jack smiled as he laced them up. "Not everything's as big as you think, young lady."

Miriam blushed and ran out of the room. Giti didn't have a clue.

Jack put on his pistol, zipped his AO vest, and secured his helmet, shouldered his pack, slung the A3 sniper gun over the top, and took the Vigilance semiautomatic in hand.

"You girls grab those guns outside," he said, heading for the door. "Make sure you take the ammo vests, too.

We may need every full magazine they got stuffed in them."

Outside, the three small-size girls, none of them a hair over five feet tall, took the rifles in their little hands and put on the man-size Russian ammunition vests surrounded with pouches stuffed with full AK magazines. Jack looked at the trio of smiling sad-sack solja girls, swallowed up by the big gear, and let out a chuckle. "I guess it's just gonna have to work."

He held up the keys for the motley trio to see. "Which truck do these fit?"

Jack hoped for the blue rig with the PKM mounted on the headache rack. However, Giti pointed to the rusted-out white Nissan hunk of junk with the dented door.

"That one Yasir uses," she said, as if either truck was perfectly fine.

"I hope it runs," Jack said, going to it. "You don't think we could find the keys to the other one?"

"I do not want to look for them," Giti answered, following Jack, with Miriam and Amira tight with her.

"It'll do," Jack said as he pulled the handle.

The door popped loud as he opened it, and the seats had worn through the upholstery into the springs. Dirt covered the floors, and all the rubber was worn off the clutch and brake pedals. Instead of a regular throttle pad, it had a silver bar where one used to go.

"Oh, this is dandy," Jack said, his butt falling through the seat. "Jump in, girls, and don't let a spring stab you in the ass."

Amira cuddled next to Jack and smiled up at him, batting her eyes, then came Miriam. Both teenagers so tiny that they still had ample room for Giti. However, large-body Sabeen might be a problem.

"What about Sabeen?" Giti said, wondering which one of their quartet would ride in the back.

"Where is she?" Miriam cried out, looking around and not seeing her. "We cannot leave without our sister!"

"I will get her," Giti said, and bolted to the house.

Jack pounded the steering wheel, impatient to get going as he waited. When Giti did not return in a few minutes he ran to the house with his .45 drawn.

"She will not come!" Giti howled downstairs. "Make her come, Jack. Omar will kill her! He will kill Yasir, too!"

"Come on, Sabeen," Jack said, exasperated. "Giti's right. You stay here, you'll die. You can't save 'em all."

"I must stay with Yasir!" she said. "He is hurt, and I must care for him. I'm the one that hit him!"

"They will kill you! Yasir will kill you!" Giti said.

"No. He cares for me," Sabeen said, cradling Yasir in her lap. He began to moan, and she stroked his face.

"I will get him awake, and we will find the keys to the other truck and escape," Sabeen said. "I have family in Jordan. We can leave here, Yasir and me, and go to them."

"Why?" Giti pled.

"He finds me attractive. He loves me." Sabeen smiled. "No man ever saw me the way Yasir does."

"That old man?" Giti said, incredulous.

"He is not that old. You saw for yourself," Sabeen retorted. "You said that day that Yasir is a good man."

"Yes," Giti said, and looked at how Sabeen cared for the old goatherd. Maybe it was for the best.

"We gotta go!" Jack growled, taking Giti by the arm and pulling her up the stairs and through the living room.

The one live gunman moaned on the floor as they went by him, regaining some level of consciousness. As Jack and Giti stepped outside, the Marine started to go back and shoot the culprit but Giti grabbed Gunny Valentine by the arm.

"Leave him. Please. We must go," Giti said.

He gave a last look at the man on the floor. He wasn't going anyplace soon. So Jack nodded okay and ran with the little girl in the big ammo vest out to the jalopy, slammed the doors, and hit the ignition.

As he left, he pulled to the side of the other truck, drew his pistol and put two flat-nose hardballs through the sidewalls of the front and rear tires.

"That ought to slow them down," Jack said, taking a reading off the bubble compass on his watchband.

"But what about Sabeen?" Giti cried, seeing the ruined tires.

Jack looked at her. "Their changing flats will buy us time, should Yasir and that live one on the floor decide to come after us."

Giti looked at the house, biting her lip, worried about Sabeen. She knew Jack was right. They needed as much time to escape as they could buy. Giti painfully realized that the Syrian girl had made her choice for Yasir and would have to live with whatever happened now.

Engine sputtering out headers with no exhaust pipes, Gunny V pulled Yasir's old junker in gear and hit the gas. It died.

"Shit," Jack said, and gave the engine another crank.

It coughed, then caught hold. "I hope this rust bucket can make it."

Spinning dirt with its one pulling wheel, the four escapees sputtered off, into the desert, rattling cross-country, due northeast.

Elmore Snow had waited with Alvin Barkley and his Marines for nearly two hours before the troops finally arrived to take charge of cleaning the arms and munitions from the subterranean jihadi barracks and taking charge of the four Rattler-ravaged bandage-wrapped Hezbollah martyrs.

A US Army lieutenant showed up with a dozen soldiers under his command and two platoons of Iraqi troops with a captain in charge. Slowly but surely the Iraqis went to work hauling out enemy guns and ammo, stacking them in the backs of the six-by-six trucks they drove. The twelve American grunts took up defensive posts, relieving the Marines of their watch.

While Colonel Snow and company got ready to roll, First Sergeant Barkley got a call from Captain Crenshaw on the command radio. He had deployed a force to Rawa, per the intel, to intercept Abu Omar Bakr there.

"We got nothing," the skipper told Barkley.

"That's too bad," the first sergeant said, and Colonel Snow stepped close to hear. "Any sign they had been there?"

"Air flew recon but saw no vehicles," the captain said. "Of course, this close to the river, they can hide a battalion in the salt cedars. We took a run through the village and saw zero. But the one citizen who would talk to us reported seeing several gun trucks come through this morning, rally around, then depart to the south. One fellow wore a fancy uniform, and had a black jihadi flag flapping on his Haji Humvee."

"That would be them," Snow said.

"Could they have gotten word we were coming?" the captain asked.

"More likely Zarqawi changed his mind," Elmore said.

"Or the whole thing was a ruse from the get-go," Crenshaw said, and added, "which is a distinct possibility."

"Regardless," Elmore said, "they've departed the area, apparently south. My bet, they're headed to Omar's headquarters. We believe it's one of these water stations out in the big middle of nowhere, to the southwest of our location."

Barkley added, "Except for the gun wagons with the dozen Hajis they may have headed back here. And however many other trucks split off to go back to their outposts."

"Good point, but maybe they haven't split up yet. Or maybe they're all going to Omar's house for a festive beheading and goat roast, now that Zarqawi's obviously not a factor," Snow said, and unfolded his tactical map across the hood of the first sergeant's Humvee.

After he gave it a good look, he told the captain on the radio, "Skipper, I suggest that you will do well to collect your force and move with all haste to overtake this bunch. If they're unaware of our presence, which I believe, they will likely move at a leisurely pace.

"Bear in mind they have a goodly-sized force; therefore, I expect that they'll travel in wide intervals, scattered in small bunches, but coordinated. Close enough so they can reinforce each other. As such, they'll be difficult to spot from air assets, and challenging to engage, given the terrain and their tactics. Lots of rat holes and gullies to run through. This is their backyard, not ours.

"But, I think that if we move our forces on them from two directions, cutting off their head and running up their tails, we'll have a good shot at killing a bunch of them.

"We're going to roll fast, cross-country to the southwest, and press hard to intercept their column before they reach their headquarters. We believe they have Gunny Valentine at that location. Ultimately, all our forces will converge on Omar's headquarters. Hopefully, we will take out his army while they're in movement and arrive in time to save my Marine."

"Roger that," the captain said, his voice bouncing with his body as his war wagon ran at high speed, going south, picking up the trail left by the Jamaat Ansar al-Sunnah legion of trucks. "We're on our way."

"Outbound, too. Meet you in the middle," Barkley told the captain, and clicked off the air.

Then he looked at the American soldiers and ragged crew of Iraqi troops. "Colonel, you think these housekeeping commandos can handle a dozen Qaeda guns running at them in Haji home-built Hummers? If those boys decide to come home?"

"They'll have to," Elmore said. "We've got to roll hard to intercept Omar before he gets his force home. They beat us there, they'll ensconce themselves in their hard-ened defenses, hold us at bay, and kill Jack."

In two minutes, eighteen up-armored Hummers, tur-rets pointed to battle, fifty-four Marines riding inside, blood in their teeth, put a dust storm in the air. They ran hard and fast, racing cross-country to head off Abu Omar.

Taking a Lawrence of Arabia dramatic pose behind the driver side of the cab, his white keffiyeh fluttering down his back, gripping his Russian machine gun, tanker gog-gles covering his eyes, Omar Bakr stood tall and proud in the bed of his truck. His force motored behind his Toyota at a comfortable speed along the base of a ridge, heading south. On the opposite side from him, a trusted captain held the grips of the other Kalashnikov PKMS.

Abu Omar's soldiers had taken the black al-Sunnah flag that the legion had unfurled in Rawa, and planted it in the stake hole by the tailgate of Omar's Toyota. As the banner waved, and a sea of odd-colored gun wagons spread behind him in a series of lines like chevrons on a uniform, Field Marshal Abu Omar Bakr Abd al-Majid al-Tikriti now felt truly royal.

Zarqawi not showing in Rawa, word coming that he had fallen ill, Omar Bakr scoffed at the excuse as, "A likely story." He stood on the tailgate of his pickup and gave a great speech to his army, calling them to unite all al-Qaeda Iraq forces under his true Iraqi banner. The cause of Jamaat Ansar al-Sunnah represented the true Sunni faithful, not the Jordanian Palestinian expatriate. Omar branded Abu Musab a coward and declared victory. Now the graybeard led a glorious parade home in celebration of the propitious day.

As such, he had rallied all of his army behind his flag and commanded them to come and celebrate with him, just as Arabian sheiks of old had once done. Thus he stood in the bed of his truck, riding crop held high, pointing forward, grand in his uniform and bright sash, leading the parade like Patton.

In his self-aggrandizing daydream, Omar envisioned himself sitting on a leopard-skin-and-gold-covered throne beneath his date palms, surrounded by his warrior tribe, goats roasting on skewers over a dozen fires. In the evening, they would triumphantly sharpen their knives and cut off Jack Valentine's head.

A return to true greatness. He smiled as he daydreamed the grandeur, and his forces rode comfortably behind him.

"What did you do to me?" Yasir said as he opened his eyes. Then putting his hand on his aching head, he looked up at Sabeen, who cradled him across her lap. Tears ran off her cheeks and splashed on the old skunk.

"I am so sorry! I had to do it. Forgive me," she wept, then, having his attention, she clutched his face with both of her hands. "Please, Yasir. We must go! Quickly! My family in Jordan. They have money. They will take care of us both. We can go there, and live very happy. Please?"

The goatherd liked the thought of fleeing from Iraq and the war. Leave behind this horrible life, living in the dirt, sleeping on a stone floor. Then he noticed the open cell, and he pulled away from the young woman.

"You have killed us all!" he shouted, fighting to his feet. "You fool! You fool! Do you know what you have done?" He pulled Sabeen up by her shoulders and wrapped his hands around her throat. His eyes filled with rage, and the heavy girl screamed as Yasir squeezed.

"No, Yasir," she struggled, his thumbs pressing hard into her throat, shutting off her cries.

"Stop! What are you doing?" A voice at the top of the stairs shouted, and Yasir let up his grip.

"Why would you kill the one who chose to stay and help us? You always were the fool, Yasir."

As Sabeen stepped away from his reach, Yasir looked up the steps at the one surviving guard, and whined, "But she hit me! With the frying pan!"

Throwing his guts up had cleared Haazim the gunman's stomach of the toxic chemicals, and he began to recover from the effects that the eyedrops had had on his central nervous system, wrecking its ability to control blood pressure and body temperature, among the many other side effects. Now the angry jihadi wanted revenge.

"Those three Christian whores, they fled with the American!" Haazim said. "They had this planned. They poisoned our food. In the vegetables. I could taste it."

"What of it, Sabeen?" Yasir added.

The heavy girl blinked. "I know nothing. I only fried the meat. They made the tea and cooked the other things."

At the top of the stairs, Haazim reached in his pocket and took out a set of keys and shook them at Yasir. "My truck is here. We can take it and capture those vermin. Those girls, we will gut like fish. But at all costs we must bring the American back before Abu Omar returns. Otherwise, we, too, must flee, or lose our heads."

"They fled in my old truck?" Yasir smiled. "That is good! The motor has no power. We can catch them easily!"

"You will have to put two good tires on my pickup, first. They shot them flat, bullets through the sidewalls," Haazim said. "We have a Nissan with broken axles sitting in the barn. You can take two wheels off it. They should fit."

Yasir bowed his head, submitting. "As you say."

Sabeen gave Yasir the stink eye. She folded arms like an angry mother and frowned. "What is this, Yasir? Abu Omar left you in command. This one should change the tires. You are his captain!"

"Quiet, woman!" Yasir hissed, and staggered up the stone steps, holding his sore head. He knew better than to argue with Haazim, a man who had used his rifle many times to kill men. The old Bedouin had never fired a shot at anyone.

"I will help, then," Sabeen huffed, and frowned at the young gunman as she tramped up the steps past him.

"We will all do the work," Haazim said, following Yasir and Sabeen. "It will save time. We have none to spare."

A hand-painted light tan Shanghai Chinese-built Foton four-by-four double-cab pickup truck with broad-stroked splotches and bold stripes of dark brown down its doors and bed, driving rear guard at the tail end of Abu Omar Bakr's parade, began honking. The peacock up front turned with a big smile and raised his riding crop triumphantly skyward, believing that his men had expressed more joy at his victory over Zarqawi. Then the self-proclaimed field marshal saw the curtain of dust rising to the north and heard the distant but fast-closing heavy machine guns opening fire.

"Go! Go!" he screamed, and slammed his fist on the roof of the truck cab.

The driver hit his brakes and stuck his head out the window. "What?"

"We are being overtaken, you fool! Go! Hurry!" Omar bellowed. And then he saw more dust rising along his left flank and screamed. "Go now!"

"What about the others?" the driver said, still hanging his head out the window, his foot on the brake.

Omar took out his pistol and pointed it at the man. "Drive this truck as fast as it can run, or I will shoot you and drive it myself!"

The man got the message, seeing the business end of the Makarov pointed at him. He hit the gas before he put the truck in gear. When he popped the clutch, the launch sent Abu Omar's machine gun captain sidekick somersaulting over the tailgate.

The truck right behind them ran over the Haji, leaving him mangled but alive, yet no one stopped.

"Down in the wadi!" Omar yelled, slapping his hand on the roof of the truck. "We must get away!"

The driver stopped the truck once again and looked at the drop-off, a good four feet, then a steep slope.

"We will roll over," he said, getting out to tell his master.

Omar had no patience with this fool. He jumped off the back of the truck, walked around with his pistol pulled, and shot the man without losing stride. Two other soldiers sat inside the pickup, and the boss gave them a cold look, pointing the gun as he would his finger. "Man the guns. I will drive."

Both Hajis rolled out through the passenger door and left Omar the cab all to himself. Then the two soldiers scrambled onto the bed and took hold of the machine guns.

As Omar hit the gas, machine gun fire from two directions came hot into the dry riverbed and followed them as dirt sprayed in twin rooster tails behind them. Two other gun trucks followed Omar while the rest of the legion turned to the flank and the rear to stand and fight.

At the lead echelon of the rear guard, a tan-painted heavy-duty T-King two-ton diesel truck pulled a large trailer with a high canvas-covered square object mounted on it. As Haji home-built Hummers formed a line with the bigger vehicle, their PK machine gun crews laying down opposing fire against the Marines, who closed on them from two sides, six volunteers bailed from their small wagons, and pulled the canvas off the trailer. The two men who drove and rode in the Chinese truck took charge of the volunteer crew and a four-stack-high-by-four-rail-wide rack of Katyusha rockets.

The two men who knew what they were doing took hold of the gear cranks that maneuvered the angle and trajectory of the launching platform and eyeballed a best-guess aim at the fast-closing Marines. Then the rocket gunner and his partner knelt behind the side of the big truck, taking cover from the rockets' back blast as well as incoming fire.

The gunner held a long control line in his hands, and before he fired, he searched around for the six volunteers who had helped rig the rockets. Finally, he saw them taking cover on the back side of the missile trailer.

"Move away!" he yelled, and waved for them to clear from behind the launcher. "Come here! You can't stay there!"

The jihadi *jefe* in charge of the men pointed his rifle at the rocket man, and yelled, "Fire!"

So the man with the launch cord pushed the button.

A blowtorch of white-hot burning rocket exhaust from the sixteen missiles incinerated all six men. The pro who had pushed the launch button and his partner jumped in one of the now-empty desert-rat pickups and sped away, leaving the big, slow-moving T-King for the Marines.

Sixteen 122-millimeter Katyusha rockets rained onto empty ground, due to the firing delay. Captain Crenshaw had seen the Hajis pulling the cover off the launcher, and managed to maneuver his Marines away from the line where the gunner had aimed the missiles.

Now half of his company raced around the right flank of Abu Omar's army while Colonel Snow closed from the left. The skipper and the other half of his company closed from the rear, hell-bent on annihilating the enemy as the pincers closed on their flanks.

"I am the Borg!" Crenshaw growled in his favorite *Star Trek* voice over the command radio, seeing the plan come beautifully together. "Resistance is futile."

Part of the al-Sunnah legion tried to make a stand and fight to the man, as their general had ordered them. But most of the Hajis now tried to evaporate into the desert, following the example of their fearless leader.

As the two rocketeers fled the battlefield, churning dust, racing for the wadi where Abu Omar had escaped, Sal Principato locked on the driver with his .50 caliber Special Application Scoped Rifle gunsights. Sergeant Carlo Savoca rested his spotting scope on the ground behind his corporal on the M82A3 Barrett.

"Go ahead and fire, Pizza Man," the Iceman said.

A hundred yards left of where the two Marines had parked their Hummer and moved forward to a nice little hill that overlooked the Haji stream of trucks, Nick the Nose Falzone had snuggled into a second .50 caliber Barrett sniper rifle while Marcello Costa, the Hoboken oddity in the otherwise all–New York City Mob Squad, spotted for him.

When Sal Principato's big gun reported, Momo barely got out, "one thousand one," when the ADI 655-grain bullet, running just a breeze faster than three thousand feet per second, splashed through the moving pickup's side window. It destroyed the upper half of the rocket man's body and blew out the windshield.

"Nice lead, Pepperoni," Corporal Costa said, watching the truck go sideways and stop. "We got another customer running from the passenger side," he said to Corporal Falzone. "Take him, Hawk-face."

"Fuck you, Momo," Nick said as he watched the man dig hard to get away, calculating the drift of his bullet, the light wind that came from the west, and took a two-ball lead with his Mil-Dot range-finder reticle on the soon-to-be-dead jihadi.

Costa took a breath, let it slide out, and held it as he relaxed into the big gun while oozing on trigger squeeze.

Boom! The mark 82 belched, blowing a dust cloud from the exhaust that came from both sides of the triangular compensator at the Barrett's muzzle.

Again, less than a second passed while the bullet arced two thousand yards and splashed home, leaving the running man scattered in pieces across the sand.

"Nice shooting, Mob Squad," Colonel Snow said on the intercom, seeing his MARSOC operators claim two clean kills with two shots. "What was that, two grand?"

"Twenty-one hundred," Iceman said.

"Short of a record, but awesome," Elmore said.

"It's just business," Iceman came back.

Momo added, "Nothing personal."

Jack Valentine kept his foot pushed to the floor on Yasir's piece-of-shit worn-out bucket of bolts. Giti, Miriam, and Amira sang in harmony. "I come to the garden alone, while the dew is still on the roses. And the voice I hear falling on my ear, the Son of God discloses."

The happy gunny joined the refrain as the old truck's wheels churned dust. "And He walks with me, and He talks with me. And He tells me I am His own. And the joy we share as we tarry there, none other has ever known."

The three teenage girls sang every old hymn that Jack had ever remembered from those long-ago times, sitting with his mother and father at Coronado Baptist Church in El Paso.

The old truck rattled, and the girls and Jack bounced on the springs that stabbed them in the ass. Each time they hit bottom, all of them laughed. Successful escape, moving toward friendly lines at a good pace, no matter the pain or misery, it all seemed good.

"Where will we live?" Giti asked, looking across Miriam and Amira at the cheery Marine.

"What do you mean, where will we live?" he asked, his mind focused on keeping his northeast heading. Crossing the desert, like driving a boat on open water, he had to make sure he didn't drift off course.

"In America?" she said.

Jack pondered and took a breath. He didn't know. He had never gotten beyond the idea of making sure the three sweet Christian girls, who had lived as slaves the past year and risked their lives to help him escape, got a green card and a life in the United States of America. It was the least a grateful nation should do for three such heroes.

"Geez," he puzzled. "I never thought about it."

Amira began to cry.

"We have no one there, and we have no one here," Giti explained. "What will America do with us? What will we do!"

Jack thought about it, and all kinds of horror pictures flashed in his mind. State Department turns them over to the Iraqi government, run by hard-thinking Shiites. Bureaucrats take charge of the three young Christian girls' futures, one of them about three months pregnant. A total nonstarter.

"I'll call my mom and dad," Jack said. "Judge Darius Archer, he's old now, retired, but he knows people. My girlfriend, Liberty, is an FBI agent. Her dad's a big-time lawyer. They'll help. So will our church, Coronado Baptist."

He looked at the girls, the three staring up big-eyed at their hero, and not having a clue.

"You'll come home with me," Jack said. "Live with my family. We have people who can get you in school, give you a good life. I promise. You'll have a great place to live, with the best people you ever met."

Giti smiled at her sisters. "See? Jesus has answered our prayers all this time. He brought Jack to us, to take us to America, and our Lord gives us a wonderful life!"

They began singing again, "Oh, how I love Jesus . . ."

Jack drove on, not having a notion where to start. But he swore to God while the girls sang that he would make sure that the three sisters in Christ got to El Paso. It would be over his dead body if they didn't. And he knew that Elmore Snow would make sure they got to El Paso, too.

A half mile ahead, Jack saw a rise in the land, and he slowed the truck. Sometimes, crossing the desert, the earth can open up. A deep drop-off appeared, not on a map, caused by a subterranean cavern, which had once held water but ran empty, collapsing on itself. It opened a sinkhole or a rift if it was an underground river that had died.

As he crept forward, he saw the ravine, sheer sides twenty feet deep. He stopped the truck and looked up and down the land rip. In the bottom he saw a dusty, well-used road, cut by jihadi homemade Hummers no doubt.

"If they got the trucks down there, they got to have a road out," the gunny told the girls, who also stretched their legs, looking at the great break in the landscape.

Jack rubbed his back against the cab, scratching the

scabs and scrapes that now itched. He thought about his kit unharmed, but his clothing shredded off, and he called to Giti, who stood with her hand shading her eyes, looking up and down the ravine, searching for a way across.

"Say," Jack said. "How'd my uniform and my back get cut to pieces but my gear not have a scratch? You know anything about it?"

"The men dragged you behind a truck," Amira answered. "You don't remember?"

"No," Jack said.

"How could you not know something so terrible?" the girl said, surprised.

"Because I was knocked unconscious?" Jack said.

Giti smiled, then told Jack, "Yasir said that some of the men found you where the jets had bombed.

"They took your equipment, put it in their truck, and tied you to the bumper. Yasir said he found them dragging you. He stopped them so they would not kill you, and told them Abu Omar wanted you alive. Then he took you home."

"Right. He saved my life so they could cut off my head on YouTube," Jack said, taking his little binoculars out of his operator's vest and searching north, up the rift.

"Well, at least Yasir saved you from death at that time, or you would not be alive later, so you can escape and live," Giti said. "He is not a bad man."

Jack smirked at her and kept searching.

"This sinkhole looks like it shallows enough, way up ahead, so we can drive across," Jack said. "Couple of feet drop on this side, but a decent-looking slope the rest of the way down and all the way up the other side. Looks like we can angle up, as long as we don't roll over."

"We will get out and watch at that point," Miriam said.

"Yeah," Jack said, getting in the truck. "Let's roll."

When the three girls got inside and shut the door, Jack ground the gears and got the old jalopy moving.

"We'll do well if this collection of crap holds up much longer," he said. "Clutch is shot and the gearbox totally worn-out. I don't know what's holding the engine together."

"Yasir drives it to Haditha all the time," Giti said. "He seems to have no trouble."

"I hope you're right," Jack said, running north, along the side of the land cut.

He looked at Giti. "Why do you suppose Omar lied to me about my stuff? He told me that it got blown to bits. One gun broken in three pieces and the barrel bent on the other?"

"He tells lies at a whim," Miriam said. "Why does a viper bite? He could so easily lie hidden, unseen, and do nothing. But he jumps from the grass and bites us."

"Omar has no soul," Amira added. "He gave it to Satan."

"That is the kind of man that Omar is. A son of perdition," Giti said. "The devil lives within him."

"Drive faster!" Yasir called from above the cab, slapping his hand on the roof. "I see them! Far ahead! They reached the wadi and now search for a place to cross. We have them, Haazim!"

Sabeen sat on the passenger side of the pickup, gripping

white knuckles on the handhold screwed to the doorjamb. She looked hard and saw no sign of the people.

Haazim squinted his eyes, too, and saw nothing. "It is like the white oryx, that old fool. He imagines what he sees, and nothing is there, except sometimes a wild goat."

"He has seen the oryx, I know it," Sabeen argued, defending her Bedouin warrior who found her desirable. "If Yasir says that he sees the infidels, then he sees them."

"Okay, old man!" Haazim shouted out his driver-side window. "Point the way!"

Yasir shot the machine gun toward his old truck, a good three miles away, leaving a line of dust pops pointing the direction.

"You see, Haazim?" he yelled.

"I see where the bullets hit," the mastermind driving the truck yelled back. "But I see nothing of your truck."

"It is there, I see it!" Yasir said.

"I hope you do," Haazim shouted.

"He sees them!" Sabeen said. "Don't doubt his word."

Haazim shook his head. "What do we have to lose?"

"Correct!" Sabeen said.

Yasir turned loose another blast from the PK, arcing these shots high and splashing them a mile ahead.

Jack stopped the jalopy and let its tired old engine idle. He put his head out the window.

"What is it?" Giti asked, putting her head out, too.

"I thought I heard gunfire," Jack said.

"I hear nothing," Giti said.

"Desert madness," Valentine said, and hit the gas, the old pickup sputtering along the edge of the rift.

Abu Omar slid his truck sideways in the dooryard at his headquarters. He left the motor running and ran to the house, tripping over one dead man. He walked to the kitchen and saw the other two guards lying lifeless on the floor.

"No!" he bellowed. His machine gunners and the men in the other truck who had just parked heard him and stopped outside, worried. They walked to the house, guns ready.

The old graybeard ran down the steps into the basement and saw the cell door open. He rushed inside and picked up the empty chains.

"No!" he roared, as loud as his lungs could project.

His men from the other gun wagon, who had managed to escape the Marines with him, stood in the house, taking in the sight of their dead brethren. They waited anxiously with their guns ready, knowing their leader's wild temper. If Abu Omar opened fire on them in his fit of rage, they might have to kill the boss and just call it a day.

Omar came back up the stone stairway, dragging Jack's chains. He dropped them in the doorway that led to the kitchen.

"He escaped!" Omar said, bewildered. "How could he escape? I left six of my best here."

"It is God's will," one Haji offered.

Omar stared at him, studied his face. Then he drew out his pistol, pointed it at the fool, and shot him.

"It was not God's will!" Omar screamed, and the other five men backed up, ready to fight, but lifted their fingers off their triggers, glad to be alive, as the graybeard holstered his pistol.

He walked back in the kitchen, looking around, and stepped on the empty Visine bottle. Omar picked it up, then tossed it at his men. "They even poured out my eye wash."

A third gun crew rolled up. They began yelling to Omar and his other two crews, "The Marines, they come this way!"

"Abu Omar," one of the men asked. "Should we stand and fight here, or should we retreat? If we choose to fight another day, we should depart immediately."

The old graybeard glared at the man, put his hand on his gun, but the soldier raised his rifle and locked eyes with the boss, cold steel. Omar moved his hand away from the Makarov and stared at the empty chains on the floor.

"We retreat, of course," Abu Omar said. "But we will go after the American and those whores and other traitors who fled with him. You can have the women. Shoot the two men. But I will cut off the American's head."

Elmore Snow intentionally allowed the third truck to escape down the wadi where Omar's pickup and the other one behind it had fled.

"We'll follow that guy to their hideout," he told Alvin

Barkley, who wheeled the Hummer close enough to keep the fleeing vehicle in sight but far enough behind to encourage him to keep running home.

Colonel Snow had rallied his fourteen MARSOC Marines to follow him and the first shirt. Sergeant Jorge Padilla sat in the backseat with Rattler, and Cochise Quinlan manned the Maw-Duce in the truck's turret.

Sergeant Rasputin Romyantsev drove the Hummer behind the colonel, finally getting his feet wet in real combat. Cotton Martin sat in the right seat. Bronco and Jaws sat in back and ran the guns.

Sammy LaSage rode shotgun in the next truck with Ironhead Heyward at the wheel. Jewfro Clingman and Hub Biggs manned their turret guns.

Hot Sauce McIllhenny drove the next war wagon, with Bobby the Snake Durant in the right seat. Staff Sergeant Dennis Drzewiecki, the senior armorer, took charge of the M-2 .50 in the turret. Short one man, he had assured the boss it was no problem. No one knew grandma better than the man from Whiskey Run, Pennsylvania, nor could anyone run it with his skill.

Mob Squad brought up the rear: Momo driving, Iceman in the right seat, Pizza Man and Nick the Nose on top guns.

With Captain Crenshaw and the bulk of Company D, Fifth Marines closing ranks around the majority of Abu Omar's lost legion, the remaining thirty-six Marines whom First Sergeant Barkley had taken with him and the MARSOC crew, merged back with the company. Closing the jaws of their pincer movement, they commenced the annihilation of Jamaat Ansar al-Sunnah.

Jack had driven two miles along the rift when he finally reached the place they could cross. That's when the right-front tire blew.

As the tread and sidewalls fell to pieces and the rim chewed into rock, the force of it pulled the steering wheel. It took all of Gunny Valentine's strength to hold the wheels straight and get stopped without dropping off the cliff.

He managed to chug the jalopy twenty feet away from the drop, amidst the screams and wails of the three girls.

"What do we do now?" Miriam asked, and huddled tight to the Marine, now imprinted on him like a puppy on a kid.

"I don't know! Pray for Jesus to materialize a new tire on the truck?" Jack said, out of sorts.

"We could also get out, jack up the truck, and put on the spare tire," Giti said, not liking Jack's mocking of their faith and their prayers. "Yasir has tools behind the seat and a good spare under the bed."

"Well then, I guess we get out and change the bloody tire," Jack said, popping open the door.

Giti and Amira had already crawled under the back of the truck and spun off the big wing nut that held on the good tire and rim. They had it rolled next to the right front and leaning on the bumper before the gunny had gotten out the spinner wrench and the screw jack stored behind the seat.

"I'm amazed he has a spare and tools," Jack said.

"Don't be amazed," Giti said, helping Jack. "As I have said, Yasir is a good man."

"Would you shoot him if you had to?" Jack asked, cracking off the wheel nuts with the spinner wrench.

"No, I would not," Giti said. "He would not shoot me, and I will not shoot him. He is not a bad man."

"Just a good man in a bad spot," Jack said, tossing the old rim into the rift and pushing the spare tire in place.

"I will shoot evil men, though," Giti said, threading on the lug nuts so that Jack could spin them tight.

"Good Book says, 'Thou shalt not kill,'" Gunny Valentine said, twisting the nuts tight with the wrench.

"Do not murder is what it truly says," Giti retorted. "Shooting evil men who murder innocent people is righteous with the Lord."

"My colonel says the same thing." Jack smiled, dusting his hands, and noticing a plume rising in the southwest, a truck coming toward them fast.

He reached in the cab, took out his Marine M40A3 sniper rifle, and pulled the bolt back. He loaded the magazine full and shoved one in the chamber. Then he grabbed the Vigilance and told the girls, "Speaking of evil men who murder the innocent, looks like some are headed our way."

"Where do we go?" Giti asked.

"Grab your guns and drop into the gully," Jack said, looking down the rift and seeing a nice slope with good footing about four feet below the sheer side.

"That could likely be Yasir and Sabeen," Giti reminded the Marine as they climbed over the edge, holding the AK rifles and wresting the oversized ammunition vests that hung down to their mid thighs.

"What do you suggest?" Jack said as he looked through his rifle scope across the hood of the truck.

"If it is evil men, then you shoot them," Giti said. "If it is Yasir and Sabeen, then do not shoot them. That is quite simple."

"And what if Yasir decides to shoot us?" Jack asked, now seeing the old goatherd holding on to the Russian PK machine gun, aiming it over the cab.

"He will not shoot us," Giti said, certain of herself and her faith in the man who had changed his mind about raping them and instead felt the need to wash himself and atone for his sins.

Jack moved the scope reticle from Yasir to the truck's windshield, expecting to see Sabeen in the driver's seat. Instead, he saw Haazim there, a scowl on his face.

"You didn't kill all four of the guards. One of them's driving the truck. Yasir's up on the machine gun," Jack said. "You still sure the old man won't shoot?"

"Oh no," Giti said. "What about Sabeen?"

Jack moved his reticle to the passenger side and there sat the husky teen, her chubby face looking perplexed and afraid at the same time. She was yelling and crying.

"She's not real happy right now," Jack said.

"You must kill the evil man, but do not shoot Sabeen or Yasir," Giti said.

"I splash him now, they'll roll and probably kill everybody, as fast as they're coming," Jack said, working on his shot at Haazim.

"Let them stop, then fire," Giti said, nodding at the Marine Scout-Sniper.

"That puts them fifty feet from us," Jack said. "You want to take that chance with Yasir? He's got a machine gun, and I bet he knows how to use it."

"I promise," Giti said. "Yasir will not shoot. He told me he has never fired a gun at another human being. He only hunts animals for meat."

"He's a jihadi and has never shot at a person?" Jack said, now holding the reticle on Haazim and waiting for the truck to slow to a stop. The instant it did, he'd fire.

"He is a good man," Giti said. "To shoot him, unless you had to defend your life, would be murder. Do not murder! God says so."

As the truck closed, Haazim yelled from the cab, "Shoot the machine gun, Yasir! I can see their heads, watching us! The American, he's standing behind the truck with the one girl. Shoot them!"

Haazim's face filled all of Jack's telescopic sight; the center of the reticle covered Haazim's nose. The angry jihadi had just hit the brakes, and was still yelling at Yasir to shoot when Jack sent the .338 Lapua Magnum bullet into his right nostril. The gunman's exploding head sprayed blood and bone and flesh throughout the cab of the truck and showered Sabeen with the gore.

"You're next, Yasir!" Jack yelled, and the old man didn't understand, but could not pull the machine gun's trigger either, seeing Giti, and seeing Miriam and Amira climbing out of the ravine and now running to the truck.

"Yasir," Giti called to him in Arabic. "You are a good man! He will not shoot you. Come down from there."

"I am a failure," the goatherd said, and broke into tears.

Jack watched and was glad he had listened to Giti and had not shot Yasir first. He had the shot.

Sabeen ran to her three adopted sisters when she saw them, and they embraced, all of them weeping. The girls wiped the blood from the Syrian girl's face and hair, using their dresses. Yasir squatted in front of the truck.

"What do we do now?" Jack asked. "We take them with us, too? How far are we from Haditha Dam?"

Yasir stared at Jack, not a clue of what he said.

Jack kicked a rock. "Fucking useless!"

Sabeen yelled Arabic at Yasir, and she climbed in the back of the truck, took the machine gun off its mount and threw it out, along with all the boxes of belted ammunition.

Yasir looked at the gun, then at Sabeen. "It stopped working the second time I shot it. Maybe something in it broke."

Giti ran to the old man, knelt where he squatted, and put her arms around his neck. She kissed both his tear-wet cheeks and smiled at him.

"God loves you, Yasir," she said, and the old man smiled at her.

"I am a failure," he replied, and stood. Then he looked across the wadi. His heart nearly stopped, and he pointed.

"Do you see?" he cried.

Giti turned and looked. Miriam and Amira and Sabeen stopped hugging and looked, too. Then Jack turned and saw what had them dumbstruck.

"What are they? Antelopes?" Jack asked, seeing the Arabian oryx buck and his three oryx doe.

The beautiful white animals stood broadside to them

not two hundred yards away. The doe had spear-like, straight, black horns two feet long. The buck had graceful arcing ebony horns that flashed in the sunlight, curving three feet over his back like two Arabian scimitars as he raised his head.

The oryxes had lain in the shade of a thicket of Alhagi, where they had browsed succulent leaves and took their midday naps. The buck heard Jack's shot, and roused to his feet, ready to move out. But something held him back.

Yasir fell to his knees. He began bowing and praying.

"It is an omen!" he cried. "Praise you, Allah! You are great! You are merciful!"

Jack, the girls, and Yasir watched the beautiful creatures casually walk over the top of the dune where they had napped. The buck stopped on top, gave the people one last look, put his nose in the air, then disappeared with his harem of doe.

Yasir looked at Jack, then at the three Christian girls. He walked to Giti and put his hand on her belly. "You carry a child, just as the one doe with the buck carries his offspring. God has spoken to us. We must obey His word.

"Go with this man, you three girls. He is the white oryx and you are the doe. Allah did not want me to shoot the oryx and his brides, just as Allah does not want me to shoot you and the American. Go in peace," he said, and bowed low to Jack, giving him the Bedouin salute with his palm-up fingertips touching his forehead.

Giti smiled. "We go in peace. It is God's will."

"He sees those oryxes, and God spoke to him?" Jack said.

"God showed him those animals weeks ago," Giti said.

"No one else has seen them except Yasir, until today. God showed them today to you, to me and my sisters and Yasir.

"This poor man has suffered great humiliation because God only showed the white oryx and his three doe to him alone. It was for a reason. A message from God."

Jack looked toward the dunes where the four antelopes had disappeared, and looked back at Yasir, who stood there still bowing to him.

"Works for me." He smiled. "What about them?"

"Yasir will go to Jordan with me," Sabeen said. "I have family there. Wealthy people! We will live with them!"

"You and that old goat?" Jack said, pointing his thumb at the humble old Bedouin.

"He is a good man," Sabeen said, then she turned to him. "Yasir, take Haazim from the truck, my sisters and I will clean the seat. Then we go to my family in Jordan."

The old man smiled at her and went to the truck, dragged the dead Haji to one side and dropped his body.

The girls piled sand in the seats and scrubbed them out with it. Soon they had the pickup fit to drive.

"I don't recommend driving that Haji gun wagon to Jordan," Jack told Sabeen. "Trade it to somebody with a car and get to a city. If your family has money, they'll get you out of Iraq."

"I will call my grandfather when we get to Hit," Sabeen said. "I know they have searched far and wide for me. They will be so pleased to meet Yasir!"

"Oh, I'm sure they'll be thrilled to death, Sabeen," Jack said, and a big grin spread on his face. He told himself, "Love to be a fly on that wall."

Yasir got in the driver's seat and put his finger in the spiderweb of broken windshield surrounding the big bullet hole. He closed one eye and looked through it, and smiled at Jack, saying something in Arabic.

"We love you!" Giti and Amira and Miriam all shouted, waving at their sister as the Bedouin goatherd drove along the rift to the south, where he would pick up a back road that would lead him to Hit.

_ 18 _

"Good-bye, Sabeen!" Giti cried, and waved farewell to her sister. Miriam and Amira stood by her, crying and waving, too.

Sabeen put her head out the window and waved back at them. "I love you!"

"We love you, too!" the three girls shouted to her.

"We gotta roll," Jack said, gathering their gear and returning it to the back of the truck.

He started the engine. It sputtered and began knocking, worse and worse.

"Get in!" he yelled, and rolled up the window to cut off the fumes that came in the truck.

The words had no more than cleared his lips when from the front of the pickup came a loud, "Bang!"

Jack dropped to the seat, ducking for cover, and the girls all hit the deck outside.

"Someone is shooting!" Amira cried.

Gunny V put his head up, and peeked around. All quiet. The engine had died with the bang, and he tried to restart it. Nothing but a groan.

Jack thought about the knocking. "Well, fuck me to

tears!" he swore as loud as he could, getting out of the truck and slamming the door so hard that the driver-side window cracked into a million spiderwebs.

"Beautiful, just fucking beautiful," Jack grumbled.

"I wish you would not use such vulgarity in my presence," Giti said, coming to the truck to help Jack check out the problem, as if she had a clue.

"I'm a Marine," the gunny fired, a head of steam now driving his train. "That's how Marines talk."

"Did it blow another tire?" Miriam asked, coming to help check the problem, too.

Jack had the hood up, looking down at the engine. A hole the size of his fist had broken through the side of the block. A piston drooping off a connecting rod lay like a dead man, half-in and half-out of the hole.

"No, Miriam," the Marine said, slamming down the hood, "we didn't blow a tire."

"What then?" Amira asked, trailing him.

"We threw a rod," Jack said, and looked at Yasir and Sabeen, too far away with the other pickup.

"Threw a rod? I do not understand," Giti said.

"Blew up the motor," Jack said. "Unless Yasir carried a spare engine, we're on foot."

All three girls turned and ran toward the departing truck. "Stop! Sabeen! Stop! Come back!"

"Ladies, it's like shouting at an airplane," Jack said, his hands on his hips.

"They might see us," Giti said, waving at Sabeen.

"They might," Jack said. "Probably think you're just saying more good-byes."

"Ugh," Amira let out, hanging her head, the oversized

ammo vest making her look even more dejected. "I do not like walking in the desert. I do not want to carry all these heavy guns and bullets."

Jack let down the tailgate and sat on it. He reached inside the liner of his operator's vest and pulled out the little intercom radio, its battery he had saved so he could use it to call to his boys when they got close enough to Haditha Dam for his brothers to hear him. The gunny pushed the switch and listened at the headset inside his helmet.

He could hear talking. Familiar voices. Busy jaw jacking, and on the move in their Hummers.

"I ain't a scared of no ghosts!" Jack Valentine yelled on his radio, a big grin spread across his face.

Cotton Martin came back. "Jack? That you?"

"Cotton! What a treat for my tired ears!" the gunny answered. "Yeah, it's me!"

"Jack! Where are you?" Elmore Snow broke in. Suddenly, he was drowned out by a dozen other MARSOC Marines talking on the intercom at once.

"Gentlemen, please," the colonel said.

"Ghost One, what is your location?"

"I'm like those Fuckawi dudes in the joke. They travel at night and when they get up in the morning, they say, where the Fuckawi?" Jack said, happiness overshadowing radio discipline.

"You don't have a clue, do you?" Cotton laughed.

"We left Omar's hideout in this broken-down piece-of-shit rust-bucket grocery wagon, heading northeast, and got to this big-ass wadi with cliffs for sides. Blew a tire, and now we blew the engine. Does that help?" Jack answered.

"Not much," Alvin Barkley said, now with a map unfolded, looking at the red dot that was Omar's headquarters and running his finger out to the northeast.

"Better question. Where are you guys?" Jack asked.

"Stopped on a hill," Elmore said, and waited.

"I'm by a wadi, and you're on a hill, in the Iraqi desert. Go figure! Big middle of fucking nowhere with about a million hills and half a million wadis," Jack said. "How about a little help!"

"We followed one of Omar's rat wagons that we let escape from a column that Delta Company, Fifth Marines has trapped, and is currently wiping off the face of Mother Earth," Elmore said. "We figured he might lead us to Abu Omar's hideaway, where you might be located. We counted on killing Omar and his minions and rescuing you."

"Little late for that, boss," Jack said. "While Omar went north for some kind of meeting with Zarqawi, me and three cute girls stole a truck and escaped. We departed to the northeast. My best-guess heading, based only on my little bubble compass, thanks to Billy-C and his asshole OCD comments, is zero four zero off Omar's back porch."

While Elmore Snow and the Marines had stopped on the blind side of the hill, Mob Squad dismounted and crawled to the crest for a look-see at what lay on the other side. The colonel didn't want to run into a hasty ambush outside Abu Omar's headquarters, or close to it, if they came bounding down the hill, hey-diddle-diddle.

Sergeant Savoca called on the intercom, "Down a half mile we got a house, goat barns, a grove of palm trees. That sound familiar?"

"That's Omar's desert getaway," Jack said. "Those guys you chased, they still there?"

"Not a sign of life anywhere," Iceman answered. "No vehicles anyway. At least not running. I see part of a pickup in the barn and what looks like a big old Russian stake-bed three-ton truck with no wheels."

"Look to the northeast from the house, you see anything?" Jack asked.

"Way out there," Savoca said. "I see plumes of dust. Three of them. One after the other."

"They're following my tracks," Jack said. "You guys need to catch them. I'll take up a defensive posture here; do what I can to hold them off. But it's just me here, with three little girls and a few rifles."

"You can explain the girls later, but hold tight, Jack!" Elmore Snow said. "We didn't come this far to have these wastes of skin kill you in a shoot-out."

"Fuckin' A, right!" Cochise Quinlan chimed in. "Give 'em hell, Gunny V. We a comin' 'round the mountain. Guns ablaze!"

"Do you see them?" Abu Omar shouted from behind his machine gun, standing in the back of his pickup, the black flag snapping in the wind off the corner by the tailgate.

"Something way ahead, I think by the wadi," the al-Sunnah soldier on the other machine gun said, and pointed.

"Yes!" Omar said, and slammed his hand on the roof of the pickup. "That is Yasir's truck!"

The driver hit the gas and honked his horn for the others behind him to pick up the pace.

Omar looked over his shoulder, his white keffiyeh fluttering like the flag, and waved his arm forward, like Peter O'Toole did as Lawrence, leading the Arabian charge.

Jack took all his ammunition from the pockets on his backpack, stacked the boxes and magazines next to his rifles, below the rim of the rift, where the two girls had stood when Yasir came up.

"Bring those guns and your ammo down here," he ordered the girls, and lined them spaced about thirty feet apart. "These are evil men. You got that?"

All three girls nodded. They knew what to do.

"We should pray," Giti suggested.

"God's already up on the situation, Giti," Jack said.

Giti nodded. "We will trust Him to deliver us from the evil that comes."

"Yup," Jack said, loading his guns and making sure that the three girls had their AK rifles ready to rock and roll. "Trust Jesus and those automatic rifles."

He gave the three girls' ammo vests a quick look. "Pull out magazines and stack them so you can load fast."

Amira and Giti stacked their magazines handy, but Miriam had a problem.

"What shall I do with these?" she called to Jack, holding two fat, green fragmentation grenades.

"Holy shit!" the gunny said, a big grin on his face. "Where did you find those?"

"In the pocket, on the side," Miriam said. "What are these things? Bombs?"

"Bombs? Be careful," Giti yelled, and hurried to her.

"Grenades," Jack said, going to the girl holding a frag in each hand. "They're just fine as long as you've got the spoons pinned down."

Jack took the two bombs from her. "I've got an idea."

He could see Abu Omar's trucks clearly now, closing fast on them, so he had to hurry.

The gunny crawled in the pickup from the passenger side, set his backpack vertical in the driver's seat, and snugged down his helmet on top. Then he took a grenade and stuffed it in the space between the seat and the driver-side door. He used a bag of MREs, ironically containing a package of Smoky Franks, the Five Fingers of Death, that he had taken from the bombed house when he was captured, and used it to make sure the grenade's spoon held tight when he eased out the pin.

With the first grenade set to blow, the pin on his finger, he backed out of the truck and closed the passenger door. Jack did the same booby-trap job on that side, this time stuffing a douche-bag delight of a poultry meal his Marines nicknamed Wild Turkey Surprise down the space to hold the other grenade's spoon in place. As he eased out the pin, he had to roll for the wadi.

Abu Omar opened fire on the truck, peppering it and the dead body on the ground, and strafing the rift in general.

"Surrender, and we will allow you to live," Omar shouted, as the other trucks took up positions.

Jack and the girls hunkered quiet, waiting to fight, their rifles ready. Locked and cocked.

One of the gun wagons with four men aboard pulled next to Yasir's pickup. A soldier jumped off the side, and seeing the helmet and backpack through the shattered window, looking like a body, he let go a burst from his AK into the back. The helmet flew off the pack and bounced against the steering wheel.

"Check it out," the driver in the Haji homemade Hummer yelled at the man. He crept forward to try to see better through the shattered left-side window.

Two al-Sunnah fighters climbed in the back of Yasir's jalopy while the Haji in the passenger seat of the gun wagon stepped out and began looking over the old rust bucket.

Jack and the girls sat tight. Just like monkeys with a box of nuts, the Marine knew that the insurgents would have to tear it open to learn what made it rattle.

One man lifted the hood and laughed, seeing the blown engine. He was still laughing when the gunman who had driven the truck walked around to the driver's door and opened it.

Abu Omar stood in his truck, parked back a few feet, and his other gun wagon had pulled across the front of Yasir's pickup, as if it might drive off.

All of the Hajis, including Abu Omar, had totally focused on the men checking out Yasir's old wreck when the first grenade exploded, blowing both the man by the door and the man at the hood to pieces. Shrapnel from the grenade killed both gunmen watching from the back of the pickup parked across the rust bucket's front.

The first explosion blew off the roof and sent the passenger door into the rift. The second grenade blew under the truck, wounding the two guys in the cab of the truck parked across the front, plus sending deadly fragments, glass, and truck hunks flying at Abu Omar and his three remaining al-Sunnah fighters with him in the third truck.

As debris fell from the two explosions, and a fireball erupted from Yasir's gas tank as it went sky-high, Jack and the girls opened fire.

First shot, Jack killed the driver of Omar's truck. Second shot, he took down the machine gunner who stood up, wanting to open fire. Next he killed the passenger.

The two men in the cab of the truck in front of Yasir's pickup, wounded but alive, rolled behind their wagon, opening fire with their Kalashnikovs.

Like a pro, Miriam stood up and began sweeping AK fire under that pickup, going after the Hajis hiding there. Amira joined her, and they managed to kill both men.

Jack worked the bolt on his rifle when Abu Omar stood up and opened fire with his PKMS machine gun.

Amira began congratulating Miriam on their success, and Jack yelled at them to get down. But it was too late.

Both girls caught three rounds from Omar's Kalashnikov, Amira two in the chest and Miriam one in the heart.

When Giti saw her sisters go down, she crawled out of the ravine, her AK braced against her hip, and began hosing down Abu Omar's truck. He managed one more shot before Jack put a .338 Lapua Magnum through his neck, which sent his head tumbling past the black flag.

Giti turned and smiled at her hero, then collapsed.

One of the .30 caliber bullets from Omar's gun had

caught her through the left side, and blew a two-inch chunk out her back as it exited. She bled bad and fast.

Jack scrambled out of the ditch and grabbed the girl. He pulled the scarf off her head and stuffed it in the hole in her back. Then he took his scrubs shirt off, ripped it in half, and tied a pressure wrap over entry and exit wounds.

"Where are you, Jesus? She is Your devoted child!" Jack yelled to the sky, his eyes filling with tears.

"He is with us always," Giti whispered, her eyes fluttering open and her mouth red with blood.

"Help's coming, baby," Jack said, gushing tears.

"Don't worry." The little girl smiled at him. "We are saved from all evil of this world. Miriam and Amira, they have gone to our Lord. I will, too. Don't weep for me, Jack Valentine."

"Stop it!" Jack yelled. "You're going to make it. I promised you that I would take you to America."

Giti smiled at Jack. "You killed Abu Omar. Just like you told him in the prison."

"Yes, I did," Jack said, and kissed the girl on her forehead. "I promised him I would. I keep my promises. Now, you stay awake."

It took ten more minutes for Elmore Snow and the MARSOC crew to arrive on scene. The colonel called for a medical evacuation helicopter, and Cotton Martin grabbed the medical kit from the Hummer and went to work with Jack getting Giti stabilized.

Rattler trotted around the trucks, inspecting the enemy dead. When he was satisfied he had no work to do, Sergeant

Padilla took out the Kong. The dog commenced running and retrieving like a day in the park, doing the one thing that made his life worthwhile. Jorge and a little rubber toy.

Cotton and Jack had Giti's feet elevated, keeping her blood high in her body, talking to her until the rescue helicopter arrived. She watched Rattler play, and smiled. It kept her mind busy, thinking of living.

Bronco, Jaws, Sage, and Jewfro took care of Miriam and Amira, zipping them in body bags that the first sergeant had packed in the back of his command vehicle. Items they hoped they never had to use, but too often did.

Alvin Barkley walked to the back of Abu Omar's truck and took off the Jamaat Ansar al-Sunnah black battle flag, rolling it around its staff as he walked up to Jack and Cotton, and nodded down at Giti.

"I've seen worse, little girl," the Marine with the big knife hanging down his thigh said. "You're going to be fine. Those through-and-through gunshots, they bleed a bit, but you'll live. Got to watch out for infection, though. Docs at Al Asad Air Base medical will get that all cleaned up. Get you fit as a fiddle in no time."

He looked at the Marines carrying the bodies of Giti's sisters. "Sure hate to see that happen to those other two children."

"Miriam and Amira," Giti said in a weak voice. "My baby, if she is a girl, she will have their names."

Jack rode the medical evac chopper to Al Asad, along with Elmore Snow. The colonel left the MARSOC team with Staff Sergeant Martin and First Sergeant Barkley. It took them the rest of the day to get back to Haditha Dam and catch Osprey flights south to the air base. They would fly to Baghdad with Gunny V and the boss.

When they landed at Al Asad, Jack and Colonel Snow went to the hospital with Giti and did not leave until the doctors had her out of surgery, safe in the recovery module.

The gunny sat by her bed, holding her hand, waiting for the girl to awaken. Colonel Snow sat with him.

"Does this young woman have any next of kin who need to be called?" the doctor asked, coming into the room.

Jack shook his head no. "All murdered by the Hajis."

"She lost a lot of blood, but she's a super trooper. Hung in there," the doctor said. "Baby looks good, too."

"It made it?" Jack asked, surprised.

"Yes. We could have terminated the pregnancy during surgery," the doctor added. "But before we put her under, the little mother told us to save her child at all costs."

"She's a Christian," Jack said. "More faithful than anyone I ever met. Presbyterian from up toward Mosul."

"These Iraqi Christians tend to be pretty tried-and-true," the doctor said. Then he added, "Would have been a lot easier for her long-term recovery if she let us take it."

Jack thought about Yasir and Sabeen, started to say something about how Giti's faith had made the difference there. About the white oryx and his three doe, too. But he decided to just nod and agree. He didn't mention Sabeen or Yasir to anyone, thus he couldn't tell the story of the Arabian oryx. It would remain his and Giti's tale. Perhaps she would tell her daughter one day about the beautiful animals and the old goatherd and her only surviving sister,

Sabeen. He figured that Yasir and Sabeen would have an easier time getting away if no one looked for them.

Then a light came on in Jack's head.

"How about her clothes?" he asked.

"We bagged them," the doctor said. "They're pretty ragged and full of blood. We can toss them out."

Jack shook his head no. "We need them. And the clothes belonging to the two girls who were killed."

"You looking for something?" the doctor asked.

"A piece of paper, folded up. A note," Jack said. "I thought Giti might have it in her pocket, but it could be in Miriam's or Amira's. Definitely, one of them had it."

"Is it important?" the doctor asked.

"Very important," Jack said.

"We'll search the pockets and bring everything we find to you," the doctor said. "Where will you be?"

"Right here," Jack answered.

"You don't want to get cleaned up? Grab a shower?" Elmore said, looking at the gunny, who was wearing blue scrubs pants and a hospital gown over his bare upper body.

"She has to see my face when she wakes up," he told Elmore. "She has no one else."

"What do you propose to do?" Elmore asked. "She's not a puppy, Jack. You think Liberty can accept her, competing for your affections? Regardless of the circumstances, she is human, and jealousy can get to even the best among us."

"We'll work it out," Jack said. "I promised Giti that I would take her to America. Her and Miriam and Amira. If we escaped, I would take them to America.

"Giti made it, so I have to keep the promise. She will live with my mom and dad. Have her baby in El Paso, and live there, where people will take care of her."

Elmore looked at Jack and took a big breath. "What about you? What about that FBI agent girlfriend of yours?"

"I'll be her big brother, and Liberty will have to accept it on those terms," Jack said, holding Giti's hand.

"So you've got it all worked out," Elmore said.

"Yeah, so far. Pretty much making it up as I go along," Jack said, then smiled at his old friend. "Got it all figured, except the part of how we get her out of Iraq and to El Paso, Texas."

"That may take some doing, but I'll bet that we manage," Elmore said, smiling, and put his arm over his gunny's shoulders and waited for the little pregnant Iraqi girl to wake up.

"By the way, Jack," the colonel said, still looking at Giti and now noticing her eyes flutter. "What's on that note you got the doc fetching? Something sentimental?"

"You could say that," Jack said, and spread a wide grin at Elmore. "The directions to Zarqawi's safe house. Where he's hiding right now."

_ 19 _

"**G**host in the hide," Jack said on the intercom that Lieutenant Colonel Elmore Snow also had patched into a covered command frequency, with an on and off switch. All ears at the unified command headquarters listened. So did several sets of important ears in Washington, DC.

"Roger," Elmore responded. "Call when target verified on location."

Jack gave his microphone button two clicks and switched off the command channel output so he could talk to his Marines without the world listening.

"Cotton," Jack called.

"In the hide," Staff Sergeant Martin replied, Sergeant Sammy LaSage tucked at his side. Covering the back half of the house outside Hibhib, he had a powerful night-vision and daylight, high-definition spotting scope with satellite uplink of supersharp video feeding real-time action to monitors and recorders watching from Baghdad to the Pentagon and the White House.

Sergeant Cochise Quinlan lay next to Gunny Valentine, covering the front of the same al-Qaeda Iraq safe house where they believed Abu Musab al-Zarqawi hid. With the same HD high-power lens, the eight-man team had two sharp pictures feeding the satellite both front and back views.

Bronco Starr and Jaws covered the left corner of the house, angled off Jack Valentine's flank. And likewise, Hub Biggs and Bobby Durant covered Cotton Martin's flank.

The four two-man sniper teams had set their hides at eight hundred meters from the house, covering quartering angles, eliminating every inch of possible dead space. If anyone showed up, they had him dead to rights, and on worldwide video for verification.

The eight-man squad had parachuted into position around Zarqawi's safe house at four o'clock in the morning, counting on the al-Qaeda leader's guards standing the late shift with heavy eyelids. No one in or around Hibhib paid attention to the high-flying Marine Corps C130 Hercules as it cruised overhead, spilling out its passengers. Nor did anyone see the eight dark canopies of the Special Operations Marines' MC5 free-fall, ram-air parachutes as Jack and his boys silently dove from a high-altitude deployment at twenty-nine thousand feet and steered from their low opening at twenty-five hundred feet to exact landing points. Each of the two-man teams precision glided to four landing sites, each one a mile from the four corners of the house.

They shed their oxygen tanks, masks, helmets, and skydiving rigs, and hid them well. The Marines would pick up their expensive gear en route to their extraction point.

As the four teams lay invisible in their hides, the sun

slowly broke light across the eastern horizon. Jack hoped that Zarqawi might step outside for a breath of morning air. But that wasn't happening. So the Marine Scout-Snipers lay in their hides, chilling and watching.

As he waited for the al-Qaeda leader to show his face, Jack fought the urge, but had to chuckle.

"What's so funny?" Cochise whispered.

"Thinking about yesterday, when we got back to Baghdad," he answered, and giggled more.

"You know, Billy's good about shit like that," Cochise said, and couldn't help but snigger, too.

Keeping his promise, Elmore Snow had called Liberty Cruz, who waited in Baghdad with Smedley and Captain Burkehart. The colonel had said that he would tell her the minute he got word on the gunny, just before they launched on the operation from Haditha Dam. His first opportunity to keep the promise came when he landed at Al Asad Air Base, thus he called when Jack finally showered.

Chris Gray and Elmore both tried to get the FBI agent approved to fly out to Al Asad, and see Jack there, but the general saw no good reason for the risk. She would see her beau soon enough. She should thank her lucky stars that she was in Baghdad, he reminded them. Any Marine wife would trade places with her in a heartbeat. The colonel couldn't argue, nor could Miz Cruz. So she waited for Snow's next call when he knew what time they would land at home base. Liberty wanted to keep her presence in Iraq a surprise for Jack, so the whole team played dumb.

"We're inbound late this afternoon. Should be there just at dark," Elmore told her, and Liberty went to work.

She showered and put on ample squirts in all the right spots of Christian Dior's fancy-smelling perfume that Jack really liked, J'adore. A rich and sexy fragrance that always brought the gunny's nose straight in for a deep landing.

"If that stuff don't make a man's dick hard, then he's gotta be dead," Jack would say.

After her shower, a little lotion, body powder, and ample clouds of J'adore mist sweetening her from little toe to top knot, she brushed out her long, beautiful black hair and let it fall free all around her shoulders and face.

From her suitcase, she pulled out a clean, black silky thin Under Armour T-shirt and put it on with no bra. Jack always loved that. Naked body beneath a thin layer of nearly nothing.

"Like two babies fighting under a blanket," he'd say, watching her walk around braless in a T-shirt.

To finish off the whole effect, Liberty slipped on some nice-fitting supersexy, black-silk, low-cut underwear with black lace around the legs and waist. Then, as an afterthought, she took the back of her T-shirt and tied an overhand knot in it, so that it rode high up, showing off her panties.

Then she took a seat on Jack's bunk and waited.

It seemed like forever had passed, then Liberty finally heard a rattle at the operations hooch front door. She got on her feet, shook her hair good, and gave herself a bounce on her toes. A big, sexy smile spread on her face.

She had told both Captain Burkehart and Corporal Butler to stay out of the operations building because she had a special something planned for her gunny's home-coming. They agreed and stayed away.

Liberty peeked around the hallway corner, after the overhead lights came on, and a familiar-looking back and flop hat sat down at the gunny's desk. Barefooted, she padded her way behind him, J'adore wafting through the air, and in a sexy slur, she said, "Hi there, Sailor. Looking for a good time?"

Billy Claybaugh spun around in Gunny Valentine's chair and fell out of it when he saw Liberty Cruz in all her heart-stopping glory.

"Holy shit!" he wailed from the floor, and scrambled to his feet. He stood dumb stupid, eyeballing her from top to bottom and back up again. "Who the hell let you in?"

"Who the hell let you in!" Liberty fired back, her hands on her hips, ready to kill.

"Gunny Valentine's on his way from the flight line with Colonel Snow, and I just got back from Haditha Dam with Chico and Petey," Staff Sergeant Claybaugh said, fast as he could think. "Cotton and everybody else, and those three other guys, Hacksaw and Kermit and Habu, they're coming, too. Liberty! You need to put some clothes on!"

"Captain Burkehart didn't get hold of you guys and warn you?" Liberty asked the Marine, fuming. The same knucklehead had once again stepped into her romantic surprise for Jack.

"I guess not," Billy said, wringing his flop hat like a rag but still totally enjoying the view, memorizing it.

Frowning at MARSOC's duty clown, she asked, "How did you manage to slip up here ahead of the crowd?"

"I wanted to fix up a surprise on Jack's computer. You know, welcome home. Sort of," Billy explained, and then clicked open the greeting on the gunny's screen.

It was that favorite photo of Liberty in the bikini on the beach, hard nipples and all, and Claybaugh had floated large red letters across the top, "Welcome Home Big Boy!"

"You've got to be kidding!" Liberty huffed.

"It sure as hell isn't as nice as what you had planned," Billy-C said. "But you really ought to go put something on. All those guys are coming with the gunny and the colonel. I'm embarrassing enough for you, and you don't need to fuck up their minds like you've fucked up mine."

"Serves you right, you little twirp," Liberty said, and tramped back to Jack's room, where she put on her shoes, cargo pants, and matching tan jacket, but she left her hair down, bra off, and still smelled awfully good.

Midmorning, Bronco Starr called Jack on the intercom, and asked, "What if I went up and knocked on the door and asked if Abu Musab can come out to play?"

"Shut the fuck up, Cortez," Jaws grumbled.

"Dude, it's like nobody's home," Jesse complained.

Jack checked his watch, clicked on the command radio, and called Elmore. "Pushing ten o'clock and no movement."

"Remain in place," the colonel responded.

"You get that, Bronco?" Jack said.

"Roger that, Ghost," the short guy answered.

"We got movement at the back door," Cotton Martin broke in. "Two guys with AKs. Taking out trash. Raking out scraps to a couple of dogs."

"Barking alarms," Jack said. "Probably finished break-fast. Those guys must get up late."

"Naw, that's probably normal for civilians who don't work," Cotton said. "Are you copying our video feed? Kitchen help went back inside, but we got two more in suits."

"Roger, I see it," Jack answered. "Those suits look familiar to you?"

"Not to me," Cotton answered.

"Tell Sage to zoom in some more," Jack said. Then he asked Colonel Snow, "You seeing this? Those guys dressed real nice look familiar?"

Elmore had both Chris Gray and Speedy Espinoza crowded around the monitor with Liberty, and behind them the entire remaining MARSOC crew, along with Hacksaw, Kermit, and Habu.

"That's Cesare Alosi's buddies, Davet what's his frog, and Jean René the other frog," Hacksaw growled.

"Shit, it sure is!" Kermit confirmed. "We saw both those sweet peas at Alosi's office at least a dozen times. Them always bringing thousand-year-old ashtrays and crap."

Then Francoise stepped out on the back porch with them, wearing men's pajamas, her head uncovered, and smoking a cigarette.

"Ray-Dean Blevins's sweetheart from the Baghdad Country Club. The one he thumped. What's her name?" Liberty said.

Chris Gray was busy writing notes and answered without looking up, "Francoise Theuriau. Ace correspondent for that fish wrapper, the *Massachusetts Democrat and Morning News*."

"That's how Abu Omar got the operation plan," Liberty said. "These three are al-Qaeda spies. Francoise screwed Blevins, and he gave her the plans."

"Or she stole them from him," Gray said. "I still can't buy that even a shit-turd like Cooder-with-a-D Blevins would knowingly give al-Qaeda a top secret plan that could get Americans killed. Jury's still out on Cesare, but I like to think that even the worst Marines are better than that."

"Action at the front door," Jack broke in. "I've got a minivan, Chinese, King Long, parking. A man and a woman got out. Someone just stepped from inside to the front porch. Two other men now getting out of the van."

Cochise Quinlan zoomed his powerful spotting-scope lens to full out and captured each person's mug. "You recording these faces?"

"We're getting them clear and bright, high-definition color. Going to all commands here and to Washington as we speak," Elmore said. "Beautiful job."

"The guy on the porch, Cochise. Get on his face," Jack told his sergeant. "Now, if he'll just turn this direction."

Gunny Valentine had no more than asked, and the man wearing a black kufi that covered the back half of his head, turned his face to them. He had a short, scruffy black beard, chubby round cheeks, and a round nose. Jack knew the face because he had dreamed of it time and again after he had missed the shot that day, it dropping between the al-Qaeda chieftain's feet, a year ago on the bridge crossing the Euphrates at Haditha.

"It's Zarqawi," Jack said, his crosshairs on him.

"Take him, Gunny V," Cochise Quinlan said.

"Check that, Ghost. We have a pair of fast movers inbound to the target," Colonel Snow interrupted. "Paint the house."

Lasers shone on the target from all four sides, pinpointing the exact center. Overhead, two United States Air Force F-16C fighters dove on the run. The lead jet let go two five-hundred-pound smart bombs, a GBU-12 and a GBU-38.

Inside, one of Zarqawi's three wives, a child he had gotten pregnant at age fourteen, worked in the kitchen with her two-year-old daughter playing on the floor. In an instant, along with her and the child, Abu Musab al-Zarqawi, one of the world's most wanted terrorists, died, along with the three French spies who had come back in the house to welcome the two other al-Qaeda leaders.

"Mission accomplished," Jack called on the radio.

"You're not disappointed?" Cochise asked. "Not getting to pull the trigger on Zarqawi?"

"Kind of glad, actually," Jack said. "I never have liked killing people. But sometimes, it is satisfying."

When Jack and the team landed in Baghdad, Elmore Snow met them on the airfield, where the Ospreys had let the team off, after extraction outside Hibhib, a few miles north of Baghdad. The colonel had a one-page printout of an email that Captain Burkehart had received while the gunny and his team were on the Zarqawi mission.

"Here, check this out," Elmore said, and grinned like someone had given him a winning lottery ticket.

Jack read the page and laughed. "Boy did they ever fuck up. Are you serious?"

"Welcome to my world, Gunner Valentine," the colonel said, and shook his Marine's hand.

"I never would have thunk it, Colonel," Jack said, his head swimming a little. "I thought they just wanted Marines with about ten or twelve years under their belts, so they could give the Corps at least a good ten on top of it. I'm pushing twenty."

"They figure you've got a good ten years left in you, and so do I," Elmore said. "You've got thirty years written all over your face. Smart guy like you, I see a cross over to captain at the very least."

"Colonel Snow." Jack grinned at his boss. "No matter how hard you try, you can't make me smart."

Elmore gave his new young warrant officer an elbow.

"What is it?" Bronco Starr asked, jogging to catch up with the gang, all of them crowding behind the new Marine gunner and their commanding officer.

"Gunny V just got word that now he's Gunner V," Cochise Quinlan said. "Get ready to salute, ladies."

"Well that sucks," Bronco said, and got funny looks. "Well it does! Gunny Valentine leaving. Now we'll get some dick-sucking recruiter or bag-of-shit drill instructor who thinks he's a Scout-Sniper without training or the MOS."

Cesare Alosi always hated going to Victor Malone's castle in south Texas. It sat too close to Mexico, and the old boss had a bad reputation of making people who upset him disappear, for good. So he especially hated it today.

"Glad you could make it on short notice," Malone said, wearing handmade black alligator cowboy boots, Bermuda shorts, a Hawaii-print aloha shirt, and a silver Stetson.

"Not a problem, Victor," Cesare said. "Your Gulfstream G550 makes traveling at a moment's notice quite bearable."

"Shit, I love being rich!" the man said. "Don't you?"

"I'm not rich, not by your standards," Alosi said, trying to be humble for his boss.

"By my standards, Donald Trump ain't rich." Malone laughed. "How about that Zarqawi! You see that in the news?"

"Yes, I did," Cesare said, and walked with Victor Malone through the man cave of his castle on the Rio Grande, where he had a full body mount of an African bull elephant standing in the center of a room that was the size of a gymnasium. At the other end, he had a full body mount of a rare black rhino, an endangered species. Near it in a tree crouched a full body mount of a black leopard. A regular leopard stood below him. He had several cheetahs, a lion, a misplaced Indian Bengal tiger, and a stuffed silverback gorilla with a chimpanzee hanging by one arm in a tree.

At one side of the room, a waterfall came out of the wall, and at the other end, a fireplace taller than most men. Best guns of every size and caliber lined the wall above the mantel, Holland, Rigby, Purdy, all the million-dollar works of art hung above art-carved silver-capped elephant tusks that flanked the great hearth.

"How about that boy escaping those ragheads," Victor Malone said, taking a seat in a wide-bodied ostrich-leather sofa chair and pointing to the one across a zebra rug from him for Cesare to sit on.

A Latino man came into the room, and the boss said, "Pour us some of that good stuff, Pedro."

The good stuff was twenty-five-year-old Macallan whiskey, and all the Hispanic men who worked in Victor Malone's castle, he called Pedro, with a long-sounding E.

"Have a cigar? They're Cuban," the boss man said, and bit the end off one and lit it with a flame that popped out of the muzzle of a gold handgun with ebony handles.

"I'm not a cigar man," Cesare said.

"But you do like those cigar-smoking women, don't you?" Malone laughed, putting a spur deep in Alosi's pride.

"It was a one-night stand. I used her to gain information that helped the company land contracts," Cesare said, rationalizing his involvement with Liberty Cruz.

"Spic girl, isn't she? FBI?" the bastard said, and laughed. "Dill weed Carlson got her canned from that job."

"She's Latina," Cesare answered, then added, "I'm Sicilian, so I'm probably closer to a spic."

"Naw, the Messy-cans, they're the spic. You guineas and dagos is your basic wop greaseball. As opposed to the wetback, who're the genuine greasers. There's a subtle but distinctive difference, like fine wine, between a greaseball and greaser," Victor Malone said, holding school on his bigotry semantics.

Like so many trophy hunters with houses filled with

dead animals and their own personal jets to fly them around the world to kill more, the man who owned Malone-Leyva Executive Security and Investigations didn't worry about feelings. He had no tolerance for even a degree of human dignity.

"I liked your testimony before that piece of shit, Senator Jim Wells. What a sanctimonious asshole he is!" Malone went on, and took a pull on his cigar.

"Pedro!" he yelled. "Where's those fucking drinks!"

The servant ran to the room carrying a tray with a new bottle of the expensive Scotch whiskey and two fat glasses filled with ice and Macallan.

Cesare nodded and took his drink. "Thank you."

"You're welcome," the Hispanic servant said, and left as quickly as his feet could get him out of the room.

"As you may know, I decided to pull out of the war business. All that bullshit going on in Iraq, and the FBI snooping my porch," Malone said, sipping whiskey and smoking his cigar. "Too many potholes on that road. Our own personal United States senator, you know the one that got the Marine Corps hot on rescuing that boy, Valentine? Cooper Carlson. He's lined us up with the Department of Homeland Security."

"Sounds quite good. I had heard that you made the deal. I look forward to the work and the challenges involved," Cesare said. "It's a rapidly expanding market. I can imagine a whole multitude of opportunities."

"That's an understatement," Malone said. "However, I need you to stick close to Senator Carlson. Be his go-to man for me."

"But . . . I thought I would take the lead on the DHS

deal," Cesare said, working hard to not let his disappointment show. "With us pulling out of Iraq and Afghanistan, I am very capable of running that business."

"Son, you lied to me," Malone leveled. "You told me you didn't make a copy of that fucking secret plan that cocksucker Blevins swiped. And you made a copy anyway."

Cesare sank in the chair and took a big drink of the whiskey. He knew better than to back his lie with some tall tale that Blevins had made the copy, not him. Malone knew shit. Scary shit. Like he had a set of eyes everywhere.

"I like you, Alosi," the Malone-Leyva boss said. "But you know way too much for your own good. So I can't fire a man like that. You get my drift?"

Cesare nodded yes.

"I thought about putting you in a car accident, kind of like that boy up in Wisconsin that we got rid of," Malone went on. "Then I thought you might work harder and smarter if you knew I had your number and could push the button.

"Son, I don't trust you as far as I can throw that elephant standing out there in the middle of this castle. But you are one sneaky son of a bitch, and you might just pay off someday, trying to redeem yourself.

"So you get a reprieve. Make the best of it."

Jack Valentine had caught the American Eagle to Charlotte from Albert J. Ellis Airport outside Camp Lejeune, and connected to Dallas on an American Airlines Boeing

757. The Bombardier 700 ride to Charlotte left him cramped in a narrow cabin filled with homebound Marines, most of them dressed in jeans and sport shirts. A handful of Army guys wore their battle-dress uniforms, which Marines call utilities. Gunner Valentine, however, was the only military person aboard wearing a class-A service uniform.

Elmore Snow had taught Jack almost from day one that when he traveled, he ought to proudly wear the dress green with ribbons and badges. It helped Marine Corps recruiting and made a positive impression on everyone. Gunner Valentine found that it also made an especially strong impression on some flight attendants, who would sometimes lavish him with extra frills, the so-called "phase that pays."

A flight attendant a few years ago, waiting by him in Reagan National, had explained to Jack what the "phase that pays" meant, after she had struck up the conversation, slathering on the flirts with the good-looking Marine while they killed time. After that, Jack began to pay attention to how flight attendants smiled and winked at him, and he played into their game, getting himself another warm cookie or that little extra tuck on his pillow.

When he boarded his plane to Dallas, he had not taken two steps inside the front hatch when the lead attendant, a tall and attractive blonde named Pandora, caught him by the arm and set him in a first-class seat. The class-A uniform paid the dividend. As she thanked him for his service, Jack smiled back and asked, "Phase that pays?"

Pandora laughed. "You've been talking to someone."

Jack kept smiling, and she brought him lots of extra good stuff, warm cookies and more, always delivered with a gentle touch of her hand on him.

From Dallas to El Paso, Jack sat just past the wing on the left bank of seats on an American Eagle Canadair commuter jet. One side of the cabin had two seats, side by side, and the other side had a single line of seats. It gave Gunner Valentine the best of both worlds, an aisle slot with a window. While he missed the hot towels and warm cookies, and generous cocktails Pandora had served him in first class on the big plane, this flight wasn't so bad. A nice seat by himself where he could watch the dry Texas world below race by at 250 miles per hour, and think.

Jack raised the lid on his MacBook Pro notebook that he had bought himself as a graduation gift upon departing The Basic School at Quantico. He opened a document he had begun writing, a worksheet and list of objectives he planned to have his MARSOC platoon accomplish in the next ten months as they prepared to go downrange. This time to Afghanistan.

He had as of yet told no one about the deployment. Of course, Elmore knew, and so did Cotton, Billy-C, and the rest of Jack's old detachment. Colonel Snow had moved them and another detachment into the newly formed platoon, Gunner Valentine's first command. Fifty Marine special operators plus their armorers, supply chief and crew, and a hard-charging staff sergeant from Chicago they called Bugsy, who ran the office with a lance corporal clerk named Dugan. However, Jack had not breathed a word to anyone outside his MARSOC band of brothers.

Ten months out, family, friends, and especially Liberty, didn't need to get their worry caps on just yet. Especially after his eventful tour in Iraq. So the newly installed MARSOC platoon commander kept his next trip down-range to himself. He'd tell Mom and Dad, and Liberty, soon enough.

Jack had taken off his blouse, draped it over his lap, and had hardly gone to work on his deployment plan when a healthy, trim young flight attendant with STACEY emblazoned in black letters on the silver nameplate pinned to her uniform interrupted him. "Want me to hang that up?"

She took the blouse off his lap before he could answer, and the Marine looked up as she walked away with it, her tight, firm ass moving all too nice under her snug-fitting blue uniform skirt. As Jack watched and liked what he saw, he answered to no one who could hear him, "Sure."

Stacey had long wild curly blond-tipped hair that brushed off her shoulders, dark underneath the blond, and even darker eyebrows, but bright blue eyes like turquoise jewels. Jack couldn't help but stare at her pretty face as she came back toward him.

When he caught himself staring, Gunner Valentine blinked, and said as she came past him, her hand gently patting his shoulder, "Thanks a lot." Then he added with a smile, "Phase that pays?"

Stacey laughed and headed to the aft of the plane. A

few minutes later, she wore a blue apron and pushed a drink trolley up the aisle with the other flight attendant, a young, slim, redheaded girl named Patricia. Skinny but athletic, with a nice rack and can.

Jack took a Dr Pepper and a pack of pretzels. As Stacey pushed past him, she nudged his shoulder with her butt, and chortled. When he looked up at her, a big grin on his face, she gave him one of those smiles.

"What do you do in the Marines?" Stacey asked Jack a half hour later, and about that much time left in their flight to El Paso. She had wandered down the aisle, as if she was making a second check for trash and empty cans when she stopped by the Marine's seat.

Closing his notebook, Jack looked up at her, and shrugged. "Mostly sit behind a desk these days, I suppose," and pointed at the rank on his collar.

"Sure a lot of fruit salad and glitter on your jacket for a guy who just sits behind a desk," Stacey said. "I recognize your face."

Jack was surprised. "You do?"

"You're that guy," she said. "They had your picture in *TIME* magazine. I read the whole story. Al-Qaeda took you prisoner and you escaped and rescued some girls the insurgents had taken into slavery. The story said two of them got killed, but one made it out alive with you. That senator. What's his name?"

"Carlson," Jack offered.

"Yeah, that's it. Carlson from Nevada," Stacey continued. "He called you a special kind of hero."

"Don't believe everything a politician says," Jack said. "I'm nobody special. Honest!"

The flight attendant smiled big and knelt by Jack. "We're laying over in El Paso tonight. The flight crew. Patricia and I split a room. We're at the Del Norte Hilton."

"Nice place," Jack said, and looked again at her blue eyes and the dark underlayer of her curly blond hair. She had him tempted.

"So, with us landing fairly early," Stacey said, then blushed bright red. "If you have a friend . . . Patricia and I want to go dancing. Or if you don't have a friend, maybe you can dance with us both?"

Then Stacey quickly stood up, beet-faced, and rolled her eyes. "I've never done this before, so I feel a little awkward. Hitting on you?"

"Hey, that's cool," Jack said, and instinctively gave her a pat on the hand. "I haven't been home much in the past fifteen or so years, so I wouldn't know where to start when it comes to picking places to go dancing. Besides, I have family and friends waiting to see me. I doubt I'd have time. But wow, it really is tempting. Seriously."

Stacey reached in her skirt pocket and took out a silver case with her personal calling cards inside it. She took one out and handed it to Jack.

"My cell number's on the card, also my address in Dallas, and my email, too," she said. "Think about it and maybe give me a call. Even down the road if you can't make tonight."

She walked away before Jack could say anything else. He looked at the card and didn't quite know what to do. So he tucked it in his shirt pocket and opened his computer.

As the plane began to descend, it banked into a standard

rate turn, entering the terminal control area approach. Gunner Valentine looked out the window and saw El Paso coming below. He found his notebook case and tucked the MacBook inside, then looked straight down. His hometown.

Below, like looking down on a bad dream, he saw the Devil's Triangle. City fathers and law enforcement had worked for years to improve El Paso's notorious hood, but it still remained the hood. Land of Barrio-Azteca outlaws, drugs, violence, whores, addicts, chronic gloom, and short lives. A ways over, but still in the valley, Jack could see his own neighborhood. Coronado High School just past it, where he had played his glory days of football. Liberty Cruz had cheered him as he ran long for touchdown passes.

On the hill, he saw the plush streets where Liberty had grown up. The rich hood, where the money flowed. Most kids there went to private schools, but Paul Cruz had sent his daughter to the public schools. Deep down, Jack liked Liberty's dad, who never forgot his poor roots and did a lot of lawyer work helping the poor kids in the real bad hood, down in the Devil's Triangle.

"Fucking shit hole," Jack grumbled under his breath as his eyes followed Hondo Pass from Dyer Avenue to Gateway Boulevard, and the blocks and blocks of poverty, violence, and crime they surrounded.

Devil's Triangle had changed Jack's life forever. Not the hood but the thugs the hood had bred. One bad night. That's all it took. One really bad decision by an angry, seventeen-year-old Jack Valentine.

As the plane made its final descent into El Paso, Jack

wondered how his life might have turned out had he not gone to Sonny Gomez's bloody bucket biker bar that night, so many years ago. On the positive side, however, it did put him on the tracks that led to the Marine Corps and this life he now led.

— 20 —

Red neon from the sign outside slashed through the front door of the El Gomez Club as Jack Valentine and three big boys trailing at his heels pushed their way inside the filthy dive and headed to the bar.

Two buzz-cut *cholos* in high-belted khaki pants and untucked blue-plaid shirts, single buttoned at their tattooed necks but wide open from there down, beer bellies protruding, stretching tight the rib knit of their wife-beater undershirts, stepped aside and watched as the four teenagers ambled past them.

"*¡Hijole! ¿Que la chingada?*" one whined in subdued breaths to the other, knowing trouble had just walked in.

"That *baboso*'s back again?" the other sang back.

"*Pendejo* must not have got his fill," the first one said.

"Looks like he brought help this time, *ese*," the other said, and they both nodded like bobbleheads, watching.

Across the nasty saloon, a yellow light shone over a game of Nine-Ball that fell dead quiet. Every eye in the joint now watched the outlander quartet belly up.

This stinking swill house with the red neon flashing GOMEZ outside sat at the corner of Norton Street and

Hondo Pass Avenue on the top end of what Texans in El Paso in 1988 called "the Devil's Triangle." Bordered by Hondo Pass on the north, Gateway Boulevard on the west, and Dyer Avenue on the east, this wedge of slum blocks had the reputation of the worst of the worst in an already rough city sharing the same stretch of border with Ciudad Juarez, Mexico.

Lives sell cheap here in this *Paso del Norte* outlaw hood. Drugs and guns flowed like the piss and beer at Sonny Gomez's gangsta water hole. Sane people avoided this slice of ugliest El Paso life, but anyone calling a barely seventeen-year-old Jack Valentine and his three sixteen-year-old fellow Golden Thunderbirds from the Coronado High School football team anything resembling sane or even remotely rational tonight had better think again.

"Chui," Jack fired through clenched teeth at Sonny Gomez, a middle-aged motorcycle head tending bar with jailhouse tattoos on both thick arms and a black Fu Manchu wrapping his tight-pressed lips. "I want Chui."

"Just like I told you last time you came in here making trouble, *ojete*. I don't know nobody called Chui," Gomez growled at the kid.

Jack panned his eyes at the holmes leaning on cue sticks surrounding the pool table, ready for another brawl.

"El burro sabe mas que tu," Jack said loudly for the audience, showing them his Latino side, then glared at Sonny Gomez. *"Tu eres mas feo que el culo de un mono."*

"Vete al infierno," Gomez let go, his voice thick, gravelly from years of heavy smoking and bad whiskey, and he laid a baseball bat across the bar as he said it.

"I'll go to hell, monkey butt, and take you and those

cabrones with me," Jack snarled back, and gave the boys at the pool table the stink eye.

"You looking for Chui?" a voice from the dark back corner called out. A girl squealed as the Latino hood pushed her off his lap, and she flopped bare-assed on the floor.

The mid-twenties gang lord zipped his pants and buckled his belt as he walked into the light that shrouded the pool table and the thugs gathered round it.

"I'm Chui," he said, cold-eyed, deadly, still walking toward the bar, cool-dude gangsta style. "What you need with me, *pendejo*?"

Behind him, nine Barrio-Azteca soljas fell into a loose echelon and sashayed to the bar with their boss banger.

"I came here to kill your murdering ass," Jack said, and his three sixteen-year-old large-bodied wingmen shouldered up behind him, scared shitless. Reality suddenly sucked all the air out of their overinflated *cajones*.

"Murder?" Chui frowned. "That's some serious shit, *ese*. Who did I supposedly murder?"

"Marco Gonzalez ring a bell?" Jack told him.

Chui half smiled and looked at his holmes close by, all of them smiling and nodding.

"He that big fat piece of shit *maricon* that played center on the Golden Thunderbirds last year?" Chui said.

"Yeah, that's him," Jack fired, his lips curled. "You dragged him to death behind your car and dumped his body on a dirt road across the New Mexico line, by Anthony."

"Never heard of him." Chui shrugged, and the whole gang behind him nodded. A sadistic smirk then spread on Chui's face as he looked cold in Jack's eyes.

"You knew him!" Jack snarled. Anger deep in his bones

took over, and his voice rose as a tear driven by hatred trickled from his eye. "You killed him because he came out gay. He never did anything against you or anyone. Marco never hurt a fly. He was a big, gentle, sweet soul. My best friend! You murdered him for the fun of it!"

Jack wiped his face with his hands and glared at Chui, and in a cold, slow voice said, "Now I'm going to make you pay."

Chui laughed. He looked right and left at his minions, lined abreast behind him, ready to pile drive some seriously medieval hard shit on the four young fools.

"So, you and your three *mariquita* chums, here, just waltz in the belly of the beast to kill Chui? Come on then, asshole. Take your shot," the hood said, smiling large, daring. Then he casually tucked his fingertips inside the waistband of his tailored brown-silk-and-wool-blend pleated-front trousers and smirked.

A fine gold chain with a tastefully small crucifix glittered against his hairless brown chest and perfect white wife-beater undershirt. A light brown long-sleeve silk shirt hung loose on his shoulders, opened down the front, the cuffs turned up one neat fold above his wrists. He had a teardrop tattooed under his left eye and an Aztec warrior's head tattooed on his right forearm with the Roman numeral XXI beneath it. A tasteful gold-chain bracelet dangled on his right wrist and three gold rings with large diamonds sparkled on his well-manicured fingers, two on the right hand and one on the left. A diamond-trimmed gold Rolex President wrapped loosely around his left wrist.

Jack snatched a beer bottle from the counter, and

Sonny Gomez grabbed his bat, but Chui frowned at him and shook his head no.

"I admire courage, *ese*. Even from a half-breed fool like you, Jack Valentine," Chui said, and smiled wide, showing off his movie-star-white enamel-veneered teeth.

Wide-eyed, Jack suddenly felt panic clutch his insides.

"You're surprised I know who you are, Jack?" Chui laughed. Then he got serious. "You came here looking for me three weeks ago, right? My boys gave you a good spanking, too, while Sonny called the cops. You don't think I'm going to check out somebody that comes to my side of town, into my house, wanting to kick my ass? Oh, correct that. Kill me?"

Then Chui got right in Jack's face, and roared, "You got off light, you sniveling little son of a *puta*!"

Chui took a cold beer from the bar that Sonny had set up for him and swallowed a long pull. Then he cocked his head at Jack. "Yeah, I know all about you, Jack Valentine. Where you live, your family, everything, holmes.

"Your mother worked on her back over in Boy's Town, and your daddy, just another Fort Bliss dumb-ass doggie, fell in love with that Mexican whore. Now he fixes air conditioners and she cleans houses and irons clothes for the *gringos*."

Hellfire rose in Jack's eyes while his three large friends, two guards and a tackle from the Golden Thunderbirds' offensive line, quivered in fear like fat girls on a high dive.

"I watched you dudes play football. Not bad. I won some pretty good bones betting on you," Chui said, taking another drink of beer and eyeballing each of the linemen. Then he focused on Jack. "Number eighty-nine, right, Jack? You're a hell of a wide receiver, or is it tight end? I bet you got a really tight end about now, dog, don't you?"

All of the gangsters behind Chui laughed, their face tattoos and glittering gold grills making them look more like devils than humans.

One of the scared boys shuddering behind Jack let out a whimper. "Let's go home, Jack. This was a bad idea. Dude, they know where you live and can hurt your family."

The boy next to him said, "Yeah, Chui, we're sorry. We made a mistake. Please let us leave."

Chui shook his head no. "You gotta pay the toll, *ese.* Don't you know? Come to my *barrio* with your cocks out, gonna fuck me and my *carnales*? No, bro, you gonna pay the toll."

Just as Chui spoke, Jack spit in the gang lord's face, and took his best swing, grazing Chui's cheek as the gangster deftly dodged the blow.

Two Aztecas stepped up, guns drawn, hammers cocked, pressing their muzzles against both the angry boy's cheeks. Jack stopped cold.

Chui eased back, took a blue-silk handkerchief from his pants pocket, and wiped the spittle off his face.

"*¡Puta madre!* Fucking disgusting! You know that, Jack?" Chui said as he moved out of the way.

Then Chui's nine Barrio-Azteca hood soljas, hands loaded with lead-filled leather slaps, brass knuckles, batons, and beer bottles, went to work on the four boys.

Sonny Gomez waited until Chui and his crew had cleared out before he called the cops to clean up the bloody but still-breathing mess they left scattered on the sidewalk outside his nightclub's front door. After a trip to Providence Memorial Hospital emergency room, the three sixteen-year-olds, just under the Texas adult-age wire, went to juvenile detention and waited for their moms and dads to pick them up. At seventeen, Jack went to the big-boy slam.

"Oh, you again," El Paso District Judge Darius Archer grumbled. He spoke with a coarse voice accented by a heavy west-Texas drawl as he looked over the tops of his silver-wire-framed half-lens reading glasses at the shaggy-haired delinquent in bloody, torn, blue-check college-boy sport shirt and bloodstained Wrangler jeans. Split lips and eyebrows, red and purple knots elsewhere on his face, the look told of a battle gone way wrong.

Jack Valentine peered back through bare slits between black-and-blue swollen eyelids. "Sorry, Judge Archer."

"I'll bet you are." The judge groaned and looked to the back of his courtroom, where young Valentine's father stood, visibly nervous, twisting a Dallas Cowboys ball cap in his shaking hands.

Before the judge could ask the man to come stand alongside his son, the double doors behind Jack's dad eased open, and a brawny man with a silver-and-black crew cut and a dark blue pin-striped suit stepped through.

"Can I help you, Counselor?" Judge Archer said to the sharp-dressed man who had entered his courtroom.

"I'd like to help the young man standing before your bench, Your Honor," the lawyer said. "Pro bono." Then he put out his hand to Harry Valentine and introduced himself. "Paul Cruz, Mr. Valentine. Do you mind if I represent your son? It would be a big favor to me and my daughter, and won't cost you a dime."

Jack's dad smiled, and his face washed with relief.

"Why, yes!" Harry said, and shook Paul Cruz's hand hard. "I mean, no! I, uh. We won't mind at all! Please help us! He's not a bad boy!"

Harry Valentine looked at the judge, then at his son. "Jackie, you don't mind, do you?"

Jack Valentine looked with blurred vision at the man who had the build of a retired NFL linebacker and nodded his approval.

Judge Archer motioned both Harry Valentine and Paul Cruz to come forward and join their young thug at the bench, and gave El Paso Police Sergeant Freddy Montoya a look. Montoya nodded approval. Then the judge locked eyes with Alice Montoya, the police sergeant's cousin, who had joined the El Paso County District Attorney's Office six months ago, after graduating University of Texas at El Paso Law School and passing the Texas Bar.

Alice blinked at the judge, her face flushed red, at a complete loss of what to do.

"Tell you what, Alice," Judge Archer said, bearing a small hint of a smile at the fledgling lawyer. "Just don't say anything, and let me talk to these gentlemen."

The judge leaned back in his chair and eyed the men and boy standing in front of him.

"What's going on, Paul?" the judge asked. "Pro bono? I'm impressed. Defense business must pay well these days."

"Did you watch this boy play football?" Cruz asked.

"My grandson, Ken Archer, plays quarterback for the Golden Thunderbirds, but you know that, Paul," the judge said. "I've watched him connect many a pass to this young man. Jack Valentine is very likely the best tight end to ever play the game at Coronado High School. He's a big reason we won the bi district championship. That's why I'm out of sorts that he stands before me today. Second time in about a month!"

Paul Cruz nodded. He'd often seen the judge sitting under a blanket, first row of bleachers behind the barrier at the home benches, on the fifty-yard line.

Judge Archer scowled at Jack. "Master Valentine. You promised me! I threw out the last case of you brawling, and got the arrest record tossed, your seventeenth birthday and all. You promised me you'd walk the straight and narrow. Yet here you stand. Why, son?"

Jack Valentine looked at the scuffed toes on his cowboy boots, and tears ran out of his swollen-shut eyes.

"What in hell's going on, Jack?" the judge blew up. "That Gomez lounge is a bloody bucket rod-and-gun club for every *cholo* outlaw on this side and the other side of the border. You just hate living? Is that it?"

"Your Honor," the lawyer interrupted, his hand raised. "How much do you know about why Jack was in that bar?"

"Not one bloody word of it," the judge fumed. "Sergeant Montoya pleaded to me to let young Valentine go last time because he and Harry here are old friends, the lad just turned seventeen the day of the fight, and he had no prior trouble. Freddy vouched for the boy. Now look."

"May we go off the record for ten minutes?" Paul Cruz asked. "Talk as friends and concerned fathers."

"Why not. Consider this a recess," Archer told the clerk and stenographer. "Doris, you and Cynthia take a coffee break. Check back in twenty minutes."

"My daughter, Alicia, and young Mr. Valentine have a relationship," Cruz began.

"I thought that pretty little girl named Liberty something or other, the cheerleader, was your girlfriend, Jack?" Harry Valentine blurted at his son.

"That's her nickname, Pop," Jack mumbled. "Her Christian name is Melita Alicia Cruz, but everybody calls her Liberty."

Paul Cruz smiled. "When Alicia was a little girl, every Halloween, instead of goblins or ghouls, she wanted to dress up as the Statue of Liberty. Little Miss Liberty, her mom and I called her. Then it became Liberty and stuck."

"Well, that's a nice daughter you have there, Mr. Cruz," Harry Valentine offered.

"Call me Paul, Harry, please." Cruz smiled.

"I know Liberty," Judge Archer said. "She applied to work here this summer as a student clerk. Headstrong girl, that one. Smart, too. Up to a point," and the judge glared at Jack Valentine when he said it.

"Do you recall the grisly story last year, about the boy from Coronado High School getting dragged to death behind a car for miles down a country road, and his body dumped just across the border, out by Anthony, New Mexico?" Paul Cruz said.

"Who can forget it?" Judge Archer sighed. "Gang thing, wasn't it? The kid was supposedly gay and had just started telling people?"

"Barrio-Azteca gang we think did it, but nothing solid

on any of them to make an arrest," Freddy Montoya offered. "New Mexico police have jurisdiction since the body wound up across the state line, and apparently the murder occurred over there. Abduction here, murder there, FBI supposedly looking into it. Hate crime and all."

"Case has gone nowhere, Judge," Cruz interjected. "Poor kid from El Paso. Just another dead Mexican. Who cares? Right? Plus, he had come out gay right after he graduated from high school, and nobody wants anything to do with that can of worms. Why stir up trouble? Kick it under the rug with all the other poor dead Mexicans."

The lawyer paused, letting the sense of injustice set in, then asked Judge Archer, "Do you recall the boy who snapped center for the Golden Thunderbirds last year?"

"Sure. A big boy, as I recall. Stood about six-four and weighed in at two-thirty or so," the judge answered. "Gonzalez, I think?"

"Marco Gonzalez," Cruz said, head nodding.

"Don't tell me that's the same boy dragged to death?" The judge sighed.

"One and the same." Cruz kept nodding. "Not a big star. *El Paso Times* story focused on gang violence and the gruesome nature of the murder and barely mentioned Marco had played football or even graduated from Coronado High School."

"Judge," Harry Valentine interrupted, "Marco's dad, Herman, works in my heating and air-conditioning business. Been with me from the start. That boy and Jack grew up together, hanging out in my shop, learning to bend sheet metal, machine, and fabricate. He was Jack's best friend."

"So after a year of the police doing nothing about the murder, you went hunting the killers?" the judge asked Jack.

The boy nodded yes. "I loved Marco like a brother." Tears flooded Jack's eyes, and he wept. "He was my brother, Judge. Same as, anyway. Besides, Marco never hurt anybody, not ever. He was shy all the time, embarrassed real easy. Soft-hearted, gentle."

"A darned good center on the football field, too, no matter what the newspapers didn't say," Harry Valentine added. "And a good boy. Darned good boy! Gay or not. Besides, I don't think he ever messed around with other boys. He was too shy, right, Jack?"

Jack nodded yes at his father.

"Why didn't you tell us this when we had you in here a few weeks ago?" Freddy Montoya snapped.

"I aim to kill the bastards that murdered Marco," Jack shot back. "If I told you that, what would you do then?"

"I'd help you, damn it!" Sergeant Montoya blew.

Alice Montoya gave her cousin a hard elbow. "Even off the record, Freddy, you can't say stuff like that. You're a police sergeant."

"According to the arrest report, it says that you and three sixteen-year-old boys were in the El Gomez Club drinking beer and got into a brawl with a group of men. I take it they were Barrio-Aztecas, given the location of that den of iniquity?" Judge Archer said, scanning the report.

"Your Honor, my daughter came to me this morning, after getting the news that Jack and three others from the football team were arrested, and asked me to help," Paul

Cruz said. "She told me the whole story. How Marco Gonzalez had gotten killed New Year's Eve last year, and how Jack had become obsessed, hunting the killers. A couple of months ago, a mutual friend of Jack's and Marco's told Jack that he heard a guy they call 'Chui' had bragged about giving a *maricon* what he deserved. Jack put two and two together and went after him."

"I know Chui, real name Rafael Baca," the police sergeant spoke up. "He and his crew of Aztecas hang at the Gomez club. Bad *hombres*, all of them." He looked at Jack. "Son, you're no match for those dogs. Not even the whole T-Birds football team, with guns."

Jack smiled at the cop.

"You know, for the last ten years, my wife, Patricia, has worked for the Drug Enforcement Agency at the El Paso Intelligence Center," Paul Cruz said. "If it's any consolation, Jack, DEA's close to dropping a net on Chui Baca and his crew. It's only a matter of time. Let the pros handle it."

"Mr. Cruz," Jack said, no longer caring. "That's all fine, sir, but I want to be the one who turns out Chui's lights."

"That's not happening, Jack!" Harry Valentine fired at his son. "You know how my heart breaks for Herman and Lola, losing their son. I loved Marco, too! But we can't go killing people! Those gangsters are the animals, not us."

"We're gonna get Chui. I promise," Freddy Montoya added, and put his arm around Jack. "Let the law kill him."

Darius Archer looked over the tops of his glasses at

Jack, studying his beat-up face. Contempt still raged inside the young man, and the judge knew it.

"El Paso, Texas, grows two kinds of people, Jack," the judge said, pursing his lips between thoughts. "Those that live to serve greater humanity, like us here, your mom and dad, and like Herman Gonzalez and other hard workers just like him. Or those that die in gangs, living out their short, unhappy lives on the wrong side of the law, destroying everything good around them. Good and evil, son.

"Hunting a man to kill for revenge, unleashing your wrath, committing murder, corrupts your soul. It'll take you to those dark places where the devil lives and turn you into a beast just like Chui Baca and those other monsters.

"You need to think about that, son, and make some serious choices. A day soon comes in all our lives when we reach that moment where we each have to choose which direction we take. Jack, today's your day. You're at the crossroads."

Harry Valentine put his arm around his son, and tears ran from the strong man's eyes. He looked at the judge and swallowed hard. Paul Cruz shouldered by him and put his arm over Harry's shoulder.

"Son, since we're still off the record, let me explain a few things. This session before my bench today is supposed to be simply an arraignment," Judge Archer said to Jack, and gave a look at the prosecutor, then at Paul Cruz. "I can throw out any or all of the charges I deem have no merit, or I can bind you over for trial and charge you with this whole laundry list of mostly trumped-up nonsense that Sonny Gomez has put in this police complaint."

The judge stopped and looked at Alice Montoya. "Counselor, did you or anyone else even investigate any part of this mess? Attempted armed robbery, assault, menacing, willful destruction of property? Seriously? What were you going to do, just throw this boy's life away for a bunch of no-account hoodlums?"

Alice Montoya lowered her head, and mumbled, "I thought we might negotiate a deal for reduced charges, Your Honor. After all, he did go in there with a gang, started a fight, and caused damages, according to the property owner."

Judge Archer shook his head and sighed.

"Paul, here's the choice I want your client and his father to consider while we're still in recess," Darius Archer said to the defense lawyer, all the while looking eye to swollen eye with Jack. "Young Mr. Valentine can go to trial and face this crock of bullshit, but like the prosecution pointed out, at the end of the day, the lad will have to face judgment for the crime of going to that bar and starting a fight. No matter how we cut that piece of meat, at best your boy's facing assault and property damages. Even if he got the shitty end of the stick in that fight, Jack started it. He took it to Chui, went to his hangout for the express purposes of causing him harm. So, Jack pays. That's a criminal conviction and a life changer."

The judge waited and let his words soak in, still looking eye to swollen eye with Jack Valentine. Then he added, "Or. And that's a big or, son."

"Yes, Your Honor?" Paul Cruz answered.

"I served in the United States Marine Corps from 1968 to 1973," the judge began. "I made sergeant in three years, went to college on the GI Bill, and got my law degree at Georgetown University. That gave me a fine profession, a good life, and I sit here as a Texas district judge today."

Paul Cruz smiled, and so did Harry Valentine. Jack hung his head and stared at his scuffed-up boot toes.

"In order for my client to join the Marine Corps these days, he cannot have a police record or any arrests, much less a conviction," Paul Cruz told the judge.

"I am aware of that fact." Judge Archer nodded. "As I said previously, I have the power to throw out this whole mess of nonsense for lack of merit and evidence and wipe the slate clean. No arrests ever took place. We can do that, can't we, Freddy? And let those other three walk, too, with a good warning."

Sergeant Montoya, also a Marine Corps veteran, smiled big, and said, "Yes, sir, Judge Archer, Semper Fi."

"How about that, Prosecutor Montoya? Will this be a problem with the district attorney?" the judge asked. "Can you take care of your end, or do I need to see him?"

"No, Your Honor, I can take care of everything." Alice Montoya smiled.

"How about it, Jack? Life or death?" Judge Archer asked young Valentine.

"Yes, sir. Life," Jack answered. "It's a deal."

"No more fighting. No more hunting Chui Baca?" the judge added.

"No, sir," Jack answered.

"Freddy," Darius Archer said, looking at the police

sergeant. "Run downstairs to the military recruiters' offices and see if that Marine gunnery sergeant, Mike Seacrest, will come up here and bring paperwork to get this boy signed up. Since Jack is just seventeen, we have his daddy right here, happy to sign the papers for his son to be a Marine."

"Yes, sir, Your Honor," Sergeant Freddy Montoya said, laughter in his voice as he jogged out of the courtroom.

Second week of January 1991, Lance Corporal Jack Valentine squared away his gear inside a white hardback barracks with a white-metal roof in an expeditionary encampment built by Seabees over the past three months outside Goatville in northern Saudi Arabia. Half a million American soldiers, sailors, airmen, and Marines, along with another 436,000 troops from thirty-four other nations had massed since mid-November in similar expeditionary garrisons across the northeastern flank of Saudi Arabia, spitting distance from the Iraq border.

There they waited with knives in their teeth, poised to run across the south half of Iraq like fire on gasoline, and crash their thunder downhill at Iraqi-occupied Kuwait, like a hammer on an anvil, obliterating the enemy and cutting off all hope of escape except into the sea or through the attacking lines, where the Iraqis would surely die. This largest gathered army since June 6, 1944, when Allied forces landed 1.3 million soldiers on the beaches of Normandy, crouched, ready to pounce should diplomatic efforts fail to persuade President Saddam Hussein to give up the oil-rich state he had stolen, and return it to its people and their emir, Sheikh Jaber Al-Ahmad Al-Jaber Al-Sabah.

Hussein had accused Kuwait of slant drilling across their border and taking oil from Iraq's Ar-Rumaylah oil fields. Saddam demanded that Saudi Arabia and Kuwait cancel Iraq's $30 billion debt it owed them as payment for the oil theft. He also hurled insults at his foe, accusing Saudi Arabia and Kuwait of conspiring to keep oil prices low in an effort to pander to Western masters.

As Saddam Hussein invaded Kuwait on August 2, 1990, sending more than three hundred thousand troops across the border, he claimed as justification for his incursion that Kuwait had originally belonged to Iraq, and he was merely reclaiming that which rightfully belonged to Iraq. He said that Western colonists had created the small oil state for their advantage. In truth, Kuwait had existed years before Britain, under a League of Nations mandate, created Iraq at the end of World War I.

On August 8, 1990, Saddam Hussein formally annexed Kuwait as Iraq's nineteenth province. This final insult set the wheels in motion for the great war to come.

Just one more new arrival among the swelling numbers along the Iraqi border, Jack pulled the zipper closed on his neatly packed Advanced Operator load-out bag that doubled as an overgrown Marine Corps field transport backpack. Inside it, Jack had tucked away everything important in his now Spartan warrior lifestyle.

Gold-embroidered Force Recon jump wings and a silver-embroidered SCUBA/UBA head above them adorned the top flap of the pale OD green Gortex duffel with the name J. A. VALENTINE, USMC finely stitched in bold black letters beneath them. He had spent the better part of a paycheck buying the well-organized, compartmented bag with padded pack straps and a tubular frame inside it made of aircraft aluminum, specifically designed for special operators like him. Jack had bought it in San Diego after graduating Amphibious Reconnaissance school at Coronado Island, before heading to Camp Lejeune and joining Second Force Reconnaissance Company.

He pushed the AO bag against the foot of his plywood-bottomed wooden bunk next to a similarly pale green, extralarge parachute cargo bag, with J. A. VALENTINE, USMC beneath a Marine Corps emblem stenciled in black paint on its side. This satchel contained the bulky stuff of his combat kit. Things like his Kevlar helmet and body armor, his Ghillie suit and bonnet that he had fashioned by hand during his ten weeks of Scout-Sniper School, along with his camouflage ground cloth and portable hide. It also held his knee pads, elbow pads, ass pack, and hooded gas mask and charcoal-lined and highly uncomfortable nuclear-biological-chemical-warfare protective suit that he dreaded ever having to wear in a real war.

Saddam Hussein had a reputation of stooping to the lowest of depths and using chemical weapons on people he disliked, such as his attempted genocide of the Kurdish civilians of Halabja, Kurdistan, and across northern Iraq as part of his Ba'athist regime's Al-Anfal Campaign in 1988. Planes and artillery bombarded the Kurds with napalm and other conventional weapons, then Hussein's forces set a deadly mixture of chemical weapons on the populace, killing thousands. Among the chemical weapons were nerve agents, sulfur-mustard gas, blister agents, and hydrogen cyanide.

Jack had spent the three months before deployment training in Mission-Oriented Protective Postures, Levels 1, 2, 3, and 4. MOPP Level 4 meant everything went on the body. It must have been how armored-up knights of old felt swaggled in their tin suits, training and fighting. He wondered how he could ever Ghillie up and carry out reconnaissance, target acquisition, or sniper missions under MOPP Level 4 conditions. Yet the alternative of dying a horrifying painful death by Saddam's chemical agents made the struggle in MOPP Level 4 doable.

Although he had a month's leave coming after Scout-Sniper School at Camp Pendleton and Amphibious Reconnaissance training at Coronado, the Marine Corps' equivalent of Basic Underwater Demolition/SEAL school, Jack took only a week off between graduation and reporting to his new duty station. He wanted to hit the ground running, still fresh, hard, and focused.

Now nearly twenty years old, Jack spent his first off-duty week since his thirty-day boot camp leave at home in El Paso with Mom and Dad. He and Harry Valentine took one day on their own, just the two of them, father and son in the New Mexico mountains, trout fishing. The rest of the time, it was nothing but Jack and Dad and Mom, and her good home cooking. Drippy, overstuffed chicken-and-green-chili enchiladas smothered with onions, more peppers, cheese, and sour cream. Jack's favorite.

Before he headed to Camp Lejeune, Harry and Elaine Valentine had arranged a special dinner for their boy, Jack.

They invited Herman and Lola Gonzalez, Paul and Patricia Cruz, Judge Darius Archer and his wife, Anita, and El Paso Police Sergeant Freddy Montoya, a divorcé who came alone.

Jack's girlfriend, Liberty Cruz, had gone off to college in New York City, at Columbia University, preparing herself for law school. She set her sights on Cornell University Law School, best of the best she regarded, but just in case disaster struck, she kept Columbia Law as her fallback. She had the inside track there as an undergrad.

Moms and dads spent the evening talking about how good Jack had turned out, and of Liberty and what Paul Cruz hoped she would do with her life as a lawyer. "She's doing it for me," Cruz boasted.

Jack said little, mostly yes, sir, and no, sir, and pass the enchiladas for seconds and thirds, but smiled a lot when Paul Cruz said what he did about his daughter going to law school for him. Jack knew the whole story.

Liberty was a rebel through and through, but she loved her daddy, and honored his wish for her. Law school it was. No arguments. While Father envisioned she would take over his successful criminal defense practice in El Paso when he retired, she had radically different ideas. Ideas she had shared only with Jack.

What Jack knew and what he didn't think either Paul or Patricia Cruz even suspected was that Liberty wanted nothing to do with defending criminals. She wanted to hunt them on the streets and throw them in the slammer. She wanted to be a gunslinging hard-ass operator. A special agent of the "Efah Bee Eye" she joked. Then in time, she planned to open her own business, executive security and special investigations.

"Big money in it," she told Jack, as they sat in his dad's Ford pickup truck sucking face and imagining their futures the week before Jack headed off to boot camp.

Liberty dreamed of one day owning a fab villa overlooking the Mediterranean, along the French Riviera, well east of that shit hole of a steamer town, Marseilles, maybe in the hills above Saint-Tropez, or perhaps in Italy, near Milan. She wanted a life of splendor, exotic sports cars and jet planes. She could not imagine sitting in a courtroom next to some sleazy, foul-smelling scumbag drug dealer, pimp, and gangster that her father spent his life dutifully defending. Young Miz Cruz assessed a big fat zero for idealism, but Machiavellian pragmatism ordered her life's agenda.

Oh, she had a heart, but she also had a brain. A very good brain, and a dream for her, and for Jack. Good old noncommittal slide-along Jack, who cared little about either money or one day owning a fine villa in France, but headed for the Marines. Liberty mused, there he'll learn all about commitment and discipline. He could do his Marine thing while she did college, and they'd meet in the middle, later.

"What's your obsession with money and all that crap that goes with it?" Jack had asked her on that last warm night in El Paso, sitting in the dark, making love, and imagining tomorrow.

"Money isn't happiness," Liberty told her beau, "but it's a whole lot easier to find happiness with money than without it."

Jack couldn't argue that point.

Conversely, Paul Cruz had preached the Constitution of the United States to his daughter from childhood. She dreamed up the Statue of Liberty Halloween costume more to please him than herself. Liberty, his red-white-and-blue sparkler, torch in hand, standing for freedom and justice for all. Just like Captain America and Superman.

As for bad guys, Liberty had no use for them. Put 'em away or shoot 'em. Preferably shoot 'em and save the taxpayer the bundle for defense attorneys like her dad. She saw his clients and detested them.

While Paul Cruz thought he knew his tall, good-looking, well-built, long-black-haired, dark-eyed daughter, Jack Valentine knew her best.

During the dinner party, the families also reminisced about Marco and Jack, fast friends as little boys, Marco a year older than Jack and towering over him from age nine onward. The two years of football with Jack at tight end and Marco at center had brought the two boys' families close, going to the games and all the surrounding activities for parents of players. Then when Marco was murdered, the two families bonded into one. Harry and Elaine helped them grieve and survive. His homosexuality never came up in conversation although it swam uncomfortably close, just beneath the surface.

When the dinner began, Harry had Jack make a grand entrance from his bedroom, dressed in his class-A, Marine Corps Kelly-green uniform. Proudly above his left breast pocket, Jack wore his gold jump wings and silver SCUBA/UBA head above his few service ribbons and his silver expert rifle and pistol shooting badges.

"Force Recon!" Freddy Montoya had said when Jack stepped into the living room, looking hard and sharp. The police sergeant bounced to his feet and pumped the young Marine's hand. "Put her there, bro. I was First Force Recon out of Pendleton in my day."

"Less than two years and you've made lance corporal. I'm impressed," Judge Archer added. "You've done well, son. I appreciate your parents having Anita and me over for dinner, so we could see you. Once in a while, in my court, we do strike gold."

"I have you to thank, Your Honor. I expect to get promoted to corporal soon after I report for duty at Second Force Recon," Jack announced. "I got the highest pro-con marks of any non-rates out of Amphib-Recon. My time in grade for corporal closes next month."

After dinner, while they sat on the patio under mosquito-repelling Tiki torchlights, drinking coffee in the cool desert evening, and Jack had changed into a sport shirt and slacks, Freddy Montoya gave Jack a serious look.

"Maybe I got some good news for you, Jack, and maybe it might be disturbing news," Freddy said, and gave a concerned look at the parents of Marco Gonzalez.

"Spill it, Freddy," Harry Valentine said to his pal.

"Well, Jack, I know you got here a few days ago, and you've been here at your parents' house twenty-four/seven, unless you're going someplace with Harry or your mom, right?" Freddy said, trying to sound reassuring. "But in case a detective might come calling, wanting to ask a few questions, I don't want you to get alarmed or anything. It's just routine."

"What is it, Sergeant?" Paul Cruz asked, picking up

on the policeman's awkward tone and never considering anytime a detective questions a client a matter of routine business.

"You remember that scumbag, Chui Baca? The one who beat the crap out of Jack, and we all think murdered Marco Gonzalez?" Freddy told the lawyer, then looked at the dead boy's parents and offered an apologetic grimace.

"I thought for sure the DEA had him for life on those charges," Paul Cruz added, remembering the gangster. "Chui Baca's made of Teflon."

Patricia Cruz added, "Bad warrants and federal prosecutors lost all the evidence. Witnesses vanished."

"Yeah, too bad about all that," Freddy said, and looked at Jack who sat expressionless, cool, waiting.

Everyone now sat silently, watching the cop, waiting for the shoe to finally drop.

"Somebody popped Chui," Freddy announced. "Did it two days ago. Caught him center mass, right in the chest with a high-velocity .30 caliber rifle slug. A 175-grain Sierra MatchKing, just like military snipers use. Blew his heart and lungs apart. His buds that was with him said he stepped out of his car and bam! Took him right out of his shoes. He thrashed on the ground for about ten seconds. Scared those sorry bastards real bad. They never heard the shot or saw where it came from. Just bam, when it hit Chui, and killed him like a dog."

Harry Valentine nodded at his son, then at his cop friend. Unfazed.

Herman and Lola Gonzalez both smiled with the news.

"Breaks my heart," Jack said, and shrugged at Freddy.

"Mine, too." Freddy smiled back. "But, given you wanted to kill the bastard and all, a little over two years ago, detectives might come knocking. Don't worry about it. Nobody's gonna look that hard for whoever committed this public service."

Paul Cruz looked at Jack and didn't say a word.

No one questioned Jack or Harry Valentine about it, then or anytime afterward.

Just as Jack Valentine had stretched out on his bunk a hard knock came on the barracks door, and without waiting to be asked to enter, a lean, high-and-tight brush-cut, tough-looking Marine captain stepped inside.

"Looking for Lance Corporal John Arthur Valentine," said the captain dressed in crisp desert-camouflage utilities, roughed-out desert jump boots, and a wide-brimmed desert-camouflage flop hat gripped in his left hand, along with a brown manila file folder.

Three other non-rate Marines sharing quarters with Jack snapped to attention and pointed to the last rack, where Lance Corporal Valentine lay, propped on his elbows, eyeballing the officer as he walked inside.

"That would be me, sir," Jack said, getting to his feet and standing at attention.

"Elmore Snow's the name," the captain said. "Take a seat, son."

Jack took a seat on his bunk, and the captain sat on the metal folding chair by it. He held the lance corporal's Marine Corps Service Record Book in his hands, and opened it across his knees.

Then he looked over his shoulder at the three other non-rates in the hooch, and told them, "Why don't you lads give me and John a little privacy."

"Yes, sir," the three said, and happily disappeared.

"Says here you graduated first in your class in the ten-week Scout-Sniper course at Pendleton, then shot the gap directly south to Amphib-Recon school at Coronado," Captain Snow said, looking at several pages of training. "Not even a ninety-six-hour pass?"

Jack shrugged. "Didn't want to lose my steam."

"Platoon guide out of boot camp, meritorious PFC. Honor graduate at the School of Infantry," Snow went on, thumbing through the pages. "Got picked for Recon two months after showing up at Fifth Marines. Jump school at Benning, won the Iron Mike. Then off to Pickle Meadows for survival and mountaineering. And last August you graduated top of your class at Amphib-Recon. I'm truly impressed. You remind me of me. Son, you ever take any time off?"

"A week last August, when I headed to Lejeune." Jack smiled. "By the way, sir, people call me Jack. John and Arthur, those names fit my grandfathers."

"Roger that, Jack." Snow smiled.

"What's going on, sir?" Jack asked.

"You cleared top secret just before deployment," Snow said, still thumbing through the pages of Jack's SRB. "That's good because I'm recruiting spooks."

"Spooks?" Jack asked. "Like spies?"

"Intelligence work, deep reconnaissance, possible limited contact, clandestine sanctions. Special operations,"

Snow explained. "I need a Scout-Sniper on my team, and Captain McBride, your commanding officer, recommended you."

"I'm flattered, sir." Valentine smiled.

"You've got your gold wings, I see, but you're still pretty green at this business. How are you at high-altitude low-opening insertions?" the captain asked.

"Good to go, sir," Jack said. "I love HALO. People pay fat money to do that in the civilian world, don't they?"

"Yes, they do, Jack. We take you skydiving and don't charge a dime." Captain Snow grinned.

"We fixing to cross Saddam Hussein's Line of Death, sir?" Jack said, bright-eyed.

"Some of us sooner than others," Elmore Snow said, and looked at his watch. "I've got a meeting right now, so I need to run along. We have a top secret briefing at 1430 at the head shed. You're on my team as of now. You be there waiting for me at 1400. I'll introduce you to the others. Then we sit down with Lieutenant General Walter E. Boomer and some of his key staff. Got it?"

"General Boomer?" Jack asked, blinking. "Like in a little room with a real three-star general? He going to ask me questions?"

"Yes, Lance Corporal, you're going to be in a little room with a real live lieutenant general," Snow said, chuckling. "Don't worry. I'll do all the talking. If General Boomer says anything to you, it's probably just to pat your back or shake your hand."

"Wow, sir!" Jack said, standing as Captain Snow stood, too. "I never met a real general before. I mean, I've seen them in a parade, me marching past the reviewing stand. But I never met one face-to-face. He might even shake my hand? That would be very cool, sir."

"Yup, very cool indeed," Elmore Snow said as he left.

Jack ate lunch with his three Force Recon hooch mates but said nothing about his meeting with Captain Elmore Snow. They asked, but Valentine only gave them a raised eyebrow over a fried chicken breast that he held in his fingers, accompanied by a one-shoulder shrug and a grin with his mouth full of potatoes and gravy.

At a quarter 'til two o'clock, he stood in the parking area in front of the long building with the flagpole in front of it, sizing up three Marines who waited at one side of the walkway near the front door. A gunnery sergeant, a staff sergeant, and a sergeant.

Five minutes later, another sergeant joined the three, and they shook hands. Then all four eyeballed Jack, standing by his lonesome, in the parking lot, no car or jeep or truck or newfangled Humvee. Just a very young hard charger in desert utilities and jump boots with a flop hat pulled low over his eyes, looking at them.

The gunny said something to the others, then waved at Jack.

"You Valentine?" the gunny barked at him.

A big smile crossed Jack's face as he waved back and jogged to the group. "That's me, Gunny."

"Early arrival," the gunny said. "I like a Marine who lands on deck ahead of schedule. Makes an outstanding first impression, along with a squared-away uniform and body."

"Back in high school, my football coach said we operate on Lombardi time," Jack said. "Always be where you're supposed to be fifteen minutes early."

"This ain't high school football, but I have long admired Vince Lombardi," the gunny said. "Lombardi time. Good ethic."

"This it, Gunny?" Jack asked.

"This what?" the gunny answered.

"The team. I thought there'd be more people," Jack said.

"Just us five and the skipper, far as I know," the gunny said.

"Any idea what we're doing?" Jack asked, and looked at the other sergeants and felt a little out of place being the only non-rate.

All four Marines laughed.

"Oh, I do love fresh meat," the staff sergeant said, and spit a hefty brown stream of Red Man tobacco juice into the green leafy boxwood shrubs planted in pots by the white-metal building's dirt porch area bordered with white-painted rocks.

"I suspect whatever it is will be exciting," the gunny said. "Captain Snow has a reputation for leading missions that scare the ever-living dogshit out of you."

"But we all come back alive." The staff sergeant grinned through juicy tobacco teeth.

"That's what matters," one of the sergeants said, and the other sergeant, a black Marine, nodded.

"Roger dodger," the staff sergeant said, and spit.

"Works for me," Jack said. "What missions? Like in Beirut?"

"No, not that far back," the black sergeant said.

"Colombia," the staff sergeant said. "Chile, too. Drug-interdiction operations. Gunfighting cocaine cowboys in Medellín barely a month ago."

"Oh," Jack said.

The gunny eyed him boots up, then looked him in the eyes.

"Pure virgin soul, my guess," the gunny finally said. "Ever kill a man?"

Jack looked him in the eyes, considering how to answer.

"By your hesitation, maybe you're not the virgin I imagined?" the gunny said, then smiled big.

"Naw," Jack drawled, and looked at his feet. "I'm the virgin, pure as driven snow."

"That'll all change soon enough," the gunny said, and put his arm over Jack's shoulders and eyed his mosquito wings with crossed rifles.

Elmore Snow stepped out the headquarters front door, gave the five Marines a look, and they followed him to a conference room. As they walked inside, the captain closed the door.

"Gunny Ambrose, did you take care of introductions?" Captain Snow said, laying down several folders and reaching in his pocket for something.

"No, sir." The gunny shrugged. "Thought we might have to throw the minnow back if he didn't check out with the crew."

"He check out?" the captain asked, holding whatever was in his pocket now clenched in his right hand, and looking at Jack as if he had second thoughts.

"Oh, sir," Jack said, worried, "I'll work extra hard. You

guys do what I joined the Marine Corps to do. I trained hard for this, sir. I know I'm a non-rate lance corporal, but I've been in the zone since August, and Captain McBride said he would get me promoted once I got settled in the company."

Elmore Snow laughed, and Gunnery Sergeant Raymond Ambrose gave the captain an elbow for spoiling the gag.

Jack smiled, too, and looked sideways at the gunny, who just shook his closely crew-cut head.

"You're not throwing me back then?" the lance corporal asked.

"Well, Jack," Elmore said. "I require all people on my team to at least hold NCO rank. We don't have room for anyone without a blood stripe."

"Like I said, sir, I've been up for promotion since the end of August," Jack tried to explain. "I should have gotten promoted months ago, but with my PCS move from Pendleton to Lejeune, and just getting my feet on the ground at Second Force Recon, it just hadn't happened. Not anybody's fault, just the way the chips fell."

"Good for you, Jack. Not anybody's fault. That's what I wanted to hear," Captain Snow said, and opened his hand, showing the young Marine a set of black-metal corporal chevrons. "Captain McBride said he planned to promote you at the company formation on Friday, but with you dispatched out today, I get the honors."

The captain then looked at his crew. "Form up a formation. Gunny, you will assist. Lance Corporal Valentine, front and center."

Elmore handed Ray Ambrose the chevrons as he took

a red-imitation-leather-covered hardback folder with a gold Marine Corps emblem stamped on its face from a guard mail envelope and opened it. Inside, under a clear plastic sheet, lay Jack's promotion warrant, signed by Lieutenant General Walter E. Boomer, Commanding General, United States Marine Forces Central Command and First Marine Expeditionary Force.

Gunny Ambrose barked, "Attention to orders!"

Captain Snow then began to read the warrant:

"To all who shall see these presents, greetings: Know Ye that reposing special trust and confidence in the fidelity and abilities of John Arthur Valentine, I do appoint him a Corporal in the United States Marine Corps, to rank as such from the First day of January, 1991. This appointee will therefore carefully and diligently discharge the duties of the grade to which appointed by doing and performing all manner of things thereunto pertaining. And I do strictly charge and require all personnel of lesser grade to render obedience to appropriate orders. And this appointee is to observe and follow such orders and directions as may be given from time to time by Superiors acting according to the rules and articles governing the discipline of the Armed Forces of the United States of America.

"Given under my hand at United States Marine Forces Central Command, First day of January, in the year of our Lord 1991.

"Signed, W. E. Boomer, Lieutenant General, United States Marine Corps, Commanding."

Gunny Ambrose took the right collar and Captain Snow took Jack's left collar. They removed the lance corporal chevrons, handed them to Jack, and together put the steel pins on the backs of the chevrons through the uniform-collar material. Then, together, they drove the pins down hard into Jack Valentine's collarbones.

His eyes lit up with the sudden sharp pain, but he held his position. Then, one at a time, the staff sergeant and two sergeants took turns pinning on the stripes. As they drove them in the collarbone, they also added a swift punch with their knees across the new NCO's thighs, pinning on his blood stripes, too.

"Welcome to our wonderful world of fun and games," the gunny then said. "Gunnery Sergeant Ray Ambrose at your service, Corporal Valentine. On the team, I go by Mutt, like a mongrel dog that doesn't care whose ass he bites. Anyone outside the team calls me Gunny. That clear?"

Jack nodded.

Next up the staff sergeant introduced himself, still smiling tobacco juice and swallowing it. "Staff Sergeant Walter Gillespie. On the team, I'm Hacksaw."

"Sergeant Kermit Alexander," the black sergeant said, and shook hands with Jack. "Call me The Frog. Not just Frog but The Frog. Dark green like a frog, but not just any frog, I am The Frog. Got it?"

Jack laughed. "The Frog, I got it."

"Cory Webster," the other sergeant said, giving Jack his hand. "Skipper named me Habu. Okinawa Japanese for snake. I'm an oh-three-twenty-one slash eighty-five-forty-one, same as you. You and I will be primary Scout-Snipers, and these other nonshooting knife fighters will work as our spotters. Kermit The Frog runs with me, so Hacksaw's your problem."

Jack looked at the staff sergeant, grinning a nasty smile at Webster, oozing tobacco juice between his teeth, sucking it back and blowing Habu a kiss. "Bro, you just wish you had a problem like me when we get in the shit. Don't forget who pulled your pork out of the fire in Medellín, when you and Dirty Harry got bushwhacked by that Escobar crew."

"Yeah, bro, I owe you. I don't forget," Habu said.

"Fuck it, dude. Comes in a day's work," Hacksaw said.

"Ray, help me with this," Captain Snow said, unrolling a tactical map with several clear-plastic overlays on it and fastening it onto a display board at the end of the conference table.

"That's Iraq," Jack said, seeing that the overlays had red, blue, green, and black markings on them.

"No shit, Sherlock," Staff Sergeant Gillespie said. "Where'd you think we're going, Disneyland?"

On the display board, next to the map and overlays, Elmore Snow pinned six color eight-by-ten portrait photographs of Iraqi officers.

"High-value targets?" Jack asked.

"They are the targets," Elmore Snow answered, stepping back and giving the display a good look to see that everything appeared straight and presentable for General Boomer. Then he looked at his crew. "Gather round, gentlemen. I don't want any gasps or whining while I brief the general. So I will give you a quick one-two-three before our audience arrives."

"Fuck you, Elmore, nobody's whining," Hacksaw guffawed.

Captain Snow shook his head. "That's why you have so

much time in grade as a staff sergeant, Walter. And you're lucky to hang on to that rocker. You've got no couth."

"I wipe my ass with couth every morning," Gillespie said, and paused before he added, "Sir."

"How come the skipper don't call you Hacksaw, or the gunny, Mutt?" Jack noticed, and queried the staff sergeant in a low voice.

"Captain Snow?" Hacksaw said, not bothering to lower his voice, not caring that Elmore Snow heard him. "Well, he's an officer and a gentleman first and foremost, so nicknames aren't his bag. And he's a Christian, above all else. The man prays at dawn like an Arab, bowing toward the rising sun, and on his knees at night like a child, praying forgiveness for all us sinful jarheads.

"He called Gunny Ambrose a Mutt one day, when brother Raymond nearly chewed the arm off a cocaine gunslinger on a back trail in Chile. They were going at it hand to hand, when we come up on them. Gunny trying to disarm the scoundrel of his .45, and keep from getting shot in the process, so he just started biting the shit out of the poor bastard. Got hold of his arm and made the blood gush. That's when the poor fucker turned loose and Ambrose killed him with that .45. Captain Snow said, you didn't have to kill him. You're nothing but a Mutt. We started calling brother Ray the Mutt after that. It really works on him, too, don't you think? Block head, big jaws, chewed-off ears like a pit bull fighting dog. He is the Mutt.

"Other than that one time, Skipper never uses nicknames. We do. Except for himself, Gunny does the naming. He'll come up with something cute for you. Just wait."

Jack looked at the gunny. "Any ideas?"

Ambrose shrugged. "Give it time, little brother. You'll do something or I'll see something. It'll come."

"Yeah, like that joke about the Indian chief who named all the village children." Kermit smiled. "When a baby is born, I name them after the first thing I see."

Hacksaw laughed. "Why you ask, Two-Dogs-Fucking?"

"At ease, gentlemen," Captain Snow said. "Here's the skinny. The six faces you see are the top Iraqi field commanders of Saddam Hussein's elite Republican Guard. We see one of these men, we take him out."

"Where are we going that we might see commanders of the Republican Guard?" Cory Webster asked.

"Once President Bush raises the flag," Elmore Snow began, "we'll launch on a night insertion. High-altitude low-opening drop. Military free fall fifteen grand. Deploy your parachutes below a thousand feet and above five hundred, your discretion. Night insertion, we're coming in black."

Gunny Ambrose looked closely at the overlays. "Which color are we?"

"Green, of course," Elmore said.

"That puts us well up the crotch of where the Tigris and Euphrates Rivers flow south," Ambrose said, tapping the map. "What's this city? Hillah? Like a hundred klicks south of Baghdad?"

"A hundred kilometers exactly, Gunny," Captain Snow said. "Saddam Hussein has his summer palace there, overlooking the ruins of Babylon, and the new Babylon he has constructed over the top of the ancient city."

"Told you his missions would scare the dogshit out of you," Hacksaw mumbled to Jack, giving him a hard elbow.

"We are the forward eyes and ears of the command

element," Snow told his men. "Eight teams of Delta Force, Navy SEALs, and Marine Force Recon will deploy to strategic forward positions. Primarily deep reconnaissance, target acquisition, and laser guidance for the air campaign, but contact is authorized if we see one of these six high-value targets. Kills must be absolute. No wounded ducks. And we will remain invisible. Dying or being taken prisoner is not an option. We have no realistic egress until friendly forces move well forward. That could take a while."

"Fuck me to tears, Skipper," Habu let go. "We lose Dirty Harry in that shit outside Medellín before Thanksgiving, and I thought that was bad. Sir, this is insane bullshit, just to put it bluntly. You said to not hold back our opinions anytime, so that's my opinion. We saw it coming in Colombia, and Leroy paid the price. Now we're all gonna die."

"Quit your fucking whining, Habu. Ya didn't want to live forever, did ya?" Hacksaw said, and laughed. "Go ahead, Skipper. You know sister Habu. He's always got a shit weasel up his skirt."

"Shit weasel?" Gunny Ambrose laughed.

"Yeah," Gillespie said. "Shit weasel."

Jack nudged Kermit. "Who's Dirty Harry or Leroy?"

"Sergeant Leroy Griffin. The Scout-Sniper you replaced," Alexander answered in a low voice. "We called him Dirty Harry because he was one badass gunslinger. Don't take it personal. Nobody's looking at you like you robbed Leroy's gun smoke or anything. Shit just happens."

"Sergeant Webster," Elmore Snow said. "This does seem like an impossible mission, but we do have our backup. Should we get into an engagement, which I strongly caution against. Contact only being a sniper shot and immediate clandestine movement. But should we engage and hold contact with enemy forces, we have Black Hawks at the ready. They will immediately come to our aid and extract us."

"Right, sir," Kermit said. "We just got to hold off Saddam's entire Republican Guard for what, two hours flight time from here to there?"

"About that, plus some change," Snow said.

"No comment, newbie?" Ray Ambrose asked Jack.

"Like Hacksaw said, do you want to live forever?" Jack shrugged, hiding the real fear that now twisted his stomach.

A knock came at the door, and a captain put his head inside. "General Boomer and the staff are headed this way."

"Thanks," Elmore said, and looked at his Marines. "You know, Lieutenant Colonel Jim Conway has command of Third Battalion, Second Marine Regiment these days. I taught at the Infantry Officers Course at The Basic School, with my pal, Captain Ed Gregory, and Jim taught tactics, as well as commanded a couple of companies. He and I had a long, heart-to-heart talk about this mission last night. Shit hits the fan, he's coming our way.

"Like you, I don't like to depend on some Army air group of reservists that I never met to save my life. Colonel Conway's got the big balls to do what's got to be done to get us home. That's a promise. Push comes to shove, he intends to bust fences and get us. He told me when this thing cooks off, he wants to drive up Saddam's Highway of Death, right up to the Son of King Nebuchadnezzar's Summer Palace, and build a barracks on top of the ruins of old Babylon."

"Let's just live low like lizards, like we always do, and don't sweat the small shit," Kermit The Frog said. "Ain't nobody out there gonna be looking for any loony tunes Force Recon scouts snoopin' and poopin' straight up their asses, right? We goin' where they think we ain't. We keep it that way, and we be fine."

Everyone shrugged and agreed.

"Yeah, we got this, Skipper," Kermit said, confident.

21

"Just live like lizards. Stay low like we always do and don't sweat the small shit." Jack Valentine laughed at himself in the mirror of the bathroom just past the gate where he had debarked from his flight home. Living like a lizard had become second nature to him, and it had taken many years with Elmore Snow to learn that fine warrior art. He didn't really need to go to the restroom, but he wanted a few more minutes alone to saddle his mind straight. No telling what would greet him past the security gate.

As Jack walked out of the restroom, he heard the click, click, click of rolling suitcases coasting along the ceramic-tile floor of the airport hallway that led from the passenger gates to the front lobby, and the crowds awaiting loved ones. Stacey and Patricia followed dutifully behind the plane's captain and first officer.

Stacey saw Jack and elbowed Patricia. She looked, too, and smiled large. Gunner Valentine smiled back and gave them a salute.

Both young women saluted back, then Stacey put her thumb next to her ear with her little finger down, mimicking a phone, and mouthed at Jack, "Call me."

Jack had started to toss her calling card in the trash in the restroom, but on second thought changed his mind. He rationalized to himself that with Liberty Cruz, a guy never really knows where he stands. What's wrong with keeping a few backup options open? Right? You never know.

So he had tucked the card back in his shirt pocket and buttoned up his blouse. When he saw Stacey, he patted his breast, letting her know he still had her card and just might ring her phone.

Then as he waited, watching the flight crew go on past the security barriers, and disappear around that turn, the knot that grew in his stomach finally took hold of the Marine gunner's better senses.

"I'll never call her," Jack said to himself as he walked toward the front of the airport. He reached inside his green blouse and took the card out of his shirt pocket. Flicking it with his fingers as he stared at Stacey's name and number, he thought about it and smiled as he saw the trash receptacle just before the security exit.

"Sorry, Stacey. It's just not meant to be," Jack said as he headed down the last leg of the hallway. As he passed the receptacle, he gave the pretty girl's calling card one last glance and tossed it in the bin.

Harry Valentine stood in the outer-lobby waiting area at El Paso International Airport. He held a baby girl in his arms, and Giti Sadiq stood next to him.

Elaine Valentine stood on the other side of her husband, and next to her, Liberty Cruz with her mom and dad, Patricia and Paul. Behind them waited Marco Gonzalez's father and mother, Herman and Lola. Herman still worked with Jack's dad at Harry's Heating and Air-Conditioning.

Freddy Montoya also showed up, with his newest young squeeze after a failed third marriage. And so did Judge Darius Archer, showing his years and now alone in life with the recent passing of his wife, leaning on a cocobolo walking stick with a brass duck's head for a handle.

When the plane let out the passengers, and everyone had rushed up the hallway to the lobby, Marine Gunner John Arthur Valentine casually sauntered far behind his fellow travelers now hurrying to get their baggage. By the time he had made his head call and ambled up the long hall past the security gate, nearly all the other passengers on his flight had disappeared to the baggage claim area.

As Jack finally came into the airport's outer lobby, his family and friends cheered, clapped, and whistled. Total strangers going to and from the ticket counters then joined in when they saw him. Everyone applauded the good-looking Marine in his green dress uniform with six rows of ribbons above his left breast pocket, gold jump wings with a silver SCUBA/UBA head above them, and silver crossed rifles and pistols, expert shooting badges. It made Jack blush.

"Hell if you don't look like a regular war hero," Freddy Montoya crowed, and grabbed Jack's hand first. He shoved his large-breasted trophy doll up for the Marine to meet, and she couldn't help herself but give the still-flushing gunner a red-lips smack on the cheek that left a mark. That didn't help Jack's embarrassment one bit.

"Good to see you, Sergeant Montoya." Gunner Valentine smiled. "You, too, and thanks for the kiss. What's your name?"

"Lolly." Freddy grinned. "My little Lolly Pop."

Jack had finished his tour in Iraq, waltzed through a short psych-eval at both Walter Reed and Bethesda, then endured six months of housebreaking and paper training in his Warrant Officer Basic Course at The Basic School at Quantico. On graduation day, Gunner Valentine drove nonstop to Camp Lejeune and dusted out his home on the waterfront in Swansboro. That Monday, he reported aboard at Marine Special Operations Command.

It took Elmore Snow's best efforts and a good dinner from June to convince the new gunner that he owed it to himself and the men he led to include his family as a priority with God, Country, and Corps.

"Family makes a Marine a more balanced leader," June had said at the table that night.

"I made a command decision and cut you a set of leave papers. June bought you a plane ticket. We think you need to take some time off," Elmore told his newest subordinate officer over glasses of Jameson's best Irish nectar.

"Colonel Snow," Jack said, "I need to get settled here first, then I will take the time off. I promise. We have a lot going on. The surge, and then my platoon going downrange to Afghanistan. Ten months is not much time."

"You're not the only Marine in the Corps, Gunner Valentine," Elmore reminded him. "Despite what those Army shrinks said about you, tough skin and all. I think you need a little time with your feet up."

When Jack had come off the Zarqawi mission back-to-back

with his ordeal with Abu Omar, two Air Force psychiatrists, a Navy doctor, and a female Army contract Post-Traumatic Stress Disorder specialist did their best to analyze the newly selected Marine warrant officer. They felt certain he would need long-term care in a German hospital. No normal human can endure what he did and still have all his marbles.

Jack Valentine sent them screaming out of the interview rooms, pulling out their overeducated hair, at three hospitals. He laughed at all the right jokes, felt sad at all the right sob stories, and told them he would love to hang out at a crowded shopping mall or go see a movie like *Saving Private Ryan* with any of them, anytime.

He didn't flinch. And all the Rorschach ink blots looked like butterflies, wild flowers, angel wings, his mother's apron, or a leaf on a peaceful stream.

"You've been prepped!" the Army shrink accused him. "You're a dangerous man, Mr. Valentine. I can't prove it, but I know it!"

"Put it in your report, then," Jack said, and left.

When he saw Giti Sadiq, and his dad holding her baby, Jack's heart leaped. Liberty right there with her, and his mom. Elmore was right. He always was, and Gunner Valentine told himself he needed to listen to the old man more often. At this moment, he was really glad that he had tossed the flight attendant's calling card in the trash, too. That kind of temptation did him no good, and right now he swelled with love.

"Hello there, baby sister," Jack said, and gave the girl from Iraq a big hug and a kiss on her cheek.

Then he held his arms open for Liberty. She came

around and locked her lips on his mouth hard and long, in front of her parents and his.

"Saving best for last," Jack told his sweetheart since high school, and she smiled, seeing the gold-and-red bars on his shoulders and the black bursting-bomb insignia inboard from them on the epaulets. Then she put her finger on the black bursting-bomb insignia pinned on one side of his shirt collar and looked over at the warrant-officer bar pinned on the opposite side.

"So this is a Marine gunner." She smiled.

"Yes, ma'am," Jack answered.

Darius Archer came close to Jack, his voice nearly gone from age and surgery to remove polyps off his vocal cords.

"You far exceeded all my expectations," the old judge said.

"We got that girl you saved on the road to full citizenship. And her baby couldn't be in a better home than with your mom and dad.

"I am proud of you, Jack. My years on the bench, putting people in prison. You made all the bad days worth that good one, when I sent you to the Marine Corps."

"That girl and her sisters saved me, Judge Archer." Jack smiled and pulled Giti close to him, her self-proclaimed big brother. Liberty kissed the girl on the cheek, then kissed Jack once more.

Special Agent Cruz had resigned from the FBI, just as she had planned, but a few years ahead of schedule. Her torture episode with Cesare Alosi and the CIA drew heat from one particular United States senator. He wanted her head but couldn't have it since she had departed government employment.

As for the CIA boys, Chris and Speedy, they walked on water, had Teflon underwear, and kept their station in Baghdad rocking and rolling.

"I'm headed back to Washington, DC. Have my own security business now, Judge Archer. A contract with the Drug Enforcement Agency, Treasury, too, and a little something going on the side with the CIA," Liberty said, adding to the conversation.

"Going to hire Cesare Alosi to run your shop?" Jack joked, and the long cool woman gave him a mean knuckle shot to the arm.

"Not funny, Gunner Valentine. And I still outrank you." She laughed, with the family and friends circled around them.

She took Jack's hand. "I have two more days here, and I intend to make the most of them with this Marine."

"We have a fiesta waiting at the house," Harry Valentine said, holding the baby. "Instead of standing in the airport for the rest of the day, let's get home and celebrate!"

The Marine gave Liberty a kiss and turned to Giti, close to his side. "A senior at Coronado High School, I hear. Top of your class."

"I tested up." The girl smiled. "I want to go to college now. University of Texas at El Paso, and study law."

"Just what we need." Jack laughed. "Another lawyer."

"I want to help people, like Mr. Cruz does," she said, and Liberty gave Jack a look and pointed a thumb at a smiling Paul Cruz walking behind them, listening.

"Miriam Amira Sadiq, such a wonderful name for your daughter," Jack said, but then paused, thinking about what he wanted to say next. The hesitation stopped them from their walk. He looked at Giti and took a cautious breath, then spit it out of his craw. "Don't misunderstand me. I love this child without exception. She's my family, like you. But does it ever bother you that her father was such a monster? Like it or not, she is still Saddam Hussein's cousin."

"Miriam Amira is none of those things, big brother," Giti said, and squeezed his hand. "She is my daughter. A child of God. He put her in my belly and saved her from all the horrors we saw. He brought her here to be born an American citizen. Our Lord has something special planned for her. You wait and see."

Ready to find
your next great read?

Let us help.

Visit prh.com/nextread

Penguin
Random
House